ELIZABETH EDMONDSON

The Villa in Italy

HARPER

Harper
An imprint of HarperCollins*Publishers*
77–85 Fulham Palace Road,
Hammersmith, London W6 8JB

www.harpercollins.co.uk

This paperback edition 2006
1

First published in Great Britain by
HarperCollins*Publishers* 2006

A catalogue record for this book
is available from the British Library

ISBN-13: 978 0 00 722377 0
ISBN-10: 0 00 722377 3

This novel is entirely a work of fiction.
The names, characters and incidents portrayed in it are
the work of the author's imagination. Any resemblance to
actual persons, living or dead, events or localities is
entirely coincidental.

Set in Sabon by Palimpsest Book Production Limited,
Grangemouth, Stirlingshire

Printed and bound in Great Britain by
Clays Ltd, St Ives plc

For Teresa Chris
Thank you!

PROLOGUE

The package from the lawyers arrived early one foggy April morning. It was wrapped in brown paper, tied with string and sealed with red wax.

The postman came whistling through the door to the offices of Hawkins & Hallett, bringing with him a gust of cold, damp air, and greeted the thin-lipped, middle-aged receptionist with a cheery, 'Good morning.'

Miss Jay looked at him over the top of her half-moon spectacles, her eyes cold and disapproving. 'What's this?' she said, as he handed her the package. Her mouth tightened as she saw the seal, complete with crest; really, these authors did give themselves airs. She turned it over, and saw the sender's name: Winthrop, Winthrop & Jarvis.

'Lawyers, I reckon,' said the postman. 'What have you lot been up to? Or maybe it's the juicy memoirs of a judge. Anyhow, it's to be signed for. The rest will be along later, same as usual.'

She signed the slip in neat, upright strokes, and handed it back to the postman. Then she drew the post book out of her drawer and made an entry. As she did so, the door opened again, letting in another blast of chilly air and a girl in a duffel coat.

1

'Good morning, Miss Hallett,' the receptionist said icily, and looked pointedly at the large clock. 'Five minutes late again.'

The girl grinned and heaved herself out of her coat, which she hung on the hatstand behind the door. 'What's five minutes between friends, Miss Jay?'

'Please take this package upstairs to Miss Hawkins. Right away.'

'Okey-dokey,' and the girl bounded up the brown lino stairs two at a time, her pony tail swinging as she went.

Miss Jay winced. Susie Hallett might be a partner's daughter, but taking on a girl like that was a mistake, even if she only came in two mornings a week.

Susie swung herself round on the polished curve of the banister rail on the first floor and skidded to a halt outside a panelled door with 'Miss Hawkins, Publishing Director' written on the name board in bold gold letters. She knocked on the door, and went in without waiting for a reply. 'Hello, Miss Hawkins. Post.'

'Good morning, Susie. Why has Miss Jay sent it up to me unopened? What's got into her?'

'Dunno. She just told me to bring it up. Looks important, string and sealing wax.'

Susie lingered, curious, as Miss Hawkins snipped the string and unwrapped the parcel. Inside was a manuscript, and on top a covering letter.

Olivia Hawkins read the letter swiftly, and then put it down. She said nothing, but looked out of the long, elegant sash window, not seeing the raindrops dribbling down the panes, or the dingy light of a bleak spring morning, but instead, brilliant sunlight on an Italian landscape; in her mind, she was in Italy, sitting under the colonnades, laughing, drinking a toast with a woman no longer young, yet every bit as full of life as young Susie.

She blinked, and reached down into her handbag for a handkerchief.

'Is something the matter? Is it a book?'

'Yes, it's a book. The memoirs of Beatrice Malaspina.'

'What a lovely name.'

'The letter is from a firm of lawyers, who had instructions to deliver the book to me after Beatrice Malaspina died.'

'Is she dead? Was she a friend of yours? I'm sorry.'

'Don't be. I shall miss her, but she was born in 1870, so she had a long life. And a very full one.'

'Eighteen seventy, goodness, so she lived to be eighty-seven.' Susie tried to add seventy years of life to her own seventeen; she couldn't imagine it. 'Was she an Italian?'

'No, she was English, but she married an Italian. Her own family had Italian connections, they owned a house in Italy called the Villa Dante, which she inherited. It is the most beautiful house, magical, a place of enchantment.'

'How did you know her?'

'We met during the war. She was a compelling personality, and she'd led a fascinating life. Rather a bohemian in her way; you would have liked her. She moved in artistic circles and knew most of the great painters and writers of her time. Many of them were her friends, and came to stay with her at the Villa Dante. She was a complex woman, and a great organiser. It annoyed her that people's lives were so muddled; she used to say, "It only takes clear thinking and energy to change a life for the better, to set it off in a new direction."'

'She sounds fun.'

'She was.'

'And these are her memoirs? Are we going to publish them?'

'Oh, yes. What she'll have to say about all those artists will make good reading, quite apart from the story of her own adventurous life.'

Susie was standing by the window, looking down at the dismal street, slick with rain. A rag and bone cart was going by, the horse's back covered with an old sack to protect it from the wet, the driver shouting out his incomprehensible Londoner's cry.

'Oh, I meant to tell you, there were a couple of shifty-looking men hanging around when I came in. They're still there, look, lurking outside number nine. Do you think they might be casing the joint?'

Olivia got up from her desk and joined Susie at the window. One glance was enough. She laughed. 'You read too many thrillers, Susie. Those aren't crooks – well, not the kind you were thinking of. Those are reporters. The man in the tweed coat is Giles Slattery of the *Sketch*. The one in the grubby mac with a camera is a photographer.'

'Giles Slattery, the gossip columnist?'

'Yes. I wonder who they're waiting for.'

'Somebody famous, do you think?'

'What, here in Bloomsbury? I doubt it. Not the kind of famous Slattery goes in for, at any rate.'

The Journey

ONE

Delia Vaughan was hanging on to the steering wheel as if to loosen her grip would be to admit defeat. The wind had risen to a deafening shriek, coming in wild gusts that made the canvas top of the car bang and flap as though at any moment it would fly off.

They had stopped two hours before, to put up the hood, when the wind had whipped Jessica's hat off, and Delia had only just stopped her silk headscarf going the same way.

'We should find a hotel,' Jessica said. 'The weather's getting worse.'

Delia didn't want to stay at a hotel. In her mind, the Villa Dante had come to represent a refuge, a haven from the storm, a destination that was more than journey's end. It was irrational, but she was determined to press on, despite her exhaustion, her hacking cough and Jessica's urgings for her to be sensible and get off the road and out of the storm.

'We're only about thirty miles away, let's keep going.'

'Let me find something to wrap round my head, then,' said Jessica. 'This car is full of draughts, and I can't hear myself think with all the noise in my ears. When I get back to England, I'm going to sell it, and buy a saloon.' She extracted

7

a silk scarf from her bag and put it over her head, tying it under her chin. 'Come on then, if you must.'

It was slow going, and Delia was as relieved as Jessica when they came to a sign that read San Silvestro. 'We take the road going south, the lawyer said, and turn off immediately after we've gone under the railway bridge. Then it's uphill, and we'll see the gates and the villa.'

'How can we see anything in all this?' said Jessica.

Miraculously, as they went up the hill, the skies lightened for a moment, and they could see a pair of tall, wrought-iron gates silhouetted in the blazing wind.

'It's astonishing,' yelled Delia, an unreasonable surge of excitement rising in her as she caught a glimpse of the classical façade of a large house. Then it was gone, and she pressed her foot hard down on the accelerator, hoping the strange noises the engine was making didn't mean it was about to conk out.

They made it to the gates, and stopped the car, although Delia left the engine running, 'Just in case,' she shouted to Jessica.

The gates were shut, with a rusty chain looped round the bars to hold them together. The wind was rising by the minute, and now the air was full of flying sand: that was the sound like hail that had rattled against the hood of the car. 'Are you sure this is the right place?' Jessica said. 'There's no name anywhere.'

'It's where the lawyer said it would be, and we didn't see a sign of any other house in the vicinity. Do you think this sand is blowing off a beach? I never asked how close the villa was to the sea.'

'Do Italian beaches have red sand?'

'I don't know.' Delia's hair was whipping about her eyes, and she pushed it ineffectually back from her forehead, trying to wedge a strand behind her ears.

'Is there a bell?'

'Only this.' Delia pointed to a brass bell attached to one

of the stone gateposts. A frayed rope with a knot at its end swung from it in the wind.

'Give it a tug,' Jessica said.

They could hear a faint clang from the bell, but the sound was carried away by the wind.

'It's so hot,' said Jessica. 'Like a wind from the desert.'

'Villa Dante or not,' Delia said, 'we're going in. Or we'll be flattened by this blasted tempest, and I hate to think what'll happen if any more of it gets into the engine of your car. Stranded is what we'd be then.'

She gave the gates an impatient shake, and let out a cry of triumph, carried away in the wind, as the chain slithered to the ground. A sudden gust tore the gates apart, driving them inwards to land with a crash against the stones set alongside the driveway.

'Watch out,' cried Jessica, as the gates began to swing back towards them with squealing ferocity.

Delia flung herself against the left-hand one, and, hanging on to it, looked around for a stone to wedge it open.

'There, on the grass,' shouted Jessica, who had got back into the car and started to edge it forward.

Delia kicked the stone into place, then forced the other gate back and held it as Jessica drove the car through.

Jessica was gesturing at her to get into the car, but Delia first picked up the chain and waited for the moment when the gates clanged together to wrench it through and twist it round the bars.

'It won't hold,' she yelled, as she got back into the car.

'The gate's the least of our worries,' said Jessica. 'I just hope there's someone here to let us in.'

They drove up to the house, not noticing anything about it, intent only on getting the car and themselves under shelter, out of the terrifying, sand-laden wind.

'This is the back of the house,' yelled Delia. 'Look for somewhere to put the car.'

'There,' Jessica said. 'A stable, or is it a garage?'

'It doesn't matter, it's shelter.'

The doors were banging to and fro in the wind and Delia struggled to hold them back while Jessica drove the car in.

Delia leant against the stone wall, blinking the sand out of her eyes. 'What a relief to be out of that ghastly hot wind,' she said.

'We can't stay here,' Jessica said. 'How do we get inside the house?'

In fact, Delia was perfectly happy to stay there, out of the wind, the engine switched off, every nerve in her body throbbing. Even a single step seemed beyond her, but Jessica was at her side, forcing her out once again into the maddening wind, so strong now that the sand stung her cheeks, and then, oh miracle, Jessica found a door, and opened it, and they were inside, out of the wind, and heat, and sand.

Wherever they were, it was blessedly cool, and the air was breathable.

Delia heard a crash and a muffled oath. 'Are we in a kitchen, do you suppose?' said Jessica, her voice seeming to Delia to come from a great distance. 'There are shutters, but I shan't open them, or everything will blow in from outside. Besides, there isn't much light to let in. But I've found a sink, and I think I collided with a kitchen table. Can you see anything?'

Delia blinked. 'I've still got sand in my eyes.' She began to cough, a deep racking sound. 'I think the sand's got into my lungs, too, blast it.'

'Hold on.'

The sound of running water, and then Jessica was beside her, wiping her face with a wet handkerchief. 'Don't you dare faint on me.'

'I'm fine,' said Delia untruthfully, her head spinning. 'I never faint.'

'Sit down.' Jessica, miraculously, set a chair under Delia

as her legs crumpled. 'Put your head down between your knees. Go on. Blood to the head is what you need.'

The dizziness receded. 'I can't think what came over me.'

'It's that bronchitis,' said Jessica. 'It's pulled you right down, and this wind and the blowing sand, it hardly makes it easy for anyone to breathe. You could do with a glass of water to drink, but I wouldn't drink anything out of the tap. Feeling better? Then let's see if anyone's at home.'

No one was. They walked through shadowy rooms, accompanied by the sudden, distant roars of the wind. Shutters rattled; somewhere a door or window was banging.

'Deserted,' said Jessica.

'Not for long,' said Delia, running a finger over the surface of a marble-topped table and inspecting it by the meagre light filtering through the shutters.

'Do you think it's always windy like this?'

'I think this is a sirocco,' said Delia. 'We did it at school, with Miss Pertinax, don't you remember? She took us for geography, and was mad about the extremes of nature. Floods and tidal waves and hurricanes, and the wicked winds of Europe. The Föhn that drives you mad, and the mistral in the south of France, and the sirocco, a blinding southerly wind that blows up from the desert into Mediterranean Europe, bringing half the Sahara with it.'

'How on earth do you remember all that?'

'Winds are dramatic. You won't remember it, because you never paid any attention in geography, and I used to do your homework for you.'

'I did your maths,' said Jessica. 'Does this sirocco happen often?'

'Quite rare, I think.'

'Then why does it have to blow on the day we arrive?'

'Fate,' said Delia. 'Angry gods.'

'There is electricity, here are the light switches, but nothing happens when I press them.'

11

'Switched off at the mains, or it could run on a generator.'

'Now isn't the time to investigate. There are bound to be oil lamps or candles somewhere. And if there's been dusting done, perhaps there's food in the house. And a wine cellar. Safer than water for drinking. You stay here; I'll find a light.'

Delia could make out little of her surroundings, although she could dimly see a pillar, and judging by the smoothness of the stone under her hand, the bench she was sitting on was marble.

Jessica came back bearing a candle aloft, the small flame sending little shadows to and fro as it flickered in a draught. They were in a large marble-floored room, with fluted columns and enormous doors set in classical architraves.

Delia sat up, sudden alarm rising in her. Faces were looking out at her, a girl peeping round a door, a woman in flowing robes strumming at a lyre – was she hallucinating?

'Good heavens,' said Jessica, equally startled. 'What the dickens . . . ?'

Delia went over to take a closer look. 'It's all painting,' she said. 'The people, this door, the columns. Trompe l'oeil. It's amazing!'

'Thank God,' said Jessica. 'It gave me quite a fright, thinking the place was full of people. Anyway, good news – I found a mesh cupboard with some food, and a bottle of wine, and bottles of water on the floor. And there's an oil lamp – see if I can get it to light.'

'Do you know how to work an oil lamp? I do, so hand it over,' said Delia. She sat down, with the oil lamp on the marble seat beside her, and removed the glass globe to get at the wick. 'We used them at Saltford Hall when there were all those power cuts after the war.'

They retreated to the kitchen, where they sat at the scrubbed table and ate the bread, cheese and cold meat that had been left in the kitchen. Fortified with food and a glass of wine, Delia yawned. 'What a day,' she said. 'I'm whacked.

What we need is beds, which means upstairs.'

Jessica tidied the remains of the food away into the food safe. 'Washing up can wait until the morning,' she said. 'Wasn't there a staircase at the end of the hall with the wall paintings?'

They went up the stairs into a gallery and then came to a wide landing, with several large, polished doors leading off it. Opening them one after the other, they found four rooms ready for guests, with the beds made and clean towels hung over the rails at the washstands in the bathrooms.

'They seem to be expecting us,' Delia said.

'Someone, anyhow.' Jessica still wasn't sure they were in the right place. 'What if we wake up and find we're at the Villa Ariosto, or the Villa Boccaccio?'

Delia said, 'Then our hosts will be in for a surprise. It doesn't matter; here we are, and here we stay, and if a claimant to my room turns up in the middle of the night, he or she can jolly well go and sleep somewhere else.'

'I can't see anyone being mad enough to be out in this wind.'

'You have this room, and I'll take the one next door. You have the oil lamp, I'll have the candle.'

From what Delia could see by the light of her candle, she was in a large and grand room, the sort of room that would belong to the master or mistress of the house. Perhaps she shouldn't be in here at all, but she was too sleepy to care.

The bed had an elaborate headboard, on which, in the flickering, shadowy light, Delia could make out the entwined initials, B M.

Beatrice Malaspina, she said aloud. Well, here I am at the Villa Dante. I do wonder what you want with me.

TWO

Until a week ago, Delia had never heard of Beatrice Malaspina, nor of the Villa Dante. She had been in her London flat when the postman's whistle was followed by the bang of the letter flap and the thud as the post hit the doormat.

She went into the small hall and picked up the letters. A brown envelope from the electricity company. A white envelope, with a handwritten address. She knew who that was from, her agent Roger Stein's wild scrawl was unmistakable. Her heart sank. He only wrote when he had something nasty to say, otherwise he'd be on the phone with a breezy, 'Delia, dear girl . . .'

And what was this? She looked at the long envelope. It had to be a lawyer's letter; why did lawyers feel the need to have different-sized stationery from everyone else? She turned it over. It was from Winthrop, Winthrop & Jarvis, the family solicitors – or at least, her father's solicitors; they were nothing to do with her these days.

Was her father communicating with her now through his solicitors? Had things got that bad?

She began to cough, and cursed at the stab of pain in her chest. She took the post into the kitchen and put it down on the table. Then she went to the stove and turned on the gas under the kettle. Coffee would clear her brain and give her strength to open the letters.

She had her back turned to the window, and hadn't seen the figure that was standing there, on the other side of the glass.

Jessica tapped on the window, softly at first, and then more loudly. Delia whirled round, startled and alarmed, then relaxed as she saw who it was. She hurried to the window, threw up the sash, and hauled Jessica in over the sill. A small black and tan dog jumped in after her, trailing its lead.

'Jessica, for God's sake, you nearly gave me a heart attack,' she said, grabbing the dog's lead and unclipping it from its collar. 'What on earth are you doing climbing up my fire escape?'

'I tell you what, it's a miracle burglars aren't in and out all day long. It's hardly difficult.'

'There's an alarm I put on at night and when I go out,' Delia said. 'It makes a terrific racket, like an air raid siren. Good thing it wasn't set, or you'd have had the heart attack and plunged to the ground. Oh, Lord; I can guess why you're on my fire escape. Reporters?'

Jessica nodded.

'Here?'

'Staked out at the front, two of them, would you believe it? They know you're a friend of mine; honestly, wouldn't you think they had something better to do than follow me around?'

Delia went into her sitting room, edged round the Schiedmayer grand piano which took up nearly all the available space, and peered down into the square.

'You're absolutely right, there they are, bold as brass, not even bothering to lurk or look inconspicuous. The neighbours will be complaining, and pointing out that this is a nice area.'

'Is it?'

15

'Not really, or I couldn't afford to live here. Respectable is what they mean. What's up? You look all in. I can see your ghastly husband hasn't agreed to give you a divorce. What's he done now?'

'Haven't you seen the papers?'

'Not that foul Giles Slattery again?'

'No, although he's one of the reporters hanging round the front door downstairs. No, this is important news, headlines in *The Times* kind: Richie's been appointed a junior minister at the Foreign Office.'

'Hell,' Delia said. 'That'll make him even keener to stay respectably married, won't it?'

Delia was Jessica's oldest and best friend, and the only person who knew and understood her predicament, the only person whose advice she trusted. Despite the fact that their lives had taken such very different paths, and despite the fact that Jessica's husband, Richard Meldon, disliked Delia almost as much as she did him, Delia and Jessica had remained the closest of friends. It was inevitable that if Jessica was in trouble she would come to Delia for refuge, advice, sympathy, good sense, and, Delia not being one to mince words, the truth.

'How long have you got before he gets back from Hong Kong?'

'One of the reporters outside my house shouted out something about him being back next week. Because of the new job, do you think? Or maybe just fed up with China.'

Jessica threw herself down on Delia's large and comfortable sofa, and her dog jumped up beside her.

Delia's sitting room was like Delia herself: exotic, larger than life and full of bright colours and untidiness. Delia, who was taller and had more curves than Jessica, liked bold colours on herself as well as in her surroundings, and she was dressed today in a huge scarlet sloppy joe jumper, with red sneakers on her feet and large gypsy hoops in her ears.

She looked at Jessica with affection tinged with anxiety. Jessica used to be a colourful dresser herself, favouring the blues and greens that suited her silvery blonde hair and the deep blue eyes set in a long Plantagenet face, but since her marriage she had become more and more neutral, camouflaging herself in camels and beiges and pale greys, none of which suited her colouring or her personality.

'Come on, what else did the damned reporter say?'

'Oh, he asked if Richie would be joining me in the Chelsea house.'

When Jessica had stormed out of the matrimonial home, a house in Mayfair, she had moved into a tiny house in Chelsea that belonged to friends who had been posted abroad, and Delia knew how happy she had felt there, in a place untainted by the husband she so hated.

They looked at each other in silence. 'You're welcome to stay here,' said Delia. 'Any time. You and Harry the pooch.'

Jessica's dog, named Harry because he had come from Harrods, had been Delia's wedding present to her. 'So that at least there'll be someone for you to love,' Delia had said with savage percipience.

Richie had disliked the little dog from the start.

'What is he, some kind of mongrel?'

'He's a Heeler.'

'A what? Never heard of any such dog.'

'They come from Lancashire. They nip at the heels of cattle.'

'You believe that, you believe anything. What a stupid little tail, curled over like that. Why didn't you ask me? I'd have bought you a proper dog.'

'Thank you, Harry's perfect.'

Delia knew that Richie wasn't a man who could easily be kept out of anywhere he wanted to be; her Chelsea house would no longer seem safe to Jessica.

'Talk about not wanting to take a hint,' she said. 'Why

doesn't he accept that the marriage is over, that it's been a failure?'

'Why ask? Nothing Richie does can be a failure.'

Delia had her own opinion about that. Richie was a failure as a human being, and not all his glowing war record as an ace fighter in the RAF, the brilliance as a speaker that had taken him into Parliament, his dashing good looks, his wealth, his connections or his influence made up for the fact that, deep down, 'He's a shit,' she said.

'I know that, and you know that, but he's no such thing in the eyes of the world, and that's why I'm now the demon woman for daring to leave him. My loving husband, so wonderful, how could I want to divorce him?'

'Yes, it's tough on you that the press eat out of his hand. Did you know that he and Giles Slattery go back a long way? They were at school together.'

Delia saw the flash of anxiety in Jessica's eyes, those eyes that always showed when a sensitive spot had been touched.

'I had no idea,' Jessica said. 'That's an unholy alliance, if you like. Oh, God, do you suppose Richie sicked Slattery on to me? Just to torment?'

'I expect so. It's a good way of keeping tabs on you, while keeping his own nose clean.'

'I'm going to have to get away. Go abroad. Only do you think the reporters would follow me there?'

'What, send out search parties all over the Continent? You aren't that much of a story.'

'I wish I weren't any kind of a story at all. Oh, why didn't I listen to you? If I had, I wouldn't be in this fix now.'

Delia had never really got to the heart of the reason why Jessica had married Richard Meldon. On the surface, it seemed a perfect match, but to one who knew Jessica as well as she did, it was doomed to disaster. Her reaction to Jessica's engagement to Richie had been openly unenthusiastic.

'Marry that man? Jessica, you can't be serious. Go and take a cold bath, or hop on a banana boat to South America, anything to make you come to your senses.'

'What's wrong with Richie? He's handsome, successful—'

'And rich. Is he in love with you, or the fact that your family goes back for nine centuries? And what about his liking for older women?'

'What older women?'

'He has a reputation, that's all. He's discreet about it, but I heard from Fanny Arbuthnot that—'

'Fanny's a tedious gossip and always has been.'

'Maybe, but she stayed with some people in the south of France and your Richie was among those present, and spent a good deal of his time in the company of Jane Hinton, who must be quite twenty years older than he is. And Fanny says he's known for it.'

'As it happens, I don't care. My past is past, and so is his. Neither of us is coming virginal and innocent to the bridal chamber, why should I mind who he's slept with before me?'

'It's who he'll sleep with after you that you should worry about,' Delia muttered.

'Make me a cocktail,' Jessica said. 'A strong one.'

'You're drinking too much.'

'It keeps the goblins at bay.'

'Yes, it's a pity you ever married the wretched man,' Delia said. 'I still don't understand how you came to do anything so stupid. It wasn't as though your friends didn't warn you.'

'Oh, trust me to make a mistake,' Jessica said. 'When you get into scrapes, you somehow manage to wriggle out of them, don't you? With my scrapes, I end up having to live with the consequences.'

'Richie's more than a scrape.'

'Unfortunately, he is. And marriage – God, what a colossal

19

mistake that was. A few words said in front of an indifferent clergyman, and bang! you're bound in chains.'

'He's still adamant about no divorce?'

'Of course he is. He won't hear of it, just shouts me down. I always thought divorce was quite simple. Didn't you think, as I did, that the man of honour hops off down to Brighton to be found in bed with the chambermaid or whoever he's paid for the privilege, and bingo, six months later you're a free woman?'

'Only Richie won't do the honourable thing.'

'Has Richie ever done an honourable thing in his life?'

They adjourned to the kitchen, where Delia rescued the coffee and they sat on either side of the kitchen table, with Harry between their feet.

'Abroad isn't such a bad idea,' Delia said. 'Where could you go? It would have to be somewhere Richie couldn't track you down. It's tricky, because even if you book yourself into some *pension* in a remote French village, you have to fill in all those forms for the police. And what officials know, Richie will be able to find out.'

'I know,' said Jessica. 'Christ, what a mess.' She looked down at the table. 'You haven't opened your letters. That's me barging in and distracting you.'

'They're hardly important. An electricity bill, a moan from my agent and a lawyer's letter.' Delia began to cough again, and Jessica silently rose and got her a drink of water.

'It doesn't sound as though you've got rid of your bronchitis.'

'No, it just lingers. The dreadful weather doesn't help, and there's nothing I can do except wait for it to clear up, which the specialist says it will, eventually.'

'You've seen a specialist, then?'

'Of course I have. All we singers rush to our favourite man at the hint of a sore throat or a chest infection.'

Delia was an opera singer, still too young at twenty-seven

for the really major roles, but she was considered a rising star, booked for Glyndebourne, Sadler's Wells, the Royal Opera House – and due to make her Salzburg debut that summer.

'That's what my agent's moaning about,' she said, opening his letter with some reluctance. 'Yes, here we go, fatal to get a name for unreliability, can I give him a firm date when I will be well enough . . .' She scrunched up the letter. 'And this one is from my father's lawyers,' she went on. 'God knows what he's up to.'

She slit open the envelope and took out a single sheet of paper. 'What on earth?' She picked up the envelope again – yes, it was addressed to her, and the letter began 'Dear Miss Vaughan'. Beneath the salutation was typed in capital letters, THE ESTATE OF THE LATE BEATRICE MALASPINA.

'What is it?' said Jessica. 'Bad news?'

'No,' said Delia, passing her the letter.

'Who's this Beatrice Malaspina? Was she your godmother or something?'

'I have no idea. I've never heard of her.'

They stared at one another. 'How odd,' said Jessica. 'And yet she must have left you a legacy of some kind, otherwise why the letter? What do they say – please call at their office at your earliest convenience? How exciting. Get changed, and off you go.'

Delia had no intention of going to the offices of Winthrop, Winthrop & Jarvis, of Lincoln's Inn Fields, and she said so. Jessica took no notice, and half an hour later Delia found herself sitting in a cab, wrapped up in a scarlet coat, 'Like a matador's cape,' Jessica said, 'but perfect for keeping out the cold,' with a headscarf wound round her head.

Jessica had insisted on her taking a cab. 'Walk, with that cough? Certainly not, and mind you come back by taxi, as soon as ever you can; don't you see that I shall be dying of curiosity to know what it's all about?'

21

Delia climbed the steep, ill-lit stairs which led to the sombre chambers of Winthrop, Winthrop & Jarvis, where the clerk eyed her with disfavour.

'There's no need to look at me like that,' Delia said. 'I've come to see Mr Winthrop. Tell him I'm here, please. Miss Vaughan. No, I don't have an appointment, but I'm sure he'll see me.'

'I'm not sure whether—'

'Just tell him I'm here.'

Reluctantly, the clerk disappeared through a dark door, to return in a few moments and, even more reluctantly, show her into the handsome panelled room which was the lair of Josiah Winthrop, senior partner of the firm.

Mr Winthrop greeted Delia with a formal, chilly courtesy that made her indignant. He was not a man ever to show much warmth, but he had known her since she was a child and there was no need to treat her as though she were one of his criminal clients. Bother him, Delia said inwardly; I know he wishes I weren't here at all, but he could try to hide the fact.

'Okay,' she said deliberately, and watched him wince at the slang, so out of place in these surroundings where every word was weighed and considered. She took off her head-scarf and shook her dark hair loose before sitting down on the hard wooden chair with arms that Mr Winthrop had moved forward for her. An uncomfortable chair, which ensured that undesirable clients didn't outstay their welcome.

'Spit it out,' she said. 'Who is this Beatrice Malaspina, and what has she to do with me?'

THREE

Jessica listened with rapt attention as Delia reported on her visit to the lawyers. Delia was sitting on the piano stool, while Jessica stretched out on the sofa, Harry curled up beside her.

'So this lawyer is claiming they don't know anything about her? But they're representing her, they must know,' Jessica said.

'I don't believe they do. I could tell from Mr Winthrop's expression that he thinks it's all most irregular. Mind you, he's hardly a talkative man at the best of times; he's the sort of lawyer who says as little as possible, as though every word came at a cost. Apparently, the instructions were from a firm of Italian lawyers, and they're simply handling the English end.'

'Are you sure there isn't some connection with your family? After all, Winthrop is your father's lawyer, isn't he? And they're a stuffy firm. Look how they've treated me; they won't represent anybody who walks in off the street.'

'I asked him, but he merely looked even more thin-lipped and said that his firm handled the affairs and estates of a great many clients. Which is true enough.'

'Are you going to ask your parents if they know who

23

Beatrice Malaspina was? Or have ever heard of the Villa Dante?'

'No. Mother won't have known her – she hates all foreigners. And you know how things are between my father and me. We haven't spoken for over a year, and I'm not going to get in touch with him about this.'

'It's about time your pa faced facts and realised you've chosen your career, and are doing very well at it, and he's not going to be able to drag you into the family firm, however much he wants to.'

'Father never sees what he doesn't want to. Anyhow, if he got wind of a will, he'd winkle the facts out of Winthrop and the Italian lawyers, or get his horribly efficient horn-rimmed secretary to do it for him. Then, if he knew I was thinking of going to Italy, he'd want to organise it all. Aeroplane? Far too expensive; he'd have all the continental timetables out, to look up the cheapest possible route, and I'd end up trundling across the Alps on some old bus.'

Lord Saltford's thriftiness was too notorious for Jessica to be able to argue with Delia about that.

'And he's never mentioned any Beatrice anybody. I don't see any reason why he should know her.'

'Maybe it's all a trick, to lure you away. Perhaps the oh-so-respectable Mr Winthrop is a secret white slave trader?'

'What, and I'll find myself being shipped out to Buenos Aires in a crate? Oh, very likely!'

Jessica fiddled with a cushion tassel.

'Are you really thinking of going to Italy? Will you follow the instructions in Beatrice Malaspina's will, and go to this Villa Dante?'

'I don't know,' said Delia. 'It's tempting, and I have to say I am curious about the whole thing.'

'Perhaps she's left you the house, the Villa Dante, and a fortune.'

'Italians leave property to their families, always. Maybe

24

a piece of jewellery, a brooch or a ring. Only why? Why me?'

'And why make you go all the way to Italy for a brooch? No, whoever she was, and why ever she wanted you to go to Italy, it must be important. And the only way you'll find out is by going. Would you ever forgive yourself if you passed on this?'

'Mr Winthrop doesn't like all the mystery, I could tell; he looked as though he had a bad smell under his long nose.'

Jessica sat up. 'Why don't we go together? It would suit me to go abroad, and it would do you good to get away from this dreadful, everlasting fog and rain and wind.' She paused. 'No, I suppose you can't really spare the time. You're hardly ever able to get away, what with rehearsals and performances and so on. That's what having a successful career is all about.'

Delia dropped her hands on to the keys of the piano, picking out the notes of 'Twinkle, twinkle, little star' with two fingers, then weaving an ornate variation as she spoke. 'As it happens, I'm thinking of taking a bit of time off. I'm not due to start rehearsals for a few weeks. Everything's rather in the air at the moment,' she added. 'With this cough of mine. And Italy might have better weather than we've got here.'

Jessica's mind turned to practicalities.

'What's the best way to get there? We could fly to Rome, I suppose, but we'd be followed by those damn reporters, and then Richie would know exactly where I was.'

'Let's go by car,' said Delia. 'You didn't leave your car at Richie's house, did you? It's a long way, but we can share the driving, and, according to the lawyers, as long as I'm there by the end of the month, that's okay.'

'Doesn't it need a lot of arranging, going abroad with a car? It won't just be a matter of driving to Dover and nipping on the next ferry, will it? There's insurance and green cards and all kinds of formalities when you want to take a car across the Channel.' Jessica knew that if she went near a travel agent or the RAC, the hounds would be on her heels. 'Oh, Lord,' she said with a sigh. 'Why is everything in my life so difficult just now?'

'I have a friend who works at Thomas Cook,' Delia said. 'Michael will fix it all up for us. What's the number of your car?'

She scribbled down the details. 'We have to be inconspicuous, or the reporters will be on our tail. How can we drive away unnoticed if the press are camped on your doorstep? They must know your car.'

'They do. I've been taking taxis everywhere to try to throw them off the trail. Pity we can't take a cab to Italy. Do you think I should try to hire a car?'

'To take abroad? I doubt if you could. No. Who looks after your car? Is it a local garage? Can you trust them?'

'Do I trust anyone?'

'You'll have to, that's all. Get them to collect the car from your house. If the reporters start nosing round, they can tell them it needs some work because you're driving north at the weekend.'

'By which time, we can be in France.'

'If Michael gets a move on, yes.'

FOUR

'Climbing in and out of windows, I ask you,' Jessica said to Delia, as she clambered in through the kitchen window once more. 'I just hope that my daily locks up securely tomorrow.'

'Does your daily know where you're going?'

'She does not. She thinks I'm going north, to my parents' house. She's going to look after Harry for me. She knows he fights with Mummy's dogs, so she won't wonder why I'm not taking him. Are you packed, is that suitcase all you're taking?'

'I'm used to travelling light,' said Delia, attempting to stuff a slip down the side of the case.

'Let me,' said Jessica. 'Honestly, with all the travelling you do, why haven't you learned to pack properly?'

'It all comes out creased, whatever I do.'

Jessica was unfolding and refolding and tucking everything in with swift and expert hands. 'There, plenty of room if you pack it right.' She shut the lid and clicked the catches into place. 'Ready?'

'Do we really need to use the fire escape? Surely no one will be outside at this time of night?'

'They know I'm staying with you; don't you think they might be out there in a parked car, with the windows steaming up? We can't risk it.'

They manhandled Delia's suitcase down the metal fire escape, Jessica wincing at every sound they made. The back way from Delia's flat led into a quiet street of Victorian houses. There was a shimmer of frost in the air, and Delia began to cough.

'Control yourself, or you'll wake the neighbours, hacking away like that,' Jessica said.

'Can't help it. Where did you leave the car?'

Jessica's racing-green MG was parked near the corner of a silent street that was inhabited only by a tabby cat slinking home after a night on the tiles. They squeezed Delia's suitcase in beside Jessica's case. Jessica got into the driver's seat and put the key in the ignition. 'There's a road atlas in the glove compartment,' she said. 'Are we heading for Dover?'

'No, we're going to Lydd airfield, in Kent. I'll map-read for you. We're flying the car over to Le Touquet. Expensive, but it's worth it. Michael suggested it. The papers have stringers at the ports, but they won't bother with a small airfield like that. And they won't be expecting you to flee the country, not if they think you're going up to Yorkshire.'

FIVE

Dawn was breaking as a weary Delia and Jessica drove the last few miles to the airport. It was hardly more than a landing field, with a man so clearly ex-RAF in charge that Jessica said in an appalled whisper to Delia, 'Let's hope he didn't know Richie.'

The plane was waiting on the runway, heavy-bellied and stubby-winged. A laconic mechanic took the key and ran the MG up the ramp and into the dark space inside. He clattered back down the ramp and directed them to some rickety steps set against the side of the plane.

'Hardly luxury travel,' Delia said, as she stooped to enter the plane. They sat down on one of the two benches that were placed on either side of the fuselage. Opposite them, a man in a grey suit was reading a newspaper, and beside him were a pair of sleepy-eyed Frenchmen who said good morning; one was smoking a French cigarette that filled the narrow space with strong, foreign fumes.

The plane lumbered along the runway and heaved itself into the air. The sound of the engines was too loud for any conversation; Delia twisted herself round and looked out of the small window. She could see the whirring propeller, and, looking down, the crests of white peaking on grey waves.

They flew low across the Channel, so low that, as they approached the French coast and flew over a fishing boat straggling back to harbour, Delia could see the face of the man at the tiller.

The flight only took half an hour, and by mid-morning, refreshed with black, bitter coffee, they had left Le Touquet and were motoring along straight French roads towards Paris. A slight mist lingered in the air, and it was no warmer than England, but to Delia it felt as though she'd landed in a new world.

'Oh, the relief of getting away,' Jessica said. 'I'm so grateful to you. I hope you meant it about the work.'

'I did. You know me, I'm a pro. If I couldn't spare the time, I'd have said so, even though you are my oldest friend.'

Jessica looked over her shoulder. Behind them the road stretched away between two neat lines of plane trees; the only other person visible was a cyclist in a beret, pedalling slowly and deliberately.

'Do stop looking round,' said Delia. 'We haven't been followed – we'd know by now if we had. Or do you think Giles Slattery will be after us, disguised as a Frenchman on a bicycle?'

'You may joke, but you've no idea how persistent those ghastly reporters can be.'

'Did you tell anyone you were coming to France?'

'Only Mr Ferguson. My lawyer. I think that was all right, don't you?'

'As long as he doesn't spill the beans to any prowling reporters.'

'He won't,' said Jessica, with certainty. 'He's not that sort of man.'

'What's he like? Is he going to put pressure on Richie?'

Mr Ferguson had startled Jessica on her first visit to his offices. Winthrop, Winthrop & Jarvis had refused to act for her, not caring for messy divorce cases, and had recommended

Mr Ferguson, of King's Bench Walk. 'He has a reputation for handling such cases with skill and discretion,' Mr Jarvis told her.

Short, stocky Mr Ferguson was altogether a different kind of lawyer from the grim-visaged Mr Jarvis. No grey striped trousers and black jacket for Mr Ferguson. He wore a crumpled grey suit that had seen better days, favoured loud ties and, Jessica was sure, never wore a bowler hat.

'A foxy man,' Jessica said. 'But very clear. There's no such thing as divorce by consent, although they did try for reform after the war, so he told me. The politicians wouldn't have it. Too risky for the stability of family life. So there have to be grounds.'

'Such as adultery.'

'Or mental cruelty or intolerable conduct – actually, isn't that the adultery bit? Or insanity.'

'You've said that Richie is crazy.'

'He is, but no judge would accept that for a moment. Then there's desertion.'

'Well, you've deserted him.'

'That doesn't count, not if he doesn't want to bring an action. Which he doesn't.'

'Anything else?'

'Rape, sodomy, bestiality.' Jessica laughed. 'Can you imagine stuffy old Jarvis saying those words in front of me?'

'Has Richie been unfaithful?' said Delia.

'Yes.'

'Then you've got grounds.'

'Not grounds I can use.'

Jessica had refused to give any details to Mr Ferguson. 'They say, never lie to your lawyer or your accountant,' he said, giving her a shrewd look.

'I'm not lying. I'm simply telling you that, yes, he has committed adultery, and no, I can't cite the other person.'

'Pity. Of course, any case you brought, especially if it were

31

contested, would be headline news. So if there's someone whose name you don't want to see dragged through the pages of the gutter press . . .'

'Richie knows I won't bring the other woman into it,' Jessica said to Delia. 'So he's sitting pretty. And I get all the opprobrium for walking out on him, and he preserves a hurt and dignified silence.' She fiddled with a thread on her glove. 'Oh, why did I marry him? Theo says . . .' She gave Delia a swift look and changed the subject. 'Heavenly countryside.'

SIX

The newsroom at the *Sketch* was a blaze of lights on a dark morning, and a hive of activity and noise, with phones ringing, messenger boys running in and out, and people having shouted conversations with one another across the room.

'Mr Slattery,' said a brassy blonde in a tight skirt, as the swing doors opened and Giles Slattery came in. 'Telephone message. Your bird's flown the coop.'

'Mrs Meldon?'

'Yes.'

Giles Slattery swore.

The blonde, who had heard much worse, took no notice. 'Her char says she's gone to the country, to her family in Yorkshire. Jim's checking that end.'

'Tell Jim to see what he can find out, but my bet is that she hasn't gone home. Doesn't get on too well with Mummy and Daddy right now; they adore Richie Meldon and are very angry with her.'

'The Meldons are in Scotland,' called out a lissome young man, who was perched on a window sill and twirling a pencil in his fingers. 'Staying with those rich cousins of theirs, the Lander-Husseys. There are a few lines about it in William Hickey's column this morning.'

Giles Slattery hooked his mac on the hatstand and tossed his trilby on to a dusty head of Karl Marx that some office wag had placed on top of a filing cabinet. He sat down and drummed his fingers on the desk.

Where could she have gone? he said to himself. His mouth screwed up at one side as he thought. 'Put Sam on to checking the ferries. Since she's driving, she could be anywhere, but I have a hunch she's heading abroad. Easier for her to hide out on the Continent, out of reach of hubby and the press, that's what she'll think. Well, she thinks wrong.'

Slattery rammed one of his thin cigars into his mouth. He struck a match and lit it, then shook out the match and dropped it on the floor.

'Tell Sam to get on to that airstrip in Kent, what's it called? Lydd. You can fly your car over to France from there, if you've got the money. She'll have gone to Paris; these bloody women escaping from their husbands always head for Paris. God damn the woman for slipping through our fingers. And get me Mr Meldon on the phone.'

'Is he back in the country?'

'How the hell should I know? Just get him, okay?'

SEVEN

Delia drove on in silence, the name Theo sounding in her ears. Theo, Theo. His name still gave her heart a jolt. Theo, Jessica's older brother, the love of her life, now married to her sister, Felicity.

'So you haven't told Theo you're off to Italy?' she said.

'Absolutely not, he'd pass it on to Richie in a flash, don't you think?'

'I'm sure he wouldn't.' Delia couldn't keep the indignation out of her voice. 'You malign him.'

'No, you idolise him. For goodness' sake, Delia, surely you're over him now? He and Felicity have been married for more than two years.'

'Of course I'm over him,' Delia lied.

They drove the next few miles in silence. Then Jessica asked, 'Where are we going in Paris?'

'I thought we'd go to the hotel I usually stay in. It's on the left bank, not smart or opulent, but clean and comfortable, with a little courtyard where one can sit out and have breakfast, if the weather's kind.'

The weather in Paris was kind. For the first time in weeks, Delia felt the tightness in her chest relax. She relished the green bursting out on the trees, the warm spring sunshine, and envied the young lovers who strolled, arms round each other, along the banks of the Seine. She and Jessica walked over the Pont Neuf, and stopped to watch the barges passing beneath them, waving to a girl sitting on the roof of one of them, and then they walked along the quais, passing artists at their easels, a girl sitting with her back against the wall, a typewriter on her knees, a group of boys fishing.

Delia knew Paris much better than Jessica, and they spent two blissful days exploring, shopping and eating.

'You've no idea how wonderful it is not to be constantly avoiding reporters,' Jessica said, after another delicious meal.

'We should drink a toast to Beatrice Malaspina, otherwise we wouldn't be here.'

'I just hope they won't trace me.'

'Madame Doisneau is holding on to the forms we filled in until the day we leave; she says she has no time for the *flics*. Besides, the reporters will be prowling around your parents' place.'

'Yes, but they'll ask questions in the village, and someone's bound to tell them that Mummy and Daddy are away, and that I'm not there either.'

'All that takes time, so while the going's good, just don't think about it. Now, if I'm going to be on time for my appointment with the French lawyer that Mr Winthrop told me to see, I'd better get going.'

The French lawyer turned out to be a Gallic equivalent of Mr Winthrop, dry and lean in a dark suit, but he did unbend enough to tell Delia that she would be joined at the Villa Dante by three other people named in Beatrice Malaspina's will. 'If they agree to make the journey,' he added.

'He wouldn't tell me anything else about them. Clams, all these family lawyers, whatever nationality they are, let's just hope the Italians have more to say,' she said to Jessica afterwards.

'So you haven't found out anything more about Beatrice Malaspina?'

'Nope, nor about the Villa Dante. You do realise that it might turn out to be a boarding house, and Beatrice Malaspina some old dink who took in English guests?'

'It could be. Or a house in an Italian suburb.'

'He showed me where it is on a map. It's near a small town called San Silvestro. Historic and picturesque, he said, but I don't know if he meant the villa or the town.'

'And no details of your fellow legatees?'

'None. I did ask when they'd be arriving at the Villa Dante, but he just said that we all had to be there by the end of the month.'

'Which gives us plenty of time to enjoy a few more days in Paris,' said Jessica happily. 'Let's go back to that shop where we saw those heavenly silk pyjamas.'

'And aren't you going to buy some new summer clothes? It could be warm in Italy.'

Jessica was surprised at that. 'Isn't it always warm in Italy?'

'No,' said Delia. 'I remember singing in Florence one March, I've never been so cold, and there were six inches of snow on the ground; people laughed at my surprise and said that the Italian winter is Italy's best kept secret. On the other hand, I've baked in April in Milan, so there's no telling.'

'I packed a few summer frocks and a sundress and a pair of shorts and bathing things, so that will do me if it's warm.'

They were sitting outside a café near Notre Dame, enjoying an aperitif before deciding where to have dinner. The city was emerging from dusk into the twinkling lights of evening. They watched the stream of people walking past: a man with a parcel dangling from his finger, tied in a neat loop, a woman with a doll-like child tripping along beside her, a pair of high-heeled ladies of the night, little fur collars making a frame for their dramatically made-up faces, an officer whose eyes flickered over them as he slowed for a moment, hesitating, before he strode on; a young couple who could hardly be out of their teens walking with her arm wrapped around his waist while he held her close to him with a protective arm over her shoulders and her other hand in his.

'I like her hairdo,' Delia was saying, but Jessica wasn't listening. She had stiffened, her eyes focused on a figure lounging against a lamp post.

'Giles Slattery,' she breathed. 'Over there, in that mac he always wears, I'd know him anywhere.'

'You're imagining it,' Delia said. 'Beasties under the bed, that's all. Lots of men wear those macs.'

Jessica wasn't imagining anything. Her mind might play tricks on her; she might have caught sight of a stranger in a mac, but no, she was sure it was Slattery; the angle of his hat, his posture, the relaxed stance of a man accustomed to standing and waiting and watching – all the details were horribly familiar. She dragged Delia inside the café and stood by the window, peering out over the letters painted on the glass.

'There he is, leaning against that cast-iron lamp post, just lighting one of those ghastly thin cigars he always has dangling from his mouth.'

Delia was at her shoulder, and saw his face illuminated for a moment by the match. 'God, you're right.'

'No question about it. Do you think he knows where we're staying?'

'Bound to. He must have followed us when we came out of the hotel, otherwise how would he know we were here at this café? Quick, there must be another way out. Let's pay and slip out through the back.'

Which they did, into a noisome alley, with refuse piled against the wall and an unpleasant film on the cobbles underfoot.

'You get the car, and wait for me round the corner from the hotel,' Delia said, as they tumbled out of the taxi which had miraculously been drawn up at the end of the alleyway. 'I'll cram everything into the suitcases and settle up with Madame.'

Delia shot through the door of the hotel as Jessica called out, 'And why not tell her we're going to Austria or Germany? To put Slattery off the scent.'

EIGHT

'Mr Grimond wants to see you right away, Mr Bryant,' said the secretary in the outer office. 'The moment you got in, he said.'

'Have I time for my tea?' Mr Bryant said, eyeing the cup on his desk, which had a saucer balanced on top, and a custard cream biscuit beside it.

'At your peril. He's on the warpath.'

'Better get it over with, I suppose,' said the youthful Mr Bryant with a sigh.

Mr Grimond's office was entirely without colour. Situated on the second floor of a red-brick building in Queen Anne's Gate, it overlooked St James's Park, or would have done if its occupant hadn't chosen to shut out the view with two dingy blinds. A square of grey carpet, of precisely the right size for his civil service rank, was laid on the floor, and on it was placed a dark wooden desk with a scratched leather top, strewn with buff files. Mr Grimond matched the sobriety of his room with his salt and pepper hair, faded tweed suit and brown tie. He sat on a wooden revolving chair that squeaked dismally every time he moved.

'You wanted to see me?' Mr Bryant said.

Grimond looked up from his file. 'Got in at last, have you?

Yes. A man's gone missing. One George Helsinger. Dr Helsinger. Alice has asked for his file. Read it, and then catch the next train to Cambridge.'

'Cambridge?'

'Cambridge. Cold market town on the edge of the fens.'

'I know Cambridge. I was at university there. But why do I have to go to Cambridge?'

'Because the man who's gone missing is one of their boffins.'

'Oh, dear. Is he important?'

'Would I be going to this much trouble if he weren't? He's one of our top men. An atom scientist. Worked on the A bomb at Los Alamos, nothing he doesn't know. And I bet my last ten-bob note he's halfway to Moscow by now.'

'In which case, why am I going to Cambridge?'

'To make enquiries. Talk to his colleagues, his landlady, find out what he's been working on, has he been moody, what are his political views, as if I didn't know. He'll be a Red, like all the rest of them.'

'When was he reported missing?'

'Yesterday, after I noticed that he was down as having been granted a sabbatical. Six months' leave of absence from the laboratory, I ask you, nobody gives us six months off on full pay. I checked to find out where he was spending his time, and it turned out nobody knew. No attachments to any foreign universities – that's what they often do, apparently, take themselves on a jaunt to America or France or somewhere they can be idle at the taxpayer's expense. "Time off to think" is all the idiots he works with could come up with.'

'Do we know if he has actually gone abroad?'

'Told his landlady he was going to the Continent, and didn't know when he'd be back. He's gone all right.'

'Have we traced him?'

'Doing it now, checking on the airports and ferries. Trail

41

will have gone cold; he left the day before yesterday. He's done a flit, defected, no question about it. There'll be hell to pay on this one, mark my words.'

NINE

Marjorie's heart lifted as the ancient taxi, reeking of terrible old French cigarettes, rumbled its way across the cobbled streets. Paris was alive; Paris had been reborn; all the harrowing times of Occupation were now only a memory, if a vivid one for someone of Marjorie's age, who remembered the war and the distress of the fall of France all too well. The houses were still shabby, with peeling paint and crumbling stucco, the roads uneven and pot-holed, the pavements cracked and disorganised; but yet, underneath it all, the vitality of the city was there, unquenched and unmistakable.

And the sun was shining. And she was hungry, very hungry, her hunger sharpened by the shops and stalls they passed, fruit piled high, a little boy walking along with a baguette almost as long as he was tall tucked under his arm, a corner stall with oysters laid out in icy baskets.

The taxi ground to a halt with a screech of uncertain brakes, and the driver heaved himself out and slouched round to let her out and hand her her suitcase.

She recklessly handed over some of her precious francs, including a tip more generous than his surliness warranted, but she was in Paris, and it was spring, and she was, for this moment at least, happy, and the tip earned her an answering smile and even a civil 'Au revoir, Madame'.

Madame! Yes, she'd been Madame for a long time now. How many years it was since she'd arrived in Paris, an eager seventeen-year-old, definitely a mademoiselle, plunging into a delightful world of cafés and jazz and endless, relentless pursuit of love and pleasure and fun. Paris had been her liberation, but it wasn't a liberation that had survived her inevitable return to England, to a necessary job, mind-numbingly boring, so boring that she'd found herself using every scrap of time when the supervisor's eyes weren't on her to scribble stories that took her out of the dull office and into a headier, richer world of the imagination. Then her second liberation, of finding she could make enough money by her pen, just enough to get by, so that she could give up her job, which she'd left with joy in her heart, swearing to herself that never, no, never again would she work in an office.

A thin woman swathed in grey garments, and with dark, suspicious little eyes, pushed a ledger towards her.

'Papers,' she said. 'Passport. How long are you staying?'

It was all so familiar, the Hotel Belfort, with its tiny entrance hall, the vase of dried flowers, dustier and more shrivelled than ever, sitting on the scruffy counter, the brass bell that gave off only a dull thud when struck, instead of the expected clang. Even Madame Roche didn't seem to have changed a bit.

'You don't remember me, Madame Roche? I used to stay here, before the war.'

Madame's eyes flew heavenwards. 'Ah, before the war, that is a long time ago. Who can remember before the war? Everything was different before the war.'

Yes, and I bet you had German lodgers, and fleeced them, just as you've always fleeced your clients, Marjorie thought, as she took the large key that Madame held out for her. Why, she wondered, knowing what Madame Roche was like, had she always stayed here when she was in Paris? Familiarity, and she liked the area: the boulangerie on the corner, the little shop that sold tin goods, the kiosk where she bought her daily paper, the old woman selling flowers from a tiny stall. Buckets and buckets of flowers; no doubt the woman and her flowers were long gone.

It was a mistake. This was a mistake. She should have gone straight through; it was madness to break her journey in Paris. If she'd left early in the morning, caught the first boat, gone straight to the lawyer's office, collected the money, then she could have been on the train to Italy even now, not stirring up old memories that were better forgotten.

Her happy mood was draining away. No, she wasn't going to look back, she wasn't going to let any regrets take her back into the glums. Come on, Marjorie, she told herself. Let's see how much money you've got, and then go out and find a restaurant.

She stared at the notes in the envelope, each bundle held in a paperclip, with a white sheet of paper beneath it. French francs, one said, and a much bigger bundle of Italian lire.

Had they made a mistake? Why on earth would they give her that much money?

'Under the terms of the late Mrs Malaspina's will, we are directed to defray all necessary expenses for your journey to Italy,' the grave lawyer in London had told her. 'We shall give you here in England the maximum you are allowed by government regulations to take out of the country. Obviously, once you are on the other side of the channel, out of the sterling area, such restrictions do not apply, and our colleagues in Paris will ensure that you have enough money to continue on your way to Italy.'

'But who is Beatrice Malaspina? There must be a mistake. I've never heard of her.'

There had been no mistake, the lawyer assured her. Her name, her full name, her address, even her parentage,

45

daughter of Terence Swift, all of it was perfectly correct. The Marjorie Swift that Beatrice Malaspina, the late Beatrice Malaspina, had summoned to Italy was quite definitely her, not some other Marjorie Swift.

She had given up wondering why. Brief fantasies of the white slave trade flashed through her mind, and then she'd laughed at herself. She'd never been the sort to appeal to any kind of white slaver, and now, well past thirty – admit it, nearer forty – skinny and grey after the last few difficult years, she wouldn't fetch sixpence on any slave market.

A scheme, a touch of spivvery? What would be the point? She had nothing that anyone could swindle her out of. Less than a hundred pounds in the world, and that would be gone by the end of the year, and then, horror of horrors, unless a miracle happened, she would be back once more in the office job she'd sworn never to take again.

Always supposing she could find any such employment. Who would want to employ a woman no longer in the first flush of youth, and a woman moreover who hadn't had a proper job for more than ten years? The familiar fear flooded over her, but she pulled herself up. A week ago, she had never heard of Beatrice Malaspina; a week ago, she had no more idea of being in Paris than of finding herself on the moon. Where there was a will, perhaps there was an inheritance, although why a total stranger should leave her so much as a Bible was beyond her.

Unconsciously, as she thrust the key into the lock, and fought the warped door, ideas began to creep into her head. Mistaken identity? Clichéd, but then everything was a cliché until you wrote it afresh. Wills? Murders were done for wills. And mystery, the mysterious woman summoning the English spinster.

She put her suitcase on the rickety stand provided for it, took off her coat – once good, now threadbare – and removed her hat. She washed her face and hands in the basin, supplied with a mere trickle of water, but enough for her purpose. Then, in a moment of bravado, she took out a powder compact, and sponged the last few grains on to her cheeks.

That day in Paris brought Marjorie back into the human race, that was how she saw it. The next morning, the memory of a meal such as she hadn't had for years still in her mouth and in her mind, she woke early, and set off to walk the Paris streets. She stopped for a café au lait and a croissant, the buttery pastry melting in her mouth, a taste so delicious that it almost hurt senses dulled by the last few years of darkness and fear and despair. How could she have thought of leaving it all? Of never again greeting glad day as the sun rose over the Seine, never feeling a taste explode in her mouth, never greedily gulping down coffee, hot and black and bitter.

She walked along the left bank, over the bridges, across the Ile de la Cité. In her mind was the France of Dumas, an untouched world of swords and kings and musketeers, not the rundown shops and streets in front of her eyes. Flaubert would provide a more realistic model, but no, on that day she saw Paris through the eyes of a Romantic, not a realist.

And so the evening brought her, weary, but with an underlying sense of happiness that was so unfamiliar she didn't trust it, to the Gare de Lyon, to catch the overnight Paris-Lyon-Nice train.

On which the French lawyers had booked her a compartment, a bed in a Wagon Lits carriage; a luxury beyond her imagining. She pinched herself as she sniffed the clean white sheets, jumped guiltily as the *conducteur* put his head round the door to enquire if she wanted anything, and then made her pillow wet with tears.

Tears for what, she asked herself, as she turned the damp object over and gave it a defiant punch. For the girl she had once been? For the fact that she was, despite her best efforts, still alive? That someone, even someone she knew no more

47

than the man in the moon, had cared enough to leave instructions and money for her to travel in this quite unaccustomed comfort? Tears of relief for being away from her wretched life in England, of gratitude for the exquisite omelette she had eaten at the station before getting on the train, of anger at herself that she should be grateful for such tiny things.

Les petits riens, she told herself as she snuggled luxuriously into her berth. The train seemed to echo the words, *petits riens, petits riens*. It was the little nothings that made life worth living, in the end.

Then she mocked herself for thinking such nonsense. The *petits riens* were all very well, but it was the greater things of life that caused all the trouble, and they pushed everything else out of the way, crashing in on one's dreams and delights, and turning happiness into misery.

TEN

In the next compartment, George Helsinger wasn't asleep. He preferred wakefulness to sleep whenever possible, only succumbing to slumber when tiredness simply became too much for him. For sleep brought dreams, and these were dreams he could do without. It was odd, that he, the least violent of men, should have become involved in the most violent act humanity had ever wreaked upon itself. And that even ten years later, his guilt and sense of moral failure should still haunt him in this way.

Pure science, that was what his life was about, so how had it ended up with nothing pure about it, and a bang that changed the course of the world? Nothing, now, would or could ever be the same again. He marvelled at how people went about their daily lives as though nothing were different, as though it had merely been another bomb among the tens of thousands, a bigger bomb, but still just death and destruction falling from the sky.

But it changes everything, he wanted to tell people. Only no one wanted to hear what he had to say. It was over now, past, history, what was done was done, and hadn't that act of extreme violence brought an end to all the other violence, and wasn't that a good outcome? And if they now all lived under its shadow and threat, well, wasn't all life a risk?

He had found recently, as he lay in a state between wakefulness and sleep, a zone where the bad dreams and memories were kept at bay, that prayers from his youth came traipsing into his mind. He had, he would have said, long put the fathers and their rigorous, prayer-filled life behind him. He had become a man of science, had turned his back on God, had played God. Along with his fellow scientists.

Yet here were those words, filling his brain with their remorseless repetitions. The Kyrie: *Kyrie eleison, Christe eleison, Kyrie eleison.* Lord have mercy, Christ have mercy, Lord have mercy. Hail Marys – how long was it since he'd said a Hail Mary? Yet the words were there as though they'd never left him: *Ave Maria, gratia plena.* Blessed art thou . . .

Was he losing his wits? Was he going to end up in a mental asylum? He'd heard rumours about some of his fellow scientists, that they'd gone bananas; well, many of them were bananas to start with.

He didn't notice the clean comfort of the sheets; he was moving in a world of bewilderment, in which French lawyers and Wagon Lits reservations seemed to be nothing to do with him. The meeting with the lawyer in England came back to him like the memory of an inexplicable dream.

'You can go?' Mr Winthrop had asked. 'There's no problem about leaving the country?'

George had stared at him. 'There is a problem, for I have no money. And even if I had, the amount one is allowed to take out of the country is, I believe, quite inadequate for anything more than a few days in Ostend.'

'Not quite as bad as that. Many people manage to go away for a fortnight or more on their allowance . . . However, that need not concern us. All your expenses will be paid, and the arrangements for onward travel from Paris will be made across the Channel.'

The late Beatrice Malaspina. Who was this mysterious woman, summoning him from beyond the grave, drawing him across Europe to he knew not what? The lawyer in England had been able to give him no details; the lawyer in Paris was working to precise instructions, he said. If he knew anything more, which George doubted, he was not going to pass on the information.

In the morning, he would be in Nice. Nice! Haven of artists and writers and aristocrats, a world away from his laboratory, from the dingy rooms he occupied in Cambridge, from rainswept, foggy England.

He could see the map of France unfolding in his mind's eye. Down through the Loire valley, the railway line running alongside the great river, down through the heart of France and so into raffish Nice; raffish but at the same time elegant, that was how Nice had been before the war. He had spent a fortnight there in the languorous hot days of 1938, guest of a fellow scientist, unusual for being of a background and wealth quite unlike most scientists.

His host, he recalled, had gone on to enjoy a distinguished war, adviser to Churchill, honours, position.

And, no doubt, a sound digestion and a good conscience, and the ability to sleep at night. Any destruction he had wrought on his fellow human beings had been a remote affair, a matter of memos and committees and impersonal, reasoned decisions.

I should have been a biologist, George told himself. Or a botanist, what harm had botanists ever done to anyone? Would he ever have imagined, as a bony boy, that his passion for mathematics could bring him to a state of such despair? His first teacher had warned him how it might be. 'Numbers will get the better of you, George; you will never be able to escape them. They will be the master, not you.'

Prophetic words, if only uttered to take a brilliant youngster down a peg or two.

Lulled by the steady rhythm of the train, George slept despite himself, overcome by sheer exhaustion. And for once his sleep wasn't trampled on by the hobgoblins of the past; he slept soundly and dreamlessly, and awoke to find the sun straining through the blind, and the *conducteur* rapping at the door to tell him that they would soon be arriving in Nice, and that *petit déjeuner* was being served in the restaurant car.

'Take your passport with you, monsieur. It is not far to the border.'

There was something about borders, Marjorie told herself as she made her way along swaying corridors to the restaurant car for her *petit déjeuner*. Red and white poles and no man's land and customs and officials, and the knowledge that you were passing from one country to an entirely different one.

The restaurant car was surprisingly full; who would have thought there would be so many people travelling to Italy at this time of the year? A waiter hurried forward, shrugging deprecatingly. Madame would sit here, if the gentleman permitted, a fellow English traveller . . .

Marjorie looked at the seat, where a tall, balding man in round spectacles was staring out of the window. The waiter coughed, and the man turned his head, looking at Marjorie with dark, intelligent eyes.

George saw the nervous, bony face of a woman whom he would have known anywhere in the world for an Englishwoman. He half rose, made a little bow. 'Of course, please . . .' with his usual courtesy, although he would have preferred to have his table to himself, not to share it with a woman who would doubtless feel obliged to make conversation. It was odd how English people had reverted to their old habits of reserve and suspicion after the war. Conversations with strangers at bus stops and on trains, being

52

invited in for a cup of tea by neighbours you had never spoken to before, the very unEnglish sense of camaraderie – all of that had vanished. While queues and saving string and old envelopes had stayed. It was very odd.

Marjorie was eyeing the basket of croissants and brioches and fresh rolls in a hungry manner. 'Please,' he said, passing Marjorie the basket; she took a croissant, and sat back to allow the waiter to pour her coffee.

How long would he be staying in Italy? The lawyer had been vague. 'In fact, Dr Helsinger, I have to admit that I know little about Italian legal procedures. It might be a few days, or perhaps longer. There are other interested parties who will be arriving at the Villa Dante, one of them is an American, and of course I have no idea as to his movements or time of arrival. Since the late Mrs Malaspina specified that all the beneficiaries of her will should be brought together at the villa, we must abide by the conditions she laid down.'

'Then there are other people going to Italy from England?'

The lawyer's face had taken on a shuttered look. 'I think I can say yes, but of course under no circumstances can I divulge any details of anyone else named in the will. That would be most improper.'

'No, indeed, quite improper,' George said, at once annoyed with himself for being drawn into the kind of language this stiff-necked lawyer used.

'Delicious,' Marjorie said. 'One has forgotten how food should taste.'

They talked in a polite and distant way about France, France before the war, Paris in the thirties, when George had been a student there, Paris now, as they had glimpsed it during their brief time in the city.

'I, too,' George said, 'was only able to stay one night and I should have liked to stay longer. To revisit old haunts, although of course nothing will be quite the same as it was. It is impossible that it should be.'

'Are you travelling on business?' Marjorie asked.

She had torn a roll apart – why did the English rip at their bread, instead of dissecting it neatly with a knife? – and was spreading it liberally with butter.

'Personal business,' he said.

'Not work. You don't look like a businessman.'

He was startled. What did he look like? He was wearing a suit, a concession to the purpose of his journey. What was there to mark him out as different from his fellow men?

'You look as though you lived by your brains. I see you in a laboratory. Not smells, though, or germs. Too much equipment around you. Are you a scientist?'

Now he was even more startled. 'As it happens, yes. But I find it strange that you can tell. Have we perhaps met . . . ?'

'No.' She was quite definite. 'I'd remember it if we had. Although during the war one met so many people, nearly all of them strangers.'

'So, then, there is something about me that marks me out as a scientist. What would that be?'

Marjorie added a spoonful of raspberry jam to her roll and took a mouthful.

George waited.

'It just came into my head that was what you are,' she said eventually, giving her mouth a determined wipe with her napkin. 'It sometimes does. Are you at a university, or do you work for a company? Or are you that mysterious thing, a government scientist?'

The habit of secrecy was so ingrained in George that he found this impossible to answer. 'I do scientific research' sounded lame, but it was the best he could manage. 'And you, are you travelling for pleasure?'

'Hardly likely or possible, with the sum the government allows us for travel. No, I, too, am here on personal business.'

54

'Are you going to Rome?'

'No, I shall leave the train at a place called La Spezia. Do you know Italy? Is it a pleasant town?'

'A naval port, I believe. Heavily bombed during the war. I have never been there.'

Marjorie seemed to lose interest, her eyes focusing on the scenery outside the window. 'It's very pretty along here. The hills and the sea. Very dramatic. I'm not staying at La Spezia, so I'm not really interested in what it's like. One just says these things, in a conversational way, does one not?'

She picked up her handbag from the seat where she had laid it. It was, he noticed, very shabby, but once it had been an expensive bag. Crocodile. He guessed that she wasn't in comfortable circumstances; there was something of a child with its nose pressed against a shop window about her. She did not look as though she were accustomed to travel of this kind.

Well, she would get off the train at La Spezia, as would he, and vanish to catch her train or bus, or be met by an aunt or a friend, and he would not see her again.

She was holding out her hand. 'Thank you for letting me share your table. Goodbye.'

She was walking away; too thin, and why didn't she hold herself straighter? Then she stopped and looked back at him, a faintly puzzled look on her face.

'Does the name Beatrice Malaspina mean anything to you?'

He was so surprised that he dropped his cup back on to its saucer with a crash that made heads swivel.

Marjorie came back to the table and sat down again. 'I can see it does. Are you named in the will as well? Is that why you're here, on the train? Because, like me, you're on the way to the Villa Dante?'

ELEVEN

Mrs Wolfson was no one's idea of a typical American grand-mother. She was sharp and bohemian, a townee to her finger-tips, and she had never baked an apple pie in her life.

Lucius Wilde had always loved her and had always been in awe of her. It didn't matter that he was a successful man in his thirties; Miffy, as she was known to friends and family alike, still provoked as much respect as affection in him.

'I've come to say goodbye,' he told her, after he'd kissed the beautifully made-up cheek offered to him.

'I shall miss you,' she said. 'I'll order martinis.' She rang the bell and a maid appeared almost at once. 'In the library,' she said, and led the way up the beautiful curved staircase to the first floor.

Mrs Wolfson lived in a brownstone in Boston and had done so since she came to the house as the bride of Edgar Wolfson. Twenty years older than her, he had been a dealer in fine arts, had made a great deal of money, and had acquired for his own walls a large number of paintings, not to mention the sculptures and bronzes and porcelain and rugs that filled every available space.

Lucius loved this house. He loved the paintings, especially

the twentieth-century ones, for his grandfather had had a progressive outlook and bought modern paintings long before the artists became fashionable or expensive.

The martinis came, and Miffy attacked hers with gusto. 'I just love the first cocktail of the day,' she said. 'Paris, and then London?'

'Paris for a couple of weeks, and then I'm going to visit some friends who live near Nice, before going on to England.'

'Nice? To stay with the Forrests, I suppose. Will Elfrida be there? Wasn't she staying with them in Long Island when you met her?'

'Yes, and yes.'

'I wonder why you didn't bring her to meet me.'

'You know why. We became engaged on the eve of her return to England.'

'Bookings can be changed. You'll bring her back to America for a visit as soon as you're married? By which time, of course, it will be too late for you to discover whether I like her or consider her right for you.'

'Come on, Miffy, a man in his thirties is allowed to choose his own wife.'

'A man of any age can choose wrong. It alarms me that your parents are so pleased about the engagement. They say she's just perfect for you.'

'And so she is.'

'You aren't in love with her.'

'Oh, for heaven's sake . . .' Exasperating woman, but of course she was right. She had always been able to see through him and out the other side. 'You'll like her. She's lively and forthright . . .'

'Organising, so I've heard. And determined. I'm sure she'll be a great asset to your career, a woman like that can take a man even to the White House.'

That made him laugh. 'I have no political ambitions.'

'You have no ambitions of any kind, not of your own. All

57

the ambition in your life is provided by other people. Have you ever thought about that?'

'Miffy, do lay off.'

'All right. Now, you've told me your plans, which I already knew: France, then a position in the English branch of the bank. That's not why you're here. Come clean, Lucius. What's on your mind?'

'Did you ever know someone called Beatrice Malaspina?'

The light was fading fast outside the windows, and Lucius didn't notice the watchful light in his grandmother's eyes. 'Because I've had an extraordinary letter from a firm of lawyers. I went to see them, in New York. They told me I'm named in the will of this Beatrice Malaspina.'

'Was she an American?'

Lucius shook his head. 'An Italian, I should think, judging by the name. The firm here are acting for her Italian lawyers. She has – had, I should say – a house on the coast somewhere in the north of Italy. Liguria. The terms of the will state that I must go there, to her house, the Villa Dante, to be able to collect this legacy.'

'Which is?'

'Haven't a clue. Could be a bundle of worthless lire, a set of spoons, her father's stuffed tiger – your guess is as good as mine.'

'How intriguing.'

'So you don't know her?'

'I've never met a Beatrice Malaspina. Of course, you're curious, and wills are wills, and if you're going to be in the south of France it won't be much of a detour – only you don't want to go to Italy.'

She said this as a simple statement of fact; it wasn't a question.

'Not really, no.'

'It was all more than ten years ago. And it was wartime.'

'It was wartime,' he agreed. 'Even so . . .'

'Don't you think it might be time to lay that particular ghost to rest?'

'How can I?'

'By not dwelling on it. Wars happen. These things happen. And your parents have done you no favours by blotting it out of their consciousness and never talking about it.'

'On the contrary, the last thing I want is for them to talk about it.'

'You went to Dr Moreton, but he didn't help.'

'Yes, I did, and no, he didn't.'

Which might be, Lucius reflected, because he didn't tell him the truth. He never had told anyone the truth, not even Miffy, although he wouldn't be surprised if she had guessed a good deal of it.

'Dr Moreton always was a fool. Your mother thinks the world of him; she's never been any kind of judge of character or professional competence. She hasn't learned that a shiny brass plate and hair going grey at the temples don't amount to a row of beans.'

'So.' Lucius leant forward, his hands dropped between his knees. He was looking at his feet, shod in shiny black Oxfords; how he hated polished laced-up shoes.

'So, do I think you should go? I don't deal in shoulds, Lucius, you know that. Have you asked your father if he knows anything about this departed person?'

'No.'

'And you don't intend to. Very wise. Any hint of an inheritance, and he'll want to take over.'

'I did ask Dolores. Whether she knew anything about Beatrice Malaspina.' Dolores had worked for his father's firm for more than thirty years, and she knew all the company's and partners' secrets. 'And drew a blank. She said it meant nothing to her.'

'You're going to Italy, in any case,' said his grandmother. 'You haven't come for advice.'

'No, not really. I thought at first that the lawyers had made a mistake, but no, correct down to the last detail, who I was, where I lived and worked.'

'They wouldn't tell you about Beatrice Malaspina?'

'Clams could learn a thing or two from them. Just acting on instructions from Italy, that's all they'd say. I asked if Beatrice Malaspina had lived to a ripe old age. I mean, she could have turned out to be my contemporary, who knows?'

'And?'

'They did tell me that she had lived to a very good age. And that was all they'd give away.'

'Naturally, you thought you'd come and ask one old relic if she knew another one.'

'Perhaps she was a friend of Grandfather's. That's what I wondered.'

'As I said, I never met anyone of that name.'

Lucius finished his drink and stood up. 'Thank you, Miffy. I'll write and let you know how I get on.'

'Mind you do. I'm intrigued. I shall be keen to hear what is the secret of the Villa Dante. And what Beatrice Malaspina has left you.'

'If it's silver spoons, I'll share them with you.'

'Like I need silver spoons. Find yourself a clear conscience, Lucius, then you can send that back to me. We can all do with one of those.'

The Villa

ONE

The mattresses of Delia's girlhood had all been uncomfortable. Her austere father was a great believer in very firm mattresses; he slept with a sheet of wood beneath his own mattress; and urged the rest of his family and staff to do the same. 'With a hard bed, the body relaxes, not the mattress.'

The mattresses at her Yorkshire boarding school had been thin, lumpy and set on a sagging mesh of strings; those at Girton College, Cambridge, were likewise meagre and designed to keep your mind on higher things than bodily comforts.

Which had left Delia a connoisseur of mattresses, and the one on Beatrice Malaspina's bed was perfect, neither too hard nor too yielding; hooey to her father and his theories of relaxation. Nothing could be more relaxing or comfortable, and when she awoke to the sound of birdsong outside the windows, and saw sunlight filtering through the shutters, it was after a deep and untroubled night's sleep, a rarity for her this winter, cursed as she was with bronchitis.

She slid out of bed and padded across the smooth dark red tiles to the windows: long, double windows stretching almost from the ceiling to the floor. She pulled them open and struggled for a few moments with the shutters before she found the catch and pushed them back against the walls.

Warm air drifted in as she stepped out on to a small terrace. The searing wind had gone, leaving only a slight breeze to make ripples on the red sand, warm and scrunchy under her bare feet.

Delia blinked at the unaccustomed brightness. It was too early in the morning for the sun to be high or hot, but there was a dazzling quality to the light that made her catch her breath. She looked out over a garden, once formal, now sadly overgrown, and saw a silvery gleam in the distance. It took her a few seconds to realise what it was. The sea! So the villa was on the coast.

Crashing sounds came from next door, and Jessica's tousled head looked out of an adjacent window. 'I say, you've got a balcony,' she said.

Her head vanished, and then she was calling out to Delia from the door of her room.

'Come out here, quick,' Delia said. 'You don't want to miss a minute of it.'

They stood together, leaning on the stone balustrade and gazing out at the green and blue and silver vista.

Jessica let out a long sigh. 'Heaven,' she said. 'Pure heaven. And can you hear Chanticleer out there?'

The vigorous cock crows mingled with the sonorous dong of a bell marking the hour.

'Was that seven strokes? Oh, the air is so fresh it almost hurts to breathe.'

'I do so hope this is the Villa Dante,' Delia said. 'We might find we have to decamp to a crumbling old house with no view and bedbugs in the mattresses.'

'I hadn't thought about bedbugs,' Jessica said. 'Still, no itchy bits this morning, and the bedrooms are quite up to date. It could have been all decayed fourposters with mouldering curtains, instead of which we get stylish art deco.'

'The villa is old, though. Eighteenth-century, wouldn't you think?'

'Don't ask me. Could be that, or older, or built fifty years ago. I think Italians, having found the kind of house they like, just go on building them. I'm going to get up, and let's see what we can do about breakfast.' Then, suddenly alert, 'What's that?'

Delia, lost in the view, came to. 'Did you hear something?'

'I think it was the gate. Hang on, we should be able to see it from one of the other rooms.' She vanished, then called across to Delia. 'A stout party in black coming up towards the house. At a guess, I'd say a servant.'

Delia didn't want to greet the new arrival in her night-clothes, so she hurled herself into the bathroom that led off her bedroom, a huge and marbled affair, with, however, no more than a trickle of water coming out of the substantial taps. Five minutes later, she was washed and dressed and running down the stairs, clutching a red clothbound book. She caught up with Jessica, who was still in her pyjamas.

Voices were coming from the kitchen quarters. Delia pushed open the door, and there was the woman in black talking at great speed and at the top of her voice to a harassed-looking man with snow white hair and a wrinkled, deeply tanned face.

'*Buon giorno*,' Delia said.

The woman whirled round, startled, and then burst into smiles and more talk, of which Delia understood not one word.

'Can't you ask her to slow down?' said Jessica.

Delia held up a hand. '*Non capisco*,' she tried.

The flow of words slowed abruptly, and the woman made tutting noises before coming closer, and, jabbing her chest with a plump finger, said as one talking to idiots, 'Benedetta.'

'Signorina Vaughan,' said Delia, pointing to herself.

That brought an immediate and delighted response. '*La Signorina Vaughan, si, si.*'

'Looks like she was expecting you,' Jessica said.

Delia touched Jessica's arm. 'Signora Meldon.' And then, '*Ch'e la Villa Dante?*'

That brought more *si, si*s.

Delia was relieved. But the woman was off again, and, seeing their incomprehension, reached out and took their hands to lead them to the open door. '*Scirocco!*' she said, pointing dramatically to the heap of red sand that had come to rest by the stone threshold.

'I think she means sirocco,' said Delia. '*Si, scirocco,*' she said, and made a whooshing sound to indicate a mighty wind.

The woman nodded vehemently, and then, catching sight of the man standing by the table, flew at him, talking once more at the top of her voice. She paused for a second, to push him forward, saying, 'Pietro, Pietro.' Then she thrust a large broom into his hands and propelled him out of the door.

'Looks like he's on sweeping duty,' Jessica said. 'What's the Italian for breakfast?'

'Bother, I can't remember,' said Delia. She mimed putting food in her mouth; instant comprehension, and Benedetta was urging them out of the kitchen. She bustled past them, and led them along to the entrance hall. There she flung open a door and led the way into a room hardly visible in the semi-darkness. There was the sound of shutters opening, and light poured in from two sets of doors.

Delia stepped out through the doors. 'It's a colonnade,' she called back to Jessica. 'With a vaulted roof.' She came back into the dining room. 'It runs all along this side of the house and there are steps further along down into the garden. Necessary shade for hot summer days, I suppose, and there are plants weaving in and out of the balustrade. Clematis, for one, with masses of flowers, and wisteria.'

'*Prima collazione, subito!*' Benedetta said, setting down a basket of bread and a jug of coffee before whisking herself away.

It was a large, high room with faded frescoes on the panelled wall. A glass table, set on ornate wrought-iron supports, ran almost the length of the room. Four places were set at one end of the table. 'For our fellow guests,' Delia said. 'We're obviously the first to arrive.'

'No one said anything to you about a host or hostess, did they?' Jessica said. 'I mean, there could be a horde of Malaspinas.'

'I told you, there was nothing to be got out of Mr Winthrop, it was like talking to a deed box. But the French lawyer did say there was no one living at the villa now. Perhaps we're all to gather here, for a formal reading of the will.'

'Or to be bumped off, one by one, like in a detective story,' Jessica said cheerfully. 'In any case, they'll have to lay an extra place, if four are expected, since they can't have known I'd be coming as well.'

'I suppose the others were held up by the wind. Or maybe they'll arrive at the last minute. It's not the end of the month yet; the others might not be able to get away as easily as us. Let's hope they'll know something about the mysterious Beatrice Malaspina. Or perhaps it will all turn out to be a dreadful mistake, and they're the grieving heirs and will toss us out into the storm.'

'Doesn't look like there's any storm in the offing just at present,' Jessica said.

Delia stood beside the French window, restless, wanting Jessica to hurry and finish her breakfast.

Jessica poured more coffee. 'Are we going to look round the house?'

'Before anything, I'd like to go to the sea,' said Delia, catching her breath after a sudden fit of coughing. 'Sea air will do me the world of good.'

'You and your fascination with water,' said Jessica. 'No, don't fidget and fret. I'm hungry, and I'm going to finish my breakfast in my own good time. Then we'll go and indulge your Neptune complex.'

Delia loved the sea, and water in all its forms, and the sight of the shining Mediterranean from her bedroom window had filled her with longing to go down to the shore. 'Besides, it's not as though we'd rented the house. It seems rather rude just to prowl around it,' she said, sitting down again and trying not to look impatient.

'Do you suppose there's a private beach?'

'Probably,' said Delia, thumbing through her dictionary. '*Spiaggia* is the Italian for beach. I shall ask Benedetta.'

'Can you manage that? When did you learn Italian? Didn't you only do French and German at Cambridge?'

'We musicians pick up quite a bit, and I bought a Hugo's *Italian in Three Months* to study during rehearsals, there's a terrific amount of sitting about. Crosswords get boring, and I can't knit, so I decided to improve my mind and expand my horizons.'

Benedetta came in to offer more coffee and Delia enquired about the beach, which brought a volley of head-shaking and finger-wagging.

'Can't we go?' Jessica asked.

'I don't think it's territorial, more concern for our health.'

Benedetta was pointing at Delia's chest and making hacking noises.

'Especially for you. She's noticed your cough.'

More Italian poured out of Benedetta, accompanied by much gesticulation.

Delia shrugged. 'She's lost me. We'll just have to find our own way. *Il giardino?*' she said to Benedetta.

Which brought more frowns from Benedetta, and a reluctant gesture towards the steps and the garden and, finally, a dramatic rendering of a person shivering, crossing her arms and slapping herself vigorously.

'She wants you to put on a coat or jacket,' Jessica said. 'I don't need Italian to understand that.'

'Compared to England . . . Oh, all right, I can see you're about to fuss as well.'

Once outside, Delia was glad of the jacket she'd thrown

over her shoulders; the air was fresh and the light breeze had none of the heat of the southerly wind of the night before. Jessica had pulled a jumper on over her shirt and thrust her feet into a pair of disreputable plimsolls.

They went out through the dining room into the colonnade, blinking in the strong sunlight.

'There are paintings on the walls,' said Jessica, stopping to inspect them.

Delia was already running down the steps to the garden, eager to be moving, to get to the sea. How absurd, like a child full of excitement at the beginning of a summer holiday, longing for the first glimpse of the sea, wanting nothing except to be on the beach. She turned and gave the frescoes a cursory glance, then came back up the steps for a closer look. The colours had faded, but the graceful lines of three women in flowing robes set among a luxuriance of leaves and flowers delighted her.

'They look old,' said Jessica. 'Or just faded by the sun, do you think? What are those words written in the curly banners above the figures? Is that Italian?'

'Latin,' said Delia. 'Sapientia, Gloria Mundi and Amor.' She pointed to each figure. 'Wisdom. Glory of the world, which is power, and Love.'

'Not the three graces, then. I must say, Wisdom looks pretty smug.'

'Love even more so. Her expression is like a cat who got the cream.'

'And Gloria Mundi reminds me of Mrs Radbert on speech day.'

Their headmistress had known all about power and possibly wisdom, but love had never tapped that severe woman on the shoulder, Delia was sure. She laughed. Jessica was right; Gloria Mundi only needed an MA gown to be Mrs Radbert's double.

The garden to the front of the house was a formal one, a

pattern edged with bedraggled box hedges, and a desolate, empty fountain in the centre.

Jessica stopped under a broad-leaved tree. 'It's a fig. Look at the leaves, did you ever see such a thing? Like in all those Bible paintings. You don't realise how apt a fig leaf is until you see one, do you? I think if we follow this path, it'll take us to the sea.'

'Through the olive trees. Only think, this time last week we were in damp and foggy London, and now . . .' Delia made a sweeping gesture. 'All this. It's heaven. And I can smell the sea.'

'No Giles Slattery, no Richie.'

'No one knows where I am except old button-mouth Winthrop,' said Delia. 'Not even my agent, who'll be furious when he finds out I've vanished.'

They were walking through pine trees now, umbrella pines that cast a web of shadows around their feet. The ground was dusty and strewn with pine cones and needles, and a smell of resin lingered in the air. It was startling to come out of the darkness into bright sunlight and find the sea stretched out before them, a shimmering, radiant, turquoise blue under a blue heaven.

Delia stood and gazed, the light almost too much to bear, the beauty and the still perfection catching at her throat. In a tree just behind them, a bird was singing its heart out.

'Perfect,' said Jessica with a sigh. 'A little beach, utterly private. With rocks. Isn't it quite, quite perfect?'

'Stone steps going down to the cove,' said Delia, already on her way down. 'Bit slippery, so watch your footing.'

She felt drunk with the colours and the light and the beauty of the place. 'Trees for shelter, rocks to lean against, and this exquisite private place,' she said. 'Lucky old Beatrice Malaspina to have lived here. What a pity it's too early in the year to bathe.'

'We don't know how long we'll be here,' Jessica pointed

out. 'Don't Italians take their time about the law, like late trains and so on? The Mediterranean sense of time, or rather non-sense of time. For myself, looking at this, I feel I could stay here for ever.' She paused. 'Of course, you wouldn't want to, not with your music to get back to.'

She perched herself on a rock and rolled up the legs of her trousers before dragging her plimsolls off and walking down to the sea.

'I'll worry about work when my chest's better,' Delia said. There was no point in fretting over her work; at the very thought of it, she began to cough. 'Besides, in a house like the Villa Dante, I'd be surprised if there weren't a piano. I've brought some music with me.'

'It's chilly,' Jessica announced, dipping white toes into the tiny lapping waves. 'About the same as Scarborough in July, though, and I've swum in that.'

'You aren't going to swim?'

'I might, if the weather stays warm. Too cold for you, though, with that chest of yours, so don't go getting any ideas. A paddle is your lot for the time being.'

'I've got stockings on.' Why hadn't she put on slacks, like Jessica?

'No one's looking.'

True. Delia hitched up her skirt and undid her suspenders. She rolled down her stockings and took them off, laying them carefully on a smooth rock, and went down to the water's edge.

'We'll be all sandy and gritty and we've nothing to dry our feet on,' she said, coming alive as the chill water swirled about her ankles. 'This is bliss.'

She looked down at her toes, distorted by the clear green-blue water, and wriggled them in the sandy shingle, disturbing a shoal of tiny fish as they fluttered past.

'It's odd,' she said as they sat on a rock and dried their feet with Jessica's handkerchief, 'to be staying in a house with no hostess. I feel as though Beatrice Malaspina is going to

71

come sweeping into the dining room, to ask if we slept all right and whether we have everything we need in our rooms.'

'She'd better not. A ghost would be too much.'

'I wonder who the house does belong to.'

'You, perhaps. The mysterious Beatrice M might have left it to you in her will.'

'Why should she?'

They sat in companionable silence, listening to the birds' joyful song from the nearby trees, and the mew of gulls out at sea.

Delia lifted her face up to the sun. 'I can't believe how warm it is. So much for Benedetta and her shivers. Mind you, the guidebook is very doleful on the subject of Italian weather, which the author says is full of nasty surprises for unwary travellers. He advises warm underwear and thick coats until May, as the weather in most parts of Italy can be surprisingly inclement.'

'Killjoy.'

'He sounds like a man after my father's heart – you know how he mistrusts warmth and sunshine, as leading to lax habits and taking the pep out of the muscles of mind and body. And also, they drink wine in Italy, how shocking!'

'Felicity drinks. Last time I saw her, she was guzzling cocktails like nobody's business. I suppose she caught the habit from Theo, he's a great cocktail man.'

The spell was broken; the mere thought of Theo, the mention of his name, took the pleasure out of the day. Delia stood up. 'Let's go back to the house, and sit on the terrace and just do nothing at all.'

'We could look round the house.'

'Later. There's plenty of time. I shall go upstairs to change into a sundress, you find Benedetta and ask what we can sit on. I'll look up the word for deckchair in the dictionary.'

Benedetta was very doubtful about the deckchairs. It seemed that April was not only a month to go nowhere near the sea; it was also definitely not a month for sitting outside in the sun. Reluctantly, she instructed Pietro to bring out some comfortable chairs. She followed him with armfuls of cushions and several rugs.

'I think she means us to swathe ourselves in these, like passengers on an Atlantic crossing,' Delia said, taking a cushion and ignoring the rugs.

Jessica pushed her sunglasses up on her forehead and lay back, letting her mind drift. It was extraordinary how easy it was here just to be, to simply exist, free from the endless round of repetitive, tedious memories of a past she longed to forget, but which refused to go away.

'The wardrobes in the bedrooms are full of clothes,' Delia said. 'Did you notice?'

'Perhaps Beatrice Malaspina was a dressy woman.'

'They can't all be hers, because they aren't the same size.'

'Family clothes. Or maybe she had to watch her weight.'

'She might grow fatter and thinner, but she can hardly have grown or shrunk several inches. Heavenly evening dresses from the thirties, do you remember how glamorous they were?'

'Oh, yes, and didn't you long for the time when you could dress every evening? And then, of course, when it was our turn, it was all post-war austerity and clothes rationing.'

'You've some lovely frocks now. That's what comes of marrying a rich husband.'

Jessica was silent for a moment. Then she said, 'Richie will have had to buy himself some new clothes. I never told you what I did before I left, did I?'

It had surprised her, the visceral rage she felt for Richie at that point. Opening his large wardrobe she had hauled out all twenty-three of the Savile Row suits that were hanging there. She looked at them, lying in a heap on the bed, and then ran downstairs to his study for the large pair of scissors he kept on his desk. She cut two inches off sleeves and hem of every jacket and every pair of trousers. Pleased with

73

her efforts, she made all his shirts short-sleeved, and hacked pieces out of his stack of starched collars.

Getting into her stride, she threw away one of each pair of cufflinks, snipped the strings on his squash and tennis racquets and dented his golf clubs and skates with some hefty bangs of a hammer. More cutting work saw to his fishing rods and driving goggles, and then she carefully removed every photo he possessed of her – not that there were many of them, only the large studio shots in heavy silver frames designed to look good on the baby grand which no one ever played. The pictures and snapshots of them together she dealt with by removing herself from the photos, leaving him gazing at nothing but blank, jagged-edged shapes.

He was beside himself with rage when he discovered the extent of her destructive efforts.

'Grounds for divorce, don't you agree?' she shouted at him down the telephone before slamming the receiver down and then, swiftly, picking it up again to ask the operator how she could change her number. 'I've been getting nuisance calls, you see.'

'Goodness, you must have been in a temper,' said Delia. 'How very unlike you. I wish I'd been there, I can't imagine you laying into his things like that.'

'It was surprising, wasn't it? But I enjoyed doing it. Very Freudian, I dare say. I wonder how he explained the sudden need for new suits to his tailors.'

'I expect they've seen it all before.'

'I can't believe I ever lived in that house with Richie. It all seems far away and unreal.'

'The Villa Dante has a timeless quality,' Delia said, closing her eyes. 'As though nothing exists except the present moment.'

TWO

Which wasn't, as it turned out, a very long moment, for barely half an hour later, when Delia was just drifting into a pleasant doze of warmth and sunshine and fresh air, and Jessica was well into her book, there were sounds of arrival, of a revving car, of voices: Benedetta's, Pietro's, another Italian man and then, unmistakably, people speaking in English.

'Oh, Lord,' said Jessica, laying down her book and swinging her legs to the ground. 'I think your fellow legatees are here.'

Delia didn't feel like greeting these people clad in a brief green sundress but Jessica, cheerful in the beige shorts she had put on when they came back from the sea, had no such qualms.

The Italian man, who had the slanting eyes and lively figure of a faun from the classical world, announced himself in a flurry of bows, eyeing Jessica's legs with evident approval, seizing her hand and bending over it, crying out how glad he was to make the acquaintance of Miss Vaughan.

'No doubt,' said Jessica. 'Only that's not me. I'm Mrs Meldon. This is Miss Vaughan.'

Dark eyes glowing at the sight of Delia's shapely form. 'But there is no Mrs Meldon expected,' he cried. 'I know nothing of any Mrs Meldon.'

'I drove here with Miss Vaughan,' Jessica said. 'The lawyers in Paris knew I was coming. Didn't they tell you?'

'No, the lawyer here, which is me, knows nothing about it; no one tells me anything. However,' he said, brightening, 'there is no problem, with the Villa Dante so large, and how pleasant for Dr Helsinger to have such charming feminine company.'

Delia was about to ask the faun what his name was when he recalled his manners, and with profuse apologies announced that he was Dottore Calderini, *avvocato*, legal adviser to the late Beatrice Malaspina, 'Such a wonderful lady, such a loss.'

Delia turned her attention to her fellow legatees. A dark woman with a bony face and angular frame, too thin for herself, and a tall balding man with intelligent, tired eyes and those round spectacles that no one wore any more. A don, by the look of him. Probably not the most exciting company in the world, but one of them might turn out to be a mine of information about Beatrice Malaspina and the Villa Dante.

The woman held out her hand. 'How do you do? I'm Marjorie Swift. This is George Helsinger. Are you here because of the will as well? The lawyers said there were four of us.'

'Only I'm not one of them,' said Jessica. 'Just a friend.'

'So there's one more to come,' said Marjorie, looking round as though she expected another legatee to leap out of a bush.

'Indeed, indeed, but as to when that will be I cannot tell you,' cried Dr Calderini. 'For I do not know when he comes, although it must be before May begins. So I am afraid here you must stay until we know he is coming, until he arrives.'

'What if he never comes?' asked Delia.

'People in wills always come,' said the lawyer with a sudden air of worldly cynicism. 'You may take my word for it.'

'I think,' said Delia, 'that Benedetta should show Miss – Mrs? – Miss Swift and Dr Helsinger to their rooms. If they've had a long train journey . . .'

'Long, but extremely comfortable,' said Marjorie. 'And I think first names, don't you, given the circumstances? I'm Marjorie.'

'My name's Delia, and this is Jessica.'

George shook hands with Delia and Jessica. 'I should be happy if you would call me George.' In the distance a church bell was tolling a single note, the sound carrying in the still air. 'The angelus,' said George.

'What?' said Delia.

'It is a bell rung every day at noon.'

They walked together towards the house and up the flight of shallow stone steps that led to the front door. At the threshold, Dr Calderini paused with a polite *Permesso?* before stepping inside.

Marjorie and George stood, amazed by the frescoes, exclaiming at the beauty of the marble-floored hall. 'And do I see a garden beyond?' said Marjorie.

'Neglected, now,' said Delia, 'but it must have been lovely once. I don't suppose they've had the staff to keep it up, not since the war, not if it's the same as in England.'

'Ah, the war,' said Dr Calderini, who had been conversing in rapid Italian with Benedetta. 'Everything was lovely before the war.'

Delia doubted it, remembering what she had heard and read about Mussolini and his fascist government, but certainly it would be true as far as gardens and houses went.

'And what's this?' Marjorie said. She was standing in front of a column on which sat a glass box.

'I didn't notice that last night,' said Delia, going to have a look.

'I thought it was part of the painting, all that perspective and detail that deceives the eye,' said Jessica.

'It's a thumping great ring,' Delia said.

'Ah, that is a cardinal's ring,' said Dr Calderini. 'A great treasure – the Signora Malaspina was much attached to it.

It belonged to Cardinal Saraceno, who built the villa. Although it has been much altered since his day, naturally. There is a fine portrait of him, also, in the house. It is a poisoner's ring,' he added casually. 'Not the ring of his office.'

'Poisoner's ring?' said Jessica. 'Belonging to a cardinal?'

'He was quite a wicked cardinal.'

That would confirm all her father's long-held prejudices as to the untrustworthiness of any Catholic priest, let alone a cardinal, thought Delia. She laughed. 'So the house belonged to a prince of the church who poisoned people. I knew the Villa Dante was extraordinary the moment we got here.'

'You will be very comfortable here,' said Dr Calderini. 'People are always happy and comfortable at the Villa Dante, even in these troubled times, and Benedetta will look after you. She is to have help from the town if she needs it. Now, I shall take my leave.'

'Hang on,' said Delia. 'Haven't you forgotten something? I mean, we want to know why we're here.'

Dr Calderini turned himself into a tragic mask of regret. 'So sorry, so sad to have to be disobliging, but Signora Malaspina's orders were laid down most strictly. I am not at liberty to tell you anything until all four of you are present at the Villa Dante, which will, I am sure, be very soon. Until then, my lips are sealed, I can say nothing. So,' he finished, bowing and smiling as he headed for the steps, 'enjoy the hospitality of the villa as Signora Malaspina wanted. You are to make yourselves completely at home. When the fourth man is here, then I will be back, and all will be made clear.'

And with a few parting words for Benedetta, he was gone.

Delia turned to Marjorie. 'You and Dr Helsinger, I mean George, travelled together? Are you old friends?'

'We met on the train, I've never set eyes on him before.'

'Did you know Beatrice Malaspina? Can you tell us anything about her?'

'I never knew her, and I know nothing at all about her;

this whole business came as a bolt from the blue. I have no idea who she may have been, and nor, I may say, does George Helsinger; we discovered that in our conversation on the train. Do you mean you don't know why you are here, either?'

'Except for the will, no.'

'Perhaps the mysterious fourth legatee will be able to enlighten us. If he ever arrives. Meanwhile, I'm perfectly amazed to be here, and I intend to make the most of every minute that I'm away from England.'

She spoke with such vehemence that Delia was surprised, but she couldn't find out any more about her, since Benedetta had appeared and was clucking with impatience to carry off the new arrivals to their rooms.

'Well,' said Jessica, as she and Delia sat on the curved stone benches under the frescoes to wait for the others. 'What do you make of your fellow guests?'

'It makes me wonder more and more about Beatrice Malaspina,' said Delia.

'It's a pity they had to arrive this morning. Now we shall have to be sociable and make polite conversation. I can't see that we're going to have anything in common with either of them.'

'I think they look quite interesting. George Helsinger – can he be English with a name like that? – has a clever, interesting kind of face. I don't know what to make of Marjorie. Dreadful clothes and no expression on her face, yet I get the feeling she's far from dim.'

'Women's Institute spinster type,' said Jessica. 'Lord help us.'

Had they but known it, Marjorie was summing them all up in exactly the same way. She had no worries about George. A kind, intelligent man, with a tormented soul. What was worrying him so greatly? An experiment that had gone wrong? Or might he be being chased by foreign agents, keen on extracting atomic secrets? In a flash, she pictured men with hats drawn low over their faces, in belted raincoats, lurking in doorways . . .

They hadn't talked much more on the train, merely exchanging remarks as to how odd this whole Beatrice Malaspina business was. Then she had returned to her own compartment, to sit by the window and marvel at the blue depth of the sea as the train wound its way down the coast.

They had met up again at La Spezia, where they transferred to a local train with wooden seats and an ancient engine, which reminded them both of wartime rail travel in England. They alighted at a deserted-looking station; what a long way down from the train platforms were in Italy, she thought, as she reached up for the suitcase that George was holding out to her.

'Now, what is best for us to do?' George said as he joined her on the platform. 'This station is a good walk from the town, which, as you see, is up the hill. Perhaps there will be a taxi.'

For a moment her imagination ran riot again. The whole thing was a set-up, there was no Villa Dante, no will, no Beatrice Malaspina, they had been lured here to be kidnapped and killed after torture to extract secret information. At least, they could extract scientific secrets from Dr Helsinger. Her mind ran on sinister lines: remote Italian castles in the style of *The Mysteries of Udolpho* . . . would there be a readership for a modern gothic? People had wanted comforting reads during the war, Jane Austen, that kind of thing, but gangster movies were popular, and so . . .

She came back to reality with a jolt, as George's voice repeated what he had been saying. 'I heard a car, and I see a man approaching. I think someone has come to meet us.'

Now, when Benedetta had whisked herself out of the room, Marjorie felt in the bottom of her suitcase and retrieved a notebook. A hard-covered notebook which she had bought in Paris, unable to resist the allure of beautiful stationery. She shouldn't be spending the lawyer's money on any such thing, but she had forgone lunch, satisfying her hunger with a ham baguette. The difference in cost would surely cover the price of the notebook.

She sat down on the bed and opened the notebook. The blank page stared up at her, as so many blank pages had done for so long. She closed it again. She had bought it hoping to keep a journal of her travels, of her Italian adventure. Nothing more. Facts, only facts. She took a deep breath, dug in her handbag for her fountain pen, unscrewed the top, opened the notebook and resolutely wrote the date at the top of the page. She underlined it, and wrote beneath it in her copperplate script, *The Villa Dante*.

She put the notebook down, and went over to the window. Delia Vaughan, rather an exotic creature, with that mass of hair and vivacious eyes, and a beautiful speaking voice. Jessica Meldon – Mrs Meldon – a typical product of the English upper classes, no doubt a crashing snob, a pity Delia had felt it necessary to bring such a friend – and where was Mr Meldon, whose name was never out of the papers? The couple were estranged, so the gossip columnists claimed. A pity she was here; the Villa Dante didn't at all seem the right kind of place for a flighty socialite who'd quarrelled with her husband.

THREE

They lunched on seafood risotto and *arrosto* of chicken, followed by cheese and fruit, and then, as they drank tiny cups of bitter black coffee, George politely asked Delia and Jessica if they would show him, and Marjorie, if she wished it, round the villa.

Jessica and Delia looked at each other.

'Actually,' Jessica said, 'we haven't seen much of it ourselves. We went to the beach after breakfast, and then you arrived. And yesterday, when we came, it was the evening, we only had candles and oil lamps, and were too tired after the drive to look at anything except our pillows, do you see?'

'We weren't sure about looking round, in any case,' Delia said. 'It seemed intrusive. But since the lawyer said we were to make ourselves at home, and there's no host or hostess to offend . . .'

'We can explore and discover the villa together, in that case,' said George. 'We can be systematic, let us go to the front of the house and begin our explorations there.'

He led the way round the outside of the house, and they stood for a moment at the foot of the shallow flight of steps that led to the three arches of the loggia. They looked up at the mellow façade, a faded cream with brown shutters at all the windows and a line of scooped terracotta roof tiles far above them.

George squinted owlishly up at the pediment. 'It is very harmonious,' he said. 'You see that the windows on either side repeat the triangular shape above them.'

They walked up the flight of steps and through the front door.

'Do you know about Italian houses?' Jessica asked George. 'I thought it must be eighteenth-century, but Delia says it's older, because of the frescoes.'

'Older than that,' said Marjorie. 'I dare say it's been altered a lot, and probably was done over in the eighteenth century, but it must be Renaissance originally, only look at the proportions.'

'Even older than the sixteenth century I think, in parts,' said George. 'Have you noticed that there is a tower at the back? That is mediaeval, I should say.'

Delia still found the trompe l'oeil disturbing as she wandered round, looking at the paintings. 'It's odd, the mixture of everyday and mythological. Here's the servant in his tights I noticed last night, but over there is the story of Ariadne. Just look at the muscles on the Minotaur's chest.'

Marjorie came over to have a look. 'That must be Theseus, looking very pleased with himself. I never thought much of Theseus, he's the kind of man who would be a politician in the modern world.' She followed the images round to the other wall. 'Here is Dionysus, on his ivy-clad ship, sailing in to find Ariadne on the beach. And here he is with all his maenads, dancing among the vines.'

'Those grapes look real enough to eat,' said Delia as they paused to look at an ebullient Bacchus with attendant nymphs.

'They've been making a night of it by the look of them,' said Jessica. 'Look at the ceiling.' She pointed upwards to a riot of gods and goddesses frolicking in billowing clouds.

'Can you imagine what your father would have to say about it, Delia?' And, by way of explanation to the others, 'Delia's father is something of a puritan.'

'I don't think he'd mind half so much about these as he would if the paintings were saints and martyrs. Those are what really irk him.'

They went through the wide central door which led into a second room, overlooking the gardens at the back.

'More wall paintings, and windows that aren't windows at all,' said Jessica.

'Classical landscapes,' said George. 'Very realistic.'

'On this wall is Prometheus,' Marjorie said. 'That's an odd choice, not nearly such a happy story as Ariadne and Dionysus.'

'Who was Prometheus?' asked Jessica.

Marjorie gave her a scornful glance. 'He stole fire from the gods to give it to humans, and so they punished him.'

Delia looked at the eagle swooping down towards the bound figure, and shivered.

'And over there,' said Marjorie, 'if I'm not mistaken, is a sibyl.'

'Go on, then,' said Jessica. 'I've got my hand up. Who or what is a sibyl?'

'Sibyls prophesied. This one is a Cumaean sibyl. She's holding the golden branch to give to Aeneas so that he can go down into the underworld. In Virgil – you have read Virgil?'

'Not to remember a word of it,' said Jessica. 'I was hopeless at Latin.'

'Dido's betrayer,' said Delia, feeling on familiar ground there; she had sung the role of Dido. 'Dido, queen of Carthage, Jessica; come on, you've heard of her.'

George had returned to the entrance hall and was investigating what was through the other two doors. One led to a marble staircase, and the other into a small antechamber, with only a pair of painted columns for decoration.

'That's the door to the dining room,' said Jessica, standing with her back to the garden and pointing to the door on her left. 'So the one opposite it is probably the drawing room. The arcade stretches right across the back. Wonderful shade from the summer heat.'

By unspoken consent, they went out of the doors into the vaulted arcade.

'More frescoes, you see,' said Delia, pointing to the female figures of Sapientia, Amor and Gloria Mundi.

'And painted columns,' said Marjorie. 'What wicked satyr faces.'

How extraordinary it must be to live in such a house, surrounded by images of classical gods and goddesses disporting themselves with frivolous abandon over walls and ceilings. 'Let's go and see what's in the tower,' said Delia.

'I think,' said George, walking backwards, 'that at one time the tower was attached to the main house. There is a wing stretching out on the other side there—'

'Which is Benedetta's territory, isn't it?' said Jessica, counting the windows. 'Where the colonnade bit ends, there's the octagonal room beyond the circular staircase, and then there's a passageway that leads into the kitchens.'

'Just so,' said George. 'So there would have been such rooms on this side. However, they are gone, and only this single tower remains.'

The three-storeyed tower was round, but had another section attached to it of a more regular shape. 'Which is not nearly as old as the tower,' Marjorie said.

'How do you know?' said Jessica.

'It's built of stones that are all the same size.'

The tower itself was built of a motley collection of stones and brick. Marjorie rubbed a finger along one of the shallow bricks. 'Roman.'

'We've caught ourselves a know-it-all,' Jessica whispered in Delia's ear, but not quietly enough, Delia suspected, for the remark to have escaped Marjorie, judging by the quick flush of colour on her cheekbones.

For a moment, she was annoyed with Jessica, who seemed to have taken one of her rare dislikes to Marjorie. Well, good manners would have to prevail, if they were to survive one another's company until the fourth man arrived and the mystery of the will was solved.

'It's like something out of the Brothers Grimm,' she said, moving away from Jessica and walking round the tower to find the entrance. A Rapunzel tower, and she was unreasonably disappointed when they reached the stout door to find it chained and padlocked. A faded notice was threaded on to a loop of chain, with *Pericoloso* written on it in red letters.

'Which means dangerous,' said Delia. 'Oh, bother. Crumbling stonework, I suppose.'

Benedetta must have seen them by the tower, for her small figure hurtled out of the house, cries of disapproval on her lips as she hurried up to them, wagging her finger in a most definite way.

'Is she telling us that the tower is out of bounds?' said Jessica.

'We can see that for ourselves,' said Marjorie.

Delia was listening carefully to Benedetta's flow of words. 'I think she's asking us if we've seen the *salotto*. That's the drawing room.' She shook her head, and Benedetta seized her arm, pulling her towards the steps and back inside.

'*Ecco!*' announced Benedetta, as she swung open the door to the main room of the house. The shutters were closed, but instead of opening them, she switched on the lights. '*Il salotto.*'

'I was right, it's the drawing room,' said Delia. 'Goodness, look at the ceiling.' She turned to Benedetta and gestured to the shuttered windows, and Benedetta shook her head and made negative tutting sounds. Then she relented, and went

86

over to the windows to open the shutters at the two windows which led out on to the arcaded terrace, George leaping across to help her.

Even with the shutters open, the light in the room was muted, but now they could see up into the vaulted ceiling, which was a deep, dark blue, scattered with stars.

'How pretty,' said Delia, tilting her head back to get a better view.

She had expected the drawing room to have heavy, dark wooden furniture, and she was surprised by the cream walls and panelling, and modern furniture, of a kind, she said in an awed way, that one mostly saw in magazines.

'Comfortable, though,' said Jessica, bouncing down on an immense sofa.

Benedetta looked pleased at their evident admiration, and burst into a torrent of Italian, from which Delia gathered that the room was entirely the work of Beatrice Malaspina. Benedetta was pointing with an air of pride at the frieze of figures painted along the walls at shoulder height. They were dressed in mediaeval costume, Delia saw, as she went to have a closer look.

'Not old, of course,' said Marjorie. 'Old in style, but modern in execution. And how varied; look, this man is almost surreal, and this poor creature has been so cubified you can't tell if it's a man or a woman. It isn't finished, either – there are the outlines of more figures that haven't been painted in. I wish we could see it properly, this part of the room is very dim.'

There was another window on that side, with a closed, slatted wooden blind over it. Delia went to pull the slats open, but the string had no effect, and Benedetta came over to take it from her hand, shaking her head again and showing her that it was firmly stuck.

'It's like the pilgrimage to Canterbury,' said Delia, peering at the figures, which were walking along a road, between buildings painted in a slanting two-dimensional way.

'Not Chaucer, but another great mediaeval poet, I think you'll find,' said Marjorie. 'Dante. Look, there he is, in the red hat, greeting the line of people. And the building he's standing in front of is the Villa Dante, I'm sure it is.'

'How very clever of you to recognise him,' said Jessica.

'There's a famous painting of Dante in a cap like that,' said Marjorie, sounding slightly defensive for the first time. 'This is copied almost exactly, so it's hardly clever of me. And, given the name of the villa, it's not surprising to find a picture of him here.'

'I wonder if the house actually has any connection with Dante?' George said. 'Perhaps he stayed here. Perhaps Benedetta would know.'

Delia was listening hard to what Benedetta was telling them about the figures painted on the wall. She shook her head, frustrated. 'She's too fast for me. I really am quite useless at Italian.'

'We have to be grateful that one of us has any knowledge of Italian,' said George. 'I regret that I never learned the language, although, unlike Jessica' – with an apologetic smile in her direction – 'I was good at Latin.'

'Oh, Latin,' said Delia. 'It isn't at all the same, you know. They pronounce all the words differently, for one thing, and then one imagines that the Romans spoke in measured tones, like stone inscriptions.'

'Whereas,' said Marjorie, 'they no doubt gabbled away like anything. Do you think that's a portrait of Beatrice Malaspina?'

The painting hung on the far wall on a panel between two flat fluted columns. It was a full-length portrait of a woman dressed in evening dress in the style of the late nineteenth century, her hair swept up, a black velvet ribbon at her slender throat. Her dress was black, and cut very low. Paris, thought Delia, and what a beautiful woman she must have been. No, not exactly a beauty; striking, rather, with that mass of hair and those huge dark eyes.

Benedetta hurried over to press a switch that illuminated the painting from above. In the brighter light, Delia could see that the hair of the woman in the portrait was very dark red, not unlike her own, but with glints to it that hers didn't have. 'And just look at that diamond on the velvet collar, what a huge stone,' she said.

Whatever else Beatrice Malaspina was, she had been rich. Or married to a rich man, which amounted to the same thing.

Or did it? Her mother was married to a rich man, but did that mean she was too? Far from it, with every penny counted, every item of expenditure having to be justified. Delia's own first act of financial independence had been to open an account at a different bank from the one where all the family had their business; goodness, what a storm that had provoked. Father hated not being in control of her money.

'I think it's by Sargent,' she said, after staring at the picture for a while longer. 'We have a portrait of my mother painted by Sargent.'

'A fashionable lady,' said George. He was doing a swift calculation in his head. 'How old would you say she was in that painting? Late twenties? Early thirties?'

Marjorie had her head on one side. 'Past thirty. She looks slightly younger than she is because of the way the painter has chosen to light the portrait.'

Delia was surprised at how definite Marjorie was. Was she going to turn out to be one of those assertive women who always insisted that they, and they alone, were right? If so, she, as well as Jessica, would find her a tiresome companion.

'In that case,' George said, 'we may make a guess as to when she was born. That is, if one can date a picture by the clothes, which is more than I can do.'

'About 1900,' said Delia. 'I know something about clothes of that time,' she added.

'In which case, she would have been born in 1870 or thereabouts,' said George.

'So she must have been in her late eighties when she died.'

'A good age,' said George. 'Let us hope that we live so long.'

'Speak for yourself,' said Marjorie, but so quietly that Delia only just caught the bitter words.

Delia had been drawn irresistibly to the piano which stood close to a window. She lifted the lid and tried a few chords, then pulled a face. 'It needs tuning, but it's a good one; nice touch, excellent tone, I should say.'

Benedetta was beside her, gesturing and talking much too fast. Delia sat back on the piano stool and gestured to her to slow down. Benedetta tried again.

'It was Beatrice Malaspina's piano. I mean, of course it was hers, this was her house, but she played it. At least, I think that's what she's saying.'

Benedetta seized Delia's hand in a surprisingly strong grasp and tugged her up from the stool. 'Okay,' said Delia, disentangling herself with some difficulty. 'What do you want to show me? Oh, a cupboard full of music, how heavenly. Here's the full score of *The Magic Flute*. Perfect; I see Beatrice Malaspina as a Mozartian.'

'Now we've lost her,' Jessica said to George.

'I take it Miss Vaughan plays the piano?'

'Delia is a professional singer. Opera.'

'Then it is a shame that the piano is out of tune,' said George. 'Otherwise we might have had the pleasure of hearing her sing.'

Benedetta clearly considered they had spent enough time in the drawing room. She switched off the light above the painting, and went over to close the shutters.

'It's an evening room, with doors open on to that big terrace and a view of the sun setting over the sea,' said Marjorie.

'We can come in here after dinner,' said George.

'If Benedetta will let us,' said Jessica. 'She's very bossy.'

As Benedetta led the way from the room, Delia lingered for a last look at the painting. She gazed up at it, the image of her mother's portrait strong in her mind; one dissolved into the other, and she was back, far back in her childhood, looking at the picture of her mother while her parents had a furious argument.

She must have been very young. Three or so. Her nurse talked about it for years afterwards. She had never forgotten the day that little Delia wickedly escaped her eagle eye and scampered away, undetected, to the forbidden territory of the gate which led through into the churchyard.

The Georgian house was built, in true manorial style, next to the village church. In former days, the family would have walked to divine service along the path, through the gate and so on to church land. But her father had bought the house and not the religion. Lord Saltford had been brought up a Nonconformist, and he would have nothing to do with the Church of England, however close at hand. He even objected to the bells as being frivolous in their exuberant peals, but that was something he couldn't fix, the village having a strong tradition of bell-ringing that no newcomer, however rich, was going to change.

So the gate was kept shut, but on the other side of the gate on that particular day was Pansy the donkey. Pansy was the love of Delia's young life, and she considered it unfair that Pansy should be allowed into the churchyard as a neighbourly gesture to graze the grass and save the aged sexton's labours, while she had to remain on this side of the gate.

The latch had not caught, the gate swung open, and Delia escaped through it. Wily beyond her years, she had closed the gate behind her, and it was several hours before the desperate nurse discovered her, curled up under an ancient yew, fast asleep.

The row was a distant memory, beyond her understanding then, but frightening as arguing parents are to a child, even to a child of her time who spent most of her life in the company of her nurse upstairs in the nursery. On that occasion, her nurse, distraught and sobbing in the kitchen, had left her with her mother, and there was her father accusing her mother of not caring for her at all, of deliberately letting her roam, of not immediately sending out searchers to look for her. The child might have been anywhere, could even have been abducted, held for ransom. She could, he bellowed at her mother, in a terrifying rage now, at least pretend to care for the child.

'I care for her as much as you care for Boswell,' had been her mother's defiant words before she flew out of the room.

The remark hadn't surprised Delia; even at three years old, she had known that her father didn't like her thirteen-year-old brother, Boswell, any more than she did.

Odd, how a scene like that, from a quarter of a century before, when she was too young according to all the psychologists to have any memories of anything, should come so clearly to her mind. Buried all that time, only to emerge now, in a place so very different from her childhood home.

She was back in the present; there was Jessica at the door, calling to her to come. With a final glance at the portrait – how the woman dominated the room – Delia went to join the others.

Marjorie fell into step beside her. 'You felt it,' she said abruptly. 'The atmosphere, the presence of this Beatrice Malaspina.'

'It's a remarkable portrait.'

'It's not just that. The whole place is filled with her presence.'

'You mean photos, and her furniture; she probably had a lot to do with the way the house looks. Unless she employed an interior designer, and none of it reflects her true personality.'

'That's not what I mean,' said Marjorie, and snapped her mouth shut.

Neurotic, Delia said inwardly. Neurotic woman on the verge of middle age, with a chip on her shoulder. I don't see that she could ever have had anything to do with the woman in that portrait, talk about different worlds.

FOUR

They gathered before dinner on the part of the colonnade they had named the fresco terrace, and Delia went in search of drinks. 'There'll be wine, but they might have the makings of a cocktail. Beatrice Malaspina looked a cocktaily kind of woman to me,' Delia said. 'Where did I put that dictionary?'

She came back triumphant, with Benedetta in tow, bearing a tray of bottles and glasses and a very up-to-date cocktail shaker.

'No problem,' said Delia, waving at the array. 'The magic word, cocktail, and hey presto, Benedetta had this out and ready. The jazz age has a lot to answer for, don't you think?'

George said he was absolutely no good at mixing cocktails, and he looked hopefully at the others.

'I'll do it,' Marjorie said, adding that she'd worked behind the bar at an hotel at one time. Let them despise her; what did she care?

But Delia was full of admiration and interest. 'Lucky you. I always wanted to do that,' she said. 'How come?'

'My cousin was manager of a big hotel on the south coast. I was staying down there one summer and all the staff left, first one thing and then another. So the barman was rushed off his feet. He showed me what to do, and I got quite good at it.'

Marjorie was mixing the contents of the bottles and adding ice and a soupçon of this and that in a most professional way as she spoke. A final brisk flourish of the shaker, and she poured drinks for all of them.

'Jolly good,' said Delia. 'I vote we appoint you cocktail-maker-in-chief while we're here. And you can show me how you do it. I wish they taught you really useful stuff like that at school, instead of wanting you to arrange flowers and manage household accounts.'

'We didn't do those things at my school,' said Marjorie. 'I expect it was a very different kind of school from yours. I went to the local girls' secondary.'

'You probably learnt more than I did,' said Delia cheerfully. 'I bet you can spell, which is more than Jessica can, let me tell you. She's a rotten speller.'

'Was yours a boarding school?' Marjorie asked, emboldened by her cocktail.

'Yes. Northern and bleak. Jessica was there, too; that's where we became friends. It was simply ghastly.'

George was sipping at his cocktail. 'Don't you like it?' Marjorie asked. 'Can I mix you something different?'

'On the contrary, I am savouring it. It is an alchemy that you make among the bottles, I think. Also, I am interested in hearing about schools. I wasn't educated in England, you see.'

'I thought you weren't English,' said Marjorie.

'I was brought up in Denmark. My mother is Danish. But I was educated abroad, at a Catholic school.'

'Are you Catholic?' Marjorie said. 'I thought scientists were obliged to be atheists.'

'You can be brought up a Catholic and then give it up as soon as you're grown up,' Delia said. 'I was brought up a Methodist, but nothing would get me into a church now.'

'The best thing to be is C of E, like me,' Jessica said. 'It means you can believe or not believe exactly what you want.

And how odd that we should talk about religion, have you noticed that English people never do?'

Delia laughed. 'My mother told me that I shouldn't talk about feet, death or religion at the dinner table.'

George raised his eyebrows. 'What an extraordinary collection of forbidden topics. How very English. But why ever should you wish to talk about feet at the dinner table?'

'You can talk about horses' feet – hooves, I should say,' said Jessica. 'Any talk of animals is fine. What a dull lot we are.'

'We can talk about religion here because it's Italy,' Marjorie said.

How obvious it was. Italy was a country steeped in religion. Not that it probably had many more truly religious people than anywhere else in Europe, yet religion was all around them. 'The Vatican and the pope and so on, and all the paintings. One associates Italy with religion. And then, when we're abroad and the sun's shining, all kinds of things come out of the woodwork, as it were. Don't you think so?'

Her words were greeted with silence, as the others thought about it.

'Our hostess had connections with the Vatican,' Marjorie went on.

'How do you know?' said Jessica.

'There are photographs of three different popes.'

'It doesn't mean she ever met them.'

'They're signed, with her name on them.'

'You call her our hostess as though she were still here.'

'I think of her like that.'

'Are there any cardinals?' said Delia. 'I dislike clergymen on principle, but I adore paintings of cardinals, as long as they're kitted out in those gorgeous robes. They always seem to be more theatrical than ecclesiastical.'

'As it happens, there are several paintings of cardinals,' George said. 'I noticed them particularly, even though

Benedetta was rushing us along on her tour of the rest of the house. There is one magnificent one in the drawing room, a portrait painted in profile, did you not notice it? The cardinal is touching a large gold ring which he wears on his smallest finger; I believe it is the same ring that is displayed in the glass case in the entrance hall. His picture faces the one of Beatrice Malaspina. I didn't notice it at first because her portrait is so striking. Then there are others that hang in the passageway beyond the dining room. I, too, very much like paintings of cardinals. These are not very respectful of the cardinals' dignity, however, there is one where he is striding along, his cloak swirling about his feet, and peeping out from underneath are little devils. Perhaps Beatrice Malaspina was not such a devoted Catholic as the pope photographs might suggest.'

'Private and public,' said Marjorie. 'Quite different, of course. The outward forms and inward truth.'

George gave her a searching look, then turned to Delia. 'I shall show you the cardinals, Delia, after dinner, to which, I have to say, I am looking forward; with such delicious smells coming from the kitchen I find I am hungry. It seems odd that you and I only arrived here this morning, Marjorie, it feels as though we have been here much longer than that.'

'I know what you mean,' said Delia. 'It's our first day, really, for last night with that sandy gale we hardly knew where we were. It's a very welcoming sort of house, I think.'

Jessica laughed. 'Not like your pa's house, then.' She explained to the others, 'Delia's father's house is about the same size as the Villa Dante, but Lord, what a difference!'

'It is bleak,' said Delia. 'It's just right for my father, though. He has a bleak nature, so he and the house suit one another.'

'What does your father do?' George asked, and then apologised. 'How rude of me, to be so inquisitive, and to ask personal questions.'

Delia shrugged. 'I don't mind questions. It's probably the

97

same thing in the air that made us talk about religion. My father's in manufacturing.'

Not just rich landed gentry then. More a grinder of the faces of the poor, and Marjorie's mind was off at the mill, toiling hands, in clogs and shawls, mean, sooty streets, brass bands . . . Factories, full of dangerous machinery . . . Not so much of a toff as all that, then, thought Marjorie. Bet her mother is, though. Delia didn't behave like the daughter of parents who'd climbed up from the gutter. He'd probably inherited some vast concern from his father; rich as anything, those northerners who made beer or mustard or sauces. Manufacturing what? There was a caginess there, as though Delia didn't care to say exactly what he manufactured. Well, Marjorie didn't mind being thought rude.

'What does he manufacture?' she asked. 'Don't tell me he's an armament king, like in Bernard Shaw.'

'Not at all,' said Delia. 'Textiles. The closest he came to anything to do with the war was making parachute silk.'

Jessica jumped in. 'Are there any armament kings left? Aren't they obsolete now, with our new blow-the-world-to-bits bombs?'

Whatever had Jessica said, to cause such a look of pain on George's face? Marjorie looked at him intently. 'I know what kind of scientist you are. You're an atom scientist,' she said.

He looked taken aback. 'I'm a physicist . . . yes, you could call me an atom scientist. It is what the press like to call us. My field is isotopes.'

Isotopes? Did isotopes have anything to do with making the bomb? Probably. Then he was that kind of atom scientist. And one with a conscience by the look of it, poor man. She'd often wished she had a gift for science, a clear, cerebral world, so much easier, surely, than her own field, she'd always thought. Now, looking at George, she realised that was a facile judgement. Haunted; he was a haunted man.

98

A gong sounded, making them all jump. Then Benedetta's chivvying voice, the tone unmistakable, even if the words meant little to them.

'Dinner, I think,' said George, attempting a smile.

FIVE

From the Villa Dante, it was possible to see the small town of San Silvestro, its tiled rooftops sprawling beyond ancient walls that hugged the lines of the hillside. Towering above the low houses were the remains of a fortress, huge and grim.

'Do let's go and see what it's like,' Delia said to Jessica when they came down to breakfast.

'All right. Shall we go in the car, or walk?'

'Oh, walk. I want to be on the move.'

'Yes, but is the exercise going to make your cough worse?'

'I'm not coughing so much, I'll be fine.'

'Liar. I heard you hacking away during the night.'

Delia was secretly relieved when Marjorie and George refused her invitation to join them on their walk, an invitation that had caused Jessica to make faces of dismay at her.

'I'd planned to explore the gardens today,' Marjorie said. 'What about you, George?'

George hesitated, and Delia had the strong feeling that what he wanted was to be on his own. 'I, too, should like to see around the gardens,' he said politely.

It was nearly midday by the time they set out. They had lingered over breakfast, and then Delia had wanted to iron her skirt, creased after its time in her suitcase. The iron was electric but erratic, and then it had seemed a pity to go without joining the others for more coffee, brought out on to the terrace by a reluctant Benedetta, who clearly considered that mid-morning coffee was not good for the system.

It was tough walking at first, along the stony track that led to the road. 'I shouldn't have worn sandals,' said Delia ruefully, as she stopped for the third time to shake a sharp stone out of her shoe. 'Look at my toes, white with dust.' She flexed her foot, and leant down to blow the dust off her toenails, which were painted a brilliant scarlet shade. She was a colourful figure, in a green swirling skirt and a red top, especially beside Jessica who wore white Capri pants and a cream blouse.

Jessica undid the buttons at her wrists and pushed back her sleeves. 'It may only be April, and it may be about to snow, or whatever you warned the weather did in Italy, but I find it hot.'

'It is warm, and just smell the air. Pine and sea and I don't know what else, but it's heavenly. And listen, I hear a cuckoo.'

'The herald of spring.'

'Spring is already here, so it isn't a herald, more a celebrant, wouldn't you say?'

As they rounded a bend, the town came into view again, silhouetted against the cloudless sky.

'Fairyland,' said Delia. 'Just like in a painting. I always thought those Italian painters made up their landscapes, but here it is, all around us.'

They walked on through a grove of olives, and out on to the road, which had a pitted surface that was scarcely better than the track. An aged woman in black, bent double, and leading a laden donkey, passed them the other way, her wrinkled face breaking into a toothless smile as Delia greeted her with a friendly 'Buon giorno'.

'She's probably about forty,' said Jessica, standing in the road and looking after the woman and the donkey.

'Or she might be eighty,' said Delia.

They were at the final approach to the town and the road ahead led steeply up to a stone archway. Inside the walls, the narrow street was paved with large, smooth stones and, after the bright sunlight, it was dark and somewhat sinister, with tall buildings on either side looming over them.

They jumped out of the way as a horn pooped behind them, and a laughing girl on a scooter with a small boy clinging behind her whizzed past.

Above them, washing fluttered on lines strung out across the street, sheets and petticoats and extraordinary knickers. A dog, all ribs, gnawed at fleas in a doorway, and a thin brindled cat slid through a narrow gap between brown shutters.

The street curved round and upwards, and they came out finally into a small square, empty except for a couple of pigeons sitting by a round marble basin in one corner.

'It might be a fountain,' said Jessica, inspecting it. 'If there were any water.' Delia looked round at the shuttered façades. Not a soul stirred, and although a faded sign said *Bar*, beneath it was another rolled-down shutter. Did no one live here? What about the girl on the scooter? There were no voices, no laughter, no echoing footsteps. Just silence. It was like a stage set, just after the curtain had gone up; surely at any moment people would spill out into the square, talking and strolling and forming little groups.

'It all seems frightfully shut,' said Jessica.

'We're stupid – we shouldn't have hung around at the villa, now everything's closed for lunch. It won't come to life until four or five; Italians take a long break in the heat of the day.'

'Shall we go and take a look at the fortress?'

They climbed up long flights of steps, which took them beneath buildings and under vaulted arches, until they came out in another deserted piazza at the foot of the fortress.

Delia gazed up at the square, crenellated tower, far above

their heads. 'They can't have been on good terms with their neighbours.' She reached out to touch the large rusticated stones at the base of the tower. 'Look at those huge iron rings and torch holders. Can't you just see the scene on a hot night: horses, courtiers, flaming torches . . . ? Just like something out of Italian opera, in fact.'

'It's a disappointment,' said Jessica, as they walked back through the empty streets. 'I'd imagined a place bustling with life, fruit and veg spilling out on the pavements, lively Italians talking and gesticulating.'

'Another day,' said Delia. 'You'll have to make do with Marjorie and George, I'm afraid, and I can't say they're a lively pair.'

'No. Marjorie's a bore, with a chip on her shoulder, and isn't George like every don one's ever known? Only it's sad, because he's obviously deeply troubled by something.'

'An errant isotope, I expect,' said Delia lightly. 'Let's hope he found the gardens soothing.'

SIX

Marjorie and George went out into the colonnade, and down the steps to the parterre. The air was warm and heavy with a fragrance of pine and cypress and box, and a faint tang of the sea.

Marjorie knew that George would rather be on his own, but she told herself that he would be the better for company. She was feeling out of sorts this morning after a poor night's sleep, and George hadn't slept too well either, by the look of him, dark shadows under his eyes and a strained look to his face. 'Do you suffer much from insomnia?' she asked, as they walked along between the curving low hedges, their once flat tops now straggly and sprouting with new shoots and entwined weeds.

George paused before answering.

'You have a habit of asking questions based on information which you cannot have. Is it guesswork, or are you extremely clever at reading faces, do you do it to impress, hoping that people will only remember your lucky guesses?'

'I don't guess. You look tired; it's not so easy to hide. I sleep very badly, and so I recognise the signs in someone else. That's all.' Which was the partial truth, and certainly the truth with regard to his lack of sleep, if not to how she suspected – no, knew – that he spent the same kind of tortured hours of wakefulness as she did.

'I don't need so much sleep as I did when I was younger,' George said.

'How can you take time off from your isotopes? Or can't you, are you worried about getting back to your laboratory in Cambridge?'

'It is customary for academic staff to be given a lengthy leave of absence, to reflect and plan new work.'

George's voice was stiff, as were his shoulders; this was delicate ground. Marjorie wished she had a less relentless urge to know about other people, and more tact and consideration for their feelings. But she didn't.

'A sabbatical, you mean? Requested, or foisted upon you?'

Exasperated, George stopped. 'Marjorie, to walk in the garden can be pleasant, but to be subjected to an interrogation—'

'All right, I'll shut up about your insomnia and your work. At least you have a job to go back to.'

'Don't you?'

'No.'

'What is your work?'

As if he were in the slightest bit interested, Marjorie said to herself, but without resentment.

'Oh, nothing important,' she said. 'Not like science.' Then, 'It must be rewarding to be a musician, like Delia. I wonder if she's any good.'

'I think so, from her attitude and what Jessica says about her career.'

'Attitude! Anybody can have an attitude, and a friend's assessment of one's abilities counts for little in a wider world, with critics and fellow professionals waiting to pounce.'

'Until we hear her sing, it is impossible to say.'

'You would know then?'

'Yes,' said George. 'Music is my greatest pleasure, outside

105

my work. I have heard a great many musicians of varying quality and it isn't hard to tell which have that extra something. Do you like music?'

'I used to go at lunchtime to hear concerts when I could, and to the Wigmore Hall. I love Mozart, I could listen to Mozart for hours. But I also have what you would consider vulgar tastes. Noel Coward songs and rousing choruses from the shows are more my line.'

They had left the formal garden, and were going down a wide flight of steps that led to an olive grove. The songs of the birds were exultant and somehow a great deal noisier than Marjorie was used to. 'Why do they sound so loud?'

'The birds? Because there is no noise to drown their song. No traffic, no voices.'

'Just the distant murmur of the sea.'

'Murmur? I hear no murmur, and the sea was very still and calm this morning, I walked down to the beach just as the sun was coming up.'

'One hears the sea in one's head. And the sea in England is always murmuring or crashing or coming in or going out. It is a restless sea. The Mediterranean has no tides.'

'It does, but a very small one, only a few feet. And it is racked by storms of extreme violence.'

'Yes, I read that the floor of the sea is littered with thousands upon thousands of wrecks. All the history of Europe is down there.' Her mind was racing into the green depths. 'Phoenician boats, and triremes, and Roman ships, and pirate vessels and gallant galleons. Skulls and chests and cannons and amphorae and caskets of treasure and gold, the whole panoply of civilisations all in the salty deep.'

'If I were to make a guess,' George said, after giving her an appraising look, 'I would say you made your living through your imagination and through words.'

'Oh, no,' said Marjorie quickly. 'I don't make any living at all; I told you, I have no work.' She stopped to look more closely at a gnarled tree. 'These are olives, I think. They seem sadly neglected. Since they are sacred to Athene, I would have thought it unwise not to tend them.'

'My dear Marjorie . . .'

'Now you're going to say something patronising,' said Marjorie. 'Men always do when they begin a sentence "My dear Marjorie". I don't expect you to have any truck with Athene, although come to think of it, she is a goddess of war.'

'Why should a goddess of war have anything to do with me? I'm not a warrior, nor ever have been.'

'No, but you make the instruments of war.'

'I do not.'

'Well, you did once, didn't you? Isn't that what atom scientists are all about?'

'I wish you would not harp so on my being an atom scientist. I am a physicist and physicists uncover the secrets of the universe. No, not the secrets, the rules and system of the universe.'

'I thought that particles were very unruly. And Athene and her like are just as much the secrets of the universe as atoms and isotopes and all that.'

Just when had she developed this irresistible urge to tease her fellow men, to irk them and goad them? It was something she never used to do. In her former life, she had been the most tolerant of people, but now she wanted nothing more than to pin people down, to understand them, and, what was worse, to make them understand themselves. A wave of depression swept over her. She was back to that nagging question: what use was she, to herself, to anyone else? Here was this perfectly amiable man, clearly suffering from some nervous strain – it oozed out of him – and here she was, poking and prodding at him as though he were the subject of some psychic dissection.

'I'm sorry,' she said abruptly. 'My tongue runs away with me.'

'It does. I'm not so surprised you do not have a job; I imagine your colleagues would find it very difficult to work alongside you.'

That struck home, but it was no more than she deserved.

'In the modern world, we are obliged, if we have to earn a living, to work in a team,' she said. 'That's difficult for some people.'

She wasn't surprised, or bothered, when George said that he was going to have a pipe. 'There will be time to see the rest of the gardens, although it seems to be little more than a wilderness.'

She watched him make his way along the path that wound its steep way down to the cove which Delia had told them about: 'A heavenly little beach, with rocks and amazingly clear water. We paddled.'

You could tell from her face that Jessica hadn't wanted Delia to tell them about the cove. The three of them were here, as far as any of them knew, on equal terms: why should not she or George enjoy the beach as much as Delia and Jessica? And if they had found it, then she and George were perfectly capable of discovering it for themselves. But that was Jessica's type all over. Dog in the manger. The war had been supposed to sweep all that nonsense away; in the brave new world of post-war England there would be no class, no us or them.

What rubbish. Five or six years of war and the following years under a grim socialist prime minister and an austere chancellor couldn't undo centuries of feudalism. Jessica belonged to the upper classes, unmistakably and irrevocably. And while she lived and breathed, she would despise a woman like Marjorie who hadn't been born with a silver spoon in her mouth. More like a carrot or a turnip, she told herself with a flash of humour. Her father had been a market gardener.

So it was Marjorie, exploring on her own, who discovered

the water garden, with its extraordinary sculptures and empty stone rills, its riotous invention of twists and turns and strange symbolic and mythological figures.

She had walked round the side of the villa, heading for the part of the garden that stretched up the hill, behind the house. Following a wide, overgrown path, she came to a wall overhung with greenery, with formal stone steps going up beside it. It must once have been a fountain, with a low curved stone wall around the basin, and heads set along the semicircle of the wall, classical heads by the look of them.

She climbed the stone steps, and at the top found a pitted marble balustrade from which she could look down on the empty fountain below. Once, there must have been plenty of water here; where had it all come from, to keep these fountains flowing, and the one in front of the house, with its trefoil shape and the central figures overgrown with ivy?

She turned and looked up the slope of the hill. She could see a rough wall, a kind of grotto, with two figures reclining on either side, overlooking another pool beneath it. That must have been a waterfall, water tumbling over the rocky surface to splash into the pool, before flowing down to the first fountain. Curved steps, one on each side of the wall, led still further up, and there was a channel, coming down the hillside in long steps, a channel running between plaited stone. She ran her hand over the fat curves, and tried to imagine it as it must have been with water running down to the fountains below.

Who had made these fountains? Skilled artisans, but who had ordered the work? Someone rich, creating a garden full of water conceits to impress his friends. A cardinal, coming here for the summer, bringing with him intrigue . . . Images of women in sweeping frocks appeared before her, laughing, moving with ease and grace, men in parti-coloured tights. Then darker forms, with poison hidden about them, stilettos ready for swift and bloodless ends, rustling robes mingling with whispering voices, all the passion and wickedness of the Renaissance.

It was a wrench to come back to reality, to the crumbling, blackened stone, the lifeless fountains, the air of sterility and sense of a time gone for ever.

Almost, she was tempted to keep the delights she had found to herself, but that was to behave in the same selfish way as Jessica, and besides, she wanted other people to share its pleasures.

SEVEN

After lunch, Delia felt restless, and wanted to be on her own. She left the others sitting on the terrace, Jessica deep in a pile of twenty-year-old *Vogue*s that she had found in her room, George and Marjorie bickering mildly about the Latin name of an uninteresting shrub with white flowers that grew up against the balustrade.

Without being aware of what she was doing, or where she was going, Delia walked towards the unkempt grass slope to one side of the house, which ended in a bosky wilderness. She wanted to walk in the shade, and the over-grown paths and trees suited her mood. Marjorie had told them at lunch about the statues and fountains she had found, but Delia had no desire to see them. What was the point of looking at a fountain if there was no water flowing through it?

Now the gloom among the trees was beginning to depress her. In fact, she had felt a tug of melancholy all day. The sunshine and the blue sky and the sea had raised her spirits for a while, but nothing had changed; the problems that worried her in England had travelled with her. The only solu-tion to the fears and sadnesses of life, in her experience, was work. Music always brought balm to her soul, but now she couldn't sing, there was no music to listen to, and the piano was as out of tune as her mood.

Snap out of it, she told herself. Her cough would go, she would recapture her old joy in singing, and in singing she would forget the aching sore of Theo. She would move from her flat, she decided, find somewhere new, throw out her clothes, chivvy herself back into the flow of life.

Easy to say while she was here in Italy, and in this no man's land of the Villa Dante, but when she got back to dreary old London, it would all be the same, and she knew the impulse for transformation would vanish. People said there were only two things that could change you completely and dramatically: a nervous breakdown, or falling in love.

Well, she wasn't going to have a nervous breakdown, thank you very much. Her mother was enough of a neurotic for one family, and besides, what a triumph it would be for her father if she showed that the life she had chosen for herself had been too much for her. As for falling in love, she'd done that, and it had brought her a few weeks of fragile joy and then months, years, even, of unhappiness.

She knew she had an inner resilience and a strength, so why had it deserted her?

Illness, and being run down after it, that was all. She must make the most of the warm, dry air here, get herself better, ready to return to the fray. Her mind ran on to the summer season; she'd have to work hard to be ready for Glyndebourne, let alone Salzburg.

If Roger hadn't cancelled for her, made arrangements for another of his promising singers to take over her roles. Would he do that?

Not without consulting her, and she'd made that impossible by scooting off to Italy, without leaving a forwarding address. She'd better write to him, tell him she was here to get rid of the last traces of her cough. She would say she was working hard, mention that she might be going to see

Andreossy in Milan for some sessions on her breathing technique. That'd keep him happy until she got back.

She walked on, not noticing her surroundings, until she was startled back into reality by finding Marjorie sitting in a clearing among a particularly dense patch of trees.

'Look,' said Marjorie. 'It's a temple.' She rose from where she was sitting on shallow steps at the base of a circular building, with steps all round leading to a trio of plain, battered columns that supported a dome. 'It's a temple of love.'

Drat the woman, for being here, when Delia wanted to walk alone with her thoughts. 'Why a temple of love, for heaven's sake? Isn't that rather fanciful?'

'Look up inside the dome,' said Marjorie, rather huffily. 'The paint has faded, but you can see it's Venus and Mars. If it's got Venus painted on it, it's dedicated to her. Therefore a temple of love.'

'If Mars is there, why not a temple of war?'

'I'd give the preference to love over war any time, wouldn't you? And Mars was completely mad, of course; why would anyone want a temple to him in their garden? Well, since you don't want my company, I'll take myself off.'

Mars. Mad Mars. Delia's brother Boswell must have been born under the sign of Mars. Red with rage, red the colour of war, the colour of blood. She remembered Boswell in the summer of 1939, alive at the prospect of war. 'Spain was all very well, but this is the real thing. Now we'll see some fun!'

Fun! Only someone with as warped a mind and heart – if he had one – as Boswell could have rejoiced in such a way at the prospect of the violence of war. And when war did come, and he was an officer in uniform, he was in his element. 'I get a kick out of killing,' he'd said.

Another memory came vividly into her mind: herself, a little girl, at Sunday lunch, when she was allowed down from the nursery to join the grown-ups. She'd looked solemnly over the polished table and gleaming silver at her mother, sitting silent and self-absorbed at the end of the table. 'Why is Boswell called Boswell? It's such an odd name.'

Young as she was, she sensed the sudden tension that hovered in the room. At last, in a rather stilted voice, her mother said: 'It's my maiden name, Delia. Since it's also a boy's name, I – we – decided to give it to your brother. Now, eat up your greens, and I don't want to hear another word out of you.'

Another scene, at the end of the summer holidays, with Nanny sitting comfortably in front of the fire, stitching away. 'Boswell goes back to school tomorrow. You'll miss him.'

'I won't. I hate him. I wish he'd go away and never come back.'

Which had earned her a mouth washed out with soap, bread and water for supper and bed an hour early.

Yet it was the truth. Was there ever a time when she hadn't feared and hated Boswell?

No one else seemed to see it, although she suspected now, looking back, that her father knew exactly what Boswell was like beneath his veneer of good manners and charm and likeability. Even her mother knew, perhaps, but Boswell was her golden boy, her ewe lamb. If she admitted any flaw in his character, it was only to herself in her most solitary moments, in the small hours of the night. And Delia came to believe that her mother maybe never had acknowledged or believed that Boswell was what he was.

The girls at school were fascinated by him; he had come once to some school function, an end-of-term concert, she thought, when he'd been on his way back to Saltford Hall.

'He's handsome,' her friends said. 'And so sweet. You are lucky, to have a brother like that.' They angled for invitations, but Delia only ever asked Jessica to stay at Saltford Hall, and Jessica, she knew, had taken an immediate and comprehensive dislike to Boswell.

114

'Sorry, Delia, he's your brother and all that, but I can't stand him, and I don't trust him.'

'Nor do I,' Delia said, and they had both taken good care to keep out of his way. Not that he would have tried any of his tricks on Jessica, Delia knew. He was far too clever to soil his own nest.

In the shade inside the temple, it was difficult to see what was on the roof, but as her eyes adjusted she could see there was indeed a painting of a naked woman looking coyly down at a burly man in velvet and armour. How could Marjorie be so sure it was Venus and Mars? Then she made out the fat naked figure of a cupid hovering above the goddess's head. Cupid, with a wicked expression on his pink face, fitting a golden arrow to his ornate bow.

Of course, if you were the goddess of love, you just had to crook your finger and that was that: even powerful Mars fell at your feet. Venus wouldn't have been so stupid as to love any man more than he loved her, which accounted for the self-satisfied smile on her face in the painting. Lucky old Venus.

One who loves, one who turns the other cheek. Damn it, she was not going to think about Theo, especially not here, in what Marjorie had called a temple of love. Like something out of a sentimental novel, for goodness' sake.

'Is something amiss? Are you not feeling well?' The words came to Delia as though from a great distance, and she blinked, aware now that her eyes were full of tears. She brushed her eyes with the back of her hand, and stood up.

George was regarding her with puzzled concern. 'I am sorry if I intrude. A moment of grief, I quite understand, some loss . . .'

'No, don't apologise. It wasn't a loss – at least, not in the way you mean. Just a sudden painful memory, which caught me unawares.'

His face was sympathetic. 'Perhaps if you can replace the

distressing memory with one of a time when you were happy, you would feel better.'

'If only one could do that, order memories to come and go.'

He offered her his arm. 'You look upset. Lean on me. You have not been so well, Jessica tells us. An infection of the chest. Indeed one can treat memories in this way. I was taught to do so as a child, by my mother, and then, you know, I was educated by the Jesuits, and they teach you a great deal about what you do and don't let your thoughts do. The Jesuitical mind is never allowed to roam unchecked.'

'Jesuits,' said Delia, and found herself laughing. 'I'm sorry, it's just that my father has a perfect thing about Jesuits; he talks about them as though they were a vicious form of black beetle, invading and destroying. He reads a lot of history, and . . . I'm sorry. That's rude.'

'Not at all. I am no Jesuit; they merely gave me the precious gift of learning to think, for which I shall always be grateful. However, and please forgive me, the advice of strangers is rarely welcome, it is dangerous to the spirit and to our well-being to let our thoughts and memories wander unchecked, so they get the better of us.'

'Not a stranger, really,' said Delia. 'Given the circumstances, we have had friendship thrust upon us. I'm glad of it. In your case, anyhow.'

'I think you will come to find that the alarming and difficult Marjorie is a personality of great interest,' he said.

'So are all your thoughts and memories under your control?'

'Sadly, not. I try, and sometimes it works, but once one's life has taken a certain turn, and things have happened, then the irrevocability of what one has done can force its presence into the mind, whether one likes it or not.'

'So a Jesuit education might not have saved me from what rattles round and round in my mind.'

116

'A Jesuit education? For you? Well, that is impossible, but I see that you are making a joke.'

'Has it worked for you, confess, and then it's all fine?'

'I have committed no sin that I could confess to any priest. Modern sins are perhaps beyond the compass of the church. Nor indeed have I been to confession or to church for many years.'

'Do you believe that when you die you will be judged, and be sent to hell or wafted up to heaven?'

'That is a nursery view: heaven, hell; you are good so a pink cloud for you, you are bad, Nanny says, so it's brimstone and pitchforks for you. Besides, you forget purgatory, where the soul may be purged of its sins.'

'All souls, all sins? Hitler, for instance? I don't care to think of him in purgatory; no amount of hellfire can be enough for him. I don't feel any sense of forgiveness towards him. Sorry, but there it is.'

'Nor do I.'

EIGHT

'I don't care what Benedetta says,' said Delia, when she found Jessica idling in a deckchair and swept her off upstairs to change. 'I find it positively hot, and I'm going to bathe.'

'What did she say?'

'Oh, I don't think I got more than the gist of it, which is that my toes will drop off, I'll have a conflagration of the lungs, and not all the prayers of the saints will save me.'

'You're making it up. She was probably asking what we wanted for dinner, that's all.'

'Does she ever? No, she was prophesying woe, I'm sure of it.'

'Do you suppose there are sharks, or giant jellyfish, or wicked currents to sweep you off to the rocks? After all,' Jessica added practically, 'we know nothing about the sea around here.'

'Oh, stuff,' said Delia, shaking out her swimsuit. 'It's a cove; I'm not planning to swim out to the horizon, or to get swept on to any rocks. I shall simply splash about in the shallows, in that blissfully clear water. Come on, don't be a killjoy, get your swimming things. I did tell you to bring a costume.'

'Look at your drawers,' said Jessica. 'By your age, you

should have given up scuffling everything up like that when you're looking for something. And your clothes are strewn all over the room.' As she spoke, she was folding and tidying away with swift ease. 'I swam in the North Sea last year, on a hot August day,' she said, looking at Delia over her shoulder as she pushed a drawer back in. 'Are these things dirty? I'll put them in the bathroom.'

Delia had no interest in her laundry. 'The North Sea, we know what the North Sea is like, August or not; you only have to stand on the front at Scarborough and turn your face to the sea to be chilled to the bone and get a blinding headache from the bitter winds. This is quite different: calm, clear water, and a sun that makes the rocks warm enough to bask on.'

Jessica fetched her costume, took a towel from the bathroom and went back to Delia's room. Delia was on her balcony, peering over the railing.

'What are you doing?' Jessica said.

'Seeing if the coast's clear. I don't mind George joining us for a dip, but I'm damned if I'm going to have Marjorie splashing alongside me, telling me all sorts of things I don't in the least want to hear.'

'As to that, you're quite safe, for I saw her setting off through the gate, with what looked like a sketchbook in hand.'

Downstairs, George raised an eyebrow when he saw their towels rolled up under their arms. 'Ah, you are venturing into the sea.'

'Come and try it,' said Jessica.

'No, I shall wait to hear what you have to say when you return, or, alternatively, I shall be here to send out a rescue party should it be necessary.'

'What are you going to do?' said Delia.

'I intend to spend an hour or so browsing the bookshelves. I hope that the late Beatrice Malaspina was an admirer of

119

Jane Austen,' George said reflectively. 'I think to sit on the terrace with a novel by Miss Austen would be extremely agreeable.'

'Oh, I tried one of her books once,' said Jessica. 'Romances, women's stuff. Why would you want to read it?'

George looked shocked. 'Good heavens, didn't it make you laugh?'

'Make me laugh?' Jessica was astonished. 'Was it meant to?'

George shook his head, and escorted them politely to the doors on to the terrace before he went back inside.

'You are the end,' Delia said. 'Anyone would think you haven't got a sense of humour, and I know you have.'

'I did have,' said Jessica, pensive now. 'Only I think I mislaid it when I married Richie.'

Once at the beach, Jessica hesitated, and it was Delia who plunged into the water, diving under and then emerging, hair streaming down her back. Jessica watched from the edge of the water, little ripples of waves curling about her bare toes, thinking that Delia looked like something out of a painting, a cavorting nymph.

'What's it like?' she called.

'Not exactly warm, but better than Scarborough. Do come in, there are little fish, you can see right to the bottom. I say, I wish I had a snorkel.'

Jessica sat down on her towel, tucking her knees under her chin and wrapping her arms round her legs. Was Delia right? Had marrying Richie taken away her sense of humour? No, it must have disappeared before then, or why would she ever have agreed to marry him? It was a laughable idea, her becoming Mrs Meldon, and yet she hadn't laughed. If only she had.

Jessica had accepted Richard Meldon's proposal of marriage two hours after her older brother Theo had married Delia's sister Felicity in the Guards Chapel. Richie had proposed to her during the wedding reception at the Ritz, at a time when her life seemed particularly bleak and unpromising, and in a moment of blinding stupidity she had said yes.

They were in bed together at the time, Jessica's elegant two-piece lying in a crumpled heap on the floor beside the bed, Richie's formal morning coat and striped trousers, in contrast, hung neatly on the clothes stand.

'It's not the sort of place we can just book a room,' Jessica had said to him, when he whispered lustful suggestions in her ear. 'Far too respectable.'

'As it happens, I have a room already. I'm staying here.'

'They won't approve of a woman in your room.'

'They won't notice. At this time of day, there won't be many hotel staff about. I'll get my key from the desk, you nip up the stairs. No one's going to question you.'

Richie smelt of hormones and horse.

'Why do you smell of horse?'

'I rode this morning.'

'Didn't you bathe before getting into your penguin suit?'

'Didn't have time. I had a bath this morning. Are you complaining?'

'No, just curious.'

He had taken it as a criticism, none the less, had rolled over and lit a cigarette.

'Aren't you going to offer me one?'

He tossed the packet over to her side of the bed. She took one out and then leant over him, forcing him towards her, so that she could light her cigarette from his.

'I like the way you smell,' she said, untruthfully. 'It's masculine,' she added.

That was when he said they might as well get married.

'I need to marry, at this stage of my career,' Richie went on. 'Someone suitable, who knows how to behave. You're perfect. Bags of class and an impeccable family background;

121

combine that with my money, and you and I can go right to the top.'

'Top of what?'

'The political ladder. Come on, what better prospect is there for the daughter of a family from a crumbling manor house who haven't got two pennies to rub together?'

'Do you love me?'

'Of course I do.' He sounded almost irritated. 'Haven't I just proved that?' No, Jessica said inwardly, but what did it matter?

The announcement of their engagement was headline news: Lovely blonde daughter of country squire Sir Edward Radley weds flying ace MP. The reporters couldn't get enough of her, alone or with Richie. There were photos of her getting into and out of his car, running up the steps to his house, riding with him in the park, on his yacht at Cowes, on the towpath at Henley, with Richie wearing the pink colours of the Leander club, leading his horse into the winners' enclosure at Ascot, herself in an enormous, extravagant hat, looking more tired than the sweat-flecked filly. The whole tiresome round.

Day by day she woke up thinking, today I'm going to put a stop to this.

And every day when she went to bed still an engaged woman, she said into her pillow that the next day, without fail, she was going to give Richie back the ridiculously large diamond ring he had given her.

She'd taken Richie to stay with Delia's family, and it hadn't been a success. He was polite and well behaved, but full of complaints when he crept up to her room in the early hours.

'Why doesn't Lord Saltford like me? Everybody likes me.'

'It's just the way he is,' Jessica had said.

'A looker, Lady Saltford,' he remarked, as he pulled Jessica's pyjamas off. 'I'm going to give you a dozen silk nighties for when we're married, I hate women in pyjamas.'

'Diana Boswell, as she was then, was far and away the greatest beauty of her generation,' Delia's aunt, her father's sister, told Jessica with some complacency at lunch the next day. 'Photographers used to follow her and beg for pictures. She was hardly out of the schoolroom, but so lovely that people would stop and stare at her in the street.'

'It's a pity I didn't inherit her looks,' Delia said with sudden temper.

Her father had turned on her, oblivious to the others at the table. 'Never let me hear you say that again. Beauty is a curse for a woman, and as often as not for all those who come in contact with her. You've got brains, which last, while beauty doesn't.'

Richie claimed to find Delia hard. 'Not anything like as pretty as Felicity, and all this singing nonsense has gone to her head. She's so sure she's going to make a name for herself; I don't find that attractive, being so keen to hog the limelight.'

If Jessica suspected that a man like Richie would never tolerate a woman who threatened to outshine him in anything, she kept the thought to herself. There had been an awkward moment over the maths.

'I can't think why your father allowed you to go to Cambridge at all, let alone to read maths. A subject like foreign languages wouldn't have been so bad, although women at university are a pain, and they just take up places that should go to men. But maths!'

'I was good at maths.'

'Girls' school maths. I suppose the women's colleges feel they have to take some women to read those subjects. It's most unfeminine.'

Jessica got up and shook herself, as though wanting to be free of the thoughts that had been flowing through her head. She ran across the sandy shingle to join Delia in the sea. They swam, but not for long, then lay on their towels on the beach, basking in the sun.

'I wish I could lie here for ever,' Delia said.

Jessica closed her eyes. There was something magical about this small, private cove, so quiet, apart from the sounds of the sea, so warm, so filled with light. A haven. No one and nothing to disturb one. Above, the empty path leading back to the villa, and behind, the other way, the sea, stretching equally empty to the horizon, blue and vast. 'Utterly peaceful,' she said, with her eyes still closed.

'As though we were the only people in the world.'

'That's what it will be like for the only people left alive after all the A bombs have gone off. They will literally be the only people left alive on earth.'

'Jessica, what a ghastly thing to say.' Delia sat up, her serene mood shattered.

'Sorry,' said Jessica, sitting up in her turn, and reaching for her sunglasses. 'It's not something I give much thought to. I mean, there's nothing we can do about it, if the scientists are going to blow us all to bits, then that's what they'll do, so there's no point worrying or fretting about what we can't change.'

'You've been talking to George. He's obsessed with A bombs.'

'Is he?'

'He was talking about it to Marjorie. He knows too much for his own good. That's the trouble with being an atom scientist, I suppose.'

NINE

George stood at the windows of the drawing room, looking out at the sky, where dramatic shafts of sunlight slanted down from billowing clouds. 'As in a baroque painting,' he remarked. 'It is as well that you had your bathe this afternoon.'

'Benedetta didn't think so,' said Delia. 'I feel lucky not to be tucked up in bed with a hot water bottle and some ancient physician in rusty black standing at the foot of the bed, agreeing with Benedetta that to swim in the sea in April is definitely to risk lungs and life.'

'Well, I am glad that I walked into San Silvestro this afternoon while the sun was still shining, although the sky was beginning to cloud over as I came back.'

'Was there any life in San Silvestro?' Delia asked. 'I never saw anywhere look so deserted as it did when we were there.'

'There were certainly people in the streets, very young or old for the most part. And there were shops open. I stopped at a bar for a beer.'

'There's a storm brewing,' said Marjorie, who had got up from the table and was looking out of the drawing room window. 'That's what George is talking about. I knew it this morning. I could smell it.'

'You know everything,' Jessica muttered.

Marjorie heard her, but ignored the remark. She was aware how much she irked Jessica, and she didn't, she told herself, care a bit.

'Not another sirocco, I hope,' said Delia. 'That was ghastly.' She joined Marjorie at the window. 'It does look as though the clouds are whipping up rather fast.'

Daylight had faded from the turbulent sky in a flurry of purple and grey by the time Benedetta sounded the gong for dinner. As they crossed the frescoed hall to go into the dining room, there was a phut, the lights flickered, and then with a bang all the lights went out.

'Power cut,' said George.

Benedetta's voice, a few rooms away, rose in a shriek of indignation and then a command.

'She wants us to stay where we are,' Delia said.

'I hate this time of day without lights,' said Jessica.

'Well,' said Delia, 'I'm not standing here in the dark for goodness knows how long.'

'All we have to do is follow our noses,' George said.

Cautiously, and bumping into walls and doors, they reached the other side of the room, and edged their way in to the hall, where they could see the door to the dining room, with a dim light coming through.

'The moon has risen,' said Delia. 'We can dine by moonlight.'

There was no need. The soft, shadow-draining light of the startlingly bright waxing moon, sailing in and out of the stormy clouds, was supplemented by first one and then an array of oil lamps, guttering slightly, and with a faint sour whiff of oil.

'Goodness, this smells good,' Delia said, as Benedetta placed a small plate of food in front of her. 'I wonder what it is.'

'Our digestive systems will rebel, with so many delicious meals,' said George.

'Not mine,' said Marjorie. 'And the wine is nectar. I suppose' – to Delia – 'you're used to good wine, but cheap red is mostly what I used to drink.'

'Actually, my father is teetotal, so no, I don't know much about wine.'

'Is your mother teetotal too?' asked Marjorie, helping herself to spaghetti with mussels in a garlicky sauce.

Delia felt the food in her mouth turn to ashes. What was it about Marjorie? How could she know? She couldn't, of course; it was just a conversational remark, such as anyone might make. Not even a guess, for why should anyone guess that calm, self-contained Lady Saltford kept a bottle of gin under the floorboards, and that the lime juice she was known to be so fond of, the cordial so much approved of by her husband, was never, in private, consumed on its own.

Lady Saltford's maid, her loyal maid, who, Delia suspected, detested Lord Saltford, was in on the secret. It was she who bought the gin, who hid it, who made up a special mouthwash to remove any lingering odour of alcohol, who disposed of the bottles, who silently brought her mother a glass of gin and lime with her breakfast tray.

Delia had found out about it by chance, when she was home from school with scarlet fever. Ill, and with not much sense of what she was doing, she had risen from her bed and padded down to her mother's room, hearing sounds of life in there. Her mother rose very early, a habit her father approved of, for God, in his opinion, started the day's work with the dawn. Her mother's early rising was partly due to insomnia, partly so that she could have the drink that set her up for the morning before anyone else was around. Not that there was any danger of her husband's paying an unexpected call on her. Their life together was, Delia had known since she was a small girl, entirely a public one. In private, they led busy, separate lives; her father with his work, her mother running the house and the estate, and involving herself in charitable works.

Was her mother an alcoholic? Did four stiff gins a day make you an alcoholic? Probably. One at breakfast, one before lunch, one before dinner and one at bedtime.

Delia sniffed her wine, and let the velvety liquid slide unappreciated down her throat. She put the glass down. 'I think there's a lot of fuss and snobbery about wine,' she said. 'I don't really care for it so very much.'

George shook his head. 'That is a pity, a great pity, with such a delicious wine as this.'

Delia wanted to escape from the memories that were rattling through her brain, of the look of despair on her mother's face as she and her husband sat at opposite ends of the long mahogany table. Did her mother love her father? Had she ever loved him? Delia had assumed, with the casual, heedless indifference of youth, that her mother and father had simply grown apart, as married couples so often did, and that the estrangement was nothing to do with emotion or any quarrel; the arguments had ceased long ago.

Now she wondered. Had there been more feeling there than she knew? And if so, what had caused the terrible chasm that had opened between her parents? It wasn't surprising that they hadn't divorced; her father considered divorce unacceptable. But her mother could have left him, made a new life for herself. Or could she? There was the question of money, and there was no doubt that her mother liked being Lady Saltford of Saltford Hall, and 27 Cadogan Square, SW.

You might think you had it all sewn up, that you knew your family inside out, but how true was that? In a sense you knew them too well. How old had she been when she realised what her brother Boswell was like? Not that it took any great degree of insight; little boys who were cruel to animals, and took such pleasure in hurting a much younger sister, sent out signals loud and clear: *Don't mess with me.*

He had been ten years older than her, and so they could never have been close, even if he hadn't been the kind of person he was. She remembered Boswell's enormous energy, his braininess, his determination, his charm – yes, there was charm, buckets of it, not for his family, of course, but for anyone who could be useful to him – his ruthlessness. How could her mother, who had never shown more than a distant affection for her, have not known what Boswell was like? Lady Saltford doted on Boswell; in her eyes, he could do no wrong.

Perhaps she, Delia, was the one without feelings, because she felt absolutely nothing for Boswell now, no regret, no memories of happy family days to bring sadness or grief that he was dead. In fact, she had felt relief when she had been told about his death by a serious headmistress, used, after five years of war, to breaking sad news to one or other of her girls.

'He died in Italy?' her fifteen-year-old self had said. 'How strange. I'd have thought he was the kind to kill lots of other people, not to end up dead himself.' Inadequate, inappropriate words, and the headmistress had given her a compassionate look and spoken to the matron about delayed shock.

'Penny for them,' Jessica said, a soft voice in her ear.

'I'm sorry,' said Delia. 'I'm poor company tonight. I was miles away.'

'No very agreeable thoughts, I believe,' said George.

'She was thinking of the war,' said Marjorie. She wiped her hands on her napkin. 'Let's ask Benedetta to serve coffee in the drawing room. It will look beautiful there by lamplight. And I'm sure she will bring liqueurs, and we can raise our glasses in a toast to our hostess.'

Delia found herself beside Marjorie as they made their way through the shadowy hall on their way back to the drawing room.

'How did you know I was thinking about a time in the

war? Do you make a habit of guessing what people are thinking?'

The expressionless pale eyes, suddenly lit by the oil lamp that she was holding, held a despair that astonished Delia.

'It's not something I can help,' Marjorie said unexpectedly. 'It isn't malice, I assure you.'

Not such a nonentity, after all. Delia didn't think she would ever really like her, but her first impression had been wrong. Marjorie wasn't either dull or dim.

In the drawing room, they could feel a new chill in the air. Whatever was happening with the weather, this storm brought none of the warmth of the Saharan sirocco that had greeted Delia and Jessica on their first evening at the Villa Dante. The wind had risen, and was blowing with a howling sound.

'The storm presages changes, and arrivals. I expect Beatrice Malaspina's fourth guest will be here very soon,' Marjorie said.

George looked alarmed. 'Marjorie, you do say very odd things. Perhaps you don't realise how odd; these mysterious statements about Beatrice Malaspina . . .'

'It's as though I can hear her talking,' said Marjorie in her downright way. In truth, she did hear her speaking; a new voice inside her head, a low voice that spoke in clipped English.

'Isn't that schizo-whatsit?' said Delia. 'Shouldn't you see someone, if you hear voices?'

'I did. In London. A very distinguished psychiatrist, as it happens. He was most reassuring, said I wasn't the only one; with the war and all the injuries, very strange things were going on inside people's heads. My case, and the causes of it, were not uncommon. He was going to write a paper on me,' she added.

'He'd have done better to send you to the loony bin,' came not very sotto voce from Jessica.

130

George made a hasty intervention. 'The human mind and its tricks and vagaries are beyond our understanding, for the most part. That is a realm where science does not venture with much success, although I fear many psychologists would differ with that opinion, since they long to call themselves scientists.'

'What did cause the voices?' asked Delia.

Marjorie turned her pale eyes on her. 'I prefer not to say. But it's a classic consequence: voices, and getting snatches of the future.'

'Whose future? Yours, or other people's? Or is it apocalyptic, like St John, divine revelation and the end of the world?'

'Never mine,' said Marjorie. 'But voices tell me things I would not otherwise know. Or ideas simply form in my head, as though they were pieces of information planted there by an unseen presence. That's how I know that things are about to change at the Villa Dante.'

George wanted to argue the point, although Delia could have told him that Marjorie's voices wouldn't be amenable to logic. 'Even if you do hear things in your head, and I agree it is not so very uncommon a phenomenon when a person is under stress, it is surely better not to believe that the voices have any truth in them. They are phantasmagoria of the mind, nothing more.'

Marjorie said nothing, but Delia could see from the stubborn set of her jaw that she disagreed with George.

There were crashing sounds from overhead.

'Not thunder, surely,' Delia said. God, let the wild weather restrict itself to blowing a gale; please, she muttered to herself, please, no thunder.

'Benedetta battening down the hatches,' said Jessica. 'I left my shutters open, and she's got a perfect thing about shutters. She'd have them all closed all the time if we let her.'

'It is the consequence of living in a hot climate, where you

131

want to keep the sun's strength out of the rooms, because otherwise in summer the heat would be unendurable,' said George. 'And also in the winter they provide shelter against bitter weather and storms.'

'This is a house meant to be full of light,' said Delia. 'I hate it when everything is so shut in.'

That, Marjorie said to herself, is what comes of living in spacious houses, probably with parks and all the private space you want. Not growing up in a tiny terraced house, and sleeping in a room that was almost too small to be called a boxroom.

George saw the look of despair that had returned to Marjorie's face. It didn't surprise him; he had already come to the conclusion that she was a woman only barely holding herself together. Not an hysteric, just someone whose nerves and will were stretched as far as they would go. He hoped she wasn't going to have some kind of breakdown here; he suspected that they were all too close to the edge to be able to cope with any of them falling off the cliff of tortured emotions.

Except that some of them had an outlet for strain and uncertainty. Delia had made her way to the piano, and was sitting relaxed on the long stool, where she felt most at home, her harbour after troubled seas. She had her music, and no doubt it had kept her saner than the rest of them. It was a long time since he himself had played the piano, he hadn't the heart for it. Music had no part to play when the soul had gone out of you.

How ridiculous, soul indeed. They would be back to talking about Methodism and the Church of England if his mind went off on that path.

'It's much more pleasant without electricity,' Marjorie said, her voice weary in the half-gloom; the two lamps were barely enough to cast a dim glow over the large room. 'I hate electricity.'

'That is a very strange thing to say,' he said with surprise. 'How can one hate an inanimate force?'

'You do,' she said. 'You hate all that atom force. I hate electricity. Perhaps there are people who have a grudge against gravity, I don't know.'

Jessica's voice came out of the shadows by the window, where she was standing, looking out at the moon surging in and out of the clouds in a violent sky. 'Why electricity in particular?'

'It's too fierce, too erratic, too uncontrollable, for all we go switching it on and off and pretending we've got it caged. Think of electric storms. We seize the power and encapsulate it in a tiny bulb, and it glows, but don't you feel there's a resentment to it, that it would get out and run wild if only we'd let it?'

George, his scientific instincts rising to the surface, burst out laughing. 'My dear woman, what a very outrageous view you have of it. Electricity is charged particles, no more. It is neutral, it has no energy of its own, and certainly no animosity. You should not attribute human emotions to something like electricity.'

'I know what she means, though,' Delia said. 'Don't you think when you're in a storm, watching great sheets and forks of lightning, that it's a force too strong for us, or for our understanding. Isn't it literally beyond our understanding, anyhow? I thought, when it came down to it, although as Marjorie says we switch on and energy flows, nobody is quite sure what it is, any more than gravity. I'm terrified by thunder,' she added, 'which is just as irrational.' She tried to keep her voice light, but Jessica, well aware of how terrified she was by thunderstorms, shot her an anxious glance, and an encouraging smile.

'I, for one,' she said, her voice calm and unstrained, 'am glad of electricity. Life without would be so dark and dreary, don't you think?'

'I once stayed in an old house that was still lit by gas,' said Delia, glad to get away from the subject of storms. 'It gave a beautiful soft light, but it popped and hissed, and there was a smell in the air. You would think twice about lighting a cigarette there. I'm all for switches on the wall and light bulbs.'

'Have you seen the gas lamps in the Temple Gardens in London?' Marjorie said. 'The lamplighter still comes round with his long stick and lights them every evening at dusk. It must have been strange for Londoners when gas lighting came in, and streets were lit at night for the first time.'

'One can imagine what it was like before,' said Jessica, 'when you think of England in the blackout. I walked into a lamp post in Leeds in the first week of the war and ended up in hospital.'

'I was always falling off the kerb,' said George. 'Or riding into it when I was on my bicycle.'

Silence fell, but not an unpleasant silence. Delia had opened the piano, and was softly touching each key in turn, then improvising on the keys that weren't out of tune, a gentle, lilting tune of a modern kind that seemed to go with the room and the sudden awareness that they were, after all, a long way from present day foggy London, and even further from the dark days of the war.

The shutters were tightly closed and all the windows firmly shut, but even so it was draughty, with gusts of air blowing down the chimney, making the pages of a book on the sofa rustle, and the curtains stir as though restless and trying to escape the confines of the room. They look, thought Delia, as though they wanted to let go and sweep away into the night.

There was a sudden roar of wind, and then the clatter of hailstones. 'It's very dramatic,' said Marjorie. 'I like storms. I do wish we could see out.'

'One of the shutters is banging,' Delia said, going to the window and drawing back the curtain, wanting to see if there was lightning in the sky, in which case there was nothing for it but to make a run for her room and dive under the bedclothes before the thunder came.

She turned the locking handle on the window, and it almost wrenched itself out of her hand as the force of the wind thrust it open. Then one of the shutters, not securely fastened, gave way, and was flung back against the wall.

Outside was a transformed world. Delia felt her senses whirl, dazzled by the brilliant flashes of lightning which illuminated a tearing landscape, trees whipping to and fro, and then, quite suddenly, a sleeting wall of rain obscured her vision. She felt frightened and exhilarated at the same time; she had never seen this intensity of the forces of nature, used as she was to the wild and wicked weather of her native Yorkshire.

Wind she could cope with, but there was that lightning, and if it began to thunder . . .

It took the combined strength of George and Jessica to get the shutters properly closed, and the windows locked shut again. They were soaked to the skin, and an appalled Benedetta, bringing in more oil lamps, let out shrieks of horror at the sight of them, and uttered what Delia guessed were terrible imprecations against the folly of persons who opened windows and shutters in the storms.

Delia led Benedetta, still scolding, to the window and pointed to the catch of the shutter, which George had fastened with a piece of twine from his trouser pocket.

Benedetta's wrath subsided as abruptly as it had come, and she shook her head, muttering Pietro's name in a way that boded no good for him when he arrived in the morning. Doubtless it was one of his many duties to attend to locks and catches. But in a house with so many windows and shutters, how could you keep them all in order? Delia knew all about houses with dozens of windows; as a child during the war, it had been one of her holiday duties at Saltford Hall to do the blackout.

'The ground was dry,' Marjorie said. 'I should think the rain will be a blessing, but such a strong wind will do the trees in the orchard no good at all.'

'You show a tender concern for the plants,' said George. 'But do not worry. I think they are sheltered from a wind blowing from this direction.'

'I know about people's livelihoods depending on what they grow,' Marjorie said tartly. 'My father was a market gardener. Goodnight.'

'That is the first piece of information about herself that's she's given us,' said Delia, going back to the piano to close the lid. She managed a smile. 'I'm going to bed, too. I hate thunder.'

'I'll come with you,' said Jessica.

They picked up oil lamps, and left George wreathed in smoke, reading in the soft light, self-contained, oblivious to the storm raging outside.

Later, much later, when the storm was at its furious height, there was nothing self-contained about George, tossing and turning in his bed. He dreamed of the desert, where he was walking in the hot dry mountains, giant cactus on either side, and shadowy figures keeping pace all around him. The sun was burning red in the sky, and he had no destination, no hope, no place of refuge. A sterile place and a sterile life, he said as he forced himself to wake up and groped for the switch to his bedside lamp. But the current was still off, so he lay back, troubled by his dream. Where was God in that place, he found himself asking. Then he turned over. What nonsense; next he would be dreaming he was back at school, a little boy cherished by the certainties of the black-robed fathers, who so foolishly managed to combine a passion for science with a belief in God, such was the power and the folly of the Jesuitical mind.

*   *   *

136

Across the passage, Delia's dreams were full of noise, as they so often were. She was singing, or trying to sing, with music all around her, words and notes in her head and ears, yet she was voiceless, no sounds emerging from her open mouth. What was the music? *Tristan and Isolde.* How ridiculous. Isolde wasn't a role she had sung, nor would she yet, not for several years.

The stage vanished, and she was in a spartan studio in Vienna with a teacher, who was lecturing her: 'A singer must be strong, always strong and resilient; for the great roles that lie ahead of you, you must have strength of body and mind, calmness of emotion, a tranquil spirit.'

She was back on stage, in the enormous auditorium, trying to sing without a voice, listening to the rising hisses and boos from a frustrated audience, only to awake in a desperate fit of coughing, with thunder resounding in the skies.

'Sit up,' Jessica was saying. 'Come on, Delia, you must sit up, and drink some water. Have you any cough mixture?'

'It was only a bad dream,' Delia said, as she looked down at a hand that was trembling so violently it threatened to spill the water in the glass. Her teeth were chattering. 'This awful thunder.'

'It's past the worst,' said Jessica. 'I think that huge clap was its last fling. Shall I stay with you?'

Delia shook her head. 'I'll leave the oil lamp on and read for a bit.'

'Okay, but take care not to knock it over.'

It was many hours before Marjorie slept, lying wakeful until the storm had died down, and the wind was a whispering breeze against the shutters. But the thunder was still reverberating in her head, changing into the massive thump of an exploding rocket, as she fell into her dream.

She was back in wartime London, during the rocket attacks, at the wheel of her ambulance, peering into the eerie light of a darkness lit by a tiny beam of light from the vehicle, and by the ominous glow of fires. The stench of burning and explosives was in her mouth and nose, and the bitter taste of fear lay lurking beneath it.

She drove round a massive crater, and braked as an ARP warden flagged her down. 'Here,' he shouted. 'Over here. They've got one out alive, and they've found another.'

She was out of the driver's cab, seizing the stretcher from the back, calm, giving orders, acting with trained, mechanical efficiency. Yet all the time voices buzzed in her head: listen, someone is calling, there's someone else there, you must find them, they can't leave her, listen, listen, listen . . .

Lucius

ONE

Delia woke with a start, to find the bedroom perfectly quiet. The wind must have dropped; nothing was keening or rattling. What time was it? Five o'clock. So the light filtering through the shutters was the light of dawn, and there was the cockerel greeting the break of day in his raucous way.

It was early to get up, but she was too wide awake to have any hope of going back to sleep. She opened the window and pushed the shutters back. The scent of fresh earth after rain was intoxicating, and breathed an invitation to go out and savour the new day. She would get up, and go down to the sea.

For a moment, at the top of the stone steps, she hesitated, thinking of Benedetta's finger-wagging warnings about snakes. To hell with it. She'd probably misunderstood the Italian, and besides, any snake worth its salt would hear her and slither out of her way long before she trod on it, just as the adders did on the moors.

The ground was glistening from the heavy rain of the previous night, and the path was strewn with pine needles and twigs. The olive trees didn't seem to have been blown about too much, although of course she had no idea what a damaged olive tree would look like. With their gnarled and twisted trunks, they looked beaten about to start with. Did olive trees blossom? And when were olives harvested?

A stranger in a strange land, she thought, far removed from her native terrain of oak and ash and thorn.

She had expected a rough sea after such a storm, raging surf, crashing waves, but although it wasn't the millpond calm of yesterday morning it wasn't rough. The sea was a glow of shimmering pinks and purples, and the sky was cloudless. The moon was still visible, but dimmed by the rising of the greater celestial body of the sun.

There was some evidence of the storm on the beach, though: a line of debris at the water's edge, and an orange crate cast up and lying on its side.

It was surprisingly mild. She would have thought the storm would have left a chill behind it, but the slight morning breeze was a warm one. She sat down, her back against a rock, and looked out to sea, mesmerised by the shifting patterns of waves and light and the steady hiss as the water drew back into the next wave.

She must have almost dozed off, for she came to with a start. What was that? Surely she could hear voices. Were the others coming down to the beach?

She blinked. Beyond the entrance to the cove was what looked like a fishing boat. How long had it been there? And the noise she had heard was the sound of oars and the steady squeak of rowlocks. There was a dinghy heading into the cove with two men in it.

Good Lord, she hadn't got herself mixed up with smugglers, had she? She'd heard about Italian bandits, and visions of the Mafia, of gangsters in big hats, of shoot-ups in the alleys of Naples, crowded into her mind. What should she do? At the moment the bulk of the rock might hide her from view, but once the boat landed she would be all too visible. Could she ease herself round to the other side of the rock and make a dash for it?

142

She was annoyed by the boat and the men drawing nearer and nearer to the shore. Never mind who they were, or what they wanted: their arrival had shattered her early morning calm.

The dinghy was within a few yards of the beach, and one man was resting on his oars while the other jumped out. He turned to speak to the man still in the boat, and the sound of laughter came to her across the water. Then the man was splashing through the shallow water to the beach.

He's seen me, Delia said to herself. She was quite sure of that; he had known all along that she was there.

His voice was still full of laughter, speaking in Italian. What on earth was he wearing? Shorts, and a vividly coloured shirt, for heaven's sake.

'Hello?' He was speaking English now, did members of Mafia gangs speak English?

He walked towards her, holding out his hand. 'You must be one of the English people staying at the Villa Dante. I'm right, aren't I, this is the beach of the Villa Dante? How do you do?'

'What are you doing here?' she said. 'This beach is private property.'

It was a stupid thing to say; she knew exactly why he was here. He was the mysterious fourth man, summoned, just as she had been, by Beatrice Malaspina.

Lucius saw a woman with dark hair, glinting slightly red in the sunshine, a proud nose, lightly tanned skin and a good figure, who was looking at him with a most unfriendly expression. She was defiant and angry, he must have startled her, wading out of the sea like that.

She pushed the dark glasses she was wearing up on to her forehead, and looked straight at him. She didn't smile. There was no response to him as a man there, just a direct, appraising gaze, a hawkish look without a hint of welcome.

143

'Did you see the yacht from your window and come down to investigate?'

'No, I was on the beach already.'

'I saw you, asleep. You didn't spend the night on the sand, I suppose.'

'I was up early.'

A long pause. 'Perhaps we could start over,' he said. He held out his hand again. 'I'm Lucius Wilde.'

Reluctantly, she gave him her hand. A firm, warm hand, a brief handshake, and then she drew away. 'I'm Delia Vaughan. Beatrice Malaspina summoned you, I suppose. You're the fourth man.'

'The fourth man?'

'That's what we call you. Actually, there are four of us altogether. Two women, and now two men. I expect the lawyer told you.'

'I'm certainly here because of Beatrice Malaspina's will.'

'Well, you'd better come up to the villa. Have you breakfasted?'

'No. Tell me, Miss Vaughan—'

'You can call me Delia. You're American, aren't you? Have you travelled all the way across the Atlantic just for the Villa Dante? It's a long way to come.'

'I was coming to Europe in any case. I've been in France these last few days.'

'Why did you come ashore like that, from a fishing boat?' She was frowning. 'Don't you have any luggage?'

'Unfortunately not. A series of events . . .'

'What events?'

She wanted to know? He'd tell her, and then maybe she'd smile; he'd like to see her smile.

'Shipwreck,' he said gravely. 'An encounter with pirates and a shipwreck.'

144

TWO

Marjorie took Lucius's arrival quite in her stride. 'Hullo,' she said. 'I'm Marjorie Swift. I thought you'd come today, although not perhaps so early. Why are you wearing such peculiar clothes?'

George, anxious to smooth over Marjorie's brusque greeting, intervened with a hearty handshake, and his own introduction.

'Helsinger. Is that an English name?'

'I come from Denmark.'

'Via England, however.' Lucius was eyeing the tweed jacket and the baggy flannels.

'George is an atom scientist,' Marjorie said.

There was, Delia felt, a dreamlike quality to all this. The four of them, bound by a will, the will of a woman none of them – ah, but perhaps Lucius did know Beatrice Malaspina. Perhaps all their questions were to be answered, and his arrival would mark an end to the mystery and uncertainty.

Before she could ask, Jessica appeared, apologising for being late down for breakfast. 'I was deep in the last chapter of my book, and I had to finish it. Oh.' She stared frankly at Lucius. 'Where did you come from?' She held out her hand. 'I'm Jessica Meldon.'

'A boat,' said Delia. 'He landed on the beach.'

Why couldn't he have driven up in a taxi like anyone else? There was something about this new arrival that disturbed her. She searched in her mind for what it was. Did he remind her of someone, someone she didn't like? No, that wasn't it. He was quite unlike anyone she had ever met. There was no handle to him. Nonsense – she was just thrown by his landing on the beach and by his peculiar clothes . . . and what had happened to the rest of his things? He could hardly have flown from America in shorts and a Hawaiian shirt.

'Well, now,' said Jessica, giving a boiled egg a brisk tap with her spoon. 'The big question is, do you know anything about Beatrice Malaspina, or are you as much in the dark about her as everyone else?'

Jessica's question startled him. 'Do you mean that you don't know why you are here?'

'Not a clue,' said Marjorie. 'Summoned, instructed by the lawyers, and left totally in the dark.'

'I can't help you at all. I'm as much in the dark as you seem to be. I have to say, I thought it very odd when I was informed by the lawyer about the will of this Beatrice Malaspina, a person I had never heard of before. So it's a complete mystery to all of us.'

'It is a mystery that may easily be solved,' said George drily, 'if we can get hold of the elusive Dr Calderini, who is the lawyer in the case. Now that you are here, I am sure we can persuade him to come clean.'

Delia had brought Lucius in to breakfast while Benedetta was in the kitchen; now she came into the dining room and let out a shriek of amazement. Out poured the usual torrent of unintelligible words, to which Lucius promptly replied with equal fluency.

'Thank goodness,' said George, 'that our new arrival speaks Italian. Now we can question Benedetta, now we can begin to find out more about Beatrice Malaspina.'

Benedetta was delighted with Lucius, that was obvious. Her face broke into a beaming smile; she gesticulated, cast her eyes to heaven, and flung herself into what Delia suspected was her judgement on all those already ensconced at the Villa Dante.

Lucius was laughing now; he seemed to laugh very easily. What on earth was Benedetta saying?

Benedetta hurried off to make more coffee.

'You speak Italian,' Marjorie said, after a moment's silence. 'That will be extremely useful, for although Delia does her best with Hugo and a dictionary, Benedetta doesn't seem to speak the kind of Italian that she's learned. You obviously do.'

'I was in Italy during the war.'

'And now you're a money man,' said Marjorie.

Lucius looked at her in surprise. 'How do you know that?'

'Oh, Marjorie is full of mysterious insights,' Delia said. 'She hears voices, so she says.' She knew she sounded contemptuous and disliked herself for it, but Marjorie coming out with her cryptic utterances was just what they didn't need right now, or Lucius would be thinking he'd landed in strange company.

'Not always voices,' said Marjorie, unperturbed. 'In this case, when I look at you, I see a dollar sign in my mind's eye. When I met George, I had an idea of those diagrams they do in the papers to explain atomic structure.'

'What about Delia?' Lucius asked, clearly interested. 'And Jessica – Miss Meldon . . .'

'Mrs Meldon, actually,' Jessica said. 'Jessica's fine, though, we're all on first names here.'

'Is Mr Meldon staying at the villa?'

'No,' Jessica said quickly.

'Delia is turned inwards,' said Marjorie. 'There's a wall of reserve about her, so I don't have any flashes of insight. As to Mr Meldon, Jessica is separated from her husband.'

147

George made a sound of dismay. 'Surely, Jessica's private life—'

'Isn't private when it's been headline news in England for the past few weeks,' said Marjorie tartly. 'There's no need to pick up details of Jessica's life from any voices. I don't suppose you read the kind of newspapers I do, George, so perhaps you haven't seen the endless headlines and column inches devoted to the Meldons' marital problems.'

'Obviously, you like the gutter press,' said Delia, furious with Marjorie; couldn't she see the effect her words were having on Jessica, who had gone quite pale? Of course, she might have expected that the other guests would have read about the Meldon rift in the papers, although it didn't surprise her that George hadn't.

'I'm devoted to the gutter press, as you call it. It's all people and story based, and people's follies and foibles interest me.'

'Of course, we don't have insights, so we don't know what you do,' Delia said. 'You must have had a job once.'

'Never mind about that,' said Jessica, recovering herself. 'What I'm longing to know, Lucius, is why you arrived by sea, and why in those clothes?'

'You aren't going to believe this,' said Delia.

'It's simple,' said Lucius. He helped himself to another roll. 'I was shipwrecked.'

He'd had it all planned. A week at the Forrests' villa on the hills behind Nice, then he would catch the train down into Italy and turn up at the Villa Dante to find out what was with this will business.

The villa in France was luxurious, with wonderful views, the company consisted of mostly agreeable compatriots – and Elfrida.

Perfectly groomed, perfectly turned out from the moment she came down to breakfast in a halter-necked dress until she appeared in a Paris model for dinner, everything about her was sleek and immaculate. Hair, nails, teeth all gleamed.

'What a handsome couple they are,' he heard a fellow guest say. And another: 'Such a relief for his father that Lucius is settling down at last. He's always had a bit of a kick in his gallop, but Elfrida will put a stop to all that. What a charming girl, what an excellent wife she'll make him.' And the invariable rider: 'Pity he didn't pick an American girl.'

'Elfrida's mother was American. That's how she's related to the Forrests.'

'She seems English through and through.'

'Only the accent and the education and the manners. Inside, she's American all right. Tough, and keeps her eye on the ball. Lucius will go places with Elfrida beside him.'

It was all so appallingly true, and it depressed him beyond measure. Which was why he had jumped at the invitation of a day's sailing from a college friend who was spending the summer yachting in the Mediterranean. 'Lotus-eating,' he said, with the lazy smile that Lucius remembered so well. Ben was an investment wizard, who had given up a career in engineering, which bored him, to make a fortune on the stock exchange and retire at thirty. His friends had laughed at his plan; it took more than intentions to make and keep a fortune, they told him. The last laugh was with Ben, who made his fortune in no time at all, but then found he didn't want to retire when he turned thirty. Instead, he spent six months of the year working the markets and six months doing whatever took his fancy.

'Last year I went on an expedition in Greenland,' he told Lucius as he steered the motor dinghy through the vessels moored in Nice harbour. 'The year before that I learned to climb mountains in Switzerland.'

Lucius envied him his freedom and his relaxed approach to life, an approach that was tested to the utmost when they were chased off their course by Albanian pirates. 'I can't think what they're doing here,' said Ben. 'Mostly they hang around in the Adriatic.'

'Will we outrun them?'

'Should do. The weather's getting dirty, though. We could be in for a rough ride.'

A very rough ride, which ended in Ben's yacht going to join all the other wrecks on the floor of the Mediterranean, and Lucius and Ben coming ashore at Imperia, courtesy of a passing fishing boat.

'At least you've got your papers and money,' said Ben cheerfully, as they squelched their way to the nearest hotel for a bath and food. 'I'll see about renting a car. I assume you want to go back to Nice.'

'No,' said Lucius. He didn't, not to that sumptuous villa with its pool and hovering servants, nor to dancing attendance on Elfrida. 'I'm supposed to pay a visit near here, so I guess I'll just turn up.'

'In bathing trunks?'

'I'll be able to buy some clothes.'

Lucius dug the spoon into the honey. 'Which turned out to be a problem, Imperia being a small place and the Italians who shop there being, I guess, six inches shorter than I am. Holiday clothes were all I could find to fit, hence . . .' He gestured to his gaudy shirt.

'I would offer to lend you some clothes of mine,' said George, 'although we are not the same size, but I have seen clothes hanging in the wardrobes, and perhaps there will be something to fit you. There can be no harm in borrowing garments in your situation.'

'I'll ask Benedetta.'

An hour later, Lucius reappeared, bathed, shaved and dressed in a light grey suit.

He didn't look at all as though he'd been through all those perilous adventures, Delia thought indignantly. Fresh as a daisy.

'It's a very old-fashioned cut,' she said.

'Isn't it just? I look like something out of an old movie. Only look at the width of these trousers. However, it fits, more or less. The shoes, though, are a problem.'

He was still wearing his deck shoes, which gave him a very incongruous appearance. 'This brand new panama, however, is exactly my size, so I feel ready to face the world. George, do you fancy a stroll into the town?'

'Stroll,' Delia said to Jessica and Marjorie as they watched the two men walk down the drive, deep in conversation. 'I don't think that man does anything slowly.'

'They are going at a fair clip,' said Marjorie. 'I expect George is awfully glad to have some masculine company; I don't think he's comfortable with just himself and three women.'

'Do you think he's queer?' said Jessica.

'No, just used to being with men. There are very few female scientists, it's a male and clubby world.'

'Then it'll do him good to find out what the other half of humanity is like,' said Delia.

Which won her a rare look of approval from Marjorie.

'It seems much quieter and duller without our fourth man,' said Jessica, as the men disappeared out of sight. 'What a personality Lucius has.'

'He's going to drive us all crazy if we have to put up with him for long,' said Delia. 'Let's hope they manage to get in touch with Dr Calderini this morning, and then we can learn what the will says and be off.'

'Oh, I don't think we'll be going anywhere just yet,' said Marjorie. 'But I'm sure things will change with Lucius around.'

'I wonder what Lucius and George are talking about, they've gone off yattering away nineteen to the dozen. Who would have thought it of George? He's not exactly the chatty sort.'

151

'Lucius is talkative,' said Jessica. 'And it's different man to man. George has more to say to another man. I wonder if he has a wife or girlfriend?'

'He talks so little about himself, how could one know?'

'I expect they're gossiping,' said Marjorie. 'Men do, when they're together.'

THREE

'These vineyards are in a shocking state,' said Lucius.

'Are they?' said George, who knew nothing about vine-yards. 'I hadn't noticed.'

'That's because you are a scientist, a theoretician, with your mind focused on a world beyond the reach of any human eye,' said Lucius. 'You should pay more attention to your surroundings. If you make a habit of it, you'll soon get the hang of it. Observe the beauties of nature, of the growing world all around you; look at those amazing white irises growing on the bank there, for example, and then you'll go back refreshed to your other world of neutrons and particles and all those dangerous things you atom scientists dabble in.'

'I do wish people wouldn't call us atom scientists,' said George with a hint of impatience. 'I'm a theoretical physi-cist.'

'Just so,' said Lucius. 'One falls into these phrases. It's because of the newspapers, everyone has to have a label these days. It's sloppy thinking, you're quite right. Now, I want you to fill me in on the others.'

George was embarrassed. 'I'm afraid I know very little about them. We've been thrown together, and although I find them good company, we aren't given to heart-baring.'

'No, as you're English, one would expect reticence.'

'I am not English.'

'Not by birth, no, but those years at Cambridge have got to you. Let's do it in alphabetical order. Start by telling me about Delia.'

George gave up. There was no point in trying to sidetrack a man like Lucius, and what, after all, was there to tell? Nothing very much, no private confidences to betray.

'She is an opera singer.'

'Have you heard her sing? Has she any talent, or is she merely an upper class dabbler, whiling away the time at the tunes until she finds herself a dull husband?'

George fired up in Delia's defence. 'I can't imagine that she would ever marry a dull man; she is not at all dull herself. As to her musical ability, I am not able to say, because I haven't heard her sing. There is a piano at the villa, but it is sadly out of tune.'

'Is it? Then we should see to that. Are you a musician yourself?'

'I play the piano,' said George. 'But an amateur only.'

'We must see if we can't get some music going at the villa. What have you been doing in the evenings?'

'Reading. Talking a little.'

'The Villa Dante is a house that should be full of voices and music and laughter,' said Lucius. 'So what's Delia's background? She has that air which the English upper classes wear like armour.'

'Delia is the daughter of a textile manufacturer,' George said. 'Lord Saltford is her father. It is not an ancient title, I understand, for she told me that her grandfather bought his seat in the House of Lords. I gather that this was possible at one time, when Lloyd George was prime minister. She comes from the north of England; Yorkshire, I believe. She has been ill this last winter – some complaint of the lungs, bronchitis, the curse of the English climate. There was a

154

brother, who died in the war, and Jessica tells me she has an older sister. That is all I know.'

'I know Jessica is here because she shared the trip with Delia. What else do you know about her?'

'She is an old and good friend of Delia's, they have known one another since their schooldays. Also, there is a family connection: Jessica's brother is married to Delia's sister. I think, with the marital problems Marjorie mentioned, that Jessica is glad to be away from England.'

'Meldon,' said Lucius. 'The name's familiar. Isn't her husband some kind of a politician? With a war record?'

'As to that, you should ask Jessica yourself; I know nothing of the details of her marriage. And as for Marjorie,' said George quickly, before Lucius could carry on with his interrogation, 'I know even less about her than about the other two. She is a strange woman, a very unhappy one, with a chip on her shoulder. She resents the fact that Delia and Jessica come from upper class families. She is hard up, and she has no job to go back to. She is obviously very intelligent.'

'She has the air of a professional woman who has had to make her own way in the world.'

'Well, no doubt she has, but as to how she made her living, do not ask me, for none of us knows. You saw at breakfast how she draws into herself when the subject is mentioned.'

'And these voices she hears?'

'It is very annoying, the way she speaks her mind,' said George with some warmth. 'You never know what she's going to say next. And this habit of pretending she knows more than she possibly can is very irritating. Poor woman, I suppose she does it to make herself interesting.'

'She doesn't need to try. She is interesting. And I'm not going to ask you any more questions, since we're just about at the town, which is attractive-looking, I must say.'

'It is run down and impoverished once you are inside the walls,' George said.

'What a maze of streets. You've been here before – where do we go to find a telephone? You don't know? Right.'

He beckoned with his finger to a small, scrawny boy who was loitering in a doorway and staring at them with frank interest. The boy came running over, and Lucius spoke to him in rapid Italian.

'He will show us the way. Apparently we need the Bar Centrale, which is owned by his aunt.'

The Bar Centrale turned out to be in the main square, the Piazza Garibaldi.

'Every Italian town has a Piazza or a Via Garibaldi,' said Lucius. 'Not to mention a Via Dante.'

Inside, the bar was a gloomy place, hung with faded yellowing photos of long forgotten football heroes and bottles that looked as though they had been there for half a century. Lucius greeted the suspicious-looking woman behind the bar with a cheerful *Buon giorno*, and then launched into lengthy negotiations as to the use of the telephone.

George could see no sign of a telephone, and suspected that the boy had brought them there simply to bring custom to his aunt's bar. But no. Lucius pushed the tiny cup of coffee he had ordered along the counter to George and disappeared into the dark depths behind the bar. He emerged some ten minutes later. 'It's going to take a while,' he said. 'The telephone system isn't very advanced in Italy. However, the connection to Dr Calderini has been promised in perhaps half an hour. Which, this being Italy, could mean anything from five minutes to a couple of hours. Who's that?' he went on, as Pietro came sideways into the bar, and George greeted him with a smile and a raised hand.

'Pietro,' said George. 'He works at the villa, with Benedetta. We haven't discovered if they're married or related or simply both employees – ex-employees – of Beatrice Malaspina. They don't seem to get on very well, she hounds him unmercifully.'

'Then I should think they're married,' said Lucius. He fell

156

into conversation with Pietro at once, bought him a glass of wine, and was soon deep in what sounded to George like technical talk, although they might be discussing Pietro's knee trouble or the weather; one simply couldn't judge in another language.

Lucius, as though reading his thoughts, interrupted his vigorous conversation with Pietro to bring George up to date. 'I do apologise, it's kind of exclusive, I know, for me to talk Italian. We're discussing vines and wine.'

George was pleased to find that his guess had been right, and he drained his cup of coffee and sat waiting for Lucius to finish, or to be summoned to the phone. He was glad of a few minutes' respite from Lucius's vigorous personality; he had forgotten what it was like to have someone with that kind of vitality and energy around. He had worked for a man like that during the war, but back in Cambridge he had fallen back into his more peaceful and relaxed routine.

Now he had an uneasy feeling that his life might once again be disrupted. But no, their time in Italy would soon be over, and then it was back to the university where he must try to make his tired brain do what he wanted. Perhaps if he stayed here for weeks rather than days his rational self would restore order in his system, and he could become what he had once been. He had heard the whispers behind his back, at the university: half the man he was. Yes, used to be quite brilliant, now even his teaching – well, the students have been complaining. He starts sentences and trails off into silence, but doesn't seem to be aware of what he's said. Not surprising, when you think . . .

He tried to jerk himself out of this stream of uncomfortable reminiscence. He could do without the voices repeating themselves in his head: he was getting as bad as Marjorie.

His head of department had, tactfully, suggested a visit to a psychiatrist, he knew an awfully good man . . .

But George had no intention of unburdening his soul to

any doctor oozing with Freudian platitudes. Instead, he had come to Italy, knowing that his colleagues saw him go with sighs of relief.

Pietro seemed delighted with what Lucius was saying; George realised that he had never seen the man smile. Well, who would smile, with Benedetta harrying you every moment with such remorseless enthusiasm?

'The Villa Dante used to have a big staff,' Lucius said, drinking his cold coffee. 'No chance of that these days, not with everyone hale, male and hearty gone away. That's why the population here is all old, female or young.'

'I noticed that, but I merely supposed the men were out at work.'

'There's nowhere to work around here,' said Lucius. 'Which is why any able-bodied man between the ages of fifteen and fifty, which is old in these parts, has gone off to Milan or even to America to find work. Leaving behind mothers and wives, but not so many sisters, for a lot of them have gone to the cities to find work as well. Take Domenico here,' he went on, lifting an eyebrow at their small guide who was hovering in the doorway. 'Ten years old, although he doesn't look it; because he doesn't get enough to eat. He's Pietro and Benedetta's grandson, yes, you're quite right, they are married. Their only son, Domenico's father, has gone to Milan to work. His mother, a good-for-nothing slut, according to Pietro, went off with a soldier three years ago, which is another all too familiar story. So Domenico goes to school in the morning and gets up to mischief in the afternoons, which will go on until he, too, is old enough to leave San Silvestro and head for the city to find work.'

Although he was taller than Lucius, George had to lengthen his stride to keep up with Lucius's ferocious pace as they set off back to the villa. 'Did you make contact with Dr Calderini?'

'I did. Luckily there is only one lawyer Calderini in La Spezia, I thought we might have to work our way through quite a list.'

'How would he know you had arrived if you had been unable to reach him on the telephone?'

'I expect Benedetta has her methods of getting in touch with him. As it is, he'll be over later today. Sounds like a brisk kind of guy.'

'Brisk?' George sounded doubtful. 'You will be able to judge for yourself when you meet him. He enjoys the mystery of these arrangements, I think.'

'Let's hope this afternoon will see an end to that particular mystery. We'll find out why we're here, and what Beatrice Malaspina has to do with us.'

FOUR

The roar of Dr Calderini's car broke the still silence of the afternoon.

'Aren't you bursting with curiosity?' Jessica asked, as they hurried to join George and Lucius who were greeting the lawyer. 'All your questions answered at last.'

'Don't you be so sure,' said Marjorie.

'Oh, not more prescience,' Delia said.

'Not prescience this time,' said Marjorie unexpectedly. 'I've been doing some perfectly rational thinking. Beatrice Malaspina seems to have been a very complicated woman, in which case she wouldn't bring us all out here just to have a lawyer read a will and say bye-bye. Likewise, Mr Lawyer is as slippery as an eel. Is he likely to come up with any straightforward clear answers? I doubt it.'

'Lucius will shake it all out of him,' said Delia. Annoying he might be, but if ever she had met a man capable of dealing with a tricksy lawyer, it was Lucius.

They assembled, with some formality, round the table in the dining room, under the dancing figures of gods. Jessica had offered to leave them to it, but Delia said no, she'd only have to give her a blow-by-blow account of it all afterwards if she weren't there.

160

'If no one minds,' said Jessica.

The lawyer was all suavity. He had a polished leather brief-case, which he opened with due ceremony; Italian, English, French, lawyers the world over were the same, Delia reflected.

'According to the instructions of Beatrice Malaspina, all four of you have duly come to the Villa Dante,' he began. 'All of you are named in her will, all are legatees and shall inherit from her estate.'

'Hold it there,' said Lucius. 'I have a question. Was Beatrice Malaspina married?'

'Yes. She was. Her name before her marriage was Beatrice Stonor.'

'So, didn't she have any children, grandchildren? Why would she leave anything in her will to a bunch of strangers?'

'Are you strangers?' said Dr Calderini. 'Well, that does not concern me. You are the people named here, and I will check that now, if you would be so good. A mere formality, you have your passports with you?'

Delia and Marjorie hurried upstairs to get their passports; George and Lucius produced theirs from their inner pockets. The lawyer made a ceremony of looking through the documents, noting numbers and dates before handing them back with a flourish to each of them.

'Very well,' said Lucius. 'Formalities over. Now, what have you to tell us?'

The lawyer raised his eyebrows and lifted his hands. 'Italian law is quite strict as to testamentary arrangements, with family always taking precedence, and the part of the estate which came to Mrs Malaspina on the death of the late Dr Malaspina goes to her husband's side of the family.' He shuffled some papers. 'There is a nephew. However, the Villa Dante always belonged to her since she inherited it from her mother. Beatrice Malaspina was a clever woman, who arranged her affairs exactly as she wanted, and so was free to leave her own possessions as she wished.'

'Weren't there any children of the marriage?' Marjorie asked.

'There was one daughter, who was married and divorced. She died childless during the war. In America, I believe.'

Lucius was getting restless. 'So what's the position?'

'Ah, as to exactly what you inherit under her will, I can't tell you.'

'Why not?' said Marjorie, who had been watching the lawyer with brooding eyes.

'Because I do not know,' he said, with a charming smile. 'It seems that there is an addendum, an extra, what in English you call a codicil, to her will, which is here in this house. Her instructions are that you are to be invited to the Villa Dante. If all four of you come, as you have done, and as she felt sure you would, then you are to stay as her guests, and it is left to you to find the codicil.'

There was a minute's complete, stunned silence, broken by a hoot of laughter from Marjorie. George took off his spectacles and wiped them, shaking his head. Delia looked out into the garden with its dappled sunlight and greenery growing more intense by the day and felt a sudden joy that they weren't going to leave the villa just yet.

Lucius was businesslike. 'This madwoman has set up a treasure hunt? For people she doesn't know? Is this some kind of a practical joke? No, it won't be; lawyers never joke, in my experience. Okay, you've been through all the papers in the house, you must have done.'

'It was part of my duty. Everything was perfectly in order, and she had a meticulous mind.'

'A tricky mind if you ask me,' said Lucius. 'So this codicil is hidden somewhere in this rather large residence, waiting for us to find it. Why, it could be anywhere – in an old book, stuffed behind a painting.'

'She says in her instructions that you will not find it by searching for it, but it will come to light when the time is right.'

'Mysticism to go with the crazy mind.'

'I suppose,' said George tentatively, 'that Beatrice Malaspina was completely in her right mind when she drew up her will.'

'Oh, no doubt about that, none at all,' said the lawyer. 'She had, as you say, all her wits with her. She knew exactly what she was doing. Now, there are conditions.'

'Conditions,' said Lucius. 'Where there are lawyers, there are conditions. Come on, let's have them.'

'It is simple. All four of you must agree to the terms she has laid down: that you come, which you have, and that you agree to remain for a certain time, which is thirty-three days from the day I make known to you what she has instructed. That is today, which counts as the first of these thirty-three days.'

'Thirty-three days?' said George. 'Why thirty-three? Why not a calendar month, or four weeks?'

Dr Calderini raised his shoulders in an extravagant shrug.

'We might find it tomorrow,' said Delia.

'We won't,' said Marjorie. 'Beatrice Malaspina's too clever for that.'

'I like a challenge,' said Lucius.

'I'll stay,' said Marjorie. 'I like it here. I don't care whether all she's left me is a bag of buttons, as it happens. Just having these weeks here at the villa is a great gift, as far as I'm concerned. It may not be so special for the rest of you.'

'What about you, George?' asked Lucius.

'I am not required to be back at my university yet,' said George. 'I see no reason . . . Besides, I should like to find out what it is all about. I am intrigued, I confess.'

'Which leaves you, Delia.'

Jessica was looking at Delia. 'You can't stay that long without working, can you? Can you manage without a piano?'

The lawyer looked puzzled. 'Working? Piano?' His face cleared. 'How delightful. Miss Vaughan is a pianist, a musician?'

163

'Miss Vaughan is indeed a musician,' said George. 'A professional opera singer.'

'But that is excellent,' said the lawyer. 'As you know, all Italians adore opera, it is in our blood. Naturally, a singer must keep her voice in good order. I have noticed a cough, which is not at all good, but our Italian sun and warmth will chase that away. The music should not be a problem, however,' he added. 'There is a piano here in the villa, a very fine piano. Beatrice Malaspina was herself an accomplished pianist.'

'It's out of tune,' Delia said.

Dr Calderini's expressive face took on a look of tragic dismay.

'George told me about the piano,' said Lucius, 'so while I was in San Silvestro, I fixed for a guy from La Spezia to come tune it.'

Jessica was right, Lucius was one of those organising men. Still, it was thoughtful of him to see about the piano.

'Excellent!' cried Dr Calderini.

'Will you also remain at the villa, Jessica?' said George. 'I should not like to think of you driving back to England on your own.'

The lawyer was horrified by such a notion. He threw his elegant hands in the air in a gesture of denial. 'To drive all the way to England, across Italy and France, a young woman on her own, and such an attractive one, it is not to be thought of. How frightened you would be!'

'Oh, we Englishwomen are made of sterner stuff than that,' said Jessica.

'I know how in the war you all drove ambulances and flew bombers up and down, but that was a long time ago and now it is peace, which is infinitely more dangerous.'

'Don't get yourself in a state, Mr Calderini. You bet your life I'm staying, if the others will let me. To leave now would be like leaving after the first act of a play.'

'So you'll stay, Delia?' asked Lucius.

She looked out over the garden, felt the warmth of the sun on her skin, and lifted her sunglasses to remind herself of the brilliant light. 'What happens if we don't stay? Or if we don't find the codicil within thirty-three days?'

The lawyer riffled through his papers. 'Ah, yes, I was coming to that.'

'Were you?' said Lucius.

'If the conditions are not fulfilled, there are other arrangements for the estate. There would be four beneficiaries. Should Dr Helsinger not stay, his bequest will go to the Centre for Advanced Weapons Research in France.'

'Weapons?' said George, dismayed.

'Miss Swift's would go to the Conservative Party in England.'

Marjorie's lips tightened, but she said nothing.

'Mr Wilde's, let me see, yes, to fund a fellowship in business economics in America.'

'And mine?' said Delia.

'Yours would go to the Methodist Church, also in England.'

'And if we don't find the codicil, then that's how it goes?' said Lucius.

'Exactly.'

'Dr Calderini, just what is the bequest?'

'Ah, that I do not know. That is another condition of the will. But I am sure all this is incidental, for within the time specified you will doubtless have discovered the document, and then everything becomes evident.'

FIVE

Dr Calderini stayed to lunch, and Lucius spent most of the meal, with a quick apology to the others for speaking Italian, talking to him. After lunch, the lawyer disappeared down the drive, rather the worse for the wine Lucius had plied him with, judging by the speed and erratic path of the car.

'He's going to hit the gatepost,' said George, but he missed it by an inch, and roared off into the silence. 'I hope he doesn't meet anyone on the way.'

'They'll hear him coming,' said Lucius.

'What were you talking about so busily at lunch?' Jessica asked.

'I was pumping him,' said Lucius.

'To any purpose?' said Delia.

'Yes and no. I think he truly has no idea why Beatrice Malaspina named us in her will, or why she wanted us here at the Villa Dante; he says if we didn't know her and are not related to her, then he is as much in the dark as we are as to her motives. He buttons up when it comes to Beatrice Malaspina herself, won't talk about her at all, although you can tell he was in awe of her. A remarkable woman, he called her. And a great lady, but unpredictable. And dangerous, he said, which is a funny word to use of a woman in her eighties.

Mind you,' he added, 'some people might call my grand-mother dangerous.'

'Beatrice Malaspina might have been dangerous when she was young,' said Marjorie. 'A femme fatale, and all that.'

'Femme fatale nothing,' said Delia. 'Listen, I don't know about you, but it's those other arrangements that really worry me. I dislike the Methodists. I'd never willingly give them a penny. And I bet Marjorie wouldn't dream of contributing to the Tory party.'

'Not under any circumstances.'

'It's neat,' said Lucius. 'Stick and carrot. I take it you aren't keen on weapons research, George?'

'Most certainly not.'

'Which leaves you, Lucius,' said Marjorie. 'Beatrice Malaspina clearly believed banking wasn't that close to your heart.'

'How did she know?' said Delia. 'We're strangers, none of us had even so much as heard her name, and here she is setting up all this. Why? How did she know about me and Methodism? It's not something I talk about, or even think about; I just know that when the collecting tins are out, that one doesn't get my half-crown.'

'We'll only answer all the questions when we find the codicil,' said George.

'No,' said Marjorie. 'It's the other way round. It's only by learning more about her, and how her mind works—'

'Worked,' said Delia.

'—that we'll be able to solve the mystery of where she's hidden the codicil.'

'She's turning out to be one hell of an interesting woman.' Lucius became brisk. 'Let's hope that our searches throw up some information about her. Maybe she kept a diary. I reckon we need to get organised. First of all, do we take what he said about not finding the codicil by looking for it at face value, or do we set about searching the villa from floor to

167

ceiling? The one thing we don't need to hunt through are the books; he told me, in an expansive moment, that Benedetta took them all down from the shelves and shook each and every one before dusting it and putting it back.'

'If we are going to search, then we will need to be systematic about it,' said George.

'There are probably attics with discarded stuff going back for decades,' said Delia. 'You could start there.'

Why did men always want to organise? Why did they have that impulse to direct other people's energies into what they considered the proper channels?

'Nope,' said Lucius. 'The attics are empty. They were cleared out years ago, so Calderini says.'

'That's a relief. Well, you organise away,' Delia said. 'I'm for a laze in the sun and a bit of pondering. Jessica, you're always reading detective stories – put your thinking cap on, become Hercule Poirot or Inspector Whosit, and get deducting.'

Lucius wasn't inclined to be idle. 'Marjorie, why don't you show me around the house, to begin with, and the gardens and grounds? Is lazing what you've all been doing?'

'There has not been a great deal else to do,' said George.

'We were waiting for you to arrive. We had, after all, no idea of why we were here,' said Marjorie.

'Even so, life is too short for lazing, especially with a thirty-two and a half day countdown ticking away.'

Marjorie came unexpectedly to Delia's defence. 'Since Delia has had a bad chest, it's the best thing for her, to sit in the sun.'

'He's going to be a real nuisance,' Delia said. She was lying back in a deckchair, a broad-brimmed hat shading her eyes, which were closed.

'Lucius?' said Jessica.

'Him. One of those knows he's right, take command kind of men.'

'I suppose so.'

Silence reigned. Then Jessica spoke again. 'Do you find him attractive?'

'Not my type. You could try exercising your charms on him, but he doesn't look very susceptible. And at his age, he's probably either married or queer.'

'He could be divorced – don't Americans all get divorced quite quickly? Anyhow, he's definitely not queer.'

'There you are, all yours.'

'Actually, he isn't my type, either,' said Jessica.

Delia wasn't listening any more. She sat up and looked towards the gate, her hand shading her eyes. 'There's someone coming up to the house.'

'Not the lawyer back again?'

'No, it's a funny little man with a moustache. On a bicycle. With a black bag strapped behind the saddle. I say, you don't suppose it could be the piano tuner, do you?' She was on her feet in a moment.

The man dismounted from his bike, mopped his brow, and looked around him.

'*Pianoforte?*' said Delia hopefully.

His face broke into a pleased smile, and he nodded his head several times. '*Si, pianoforte.*'

Jessica watched them disappear into the house, and lay back, listening with inattentive ears to the pings and notes coming out through the shutters. She envied Delia her music. She wished she had something that was so absorbing, so demanding of her being.

Delia had told her to get detecting. She had a logical mind, but where did you begin with a problem like this?

George, wearing a short-sleeved white shirt that made him look much younger, came out into the arcade. He was carrying a book.

'Come and sit here,' said Jessica. 'I'm trying to sort out the facts of the puzzle in an orderly way, only there don't

169

seem to be many facts. Don't you think Beatrice Malaspina is even more of an enigma than she was before?'

'My mother said that to find something, you had to put yourself into the mind of the person who had lost or hidden it.'

'I wish you luck, because so far Beatrice Malaspina's mind seems to be a closed book, doesn't it?'

'Marjorie has insight,' said George. 'And a vivid imagination. Perhaps she may be able to understand something of Beatrice's Malaspina's psychology. Meanwhile, I found this book, and I think it will interest you; you were asking about the proportions of the rooms. It is all laid out in here.'

Jessica took the book. 'Classical architecture.' Her eyes flicked down the page. 'Not art, but maths.' She gave George a direct look. 'My maths is distinctly rusty. I've not used it since I did my finals.'

'Then perhaps it is time you did.'

'Is the piano done?' said Jessica, as Delia came out of the house, looking happy.

'Perfect,' said Delia, flopping down on a deckchair. 'Wonderful. Lucius is paying him now. I wanted to, but he's appointed himself paymaster, it seems.'

'Lord high everything, in fact.'

Delia settled herself back in her deckchair. Once, she would have been eager to get to the piano, to sing, but although she was pleased that the piano was restored to a properly harmonious state she found herself curiously reluctant to work. I can't really, my chest is still furry, she told herself, closing her eyes and letting her mind drift.

Jessica was saying something about a piano, she and Richie had a piano in their flat, which was never played, Theo had teased her about it, said it made the drawing room look like a club. Do you remember that tiny restaurant Theo was so keen on, with all the tables close together and a piano that the owner used to play and croon to?

Why did Jessica have to mention Theo? In one of the sudden, vivid flashes of memory that she so resented, Delia remembered the first time she had gone out with Theo. They had dined in that very restaurant. A dimly lit little place, with tables packed together, and overflowing with people, and a queue at the door. Theo was obviously a favoured guest, a table was miraculously found for them, and a waiter was hovering, with offers of game, fish; oysters are very good today.

Theo drove her out to the river, the next Sunday morning, where they took a boat and rowed upstream, all among the meadows, with birds soaring in a pale blue autumn sky, and trees, a blaze of colour, drifting their leaves at the water's edge.

Delia was overwhelmed by the masculinity of him, with his shirt unbuttoned and his sleeves rolled back, his arms rippling with muscles as he pulled effortlessly at the oars. 'I rowed for my college,' he said, when she congratulated him on his prowess with the oars. 'I was in the eight.'

Felicity would probably have gone to bed with Theo the first time she'd met him, in Delia's shoes. Why had it taken so long for them to make love? Theo was wooing her; at least, that was how it seemed. He was courting her, in an old-fashioned way, out of keeping with the times. When he first kissed her, not lightly, but with passion and intent, she felt dazzled and weakened, and powerless. But he had gone no further than the kiss, not then.

Would it have been easier if it had been a matter of casual lust, if there hadn't seemed to be any love behind their relationship, at least on his part? Had he ever had more than the mildest of feelings for her?

He'd known exactly what he was doing, she decided; he'd played her like a violin, so that when at last they did go to

171

bed, she was so longing for him that she would have thrown restraint to the winds and torn off all his clothes, had he not been there first, undoing her frock, standing there before her, naked, holding her at arm's length . . . So that I could admire him as much as he was admiring me.

And, typical Theo, there was no rolling about on the floor, no hurling themselves on a handy sofa. No, he'd arranged it, a weekend of snatched time at the Ritz, booked in as Mr and Mrs Sanderson, signing the name under the bored, supercilious, unbelieving eyes of the receptionist. A huge bed, sheets of a kind she hadn't slept in ever, Saltford Hall going in for strong cotton and cold linen, and the bliss of finally being utterly at one with Theo.

So she thought, until Felicity came back from a trip to America.

'Wow,' Felicity said, when she bumped into Theo and Delia one evening at the pictures. And, while Theo was apart from them for a moment, she lowered her voice and whispered in Delia's ear, 'Sex on the hoof! You do surprise me, Delia; I didn't think you had it in you. What's he like in bed?'

Casual words, but she should have known then that Felicity had her eye on Theo. Had Theo been taken with Felicity, glamorous, laughing, sophisticated Felicity, when he first met her?

'Quite a girl, your sister,' he said.

Jessica's voice broke in on Delia's thoughts, and her words brought Delia back to the present, to Italy, to a place that had no memories of Theo, except those she carried in her mind.

'I wonder if Marjorie has ever had a lover.'

'Who cares?' said Delia crossly.

'She doesn't seem the emotional type. Except when it comes to the upper classes, who obviously annoy the hell out of her.'

'She has something on her mind, I'm sure of it,' said Delia.

172

'Only I dare say we'll never discover what it is, or anything much about her. She's very secretive.'

'Secretive people in my experience have nothing but lives so dull that nobody cares whether they know about them or not.'

Lucius, however, had learned more about Marjorie in a couple of hours than the others had done in all the time they'd spent with her. She went round the house with him, making occasional remarks about the style of furnishings, scornful for the most part. 'All these rooms, all this furniture, all this comfort, and not for a large family. As far as I can make out, it was just Beatrice Malaspina living here.'

'I wonder who this fellow is,' he said, stopping beside the portrait of the long-nosed cardinal. 'Do you think he has any connection with the house?'

'He built it, I think. All those Italian churchmen were as rich as Croesus, and great landowners, none of the meek-shall-inherit-the-earth about them. Hypocritical to their bones, like so many men.'

'You could be right. Isn't that the villa there, in the background behind him?'

'All those fountains,' Marjorie said, speaking more to herself than to Lucius. 'It must have needed an army of labourers. I dare say labour has always come cheap in these parts.'

'So you see Beatrice Malaspina as a rich old woman, whose money and property should have been handed out to workers and labourers? Are you a communist?'

'No, but I vote Labour, which, in case you don't know, is the socialist party in England. And I have nothing to say against Beatrice Malaspina. One shouldn't disparage people one doesn't know, and besides, her presence is everywhere here, she was a woman with a strong personality. I like that. But that doesn't mean it isn't wrong for one person to be so rich and so many others to be so poor.'

Lucius was a man in a hurry, opening doors, glancing round a room, his eyes lingering appreciatively for a moment on a good picture, a fine bronze, an unexpected ceiling painting. 'A woman of taste, and modern-minded with it. Interesting. I take it,' he went on, after a brief inspection of the last of the bedrooms, 'that you don't like men.'

That brought Marjorie up short. How could he have come to such a conclusion? 'I have many men friends.'

'Do you?' He didn't pursue the subject, instead taking the steps down into the garden two at a time. 'What an air of neglect,' he exclaimed. 'Inevitable after the war, but what a shame. These fountains – here we have the pattern of a Renaissance garden, with this parterre, though all the box is sadly overgrown.'

'I don't care for ornamental gardens,' Marjorie said. Which wasn't entirely true, for greenery in all its forms had the power to tug at her heart. 'All this box is very static. One has no sense of growth.'

'No, but movement and colour, and then there's such an intricate pattern to it. It's so pleasing to the eye, this kind of a garden. It's on a small scale, but very typical of its kind.'

'There's a wilderness further up,' said Marjorie. 'A bosky grove. That's typical, too.'

'Ah, then you do know something about these Italian gardens.'

'All out of books; I've never been in Italy before.'

She took him up the sloping layers behind the house, past the desolate fountains and urns, and blank-eyed statues.

'Enchanting,' he said, eyeing the mossy giant carved into the grotto, a forlorn figure with his open mouth, designed to let out a stream of water into the basin below. 'This is a river god, I fancy. Arno, probably, and that even more battered one there will be Father Tiber.'

She should have known that, and it irritated her that she hadn't. 'There's Demeter,' she said, pointing to a statue that

174

stood in a niche to one side. At least she recognised her, with a cornucopia balanced on her hip.

'There is, or was, a stream up here,' Lucius said, 'which fed all the fountains. It will have silted up, perhaps, or been diverted. What a pity; these fountains and cascades must have brought such light and vitality to the place.'

He toured the olive groves, tutting at the neglect of the trees. 'No market for olives or olive oil now, but they should look after the trees. Some of these are very old.'

They took the path that led down to the side of the house, where Pietro was hoeing the vegetable garden in a desultory fashion.

Marjorie stooped and picked up a handful of soil. She let it trickle through her fingers. 'Not bad, but it needs nourishment. You could grow anything here, with this light and sun, if you had the water. What's he got? Lettuces, tomatoes – amazing to see tomatoes out, in the ground, at this time of year. I don't know what those are.'

'*Melanzane*,' said Lucius. 'Eggplant. Big, purple-fleshed vegetables. Haven't you seen them piled up in San Silvestro? Delicious, grilled or stuffed. I'm sure Benedetta will have cooked them for you.'

'Carrots and potatoes,' said Marjorie, pointing; she was on firmer ground with these humble vegetables. It stirred her heart, the neat rows, the green shoots, and brought back memories of helping her father, as a little girl, when she had first been fascinated by the mystery of growing things out of the apparently dead earth.

'You're a gardener,' Lucius said.

'And you see with an artist's eye. Do you paint?'

Lucius was bent over a tomato plant, crushing a leaf and smelling it. 'Delicious. No, as you guessed, I'm a banker.'

'My father was a market gardener,' Marjorie told him. 'So I grew up digging and growing. And he had a market stall, on Saturdays. During the week he supplied the shops, then at the weekend it was the stall. Nothing like money straight in your pocket, he used to say.'

'He's no longer alive?'

'No. Our house got a direct hit in the war. My parents were killed instantly.'

'I'm sorry.'

Marjorie shrugged. 'It happened. They weren't the only ones.'

'Do you have brothers, sisters?'

'No, I was an only child.'

Why was she telling him all this? Her life was something she kept to herself, a private and essential part of herself that she felt she had to keep away from the world, as though it might vanish, with all the memories, the good memories, if they were spoken of. She had talked about her childhood to Maria, of course; she winced at the thought of it.

Lucius noticed, she could see he had, but he made no comment.

'Let's go and look at the vineyards,' was all he said.

'How do you know these belong to the house?' Marjorie said, as they looked over the ranks of straggling vines.

'I asked Benedetta. It was a flourishing vineyard once.'

'How do you know about vines?'

'My brother has a vineyard in California.'

'You'd think they'd look after these vines better.'

'You would, wouldn't you, except that means manpower, and that's what they don't have. Didn't you notice the fields around San Silvestro, bent old women in black tending the crops? All the men who can stand up and work have left. Women, children, decrepit old men, that's all that's left. Who's to pay them for working in a vineyard like this?'

'Doesn't wine make money?'

'Yes, but it needs some organisation. I don't know if these vineyards just supplied the family, or if they sold the wine elsewhere. We can find out.'

Lucius swept Pietro out of his vegetable patch and into the house, ignoring Benedetta's shrill protests at the dust on his shoes. A brief argument, a smile and charm from Lucius, and a huge key was produced; muttering darkly, Benedetta led the way to the end of a dark passage, to a huge and ancient door. Lucius put the key in the lock, and the door swung open, revealing a dimly lit flight of steps leading down.

'The wine cellar,' Lucius said to Marjorie. 'The *cantina*. Now we shall see what's what.'

'Tonight,' Lucius said to Marjorie, when they emerged two hours later, 'we shall have a party.'

Marjorie's head was reeling. It was the most intensive lecture she had ever had, on the cultivation and making of wine, something of which, until then, she had been entirely ignorant. Growing the vines, tending the vines, she could grasp, but the whole mysterious, even magical process by which the grapes became what was in the bottle Lucius was crooning over was mostly beyond her.

'Why a party?'

'Because we are going to taste some of this wine, to find out just what has been produced here. It could be vinegar, although the wine we had at lunch was admirable in its way. And we need to do a bit of brainstorming, to see if we can get a lead on Beatrice Malaspina's schemes. So, party frocks, and if the piano tuner has done his work, then we'll have music too. Think American. Tell the girls, and I'll find George a tuxedo.'

Marjorie was about to point out that they could hardly don party frocks they didn't have when she remembered the wardrobes in the rooms upstairs, full of pre-war clothes, with evening dresses that had made Delia exclaim with delight.

'How do you know that the piano tuner has been?'

'Didn't you hear those noises that sounded like cats making

love? It's extraordinary the sounds a piano can produce when its innards are exposed. Ah, that reminds me. Benedetta!'

Reminds him of what? Marjorie asked herself, as she headed for the terrace. As she'd hoped, the others were there, Delia looking flushed and talking to George about the piano.

'Of course, I'd completely forgotten about continental concert pitch, so we had a bit of a tussle about that.'

'What's continental pitch?' Jessica asked.

'They tune to a different pitch. Higher. So, for example, a C in Germany is sharper than in England.'

'I thought a note was a note,' said Marjorie. 'How can C be C in England and something else elsewhere? Do you mean they all play out of tune?'

'There is no absolute,' said George. 'Sound is waves, and so it is a matter of vibration. The names we give notes are just that, names. The only way of fixing it properly and scientifically is by the wavelength, when you can say such a note is so many hertz.'

'Anyhow, we got it right in the end,' said Delia, 'even if he does think I'm mad and no kind of proper musician.'

Marjorie passed on Lucius's message.

'Lord,' said Delia. 'The man is a real bossy boots.'

'I don't think so,' said Jessica. 'Why not have a celebration? He's arrived, the piano's in tune, and we can drink to the success of our quest.'

'Quest?' said Delia. 'What quest?'

'To find the missing parchment or whatever Italians write their wills on.'

'We've nothing to wear,' said Delia.

'Oh, yes we have,' said Jessica. 'This is my chance to try on that slinky number in Marjorie's room.'

'Should we?' said Marjorie.

'No one else is wearing them. And we'll hardly wear them out, in one evening. It's not like stealing the food from someone's plate.'

'I think she wants us to wear them.' Marjorie saw the others were staring at her.

'You did look odd just then,' Jessica said. 'Are you sure you're all right? You aren't prone to fits or anything like that?'

'No.' She could hardly tell them that, as if she had been looking at a painting, she had seen the room behind them full of people, smoke drifting in the air, the women with shingled hair, the men in evening dress, sleek and curiously old-fashioned. Nineteen twenty-five, a voice whispered in her ears. And then the picture faded, and she was back, blinking in the sunshine, with the others looking at her, worried.

'Angels passing, that's all,' she said, in a bright voice that sounded peculiar even to her.

George knew he had drunk too much wine. How could he not have, with Lucius insisting they have a glass of this and then a glass of that.

'I thought when you tasted wine, that's all you did, taste it,' he said.

'Yes,' said Delia. 'And then you spit it out.'

'I did all that earlier,' said Lucius. 'And it was worth it; there are some fine wines here. Beatrice Malaspina knew a lot about wine, Benedetta told me, and she had an excellent wine master. So what we're drinking is my selection for the evening. Pure nectar, don't you agree?'

George did. He'd never drunk much wine, and none of the quality that Lucius had lovingly poured into their polished glasses.

'Does this wine come from the vineyard here?' Marjorie asked.

'No. In this region, the grapes are Vermentino, which is a white wine. This, so Benedetta tells me, is a Sangiovese from another vineyard belonging to Beatrice Malaspina, further south, in Tuscany.'

179

'It seems strong,' said Delia. She held her glass up to the candlelight. 'It's a beautiful colour.' Then she laughed. 'It's a good thing my father can't see me now, tasting a noble wine.'

'What's wrong with that?' Lucius asked.

'Devil's work, as are all wines of whatever quality,' she said.

'Well, wine is sacred to Dionysus, a.k.a. the Loosener, so while we're all a bit tipsy might be a good time to seek inspiration.'

'Are you planning to write a poem?' said Delia.

'No, just to see if we can crack the puzzle that Beatrice Malaspina has set us.'

'All this trouble, to hide away a piece of paper for four strangers to find,' said Marjorie. 'It's such an odd thing to do. Which suggests to me that the codicil won't be tucked away in some hidey-hole, and, moreover, that she'll have left us some way of finding it without taking the place apart.'

'For all you know,' Delia said, 'Beatrice Malaspina was a dimwit. Why should she have laid a careful intellectual puzzle for us to follow?'

'As a tease?' said Marjorie.

The others all looked at her.

'If Beatrice Malaspina at her age hadn't grown out of practical jokes, then all we're going to be left in her will is likely to be some kind of Ha ha,' said Delia. 'And I'm still alarmed by what she knows about us – see the charitable donations designed to touch a nerve with each one of us. Put together the information she somehow acquired about us, and her willingness to use it to spur us on, and I'm not sure that we mightn't find the codicil not at all to our taste.'

'You mean we've crossed her or offended her in some way, and this is her revenge?' said Marjorie.

'It's a possibility,' said Lucius. 'I've got to hand it to you, Delia, you lay it on the line.'

Delia shrugged. 'I don't want to seem negative or cynical,

but it's easy to be seduced by the gorgeousness of the Villa Dante, and Calderini's smooth talk and the sun and our gratitude for an enchanted escape from our daily lives and their problems. What if it hasn't been done from loving kindness, but instead is a kick up the backside?'

'Which brings us back to why each one of us is here,' said George with a sigh. 'We need to rack our brains and consider how, in the course of our lives, our paths might have crossed that of Beatrice Malaspina.'

'And we need to find out more about her,' said Marjorie. 'That way we'll know if she was a vindictive woman, and if she's brought us here out of spite. Which, incidentally, I don't for a moment believe. A spiteful woman wouldn't live in a house as serene as this one, nor would a woman like Benedetta have been as devoted to her as she obviously was. Bad masters make bad servants, or so they say. Not having ever employed a servant, I wouldn't know.'

'How do you propose to find out more?' said Delia. 'Calderini and Benedetta are reticence itself – and that, too, could be grounds for suspicion.'

'Why thirty-three days?' said George. 'You asked that, Lucius, and of course Calderini gave us no answer. I think we must write down all the facts, every piece of information we have about Beatrice Malaspina, and the villa and how we were brought here. Somewhere, there will be a clue, a pointer as to where and how we begin our search.'

Lucius, who had fallen into a brooding silence, raised his head as Delia went over to the piano and lifted the lid.

'Schubert, George?' she said.

'I am very much out of practice.'

'And I'm bound to cough, so it'll be quite a performance.'

The words and the music captured all their hearts. Benedetta, who had brought a tray with coffee, stood stock still at the open door, listening intently to Delia's lovely voice as she

181

sang, *Komm her zu mir, Geselle/Hier findst du deine Ruh'*.

Jessica stirred and looked at Lucius, who was watching Delia with an expression that startled her; she averted her eyes, made uncomfortable by the sudden glimpse into Lucius's soul, and moved by the intensity of his feeling. He was clearly overwhelmed by the beauty of the song and by Delia's voice, yet it was the pain in his eyes that made her fidget and look down at the book beside her.

As the last notes died away, George put his hands in his lap and shook his head. 'My playing does not do justice to your singing, Delia, but I thank you from my heart for such music.'

'How do you follow that?' said Lucius, sliding down into his chair and arching his fingers.

'I don't,' said Delia cheerfully. 'It's time to dance.' She picked out the notes of 'Heartbreak Hotel' with her left hand as she riffled through the pile of sheet music on top of the piano. 'This, to begin with,' she said, taking out a score and putting it on the stand. 'Something lively to match our frocks.'

The sound of Cole Porter rippled into the air. Lucius got to his feet and offered his hand to Marjorie, who, after a moment's hesitation, swung awkwardly into the dance with him.

Jessica leant on the piano, watching them. 'Shall we?' said George politely. Jessica hesitated, then stubbed out her cigarette.

'Why not?' And, quick to catch the ungraciousness in her voice, she smiled, and said she would like to dance.

SIX

The music sang in George's head. He was dancing with his feet and his body, but was almost unaware of Jessica and his surroundings, his mind four thousand miles away, on a December day in 1943.

'What are you thinking about?' said Jessica.

He tripped over his feet, but quickly recovered. 'I'm sorry. I was remembering . . . Have you ever been to America?'

'To New York.'

'Not to New Mexico?'

'No.'

'I was in New Mexico during the war.'

'During the war? How on earth did you get to America during the war? Oh, I suppose you went for some scientific purpose, one of those hush-hush things people at school were always saying their brothers and fathers were on. I don't believe they ever were, but you actually went, did you? What was it like?'

'I flew to Lisbon, and then went by boat to New York. I had been going to travel to New Mexico with a fellow physicist, Philip Bantam, but Philip decided to stay on in New York for a few days. So I boarded the train to New Mexico on my own. I was unsure where exactly I was going, or what or who I would find when I got to my eventual destination, since all I had been told by Sir James was that a group of British scientists were going to America to work on a secret project of the highest importance to the war effort. It was because of my work on isotope separation; Oppenheimer had asked for me.'

They made a circuit of the floor in silence, George lost in thought, Jessica curious about his uncharacteristic need to say something about what was clearly haunting him. After more than ten years, that was what war did to you.

'My journey ended on a chilly, clear morning as I stepped down on to the platform at a place called Lamy. The air was pure and dry, the altitude high, so that I caught my breath as the thin air reached my lungs. Such air would be good for Delia, I think,' he said. 'A young man in uniform approached me and asked if I were George. No surname, no Dr, which is usual, just George.

'I asked where we were going, and he said Santa Fe.'

Santa Fe! The name had conjured up visions of the wild west, of stage coaches and Wells Fargo, of sheriffs and shoot-outs and men who were men riding into town, the spirit of the frontier in a bustling, wicked town. One of George's indulgences, of which he had always been rather ashamed, was Westerns, which he'd read ever since his boyhood.

'So we're high up here?'

'Seven thousand feet. Those are the Sangre de Cristo mountains; you go up to ten thousand feet there. The air's rarefied, but the skiing's good.'

But the town into which they drove looked merely peaceful and rather Spanish, quiet in the late morning sun, although as the car came to a dusty halt in a small plaza, George saw a horse hitched to a wooden pole, a horse with a western saddle, dozing, one hooftip balanced on the ground.

'Folk around here ride a lot, along the trails,' the driver said, but next to the horse was an army lorry, symbol of war and a modern world that had far more violence in it than the gun-toting pioneers could have dreamt of.

The young man placed George's suitcase on the ground beside him.

'Where do I go from here?'

'Where do you want to go?'

George fingered the piece of paper with the address on it, but he didn't need to look at it, he knew it by heart. 109 East Palace.

'The door's over there,' said the soldier with a hitch of his thumb.

George thanked him, and picked up his suitcase, an incongruous figure in his tweed suit, too big for him after four years of wartime food. There must be some mistake; was he the victim of some practical joke? He went through a wrought-iron gate and down a short path to an open door.

The woman at the desk looked at him with clear, intelligent, sympathetic eyes. 'I'm Dorothy,' she said. 'I need to see all your papers, and then I can issue you with a pass.'

'A pass to where?' George said, sounding desperate.

'To the Hill. You'll see.'

He came to know what a key figure Dorothy was, how she had the whole organisation at her fingertips, how devoted she was to Oppenheimer, how committed to the project. But at the time, the baldness of the single name appalled him; the loss of his title and surname seemed to strip him of part of his identity, as though he were being entered at a kindergarten, or an asylum.

'Santa Fe wasn't the end of my journey,' he said to Jessica. 'I had to go on to the Hill, as we called it, which was a thirty-five-mile drive from Santa Fe, along a bumpy road, with many hairpin bends, sheer drops only inches from the wheels of the truck.'

He had sat there, feeling more out of place than he had ever done in his life. Hot, lonely and fearful of – what? He

185

must think rationally. A secret scientific project of immense importance might well be situated in a remote spot, that made perfect sense, away from prying eyes and spying enemies.

Yet his work needed laboratories, equipment, assistants. How could such an establishment exist in this isolated spot, miles from the nearest town, even further from a railway? It was only as the truck came to a rumbling halt outside a guard post, and he took in the sprawling array of buildings beyond the barbed wire, that he realised the scale of what was happening on the Hill.

'There were about twenty of us scientists from Britain, a few of us English, but most from other countries, who had fled the Nazis and sought refuge in England: Poles, Czechs, Frenchmen – and a fellow Dane. As soon as I saw Niels Bohr, I knew what we were all there for.

'There was snow that Christmas, and an air of festivity about the extraordinary town that had grown up in the last two years. Oppie told me how it had been when he'd first got there, a handful of scientists, rooms in what had been, pre-war, an elite boys' prep school, a tremendous sense of purpose and camaraderie from the beginning, which was still there, he insisted, despite the site now having several thousand inhabitants.'

He had been one of many fellow scientists and their wives, for most of the married Americans working there had brought their families with them. 'No one outside here knows where we are,' one young wife told him sadly. 'We can't visit, we can't tell even our parents where we are or anything about our lives.'

'Do you know why your husbands are here?'

'Oh, yes. Some of us know a lot about it, but we don't say. That's part of the deal.'

'The deal?'

'Yes. We put up with all this, and keep quiet and look after our husbands who work sometimes sixteen hours a day, and we work ourselves, if we can, office work, or teaching or whatever. In return, we know that we may just help to end the war.'

'There was a formality at the evening parties, everyone dressed so casually during the day that I was astonished to find myself donning a dinner jacket, and moved by the sight of women in evening frocks.

'We danced,' he went on, speaking more to himself than to Jessica, 'to this music, which Delia is playing now. We were building a monstrous thing, and we danced.'

He was back in the present, stumbling again, as the music left his feet.

SEVEN

The next morning at breakfast, Lucius was in vigorous form. 'What is each of us going to do today to find the codicil?' he said. 'We need to make a plan.'

Delia found his energy and assumption of command infuriating, and her reaction was instant. 'Plan? Oh, Lord, count me out. I've got my own plan for today, thank you very much.'

'Which is what?' asked Jessica. She stirred a spoonful of sugar into her coffee. 'George and I are going to work on a fact sheet, as he suggested last night, aren't we, George? Logical thinking can work wonders.'

'Good for you. I'm going to find out why the fountains aren't working,' said Delia. The garden needed the sound and freshness of water; it was arid and incomplete without running water. And what was the point of all the fountains if they didn't work? 'Who knows, perhaps a pipe is blocked by a codicil wrapped up in oilskin? Mind you, I expect it's a waste of time going to have a look; by means of Hugo and my trusty dictionary, I got some info out of Benedetta this morning re the fountains. They've been blocked for years, since the war, by the sound of it. Beatrice Malaspina had an expert in, but he said nothing could be done without manpower, which they didn't have.'

'I don't believe that,' said Marjorie. 'Not for a moment. Beatrice Malaspina was rich enough to bring in whoever she needed.'

'You underestimate the difficulties in this country in the post-war years,' said Lucius.

'Perhaps, but it would do the veg patch a world of good to have more water. If you want to know what I'm going to do, it's the same as George and Jessica, only my facts will be ones of mind and personality. We need to know more about Beatrice Malaspina; we need to understand her psychology.'

'Quite right,' said Lucius. 'If we can suss out what made her tick, then perhaps we'll have a better understanding of how her mind worked, and so get to the bottom of the codicil business. How do you propose to make these discoveries, by the way?'

'In my own way,' said Marjorie. 'I'm not much of a one for team effort.'

'For my part,' said Lucius, 'I think the tower warrants further investigation.'

'It's *pericoloso*,' Delia said. 'Dangerous. Crumbling, falling down.'

'Do you believe everything you read? Benedetta told me that Beatrice Malaspina locked it up when she left for Rome, and put that notice up,' said Lucius.

'Did she tell you what's in the tower?'

'Some rooms, that's all she'll say. Downright cagey. There's more to it than that, though, something she isn't telling, and I get a sharp feeling she isn't any too keen on the tower.'

'Have you asked Benedetta for the key to the tower?' George said.

'I have, and she has no idea where it is. Beatrice Malaspina didn't leave it with her.'

'Then I expect she took it to Rome with her,' said Delia.

'Or maybe it's with the codicil, everything in one hiding place. I hope you don't find it just yet. I'm looking forward to spending a bit longer here.'

Delia walked up the narrow path between the overgrown hedges, which smelled strongly in the morning sun. It was a scent she found evocative of the box walk at Saltford Hall, a neutral smell that she neither liked nor disliked, although she knew that some people hated it. Her mother, for one. 'I can't bear the smell of box,' she would say when Delia, who liked the complex herb garden with its severe box hedges, tugged at her mother's hand to take her there. 'Ask Nanny, it makes me sneeze.'

As if in response to this memory, Delia sneezed, then laughed, back in the warm present, far away from childhood and the Hall. This path needed gravel, there were only traces of it left under her feet, and in wet weather it would be muddy and slippery here. And the box had given way to the richer smell of cypress. The scents of this Italian garden were quite different from an English garden, more pungent and aromatic. What was that deep green broad-leaved plant, growing under the cypresses? Marjorie would probably know its Latin name and everything else about it.

She came out at the first of the hillside fountains, empty and forlorn. Steps rose on either side of it, uneven, mossy steps; a trap for the unwary, and she took care how she put her feet down as she walked up beside the plaited channel which provided a conduit for the water.

Above it was the next fountain, with a damp patch at its base, bright green and slimy. The path curved in an elegant loop on its upward way to the top fountain, with great figures carved out of the rock and the huge head with the open mouth which should be gushing with water, water that would flow down to feed the fountains below, and then on to Pietro's vegetable patch, so short of water. Parched, that was what this garden was, when in her mind's eye she saw it lush and green and full of the sound of running water.

Above her were trees and the cliff out of which the fountain and its basin had been carved. It seemed impenetrable, but the water must have come from up there. She went along the remains of a path to the left of the fountain, and at the end of it found some steps, steep, roughly cut steps, hewn into the rock.

Delia wasn't enjoying this at all; she didn't have much of a head for heights, and so had never gone in for any kind of climbing. Well, at the worst, she'd slip and tumble down on to the path below. She wasn't going to give up now.

What was it about Lucius, she wondered as she climbed carefully up the steps, clutching on to an overhanging branch to steady herself. Why did he annoy her so much? Was it his easy confidence, his air of superiority? Jessica might find him attractive; Delia thought he was going to turn out to be a menace. Not that she wasn't used to authoritative men, she'd been surrounded by them: her father, Boswell . . . Even Theo, although she hadn't minded his bossiness at all.

Breathless, and relieved, she reached the top of the steps. She saw, as she peered down into the empty fountain below, that she was a lot higher than she'd realised. And what a view! She looked down the sweep of the slope to the house, perfect in its setting, with the tower beside it, with its orchards and olive groves and the sea. There was the speck of a sail; perhaps it was Lucius's Albanian pirates, hunting new prey.

There was water here. There was green, lush grass where the trees thinned out, and yes, there was a big patch of bright green: another pool, man made with a low wall and just a thin layer of water covered in green. What had fed it? What had happened to the stream? It hadn't dried up, or it wouldn't be so damp everywhere. It was as though instead of flowing into the pool, and from there feeding the system of fountains below, it had been dispersed. Here was a rivulet, thin and useless, which trickled away down the hill to the side of the path she'd come up.

She paused to admire the violets that carpeted the ground under the trees, their purple glowing against the dark greens, and sniffed the fragrance of them, wafting up from under her feet. She walked round the side of the pond, and up a slope found a high stone doorway, with a larger stone head in the centre of the arch.

There was a wall behind the archway, and, stretching up to right and left, more steps. Above her she could see a crumbling balustrade.

Yet another pool?

Another pool. This one was rectangular, formal, almost like a swimming pool. And empty. But at the far end, where surely the water would have come in, was a heap of rubble and boulders. It was damp, water was oozing through, but nothing like enough to fill the pool, the one below, or the fountains; that must need a real flow.

'That's interesting,' said a quiet voice behind her, so startling her that she slipped as she whirled round.

Lucius leapt forward to catch her, seizing hold of her elbow and hauling her upright.

'What on earth are you doing, creeping up on me like that?' she said, furious, her heart still thumping from the fright.

Lucius was profuse with his apologies. 'It's lunch time – well, past lunch time. Benedetta has been beating the gong, and I said I'd come up to see where you were, if you were all right.'

Her fury drained away. 'Is it really so late? I had no idea. It took a while to get up here.'

Although Lucius must have bounded up here in a few minutes.

'I stopped to admire the view, and to think,' she said.

'As one does in gardens.' Lucius's eyes were taking in the

pool. 'This is extraordinary,' he said. 'When I came here with Marjorie, we had no idea there was all this further up. So what has happened to the water?'

'The stream must have dried up.'

'I wonder,' said Lucius. He was looking up and down the steep, rocky backdrop to the pool, and seconds later he was scrambling up the wall.

'Oh, do be careful,' cried Delia. 'You'll fall.'

She was talking nonsense, she thought, and sounding just like a woman in a melodrama, wringing her hands while the hero did amazing things. Not that Lucius could possibly be anyone's idea of a heroic figure. But he was like a goat on the rocks.

'I've done a lot of climbing,' he called down to her. 'Stay where you are; it isn't as easy as it looks.'

It didn't look in the least bit easy to Delia. 'Shouldn't we come back later?' she shouted, as Lucius vanished. 'Benedetta will be in a temper.'

Lucius landed on his feet beside her. He brushed dried twigs and grass from his trousers.

'I thought so,' he said with satisfaction. 'If you were to go up there, you'd find that the water which should be channelled to pour into this pool is just bubbling out and seeping away into the hillside, no use at all to anything below.'

'I thought streams reverted to their natural bed,' said Delia, 'and flowed down by the shortest and quickest way. So why should it spread and trickle?'

'I'm no water engineer, but it's quite straightforward. The water up there has been dammed.'

'You mean a tree . . . ?'

'Oh, no. A landslide. A great chunk of rock has broken off, and caused the blockage.' He wiped green hands on his handkerchief. 'We'd better go down, as you say.'

Delia was hard put to keep up with him, and she didn't have breath to ask any more questions.

193

'Goodness, you do look hot,' Jessica said, when they reached the villa. 'Have you been running?'

In between greedy mouthfuls of pasta flavoured with garlic and olives, Delia told them about the pools. 'And Lucius went higher still, where the stream's blocked.'

'Is there anything we can do to clear the blockage?' Marjorie asked. 'Could we clear the stones away with spades?'

'Difficult, with just us,' said Lucius. 'It'll take some shifting.'

'Explosives?' Marjorie suggested. 'They used them in the war. A controlled explosion, to clear away a site.'

'Surely that would simply blow it up into the air and then it would all come down again,' Delia said. 'Why don't we see what shovels we can find and get up there and have a go? After all, there's no point in Pietro picking away at the ground down here when it's so obviously in need of water, when it could all stream down the hill for him. I know there's a well . . .'

'But it's hard getting the water up, and I think the level is lower than it should be,' said Marjorie. 'I'm on for a spot of digging, and it's the least we can do, to try it. Think what a difference it might make to Benedetta if Pietro can grow more veg.'

'It seems daft not to try, to sit here while it all shrivels up, and it will shrivel, come the heat of the summer,' said Delia.

After lunch, they retraced Delia and Lucius's steps, all five of them eager to get to the top and see what was there, but slowed down by Marjorie, ecstatic at every new plant seen and identified. 'Acanthus,' she said, pointing to a shrub with dark and shiny heart-shaped leaves. 'And juniper.'

'I didn't know juniper was spiky,' said Jessica.

'Here's Dionysus,' Lucius said, pulling at ivy which had wound itself round a statue that Delia hadn't noticed to reveal an image of a youthful god with a carved leopard skin just visible over his shoulder.

Delia was amazed at how much she had missed, but she was too keen to get on to linger over plants or lissome statues. 'If we don't get a move on, we'll never reach the top level,' she said. 'Unless you think the codicil is concealed under his foot.'

'The view,' said Jessica, shading her eyes and looking out over the unfolding vista. 'Isn't it simply heavenly?'

'It's even better at the top,' said Delia.

'Do we really have to climb up there?' said Marjorie. 'I'm not sure that I can.'

'Nor me,' said Delia. 'Lucius went up like a monkey going up a tree.'

'There must be another way up,' Lucius said, 'since people from the villa will have needed to have access to this part of the system. I can see why Pietro's never been able to get up here and do anything about it, not with his lame leg. Not that he could have, on his own, in any case.'

Ten minutes later, he appeared away to their left, beckoning to them to join him. 'There is a path, do you see? It winds round and takes us to the top. But be careful, it's steep and stony.'

'Path?' said Marjorie, swearing as a creeper caught at her ankle.

'It is overgrown, but one can get through,' George said. He paused to brush burrs from the legs of his flannel trousers, but as Marjorie said, he'd only collect more of them as they went on.

Then they were at the top, where Lucius was waiting for them, and they stood in a line, surveying the heap of stones and rocks piled up in front of them.

'I think it would take more than us to shift this,' said Jessica. 'I wouldn't even know how to begin.'

'Even if we could clear away all the smaller stuff, look at

those boulders,' said Marjorie. 'We couldn't possibly move them.'

'We can, with leverage,' said George.

'Yes,' said Jessica. 'If we could work out the weight of the boulders, and find a crowbar of the right length.'

'Crowbars and shovels,' said Marjorie. 'Let's go down and see what Pietro's got hidden away.'

Benedetta was sceptical, they didn't need Italian to know that, and Pietro pursed his lips and shook his head when Lucius made a quick sketch of the lowest fountain overflowing with water.

'*Impossibile*,' he said. He pointed to his lame leg, then up to the hill behind the villa and shook first his head and then his finger at them.

'I wish I could make him understand that it's us not him who are going to clear it,' said Delia. 'Yes, I know it's *bloccato*, but we're going to *unbloccato* it. Lucius, do explain.'

Finally, reluctantly, after much gesticulation and a final push from Benedetta, who simply wanted them out of her kitchen, Pietro took them across to the stables and pointed to a row of tools. They had a forlorn, unused look to them, and were festooned with dust and cobwebs.

'These are all the blunt old things he doesn't use,' said Jessica.

'That's fine,' said Marjorie. 'We don't want to take his tools, the ones he uses, he'd hate that.'

'He's got a stout shovel there,' said Delia, eyeing the tools on the other side, the ones that were kept rust free and ready for action.

'Yes, but it'd be like taking his trousers,' said Marjorie. 'We'll have to make do with what we've got.'

'Look, here's a crowbar,' Delia said. 'That's exactly what George said we needed.'

'And here's a pickaxe.'

196

'The head might fly off,' said Delia, picking it up and giving it an experimental waggle.

'I,' said George, 'shall take it into the town and see if they can make it good.'

'I don't suppose you'll be able to get gardener's gloves, but you could try,' said Marjorie.

EIGHT

Marjorie had to admire Lucius's way with a pickaxe, and she told him so.

He paused, and leant on the handle of his pick, wiping his sweaty brow with the back of his hand. 'You don't have to sound surprised. Why shouldn't I wield a pickaxe as well as the next man?'

'You don't seem hefty enough to be able to do anything useful, like cracking up boulders.'

Now he was annoyed. 'Do you always say what you're thinking?'

'Mostly, these days, yes I do,' said Marjorie. She thrust the shovel deftly under the rocks that he had loosened, and tossed the load on to the growing heap of stones and rubble that they had removed from the blockage. 'It saves time, and I can't be bothered to think up polite ways of saying or not saying what's in my head.'

'I take it you aren't blessed with a large number of friends.'

Marjorie said nothing, but went on with her shovelling. He probably thought she was noticing his muscles, now that he'd discarded his shirt. Should she tell him that muscular men were no part of her fantasies? No, why should she? He knew where her tastes lay, and no doubt had her down as a dried-up spinster, probably full of repressions. Which was the pot calling that kettle black, all right.

'Now what are you laughing at?' he said. He gave the boulder, which had developed a narrow crack along one side, a neat blow, and a large piece broke off.

'Since my thoughts trouble you, I'll keep that one to myself. If you can give that bit another whack or two, I think it will split up into manageable pieces.'

It was very early on Sunday morning. Marjorie had come up to the stream to put in an hour's work. She wanted to do something physical, and knew of nothing more soothing and conducive to thought than digging and shovelling.

'I woke early,' Lucius said. 'Voices, under my window. Very inconsiderate. If Jessica and George want to wake at dawn and chat, I wish they'd go elsewhere to do it. I can't think why they were up, anyway.'

'George suffers from insomnia. And he'd have been up early in any case, because he was going to go to Mass.'

'Is George a Catholic?'

'Yes.'

'And Jessica?'

Marjorie shrugged. 'She hasn't gone to church. She's deep in Dante. I brought my copy of the Dorothy Sayers translation – since I was coming to the Villa Dante it seemed appropriate – and I lent her the *Inferno*.'

They worked on in silence. Then Lucius spoke again. 'Delia is the only one enjoying the luxury of sleep, I take it.'

'No, she's up. I saw her on her balcony as I came past. I waved.'

'Why didn't you tell her to come up and help?'

'Because I wanted to be on my own, and she could see I was carrying a shovel. If she'd wanted to join me, she'd have said. Why should she? We aren't on a rota, it isn't a duty, we're under no obligation, any of us, to shift this lot and see if the water will flow again.'

'Or if the codicil is hidden under the rubble.'

'No question of that. How would Beatrice Malaspina have got up here to plant it? If you're concerned about the codicil, you should be down there hunting for it, not up here hacking at boulders.'

'Many hands . . .'

'Nothing will make this light work. It's just slog.'

'I still can't believe that Beatrice Malaspina couldn't have had all this cleared away.'

'Who could she ask? Pietro? He'd never get up here, as you said, he's too lame. And there aren't any hale and hearty men left in the village, as you pointed out. All gone to Milan or America, every one.'

They worked on again in silence.

'Did you learn to dig so expertly from your father?' Lucius asked, resting for a moment on the handle of his pickaxe.

'Yes. And I've done some archaeological excavations, too.'

'Isn't that all trowels and paint brushes?'

'Not when the site is several feet beneath the surface. They aren't called digs for nothing.'

'We might unearth an antique pot or two here, perhaps.'

'I would be amazed if we did.'

In the two days since Delia had discovered the wandering stream, they had made a lot of progress. George put in several hours at a time, working with a steady rhythm that impressed Lucius; damn it, George must be ten years older than he was, but he didn't perspire or have to stop to catch his breath. So much for weedy scientists.

'Although George has a more stylish way with the pickaxe than you do,' Marjorie observed, as Lucius swung his pickaxe round and down. 'It's a pity really we can't simply blow this up.'

The pickaxe bounced off the rock he was attacking, and he winced and rubbed his arm. 'Can we cut out the running commentary, and just get on?' He looked at his wristwatch.

200

'Although I could do with some breakfast. I wonder if George is back, did Benedetta know he was going to the service?'

'Benedetta isn't here this morning. She probably goes to Mass as well, but in any case, it's her day off, so we fend for ourselves today. She's left a cold collation for lunch. Breakfast will be what we can find, I suppose.'

It wasn't. Benedetta had set the table in the dining room before leaving the night before, and George had found a baker open in the town. Delia made coffee, with George's help.

'Like this,' he said. 'Coffee in there, and then, when it boils, you turn it over, and the steam rises through the coffee grains.'

'Very scientific.'

'It is a very good way to make coffee. The flavour in coffee comes from acetone, which evaporates on boiling. Which is why you should never let coffee boil.'

Delia had felt a momentary pang of guilt when she saw Marjorie stalking off to heave stones, but then she'd seen Lucius heading the same way, and had stood back against the wall so he wouldn't notice her. Marjorie wouldn't stop and talk, but Lucius, with his careless good manners, might feel obliged to make conversation, and she hadn't been in the mood for talking to anyone.

The air was too warm, the sky too bright with morning promise for her to want to talk or think or do anything except let the warmth and the light seep into her bones. Into her soul. God knew, that could do with some light. If she could detach that amorphous thing, in which George believed, and she didn't, she felt sure it would hang suspended on that rusty hook up there like a lifeless bat. Probably with eyes, looking at her, hung up to warn other souls to steer clear, a message of what might happen to them.

She was startled by the vividness of this image that had

come to mar her sense of peace. What was this with a soul? And why should her soul be blacker than anyone else's? Full of sin to a religious person – well, according to her father, human beings were stuffed full of sin from the moment they were conceived – but that simply made her one of a crowd.

At lunch, Jessica was full of Dante. 'I had no idea it was so good, although I don't understand half of it. Do you know who all the people are?' she asked Marjorie.

'Read the notes.'

'Is the next part as good? Purgatory doesn't sound as dramatic as the *Inferno*.'

'The devil has all the best tunes,' said Lucius.

'Like *Paradise Lost*. Satan is definitely the lead there,' said Marjorie. 'As to Dante, I don't know, you'd have to ask an Italian. I read the *Purgatorio* when I was doing a WEA course on Italian lit. but I found it dull by comparison, and I didn't get far with *Paradiso* – that was too Catholic for me. Sorry, George.'

'Perhaps our English souls don't go in for purging,' said Delia, thinking of the bat's skin. 'Your soul must be in good order, George, after going to church. Did you understand any of the words?'

'The Mass is in Latin, and although they pronounce it differently, it is the same as any Catholic Mass wherever you are. It was sad, however, to attend a service with only old people and children there.'

'Even if the men hadn't gone away to find work, they wouldn't be in church,' Lucius said.

'Why not?'

'They'll all be communists. Communists don't go to church. Communists are atheists.'

Delia stared at him. 'How do you know? How can you possibly make such a sweeping statement? Have the communists taken power in Italy?'

'Not yet, but they'd like to.' Lucius stirred his coffee. 'We

202

aren't getting anywhere useful with our picks and shovels. I think we need to try something else. As Marjorie suggested.'

'What did she suggest?' said Delia. 'A team of slaves?'

'No, dynamite.'

'Dynamite?' said George, alert and interested.

'Dynamite! Would that be safe? You might bring half the hillside down,' Jessica said.

'Dynamite?' said Marjorie. Her suggestion of blowing the blockage up had been a flippant one. God knew, she'd had enough of explosions to last her a lifetime, and she had the feeling, that although Lucius's sensible, practical mind was considering dynamite, he also carried memories of wartime blasts, perhaps ones even grimmer than hers.

For the first few days of the Blitz she had been in a state of constant fear, dreading the sound of the enemy aeroplanes overhead, the sound of the ack-ack guns, the searchlights playing across the sky. She refused to go down to the shelter if she was going to be blown up, it would be in her own bed, not underground.

Then after yet another sleepless night of fear, her ears ringing with the roar and crash of bombs, she decided that, as with all fears, the best thing to do was to face up to it. Rather than cowering in her room, she would go out into the flames and the explosions, and if she was killed, well, so be it. She went to her local office to sign up for the ARP, but when they discovered she could drive – she'd driven her father's old van since she was fifteen – they enrolled her in the ATS, and sent her to train for ambulance duties.

'Dynamite,' Delia said in a resigned tone. What a show-off this man was, feeling he had to make a dramatic effect. Then she laughed. 'You're saying that we've been digging and picking around all this time, and a simple blast would do the job in a few seconds. That puts us in our places, don't you think?'

'There are always several ways to get things done,' he said.

'The slow way and the quick way. Right now, I like the look of the quick way.'

'Just one problem,' said George.

'Yes,' cut in Delia. 'Where do you imagine in the Italian countryside you're going to find dynamite? And, even if there were any, who's going to let you have it?'

'Oh, the mighty dollar will see to that. And there must be dynamite. There are quarries not so far from here.'

'You're crazy,' said Delia. 'You actually mean it.'

George took off his spectacles and polished them with his handkerchief. 'How do you know about dynamite?' he asked Lucius. 'The war?'

'Yes, that's right. I blew quite a few things up. It was what we did, you remember.'

'I remember all too well,' said George, a fleeting sadness in his eyes. 'That was a while ago, however.'

'One doesn't forget. I started in demolition when I joined up. A little job like this is as easy as pie. If one knows just where to place the charge, and how much, which I do.'

The look of doubt on George's face vanished. He now had the eager look of a little boy expecting a treat. 'I can give you a hand. I suggest we go up and make some calculations.'

NINE

Delia was almost asleep, tired after a busy time in the kitchen; she had volunteered to cook in Benedetta's absence, and, with Jessica acting as her sous chef, had turned out a meal she was proud of.

'If you lose your voice,' Marjorie had said, 'you could always earn a living by writing cookbooks.'

Casual, meant to be complimentary words, which hadn't amused her. Marjorie, so quick to pick up other people's reactions, had flushed, and Delia had passed it off with a casual remark, not wanting the others to see how sensitive she was on that subject.

Never mind her voice, what was that noise outside her room? Jessica's voice, raised in excitement. Who was she talking to? Marjorie by the sound of it. She considered shouting to them to keep the noise down, but was too sleepy to make the effort. Instead she rolled over and drew a pillow over her head.

She found out the next morning what they had been talking about when Jessica waltzed into breakfast waving a Penguin book in the air.

'Look, everyone,' she cried.

Delia looked at Marjorie in astonishment; she had gone a

205

brick red colour. Then she looked at the book which Jessica had thrust under her nose. 'Look at the author photo!'

George got up from his chair and came round to see what Jessica was pointing to.

'She's Marjorie Fletcher, the detective writer,' said Jessica, looking from the photo to Marjorie. 'Fletcher's her pen name. I can't think how I didn't recognise you before. I just thought you looked a little familiar, but then lots of people do, and I thought no more about it.'

'The photos on the books are so very small, and generally not much of a likeness,' said Marjorie, 'and I wore my hair differently then.' And, she might have added, but didn't, except inwardly, I was much younger when that picture was taken, and happy and successful. 'Time leaves its mark,' she added, trying to bring it off lightly.

'I've got one of your books with me, although I needn't have bothered, for there's a heap of them in the house.'

Marjorie stared at her. 'My novels? I would hardly have thought . . . it seems to me that Beatrice Malaspina was an intellectual.'

'Lots of intellectuals read detective stories, and crime novels. Half of them are written by dons and people like that, under another name of course, so as not to scare the students and their fellow academics and bring ill repute upon hallowed seats of learning. Oh, whoops, you aren't a don as well, are you?'

'No,' said Marjorie. 'I left school at fourteen. All my education came from evening classes.'

'A writer?' said George. 'But, my dear Marjorie, why didn't you tell us?'

'Are you published in the States?' said Lucius, keenly interested. 'I have an aunt who writes novels, but they aren't detective stories, they're all serious stuff about human relationships in suburbia, dull in the extreme. I'm sure yours aren't. I'm very keen on a good mystery.'

206

'Imagine your being a writer! Whyever didn't you tell us?' Delia said.

'People do write books, I know,' said Jessica, 'but however do they get through even the first chapter? It was agony for me to write a single page at school.'

'That is because your mind is better suited to numbers,' said George. 'I have friends who have written textbooks, but, I must confess, I have never met a detective author.'

They all looked so pleased, so interested, so admiring. Marjorie had forgotten that was how it used to be. People were fascinated by anyone who had been published, and of course a woman who wrote murder mysteries had a special allure. It was a contradiction in terms, some moralisers thought; the local vicar had once chided her for taking to violence to make a living. 'It seems inappropriate for the gentler sex to embark on such books,' he'd said. 'One prefers to think of woman as nurturing and caring for life, not destroying it.' He'd given a thin, braying laugh. 'Even if only with a pen.'

'Perhaps some of the women who murder their husbands might not have done so if they'd killed on the page instead,' she'd whipped back, causing him to purse up his mouth and shake his head at the folly and wickedness of women.

Where had he spent the war? Marjorie wondered. And his wife? She clearly hadn't helped the war effort by working at the munitions factory.

Somebody had to say it, of course.

It was Jessica who did. 'I say, though, isn't it a while since you had a book out? I keep looking out for a new one, and I haven't seen one for ages.'

'Five years,' said Marjorie in a tight voice. 'The last one was published five years ago.'

'Gosh, I am sorry,' said Jessica. 'I didn't mean . . .'

'I haven't written a book for six years,' Marjorie said. 'That's why you haven't seen a new one.'

'Are you working on one now?' asked Delia.

'I do hope so,' said Jessica. 'An Inspector Zeals one. He's quite my favourite detective.'

George, quicker to sense Marjorie's discomfort, intervened. 'I have a feeling that writers do not like to be cross-examined about their writing.'

'I am working on a new one, actually,' said Marjorie, defiant now. 'I just haven't got very far with it.'

It wasn't exactly a lie. She had typed out the words *Chapter One* more times than she cared to remember.

Then her devastating urge to honesty made her blurt out, 'If you want to know, it's gone. The muse. Inspiration. Whatever you want to call it. I haven't written anything for six years, not since that last book, because I can't. I want to, but nothing comes out. Which is why I don't have any money, and why I'm so grateful to Beatrice Malaspina for inviting me here.'

'Perhaps, here,' said George, in a very gentle voice, 'away from London, away from memories and your habitual round of life, you may find you can write again. This does happen, I believe.'

Marjorie managed a wry smile. 'Yes, people get over it, don't they? The infuriating thing is I want to write. I have a plot, characters. But when I put my fingers on the keys of my typewriter, it all dissolves. Nothing. It is as though my fingers have gone numb. And the writing part of my brain with them.'

'Clearly,' said Delia, anxious to steer the conversation back into clearer waters, 'Beatrice Malaspina was a fan of yours.'

'And that's the reason she put me in her will and brought me out here?' Marjorie shook her head. 'I don't think so.'

'Not what your voices are telling you?' said Delia.

'My voices come of their own accord, and say what they want to, not what I want to hear.'

'Which is a pity,' said Delia. 'Otherwise they could tell you where the codicil is, and then the mystery will be solved, and we can all go home. Except,' she added, 'I'm not sure that I want to.'

TEN

'Is that dynamite?' Marjorie asked, looking at the bundle Lucius had just put down on the hall table.

'It is.'

'How did you get it?'

'That kid Domenico knew where to go. Kids always do. He wants to help, but I've persuaded him to stay with you lot at a distance and watch the fireworks from afar. Actually, there won't be any fireworks. I'm only planning a very small explosion. Nothing dramatic.'

He went off with George, deep in discussion of fuses and charges, leaving Domenico in a state of high excitement. 'Bang,' he said. And then again, with the utmost happiness, 'Bang! I speak English,' he added, giving them a fetching look from under ridiculously long lashes.

'Come and have a Coca-Cola,' Jessica said practically.

Lucius was right. It wasn't any kind of shattering sound, no violent boom filled the air, just a dull thud, which made Marjorie go suddenly tense. But the after-effects were dramatic indeed, as they discovered when they hurried up the by now familiar path to the lower of the pools and saw water pouring in, sweeping down the rocky wall and splashing down in a steady flow.

'Beautifully done,' George said, calling down to them from above. 'Miraculous, you might say. The stream is back in its path, or will be when we have done a little more work with the pick and shovel, but already it flows where it should.'

'How long do you think the pools will take to fill?' Marjorie shouted.

'Many hours, I think. First this one, then the one below, and then we should see some fun.'

'In which case,' said Delia, 'I'm going to clean out the bottom fountain, the one in the parterre. Whatever the figure in the middle is, it's covered in ivy and there are weeds all over the place.'

She relished the work, finding, as Marjorie did, that physical work calmed the mind. She sang softly to herself as she tugged at the obstinate creeper, and felt a sense of achievement as she revealed the sculpture beneath.

'What on earth is it?' said Jessica, who'd gone to fetch a scrubbing brush to clean the floor of the fountain. 'It looks modern.'

'It's not as old as the other ones,' said Delia. Three faces looked out at her, one facing each curve of the trefoil basin. 'A girl, a woman and what looks like a witch,' she said.

'She's a crone,' said Marjorie, who had come out to see how they were getting on. 'A tripartite depiction of the feminine. Done in the twenties, I should think. I wonder who by?'

Lucius looked at it with a knowing eye, and said he didn't recognise the artist, but he'd take a bet the features of the woman belonged to Beatrice Malaspina. 'Look at the nose, just like in the portrait. Beaky.'

'That's not very courteous,' said Delia, mindful of her own nose.

'I mean no disrespect. I like a woman with a strong nose; give me that over a cute little snub number or a perfect Grecian any day.'

211

ELEVEN

Delia woke early, and almost ran to the window. Could she hear water? Yes, she could, the fountains were flowing. She took a swift shower before donning shorts and heading joyfully for the garden. It was extraordinary, the effect of the water, the whispering, splashing sound of it, the shifting, endlessly changing play of light and water. Delia sat beside the fountain in the formal garden, simply watching and watching, lost in the sound and colour and movement.

Lucius found her an hour later, standing in one of the upper fountains, up to her knees in water, her hair damp, and an intent expression on her face. She was attempting to clean the spout that nestled between the teeth of a gummy dolphin. She looked, he thought, like a girl, not a young woman.

'This spout seems to be caked up with something,' she said. 'I want the water to gush, like it does from the other one.'

'Maybe you should get a toothbrush and give his gums a going over,' he said. He held out a hand to help her as she clambered over the edge of the basin.

Delia trailed a hand in the water and watched the drops

fall from her fingers. Then she leant down to pick up her sandals and slipped her wet feet into them.

Lucius was overcome by the grace of her movements. Her gracefulness was a large part of her beauty, he decided, along with her voice.

She put on her sunglasses, which had been lying by the fountain, hiding her eyes, shutting herself away again.

'There are the others,' she said, waving, and running down the path to join them on the parterre.

It had taken a little coaxing for the water to flow from the mouths of the three women's heads.

'That's the problem,' George had said. 'We shan't know if the system is in working order until the water comes down, and then it will be a wet job to fix anything. This is the difficulty with a system like this, where a natural stream is diverted to make the fountains work.'

'I always wondered why fountains don't just overflow.'

'In a closed system, the water is recycled. It is pumped up and then it falls back into the basin and is pumped through again. But these fountains were made to work by the force of water coming down from a higher level, so there is a constant flow. If you look at the channel round the base of this fountain, you will see how the water pours away, to run as a stream again further down. It will irrigate that dry land down there, and Pietro will be able to grow vegetables to his heart's content.'

If Lucius had been a clear favourite of Benedetta's before, that was nothing to her rapturous approval of what he had done to the fountains. 'I've told her it was a united effort,' he said, 'but she thinks I'm some kind of a magician. I think she plans on bringing the whole village up to see what the *americano* has done. Mind you, Domenico said his father could have done it any day of the week, had he been here; there is nothing his dad can't do. Poor kid, he hasn't seen the guy for two years.'

*   *   *

213

So pleased was Benedetta with them that she made no demur when they suggested that they dine outside that evening. It was as warm as it had been during the day, with the stones of the building giving off the heat of the day's sun.

'Feel how warm the wall is,' said Delia, pressing her hand against it.

The light was fading fast, the last rays of the sun setting the evening sky ablaze, and then, as darkness fell, the garden began to glow with pinpricks of light. Benedetta had fried a mound of anchovies to follow a risotto made with fresh green peas, and she had brought them out glasses of a fiery local grappa.

'Fireflies,' said Delia. 'Look, everywhere, on the ground, and flickering in and out of the leaves. Hundreds of fireflies.'

They were silent, watching the fireflies flitting to and fro in the gentle warmth of the velvety evening. There was an ease between them that night as they sat round under a vividly starry sky.

'This was how the stars looked when I was little,' said Delia. 'When the lights went out in the war, it was as though there had been another world out there that you couldn't see before then. Now, in London, there's so much light, you forget what the stars are like.'

'They aren't ever like this in England,' said Marjorie. 'Not huge and looking as though you could put out a hand and pluck one out of the sky.'

'*In such a night* . . .' said Lucius, with a quick sideways look at Jessica.

'Are you talking to me?' she said, after a moment of waiting for him to finish.

'Don't you get educated in England any more?'

'It's Shakespeare,' Marjorie said. '*The Merchant of Venice*. Lorenzo talking to your namesake, Jessica.'

Delia took up the quotation, her lovely, trained voice making music of the verse.

*'Sit, Jessica: look, how the floor of heaven
Is thick inlaid with patines of bright gold:
There's not the smallest orb which thou behold'st
But in his motion like an angel sings,
Still quiring to the young-eyed cherubins;
Such harmony is in immortal souls;
But, whilst this muddy vesture of decay
Doth grossly close it in, we cannot hear it.*

'It's about the music of the spheres. Those lines are so beautiful. I learned them at school. We had to learn a lot of Shakespeare by heart, only it didn't stick with you, did it, Jessica? Your head was always full of maths and formulae.'

'The maths was easy, and apart from that, why waste time on words written by dead men from long ago?'

'Poetry is food for the soul,' said George, unexpectedly. 'That is what the fathers used to say.'

'I've made a start,' said Jessica, on the defensive now. 'I've read the *Inferno*.'

'And?' prompted Marjorie.

'The rhymes take a little getting used to, don't they? Is that Dorothy Sayers, or is it like that in Italian?'

'It's called *terza rima*,' said Marjorie.

'It's not exactly a soothing read; I thought poetry was meant to soothe you.'

'Some soothes the soul, some invigorates the spirit,' said Lucius. 'Shakespeare's the guy for me, but on stage, not on the page. I like to watch it happen and hear the poetry spoken by actors. You ever thought of giving up singing for acting?' he said to Delia. 'You could, with your voice. Although I suppose opera's pretty much the same kind of thing, or do you just stand around and belt it out?'

'Not these days, not if you want to stay in work,' said Delia.

'Isn't it hard?' Marjorie asked. 'Singing those tragic roles, and expiring, mostly, night after night?'

'It's hell, actually,' said Delia. 'Mozart's all right, Mozart's different. I adore singing Mozart.'

After dinner, with Mozart humming in her head, she propped Beatrice Malaspina's score of *The Magic Flute* on the piano and began to play the overture, more to herself than to the others. Lucius was watching her, Marjorie was wrapped in her own thoughts, and George and Jessica were deep in discussion about the proportions and mathematics of Renaissance architecture.

Snatches of their conversation drifted in and out of her mind: the golden section, Pythagoras, Plato, Leonardo da Vinci; and then George had a notebook and pencil out and was writing as he spoke. 'For the geometric mean, the equation is M over G equals G over N, or G equals the square root of brackets M times N. The harmonic mean, H . . .'

Harmonic mean. 'Are you talking about music or maths or architecture?' she called out to them.

'All three,' said George. 'In the Renaissance, the harmony of the universe was at the heart of philosophy.'

'Three,' said Delia, playing a triad. '*The Magic Flute* is full of threes. E flat has three flats, there are three trials to be undergone, three messengers, three temples . . . There are lots of threes around the Villa Dante, by the way. That three-faced fountain, for a start – I do wonder if it is Beatrice Malaspina. If so, it's slightly alarming. Two-faced one is used to, but three-faced is too much to cope with. And there are nine pools and fountains altogether, and I don't have to be George or Jessica to know that's three times three.'

'Dante's full of threes,' said Marjorie, coming out of her reverie. 'Hell, Purgatory and Heaven, of course, and the *terza rima* Jessica asked about. Three was the Trinity and so expressed perfection. And there are thirty-three cantos in

Paradiso and *Purgatorio*, but thirty-four in the *Inferno*, because of course that couldn't have the same sacred number as the other two.'

Lucius was suddenly alert. 'This begins to get interesting. Thirty-three cantos in the *Divine Comedy*, all those threes in *The Magic Flute* which Beatrice Malaspina left on top of the pile of music, thirty-three days to find the codicil.'

George and Jessica began to talk at the same time, while Delia softly played arpeggios in E flat major. 'Three what?' she said. 'I mean, it does seem more than a coincidence, but what can she be trying to tell us with these threes? Of course, *The Magic Flute*'s also full of masonic symbols, but Beatrice Malaspina can't have been a mason, being female.'

'Could the codicil be hidden in the three-faced fountain?' said Marjorie.

'No,' said Delia. 'We'd have found it. And if we hadn't, it would be sodden by now.'

She got up from the piano, and stretched. 'It's late and I'm heading for my bed. Maybe an inspiration or three will strike us in the night.'

'So many threes,' Lucius was saying. 'Graces, fates, furies, are there any of those among the statuary? Rooms with three doors, triangles in the garden?'

Delia paused by the sofa, where Jessica and George had discarded the book on architecture to talk about primes. She looked at a page filled with diagrams of columns. 'Tuscan columns, that's what those plain columns on the little temple are.'

'Temple?' said Lucius. 'What temple?'

'The one in the garden that Marjorie calls the Temple of Love, because it's got Venus disporting herself with Mars painted in the dome. There's another three for you: it's got three columns.'

'Let's go look,' said Lucius.

The moon cast a good light, riding high in a clear, starry

sky, quite bright enough for them to find their way to the temple without difficulty.

'One dome, three pillars, three curved marble seats with nothing hidden under them,' said Lucius, sitting back on his heels after a brief inspection and dusting his hands.

Marjorie was staring down at the floor. 'All these marble flags have obviously been down for ever, but what about that circular one in the middle? It's darker marble, and it looks as though it might have moved some time recently.'

'We need a screwdriver or a strong knife to see if we can prise it up,' said George. 'We can't do it with our bare hands.'

Lucius was back to the house in a flash, returning minutes later with a screwdriver of Pietro's. Then he was on his hands and knees again, with the others standing closely round him as he inserted the blade, ran it round the stone and began to lift it.

Beneath the cavity was a space, and in it nestled a small, flat metal box.

'Eureka,' said Lucius, lifting it out. 'Let's take it indoors, but I bet my bottom dollar we've found the codicil.'

TWELVE

The box had no lock, and the lid came off easily. Inside was a notebook made up of several pieces of paper stitched together and covered, front and back, with marbled card.

They looked down at it, as Lucius quickly turned over the leaves. Each page was filled with small, cartoon-like drawings and handwriting, distinctive in its flowing calligraphy.

'Does a codicil have to be written in a legal way?' said Delia. 'Can you have a chatty one with drawings, or does it all have to be in legalese?'

Lucius picked up the notebook and gave it a good shake, in case there was another piece of paper among the bound sheets. There wasn't.

'It's a kind of journal,' said Marjorie, who had taken the notebook from Lucius and was scanning the first page. 'She's written here, "My first visit to the Villa Dante, when I was seven years old." This is her at the gates, just the same as they are now.'

They looked at the pen and ink outline of a girl in a sailor suit, with pigtails under a straw hat, peering through the gates at the familiar façade of the villa. Further down the page, there was a sketch of the child stretching up to ring the bell.

'She certainly knew how to draw,' said Lucius.

The next page showed a young woman in a wedding dress at the altar, having a wedding ring put on her finger by a good-looking man in a frock coat. 'My wedding day in 1881,' was written beneath it. 'My dress was satin and I carried white roses from the Villa Dante.' And further down the page a swift few lines portrayed a tall, lean priest. 'Don Marco, who married us. Now a cardinal, and much fatter.'

'Now?' said Delia. 'When is now?'

Marjorie looked at the last page. 'The Villa Dante, Christmas 1956,' she said. 'She must have drawn all these right at the end of her life, the last time she was here.'

'And left it for us to find.'

Delia had hold of the book now. 'It's scenes from her life. Here she is at the opera. It's brilliant; she's caught the look of a large Wagnerian tenor to the life. Look at Siegfried belting it out while he forges his sword.'

Another picture of Beatrice as a girl, wearing a party dress and sneezing, with 'Atishoo' written over her head. As an older woman, about the age she was in the portrait. 'Sitting in the temple reading poetry on a May evening, with the cicadas chanting and the fireflies dancing and the moon full,' she had written. And under the picture, a quote: '*I saw eternity the other night . . .*'

A Christmas page, dated 1925, decorated with images of 'The Twelve Days of Christmas'.

London, 1940, was the date on a page which showed Beatrice Malaspina sitting on a seat in a Tube train, looking at a reflection of herself. 'I travel on the Circle line to Paddington, hoping that no bombs fall while I am on the train. I am on my way to be questioned about all my Italian contacts, so perhaps my next ride will be to the Tower of London.'

Then on to a characterful drawing of herself as an old woman, sitting on a sofa and reading a hardback book. 'My

English cousins insist I read this epic by Tolkien but I'm not sure I understand orcs and elves or even hobbits.' And on this page she had drawn a cross-eyed orc and a languorous elf and a bemused figure with hairy feet.

There was a drawing of her, hair in a turban, in the top room of a tower, looking through a telescope. It was labelled, 'An astronomer studies Saturn on a summer night while she listens to the nightingales singing.'

And then, on the last page of drawings, 'Here is another tower, the tower at the Villa Dante.'

Marjorie let out an exclamation. The tower was drawn in exquisite detail, and standing at the foot of it, looking at the open door, were four figures.

Lucius gave a low whistle.

George took off his glasses, wiped them on his handkerchief, and replaced them to take a second look.

Delia was too amazed to say anything.

'It's you four, isn't it?' said Jessica. 'Goodness, she could catch a likeness. But however did she know what you all look like?'

The Tower

ONE

'I have observed,' said George, 'that there are some people whose lives are littered with "Danger, keep out" signs, while others never come across them at all.'

'They're the ones in real danger,' said Marjorie. 'If you don't notice the danger signs, then you really are in trouble.'

'And there are those,' added Lucius, 'who see a danger sign and head straight for it.'

'Like you,' said Delia.

They were standing at the door to the tower. It was an ancient door, dark and wooden and solid, with recessed, square panels, set in an archway made of formidable, rusticated stones. The danger sign hung lopsidedly, and the chains had a severe, mediaeval, no compromise look to them.

George was looking at them intently. 'Do you know,' he said, 'I think . . .' He stepped forward, took the chains in both hands, and gave them a vigorous tug.

To Delia's surprise, the hasp of the padlock opened and the chains slid to the ground with a clatter. Gordian knot time. What a shame that one couldn't simply give all the obstacles in one's life a good tug and watch them fall to the ground. Maybe you could, if only you could find the right place to apply pressure.

Lucius was examining the door. 'The lock, however, looks as though it means business.'

He gave the door a push and then a heftier shove with his shoulder. 'Definitely not just for show. The door is locked. We have no key.'

'It must be a large key,' said Marjorie. 'Not so easy to hide.'

'Benedetta said it's this big . . .' Lucius gestured with his hands. 'And she has no idea what Beatrice Malaspina did with it.'

'There are some letters carved above the door, in the centre of the arch,' said Delia.

George went closer, to take a better look, while Marjorie stepped back. 'Dante,' she said. '*Lasciate ogni* . . . It's what's written over the entrance to hell. Abandon hope all you who enter here.'

'A cheerful quotation,' said Lucius. 'Probably more effective than the chains for keeping you out.'

Marjorie was still squinting at the letters. 'Those words are annotated,' she said.

The letters were carved into the stone, each one about an inch high. But someone had written on the stone, as well, in ink, now faded to a pale, almost invisible, grey.

'It actually reads,' Marjorie said, '"Abandon hope all you who try to enter here without looking in the obvious place."'

'Someone is playing tricks on us.'

'Beatrice Malaspina,' said Marjorie. 'Who else?'

All four of them were brimming with a certain sense of excitement, each of them convinced that the codicil would turn out to be hidden in the tower. 'Otherwise, why the drawing of the tower and us?' Lucius had said.

'What is the obvious place?' said George.

'Does she mean the key?' said Lucius.

Delia's eyes were on the ground. 'I don't know what you do in America,' she said, 'but in England it's traditional to keep a spare front door key under a flowerpot by the front door.'

'Very unwise,' said Lucius. 'Leaving keys in an obvious place like that is simply saying, "Burglars, walk this way."' He stooped and tilted the large terracotta flowerpot that stood a few inches from the door, then jumped back with a cry of surprise.

Delia froze; that was definitely something she'd never found under a flowerpot. It was only an insect, but how could anything so small look so menacing? The scorpion was motionless, tail curled over. Marjorie stamped her foot, and it darted towards George. Unperturbed, he picked up a large sherd of broken pot from a little heap near the door, and set it swiftly in the scorpion's path.

Lucius nudged the insect on to the piece of pottery with his foot, and George carried the scorpion away, accompanied by instructions from Marjorie to heave it somewhere they never went.

'It was only a small scorpion,' he said, when he came back. 'It is the price you pay for living in a warm country such as Italy.'

'They probably had scorpions in the garden of Eden,' Lucius said. He picked up the large iron key which had been keeping the scorpion company under the flowerpot. 'So, no burglars, but instead a scorpion guarding the door. Bet you don't find that in England, Delia.'

'No, thank goodness.'

'Shall we go in?' said George.

For a moment they stood there, looking at the door. Then Lucius put the key in the lock and turned it.

'Beatrice Malaspina kept it well oiled,' he said, as the lock slid back. He pushed the door, and it swung open, letting out a musty smell of shut-up rooms. A moth flew blindly out, disoriented by the light.

'We are going to need a torch, I think,' said George. He

227

hurried away to the house, and the three others stood around the doorway, trying to see into the darkness within.

George was back in minutes, holding a serviceable torch.

They were in a lobby, cool after the warmth outside. The floor was stone-flagged, and the only light came from the door.

'There aren't any windows on the ground floor. Just those narrow slits in the stonework,' said Marjorie.

'I expect they used to keep animals on the ground floor,' said George. 'And hay above.'

There were two doors leading from the lobby, one quite small, and the other a larger one set in an arch. Marjorie opened the smaller door and George obligingly shone the torch through it. A stone staircase with a wrought iron balustrade ran up the side of the wall to a gallery above.

'Let's see what's in the lower part of the tower first,' said Delia.

There was a large round iron ring on the left hand door, which she grasped with both hands and twisted. The doors swung apart, and she only just saved herself from toppling headlong down the three steps which descended into the dimness.

The thin shafts of sunlight coming through the slits high up the wall barely cast a glow into the large empty space.

The light from George's torch flickered over the floor, which was covered in ornate tiles laid in a spiral shape, culminating in a star pattern in the centre.

'Checking for oubliettes?' said Lucius.

'You never know,' said George. Then he played the light over the walls, turning round as he shone the beam on each section.

None of them said a word.

Eyes looked out at them, writhing figures, floating aimless shapes, burning fires. The figures had a picturesque, formal quality, and in and around them planes fell blazing out of the sky, houses burned, gaunt and hungry faces gazed hopelessly through brutal barbed wire barriers. Delia felt as though she had been punched in the stomach as the dreadful images seemed to surround and enclose her within them.

Lucius's voice, wary and alarmed, came out of the gloom. 'It's a collage.'

'It's Hell,' said Marjorie.

'Surely only a very disturbed mind would cover the walls with such scenes,' said George, in a shocked voice.

His beam of light fell on a mushroom cloud, its gigantic plume of smoke rising the full height of the wall. At its base were the ribs of a flattened city.

'Hiroshima,' said Marjorie.

George switched off the torch. His voice echoed in the sudden darkness. 'I do not care to look at this.'

'Give me the torch,' said Marjorie.

She shone the beam on to an area of the wall densely covered with images of nightmares. Eyes shone out from shadowy, gothic figures.

'Fuseli's *Nightmare*,' said Lucius, as the torch lit up the familiar, ghastly picture with the incubus perched on the sprawled, unconscious woman, and the wild-eyed horse looming out of the shadows, and then moved on to illuminate stills from horror films: haunted faces, creatures coming out of slime, a naked Ophelia drowned in green weeds.

'This is the hell we carry in our minds,' said Marjorie.

'We're all doomed, in fact,' said Delia, trying to sound more cheerful than she felt; how could anyone feel anything but grim in this place? What kind of a mind must Beatrice Malaspina have had to create this, if she had done so?

Lucius's voice echoed her thoughts. 'If this is the old lady's doing, she could have done with a trip to the shrink,' he said.

Marjorie rounded on him, lighting his face up for a second with the torchlight. 'Don't talk about her like that. She has a name, Beatrice Malaspina, never the old lady. Don't you know an artist when you see one?'

'I do, thank you, better than you can imagine, but this is – well, plain horrible.'

'It is the darkness of our souls,' said George, his voice sounding remote and infinitely sad. 'Truly, Beatrice Malaspina had a knowing eye.'

'There's more,' said Marjorie. She lit up a series of frames, each containing figures and a speech bubble.

'It's a comic strip,' said Lucius, crouching down as his eyes followed the pictures through their sequence. 'Look, this Roman in a toga and a tin hat has to be Virgil, and that man in the mediaeval gown will be Dante.'

'Why Virgil?'

'Because Virgil was Dante's guide through Hell. There's the leopard and the lion and the wolf that Dante meets at the entrance; they represent lust, pride and avarice. Then off the two poets go, down through the circles of Hell.'

'And the tin hat?'

'Bringing Virgil and the poem into the twentieth century, I suppose.' Marjorie dropped to her knees beside Lucius and pointed to the figures. 'This is the first circle, Dante's Limbo, where he put the virtuous pagans. Born before Christ, so denied redemption.'

'Oh, my God,' said Lucius, staring at the final few frames. Delia knelt down beside him.

'This is right at the heart of Hell,' he said.

'The betrayers,' said Marjorie. 'Brutus, among others.'

'Never mind them. Look for yourself,' said Lucius. 'This is where it gets personal.'

The full beam of the torch picked out a set of separate pictures. These weren't the cartoon-like figures of the rest of the circles of Hell; these were four photographs.

Delia let out a cry of disbelief. 'That's me!'

It was, almost unrecognisable, caught in a flash, and behind her were the smiling faces of Felicity and Theo, bride and groom. There was her mother, looking at Richie, who was standing next to Jessica; she had turned away from him. Watching them all with brooding, severe eyes was her father.

Marjorie saw a photograph of herself, taken on the day she came out of hospital, unhappiness etched on every line of her face. There wasn't a caption, but she could supply the text herself: *Famous writer Marjorie Fletcher leaving St George's Hospital after her near-fatal accident.*

George was one of several people in a group photograph, standing beside a tall man in a hat and sunglasses, who had one arm draped over George and the other over the shoulders of another man. The other two were smiling for the camera; George was not. He looked anguished, and ill at ease. 'That was taken on the day we knew that it would work . . .' he said, and his voice tailed away.

The fourth picture showed a younger Lucius, in uniform, his face stiff and unsmiling, about to go through a door above which fluttered the Stars and Stripes. He was flanked on either side by soldiers with rifles. Attached to it was a smaller picture, of a threatening landscape, with a lake, and a jeep, and two indistinguishable men in uniform leaning on it.

TWO

'I want some air,' said Delia, getting to her feet and heading blindly for the door. 'I can't breathe in here.'

Outside, in the sunshine, with the soft rustle of a breeze in the leaves and the determined chirrup of a bird in a branch above her head, she took deep breaths, her eyes closed, her head spinning. The single note of the angelus carried across from San Silvestro, a steadying, tranquil rhythm.

The others joined her.

'Well,' said George at last. 'This is a most extraordinary thing.'

'How the devil did she get those pictures?' said Lucius.

'It's not hard if they were ever printed in newspapers, or taken by press photographers,' said Marjorie. 'And there are agencies who find pictures for you. Cutting agencies.'

'But why?' said George. 'I am completely perplexed. I never knew her, I had never heard of her until the lawyer got in touch with me. And how did she know that moment, in the photograph, had such particular meaning for me?'

'God only knows what's in the rest of the tower,' said Delia. 'It's impossible to imagine Beatrice Malaspina working in that tower pasting and drawing – do you suppose she did it all herself?'

'Who else?' said Lucius.

'What about the rest of the tower?' said Delia, looking up at its bulk looming over them. 'Do you think there are more terrible pictures on the other two floors?'

'No,' said Marjorie. 'It's quite clear what's she's doing. The next round room will be Purgatory and the top is Paradise. I just wonder if she had time to finish it all, it would be rather distressing if she got no further than Hell. I wonder when she did it.'

'That photo of me is fairly recent,' Delia said. 'It was taken . . . it was taken on one of the most horrible days of my life, if you want to know. I don't think it ever appeared in any paper, although I can't say I went looking for it. I can't imagine how she got hold of it, press cuttings or no press cuttings.'

'It looks like a wedding photo,' said Lucius. 'Didn't I spot a radiant bride?'

'The cream-cake bride in a tiara is my sister.' And you, Lucius, Delia said to herself, are far from radiant right here and now. Green about the gills would be a good description of how he looked.

Marjorie was asking her a question. Concentrate, concentrate on the here and now, on the sun and the dusty ground under my feet and these three people whom I didn't know a fortnight ago, let alone three years back.

'I'm sorry?'

'Who's the woman in the smart hat?'

'My mother.'

'She doesn't exactly look the joyfully happy mother of the bride.'

'And the other guy in the picture, the one looking at her?' Lucius asked.

Marjorie answered for her. 'That's Richard Meldon, war hero, MP, darling of the press.'

'Jessica's husband,' Delia said.

*   *   *

George and Marjorie were walking towards the house, deep in conversation. Delia hung back, worried about Lucius. He had a look of anguish on his face, of the kind of mental suffering that had gone beyond feeling. What on earth had happened to make him look like that?

She stopped by the fountain of the three women, and perched herself on the stone edge. 'Sit down. Take a few deep breaths. Take some time to recover. You've had a shock.'

He leant over and splashed some water on to his face. Then he hitched himself up beside her, and sat with his hands resting loosely on his thighs. He was looking down at his hands as though they carried some vital message.

'Was it some important military occasion?' she asked him. 'You look tense in the photo.'

'Tense? You could say that.'

'Was the picture taken in America?'

'No, Italy. I was in Italy towards the end of the war.'

'Were you about to get a medal?'

'On the contrary. I was dressed up like that for a court martial.'

'Whose?'

'Mine.'

'Oh. What were you being court martialled for?'

'I killed a fellow officer.'

He had awoken in the morning to the sound of rain pelting down, banging on the tin roofs, bouncing off the bonnets of the jeeps. There had been a heavy storm overnight, great cracks of thunder, jags and flashes of lightning making the whole bay light up, incongruous against the constant flickering flames of the volcanic activity on the hillsides. They had driven out at dawn, a likely spot, his CO had said, just the place for a bit of fancy work.

Lucius had ended up working on deception in the war quite by chance. Since he could paint, he volunteered to help

234

with a show the unit were putting on, when he was still just a rookie. It seemed ridiculous to be there in a war, painting scenery. But the officers were keen on shows, saying they helped keep up morale and so on. So he painted this set, a landscape; it was fun, he enjoyed it and made a good job of it, finding it a welcome relief from weapons training and explosives.

Among the pots and brushes, he had been able to forget that there was a war on; the smells, the colours, the normality of it all, were in stark contrast to the sweat and fear and urgency of the final, or what they all hoped would be the final, stages of the war.

It so happened that some bigwig was in the audience, and two days later Lucius was transferred to an outfit that specialised in making the enemy think things were other than they were. It was an idea they'd taken from the British, who had been doing it since the beginning of the war; in fact, Lucius heard that they'd done it with some success in the Great War. The British had one guy, a magician in peacetime, who could build a fake city in front of your eyes and you'd swear it was real.

So they were headed out for this place where they wanted to persuade the Germans they were up to something. That meant phoney tanks, tracks in the ground, tents, the whole thing. His job was to suss out the lie of the land, to assess whether they could do what was needed. It depended partly on the surrounding landscape, light, all that, as to whether they could make it convincing, or rather, since they'd been told to make it convincing, how they could pull it off.

The events that had brought Lucius to his court martial were as clear in his mind as though they had happened that very morning. That was because he lived them over and over again; they were a ball and chain, tugging at him, reminding him that he had no business to be alive and well and prospering. And telling him that by what he had done on that day, which was, to all intents and purposes, murder, he had forfeited his right to happiness. In recompense for that wrong, he had lost the most precious thing in his life. Except for life itself.

The place they'd been sent to was near Naples, called Averno. One of the entrances to the ancient underworld, as it happened. His CO was a classicist, a Harvard man. He quoted some words in Latin: *tuta lacu nigro nemorumque tenebris, / quam super haud ullae poterant impune uolantes / tendere iter pennis*, and then he told Lucius what it meant, that no birds would fly over the lake. Lucius could believe it; it was the blackest lake and the most dismal place he'd ever been. Volcanic, of course, like everything else around there. Which probably meant that birds really did prefer not to fly across the lake, who knew? Anyhow, there they were, them and a photographer. What with the rain and the gloom of the place, they weren't any too cheerful, never mind the birds, but it was their job and so they got on with it.

He climbed up through a wooded area to one side, to get a wider view. Up at the top, he heard voices, which dismayed him, because as far as they knew there shouldn't have been any troops anywhere near. This was some guy barking orders in English. Not an American; one of those upper class English voices.

The first thing that caught his eye was a rather fine house set at the side of a valley. One of those serene Italian houses; even in the rain he could see how mellow and beautiful it would look on a sunny day when there wasn't a war going on. And there was a small contingent of troops there, milling around, looking a bit disorganised.

The guy in charge was the kind he'd have known for an officer if he'd been dressed in rags. He had a high brow and a beaky nose and he was crackling with energy, alive and intent on what he was doing. He heard Lucius, and whipped round, shouting out to him in Italian to drop, get flat on the ground. Then he pulled a gun; he must have been nuts, not to see the uniform, but Lucius yelled at him that he was American, and he lowered the gun.

'Well, I don't know what the hell you're doing here, but just fuck off out of it, there's a good chap,' he said. Not very polite as a greeting, and Lucius couldn't see what he was so het up about. He wasn't the only one, because there was a sergeant standing beside him, rain was dripping off all of them, and this little man, like one of those terrier dogs, was shouting at the officer. Arguing, which you don't do with a man like that. He was Scottish, the sergeant; Lucius recognised the accent. The men weren't looking too happy, either, and one of them was hauling what looked like explosives off the back of a truck. Lucius began not to like the look of this, although it was none of his business, but an aggressive Englishman and the weather and a heap of stuff that might go off bang, well, it looked as though it might get quarrelsome, so he thought he'd take the officer's advice and clear out. Only then the sergeant broke free from the grip the British officer had on him and came slipping and sliding over to him.

'Sir, for Gawd's sake, stop him.'

Lucius just stared at the sergeant. More than ever, he thought, he didn't want to be there. 'Look, this show is nothing to do with me. I'm with the Yanks, and I'll just get back where I belong. And you'd better do what sir over there says, or he'll have the balls off you. I can see he's that type.'

'You don't get it,' the little sergeant said. His face was red. 'There's people holed up in yon house, Germans, and he's going to blow them all up.'

'Won't they come out?'

'He won't give them the option.'

'If they came out, hands up . . . Do they know what he's planning to do? Has he warned them? If they've barricaded themselves in . . .'

'*He's* barricaded them in. He doesn't want anyone to get out. And he's not planning to blow the place sky high, nasty but quick, he wants them to burn. He wants to set the house on fire.'

Lucius still didn't get it. 'Smoke them out, do you mean?'

The sergeant was almost dancing with impatience by this time. 'No. Burn them alive. And there are Italians in there, civilians, a family. Women and kids.'

'Oh, for Christ's sake. He must get them out. And the Germans aren't exactly fighting back. Have they got weapons? Can't you just surround the house and get them to come out?'

'He won't hear of it. He wants a blaze, and he doesn't care who gets killed. He's barking, sir, barking mad. He just says, "We'll burn them all, and if they're innocent, they can just go to heaven a bit quicker, isn't that what the Eyeties are always on about, God's in his heaven, waiting to welcome you to a fluffy cloud in angel land?"'

Surely the men wouldn't carry out an order like that. But one guy, obviously afraid of the British officer, had set the charges, and now the officer was setting up the final fuses. He was going to do it himself; Lucius could see he was almost ecstatic.

Delia words came to him out of another time.

'What did you do?'

'I shot him.'

The three words hung on the air. 'I shot him,' he repeated. 'I killed him.'

He could see now the look of astonishment on the man's face as he fell to the ground. It all seemed to be happening in slow motion; he heard the crack of the gun, and, impossibly, there was a pause before the bullet struck the man, and he fell, spiralling, his blood suspended in mid-air, before he sank to the ground, and suddenly everything speeded up, shouts, men running, consternation, and the sergeant shouting

238

in his ear, 'Thank God, thank the Lord.' And then, 'You tripped, sir, I saw you trip, as you were running towards him, what a dreadful accident.'

Lucius knew all about atrocities and had no illusions about those being something only the enemy went in for. That's what war was like; it dehumanised decent men. He was filled with anger, at the waste of war, at all the destruction and pointlessness of it, all the cruelty, all summed up for him there on that Italian hillside. The enemy in that beautiful house, that's what got to him, the awareness that the house stood for what they were fighting for. And the lives of the people inside.

The Germans had come out, white-faced, glad to be out of the house, and were hauled away as grateful prisoners, and the family, well, they were alive and that was all that mattered to them. A woman was screaming. It was sheer fear, she wasn't hurt, but there was just this great ululating scream, going on and on. Lucius still heard it in his dreams, he heard it all around him; a car horn, a long drawn out note on a violin, a child yelling, and he heard the shots and the screams ringing in his head.

'That's why you didn't want to use the dynamite at first. Marjorie said you weren't keen when she first suggested it. Why ever didn't you say? Maybe you need to see Marjorie's psychiatrist.'

'I've tried that.'

'Does your family know what happened to you?'

'I've never told a living soul.'

'Not the shrink?'

'I couldn't bring myself to tell him.'

'So it's all been locked up inside your head all this time?'

'Yes.'

'What about the court martial?'

'The penalty for shooting the British officer, an ally, was death. Yet I wasn't on trial for murder.'

The lawyers had made that quite clear. An accident, they all said, just a tragic accident. It was a most unfortunate incident; the man he'd shot had died from 'friendly fire', that was the official wording. Even so, there had to be a court martial, since he'd killed a fellow officer. Well, not exactly a fellow officer, his American lawyer said. 'Let's not forget the guy you shot was a Brit. Not one of ours.'

'Does that make it any better? I shot him, he died.'

'That's war,' the lawyer said.

'Isn't that the truth of it?' said Delia. 'When you joined up, you knew it meant killing other people, whoever they were. Or were you conscripted?'

'I joined voluntarily,' said Lucius.

And that was another story, since the reasons for his joining up were complicated and had nothing to do with fighting for freedom or democracy or against the Nazis or the Japanese or for his country or the countries of his ancestors.

'It had more to do with wanting to get away from home,' he said.

Delia knew all about getting away from home. 'Don't you get on with your parents?'

'We didn't see eye to eye on what I was going to do when I graduated. I'd started at college, and they were happy with that: I was on track for my future career as a money maker in the family firm.'

'Which is what you are, isn't it?'

There was a silence. Lucius was gazing at the ground with a brooding expression on his face. 'Yup. It's what I am. It's not what I wanted to be, back then.'

'So what had you in mind?'

'Oh, I wanted to be an artist. Crazy, huh?'

'Why crazy? Have you no talent?'

'No, it's just a crazy way to make a living. At least, if you're Lucius J. Wilde the third, it is.'

'But you didn't think so then. How old were you?'

'Eighteen. No, I didn't. All I wanted to do was paint. But to keep the family peace, I agreed to go to college. Then, I told them, afterwards, I would go to art school. I thought that would buy me a bit of time, and no more would be said until I graduated.'

'You postponed the moment of decision.'

'Something like that.'

'Unwise, if your father's anything like mine.'

'I suppose it's different for girls.'

'Don't you believe it.'

Lost in his own thoughts again, Lucius wasn't listening to her. 'Actually, my mother was worse. Dad might have understood, might even have said, "Let him have a go, then when he fails we'll be there to pick up the pieces." But Mom . . . well, her parents weren't – aren't – the banking sort. They're more bohemian, and she's uneasy with that. She didn't just marry Lucius J. the man, but Lucius J. the Boston banker. I don't say she didn't fall in love with him, I mean that she took care not to fall in love with one of the crazy types, read artists, whom she met at her parents' house. And she sure as hell wasn't going to have her only son, her ewe lamb, sliding back into that world.'

'So you joined the army.'

'That made them really, really angry. I think they'd reckoned they had enough influence to keep me out, and of course they'd have let me finish my college education and by the time that was done, with any luck the war would be over. Which it was. But I thought if I could get out of the States, then I could stiffen my resolve, work things out for myself. Grow up, be able to stand on my own two feet and not be under my parents' thumb. I suppose I had this sneaking feeling that somehow they'd get their way, and I'd end up in the bank just the same.'

'Which is exactly what you did.'

'Only because of what happened in Italy. I'd made up my

mind, while I was painting bits of canvas and ply board to look like tanks, that I was going to do what I wanted. Not finish college, but go to art school. Or, best of all, stay in Europe, and work in Paris or Rome.'

'So why didn't you?'

He didn't answer. It was too complex to put into words, Delia could see, but she could also see how that equation worked out. 'The court martial cleared you. And so, since they didn't punish you, you decided to punish yourself.'

'You make it sound so simple.'

'The upshot was plain enough. I don't suppose what went on in your head and heart was simple at all. Why do we do the things we do? Why do we mess up our lives so often by doing what seems to make sense at the time, even though there's a voice whispering in our ear that we're making a huge mistake? How does your being a banker and not a painter help the guy who died? And were you to blame?'

'I told you, I shot him. I intended to shoot him, I intended to kill him, and I did so. A guy who'd been alive one minute was dead the next. Telegram to his grieving mother, father distraught, misery all round. Just because I did that.'

'What happened at the court martial?'

It had been a sunny day. He was hot in his uniform, and dismayed by the relaxed atmosphere in the court. It all seemed not to matter very much, just another routine procedure, all in the day's work.

The British sergeant was the key witness. He was completely clear in his testimony, which he shot off in a monotone, like rounds from a gun. He looked straight ahead and lied through his teeth. Lucius had come down the hill, it was steep, he'd gathered speed, tripped on the root of a tree, and his gun had gone off.

They didn't ask why he'd had a gun in his hand. Nor did they cross-examine the sergeant; he made his statement and that was that. Not a single question.

A British observer had been sitting in on the proceedings. Lucius had caught his words as the court rose at the direction of the judge, a tired-looking man with a thin, lined face, wearing the uniform of a colonel. Oddly enough, Lucius hadn't heard the judge's words, knew nothing about what had been said, only knew that he'd been cleared of any wrongdoing when his lawyer clapped him on the shoulder and congratulated him, and his commanding officer hurried forward to shake his hand. Everyone was smiling and looking pleased.

Lucius hadn't heard anything of the findings. He was listening to the British officer behind him, who was talking in a low voice to an American. Saying that it was a blessing and Lucius should be given a medal. That the guy he'd killed was a monster, and thank God Lucius had done what he had, because it had saved everyone a pile of trouble.

'What about all the lives you saved?' Delia said. 'What about all the grieving families there would have been had that nutcase set the house on fire?'

'How do I know he really intended to do it? He could have been going to smoke them out. It's an old trick, start a fire, make it smoky and unpleasant; very few people are going to hang around inside to see if you're serious.'

'You said the house had been barricaded.'

'It looked like it. The sergeant said it was. But how can I be sure?'

'The sun's come out while we've been here,' Delia said, after another long silence. 'Let's go for a swim.'

In the clear water, Delia lay on her back. Lucius watched her as she lay with her eyes closed.

'How do you do that?' he said. 'I can float all right, but not as though I were lying on a cushion of air the way you do.'

'It's a knack, that's all.' Delia flipped over in a dolphin

243

dive and surfaced beside Lucius. 'How do you manage to be so – insouciant? Positive? When that's been rattling round in your head for all this time. It would be guaranteed to make me sour and depressing.'

'It's a knack. God meant me to be insouciant, as you put it. I love the way you say that. So perfectly English.'

'And you've never said a word about all this? To your family? Friends?'

'Not a word.'

'Until now.'

'Until now.'

Delia dived to the bottom and came up with a pink shell in her hand.

'The real mystery,' said Lucius, treading water, 'is how on earth Beatrice Malaspina came by those pictures. The one taken by Lake Averno, that's a military photo. And so is the one of me going into the court martial. Those can't have come from any press cutting agency.'

'Everything we find out about her makes her seem more remarkable. I wish I'd known her. I wish she hadn't waited until she was dead to invite us here.'

THREE

Jessica was quick to notice that there was something different about Lucius.

None of them had wanted to venture back into the tower that afternoon.

'Even if the codicil's upstairs on one of the next floors up, it can wait,' Lucius said. 'It won't be going anywhere.'

Marjorie had gone down to the beach with a book; George and Lucius decided to give Pietro a hand with some belated pruning in the orchard.

Delia found Jessica reading in the shade of the arcade, and, sitting down on a marble bench, she filled her in with the details of their visit to the tower. 'Be glad you didn't come. I can't tell you the complete horribleness of it all.'

'I can see that a photo of Felicity's wedding day might give you a shock. What about the others?'

'Marjorie was snapped coming out of the entrance to St George's Hospital, looking like a tragedy queen. I don't see that George's picture was of a bad time, because he was in a photo with a very cheery-looking set of people. But it upset him, just the same.' She paused. 'I do know about Lucius's picture, though. He told me all about it when we came out, don't ask me why.'

'What was the photo of?'

'Him going into a court martial. Oh,' seeing Jessica's startled expression, 'he was acquitted, honourably and all that. Only there were some things that happened during the war that have rather haunted him since. The photograph brought it all back, and for some reason he felt compelled to tell someone about it. Pity it wasn't you sitting on the fountain. You'd have been more understanding and sympathetic than I was.'

'Do you think Lucius is the kind of man to bare his soul to anyone who happened to be passing?' Jessica said, choosing her words carefully.

'I expect so. People do confide in you; you're a much better listener than I am. Kinder. And he wasn't crying or asking for sympathy, it was just that he's never talked about it to anyone, and for some reason he had to.'

'What's strange,' Jessica went on, 'if it's been confession time, is that getting it all off his chest has made him somehow less frivolous, less light-hearted. You'd have expected the opposite.'

'He wanted to be a painter before the war,' Delia said. 'His parents weren't too keen, and that was one of the reasons he joined the army. I think talking about what happened has made him remember what he really wanted to do with his life.'

'After the war, surely he could do what he liked, couldn't he? He would have gone away a boy, and come back a man.'

True, but he had gone away a free spirit and come back with that terrible thing on his conscience, and an over-burdened sense of having to somehow make amends for what had happened. 'Parental pressure can be hard to resist.'

'You resisted your father, didn't you? He wanted you to join the family firm, when you came down from university. Only you stuck to your guns and went for the opera singing.'

'Yes, I did,' Delia said, thinking of the terrible battles she had fought, the struggle to get herself the training she needed in the face of such adamant opposition from her father, changing her surname, not just for work, but by deed poll, 'So that you needn't feel I've sullied the family name,' she'd told him, glad to see the hurt in his eyes at this gesture of independence.

Jessica was still thinking about Lucius. 'If he's an artist by nature, it must be grim having to trot along to the bank every day. Or maybe he was only ever going to be a dabbler. An amateur. Not like you, with a huge gift, the voice they all want, professional to your fingertips, your agent actually ringing you, never the other way round. You are so lucky.'

'Yes,' said Delia flatly. 'I keep telling myself how lucky I've been.'

Dinner was laid on the terrace again, and Benedetta lit a veritable forest of lights scented with citronella to ward off the swarms of insects that she clearly felt would otherwise descend and devour the diners as they ate.

The soft, wavering lights gave the table and terrace a very gay appearance. They ate pasta done in a green sauce that Delia thought was ambrosial. Benedetta told Lucius it was called *pesto*, a Ligurian speciality, made from basil leaves and pine nuts.

'Benedetta has been coaxing early basil on the sheltered sill of her kitchen,' Marjorie said. 'I've never eaten it before. Do you suppose it's the same as Keats's pot of basil, with Lorenzo's head buried in it?'

They had drunk rather more wine than usual, and Jessica was flushed and talkative. She looked across at Lucius. 'Hope it's not tales out of school, but Delia told me you're an artist, that you paint.'

Delia could have throttled her. Now Lucius would think she'd gone gossiping to Jessica, blabbing out his story, which

247

he now probably wished he hadn't told her, and which she was sure he never wanted the others to hear.

For a moment, a look of – no, not fury, but panic, for heaven's sake – crossed Lucius's face. Then he relaxed.

'Girls' talk?'

'I told Jessica that you painted. That's all.'

'I don't paint any more. I did, when I was a boy.'

There was a finality to his words, but Delia, made reckless by the wine, wasn't going to let that pass. 'I'm a singer,' she said.

'We know,' said Marjorie.

'And a very fine one,' added George. 'That Schubert you were singing the other evening – you have a gift to move men's hearts.'

'And how do you think it feels to move men's hearts like that?' said Delia, heated now herself, and sounding indignant.

'Powerful, I'd say,' said Lucius. He leant back in his chair, watching Delia intently.

She swirled the wine in her glass, looking at its rich colour against the candlelight. 'I think it's extremely interesting that there are five of us here, and none of us is doing what we want to do or what we should be doing.'

George made a tutting sound. 'In my case, you are mistaken. I am a scientist, that is my training, it is all that I ever wanted to do.'

'No, that's not quite right,' said Marjorie. 'It may have been in the past, but it isn't going too well just at the moment, is it? Because of whatever it is you did in the war, I suppose all to do with the A bomb or something else just as terrible, you've become disillusioned with science. It's been your god, and now you've discovered it's not an awfully good one.'

'I beg your pardon?' George sounded really affronted. 'Science a god? That is a most irrational and unscientific assumption, and, I assure you, quite untrue.'

248

'It isn't. You scientists make a religion out of science. You have labs instead of churches and benches instead of altars, but you're a breed apart, just like priests, and you think you have all the answers. Also like men of God.'

This assertion seemed to render George speechless and Delia plunged in again. 'George can deny it, but I think Marjorie's got to the heart of his problem.'

'Why am I doing what I don't want to?' said Jessica. She didn't care for where this conversation was going. 'I have a difficult domestic life, but that's true of lots of people.'

'You don't do anything,' said Delia. 'That's your trouble. You've got brains, and energy, and all you've done is fool around and get married to a rich man who's totally wrong for you.'

Jessica was suddenly furious. 'You think I should be at some school teaching maths, is that it?'

'The way you wasted your time at Cambridge, I don't suppose a school would have you, you took a lousy degree. A fellow mathematician of yours from Cambridge once told me you could have done much better, if you hadn't been so intent on having a good time, and had ever done a stroke of work.'

'Since I never had any intention of being a mathematician, it was just my best subject at school, why ever should I bother? I got a degree, I wasn't sent down, I didn't fail. Besides, maths is a hopeless subject. Unless you have the kind of gift that some mathematicians have, all the work in the world doesn't make any difference. There were people there who could do maths that no amount of swotting and sweating away at would make me able to handle. It's like music, Delia: you've got it or you haven't. So I'm very content with what I achieved, thank you all the same. And,' she added, plonking her elbows on the table, and giving Delia an intent look, 'if we're going to talk about time-wasting at Cambridge, who barely scraped a degree at all, because she spent all her time on music and none at all on her studies?'

'It is true, about mathematics,' put in George, who had been watching Delia and Jessica with an earnest attention. 'You should not attack your friend in this way.'

'I'm not attacking, and I can say these things because she is my friend.'

'We all make mistakes,' murmured Lucius.

'You haven't found what you want to do, and you'll be miserable until you do,' Delia pronounced. 'Give me some more wine, Lucius.'

'Perhaps you have had enough,' said George.

'No, I haven't. I feel like that person in the ancient world, what was she called? The one in the fresco. A prophetess – I know, a sibyl. I sang a sibyl once, but I can't remember when or where, or which opera. What's more, I don't care.'

'Oh, for God's sake, leave the prophetic bit to Marjorie,' said Jessica, still smarting from Delia's words.

'Shan't,' said Delia. 'You and George may deny what I say about you, although it's true, but Marjorie can't. She was a writer, and she wants to be a writer again. Only she isn't, so she's not doing what she wants to do. And you, Lucius, you want to be a painter.'

'Not quite correct,' said Lucius. 'Past tense, Delia. That's all over and done with. A boyish whim. I'm a grown-up now, a successful banker, taking time out which I shouldn't to come to the Villa Dante, which was probably a mistake, given what's lurking in the tower. I shall go on to London, where I shall work for a number of years, making a great deal of money for myself and for the bank. And, come the fall, I'm getting married.'

This pronouncement was greeted with stunned silence.

'Who to?' said Marjorie. 'Someone wholly unsuitable,' she added, 'I bet you.'

'On the contrary. Elfrida is the daughter of an English merchant banker. She is beautiful, well bred, charming, everything a man could want in a wife. She doesn't hear voices or sing or idle her time away, and it will be a relief to get back to her company.'

'Elfrida?' said Delia, suddenly alert. 'That's an unusual name. She doesn't happen to come from Yorkshire, does she?'

Jessica was looking at Lucius with an awed expression. 'It couldn't be Elfrida Harrington-Knowles you're talking about, could it?'

'As it happens, yes. Do you know her?'

Delia and Jessica exchanged glances.

'Know her?' Delia cried. 'Oh, yes, we know her all right. We were at school with her. You can't possibly marry Elfrida. Why, she's . . .'

'Delia, shut up!' said Jessica. 'If Lucius is in love with Elfrida and is going to marry her, then don't say another word. No. Nothing.' She turned to Lucius. 'We knew Elfrida when she was at school. Neither of us has seen anything much of her since.'

'You may not have done, but I . . .'

'Delia, I said shut up.'

'Oh, all right.' Delia cast a darkling look at Lucius. 'You'll regret it. That's all. It's just part of this phoney life you're leading. You want to be a painter, you aren't or can't be for some reason, and so you're inventing this terrible life for yourself, designed to make you as miserable as hell.'

Which is what his life would be, if he married Elfrida. He might as well go and shut himself up in that desperately grim room at the bottom of the tower as go on with his banking career, Elfrida at his side.

Lucius was looking amused rather than annoyed, but Delia suspected that beneath the lightness of his tone as he said, 'Thank you for the words of advice,' there was that strain of panic again.

'Well, you alone among us seems to have made all the right choices,' he went on. 'We're all failures or have come off the rails, while you enjoy a successful and satisfying life.'

251

'Don't be stupid,' cried Delia. 'How can you be so blind? Do I seem happy to you?'

'Aren't you?' said Jessica.

Delia could tell from her voice that Jessica was afraid she was going to tell the others about her feelings for Theo. Which she certainly wasn't; she hadn't drunk that much wine.

'Do you know what it does to me, agonising and often as not expiring, for hours on end? I hate it. It's nearly all tragedy and it makes me wretched, it makes me throw up, it hurts me to sing those roles. I have the voice, the technique, I'm eminently directable, I have the looks, I have stamina, I have it all. Except I simply don't have the temperament.'

'It is a mood,' George said. 'A patch of melancholy that artists suffer from. It will pass, surely.'

'The mood may, but the roles won't. Have you ever considered that in virtually every opera, the woman's role is that of victim? In opera, women are betrayed, oppressed, doomed.' She pinged her empty glass with her finger, and sang a long drawn out 'doomed' to the note. 'And the joke is, I fought to become an opera singer. I asserted myself, I saw myself as a strong, independent woman, I estranged myself from my father, I worked like a dog, and I got where I wanted . . . only now I realise I don't actually want to go through that suffering, night after night, year after year.'

Jessica sounded stunned. 'I'd no idea,' she said. 'Delia, why didn't you say?'

'Because you were too wrapped up in your own problems, you didn't need to have mine thrust on you.'

'Isn't that what friends are about?'

'Not always. Sometimes friends do best to keep things to themselves.'

'How long have you hated the kind of singing you've been doing?'

'At about the time when music, which I love, it's my life, stopped being a joy and became a duty and an obligation to others. It's not that the music I sing isn't wonderful; it is. I adore it. Or at least I do when I'm in the audience, or at the other end of a loudspeaker.'

'So a long time,' Jessica said. 'And you didn't say a word.'

'I had to sort it out for myself. And since I've been here, I've had to face the fact that it's making me ill.'

Even before she'd gone down with bronchitis, she'd been exhausted after every performance, had stomach upsets, caught a lot of colds. As she climbed up the ladder people kept on telling her how gifted she was. Lucky her.

'I've had a lot of luck; it's a fiercely competitive business, opera, not one in a thousand, not one in ten thousand, makes the grade. You need the voice and the teachers and most of all luck, being in the right place at the right time. I had all that. And it seemed like chucking my gifts back at wherever they came from to admit that it's wrong for me. Knowing it would be a betrayal of all those people who have given my career boosts along the way.'

She pushed her glass towards Lucius.

'You've had enough,' he said.

'You sound like my father, except for him even a teaspoon of the stuff is too much.'

Benedetta came out on to the terrace, carrying a silver tray. On it were five small glasses, a bottle of deep golden wine and a plate of tiny biscuits.

'What are these?' said Marjorie. 'They look like rusks with nuts in them.'

'Biscotti,' said Lucius. 'Hard as bricks, break your teeth if you bite into them. You dip one in the wine – it's a dessert wine, quite sweet – and let it soften. Then you eat it.'

'Good,' said Delia. 'Let me try.'

'This wine's much stronger than the stuff you've been drinking,' warned Lucius. 'You're going to have a hell of a hangover in the morning.'

'But for now the night is warm and full of promise, the sky

is full of stars, the air is fragrant with scents of darkness. I'm not drinking to drown my sorrows.' No, she was drinking to celebrate the revelation that she'd had here in the Villa Dante. Her life was still full of problems, and when she woke up in the morning to face the decisions that her discovery would force her to take everything would seem much worse. How different it might have been if she and Theo . . . but she wasn't going to talk or think about that, not now. 'I'd like to dance naked among the olive trees,' she said, 'but I think I'd fall over.'

'You certainly would,' said George, alarmed. 'I beg that you will do no such thing.'

'A touch of Bacchus in the night,' said Lucius. His moment of panic had passed, and now, Delia looking at him, saw another Lucius, at ease with himself, amused, full of life. What a strange man, with his layers of being and his quite different personae. He doubtless had a string of other façades to put on as the occasion demanded. One of them to come in the autumn, when he would be the second lead player in a repetition of that ceremony she recalled with such misery. Knowing Elfrida, it would be an even grander affair than Jessica's or Felicity's weddings. York Minster, probably, with trumpets. Elfrida had always had a vulgar streak. Elfrida didn't deserve a man as interesting as Lucius, and she'd certainly destroy any hopes he had of ever being anything other than a moneyspinner.

'In a minute,' said Delia in ringing tones, 'I shall fall fast asleep at the table.'

In her mind's eye she could see, as vividly as though she were sitting there, the wise old woman she'd met last year, one of the best singers of her generation.

'You can live your life to please others, and will never be quite well, never be totally alive, or you can live the life you want, to please yourself,' she'd said to Delia.

Delia had been disbelieving, alarmed. 'What shall I do if I don't sing? It's all I can do, and I love music.'

'Sing something entirely different, something that you enjoy singing.'

Delia gazed into the yellow, flickering lights. 'I should be ashamed, I suppose, to turn my back on high art, but I'm not.'

'The art,' said George, 'is separate from the singer. I have known several singers of classical music who are as stupid as owls.'

'I think they're the ones who do it best,' said Delia, with a prodigious yawn. 'They don't care, it doesn't touch them, they don't give a button about what they're going through out there in the spotlight. They just trundle on stage, belt out their numbers, die on cue and then go home for a nice cup of Horlicks.'

Lucius was laughing at her; he had slipped back once more into the persona that Delia had seen most of, laconic and easy-going. Now she saw it as a veil, drawn over a much more turbulent personality, although maybe, deep down, were he to reach the essence of himself, perhaps there would be the reality of which this was merely the appearance. She didn't feel he was meant to be tense and worried, or to be conventional and comfortable in the world he had chosen to make his way in.

'I'll tell you something for nothing,' she said to him, smothering a yawn. 'You're not happy banking, and you won't be happy married to Elfrida. No way.'

With which words, she lowered her head on to her arms, and fell asleep.

'Well,' said Marjorie.

'Was that just drunken talk, or the truth, I wonder?' said George.

'The truth,' said Jessica instantly. 'Delia never lies about herself. In fact, she very rarely talks about herself, but if she does, believe me, it's the truth.'

'What are we going to do with her?' said George. 'Should we wake her up, advise her to go to bed?'

'I don't suppose you could,' said Marjorie, dunking another biscotto in her wine. 'She won't wake up until the morning now.'

'We can't leave her here, at the table,' said George.

'When we've finished our wine, you and I'll carry her upstairs,' said Lucius. 'The girls can put her to bed.'

'If Delia had been your friend and going through all that, would you have known about it?' Jessica asked Marjorie.

'That she was facing a crisis of some kind? Oh, yes. I could tell.'

'How could you see that, when you're strangers, and me not, when I know her so well? And thought I was so close to her.'

'I observe people, it's what I do. You don't. Besides, there is only so much emotional turmoil one can put up with. We all have our limits. As Delia has discovered, and now she'll redefine her personal boundaries in a practical and satisfactory way. She's fortunate; not many of us can do that.'

'Not many of us have her gifts,' said George. 'I still think what a loss to music.'

'That's mere sentimentality,' said Marjorie. 'There are lots of singers who come and go; the music is still there. Because she won't be singing Verdi, it doesn't mean you'll never hear another Desdemona. And just think of the pleasure she'll bring to thousands and thousands of people who'd never go near an opera house if she goes in for a different kind of singing. They'll come out of any musical show she sings in feeling light-hearted – for an hour or so they'll have forgotten all their problems. And when they hum a tune from the show while waiting for their crowded train to some dull job the next morning, worrying about how they are going to pay for the repair to the boiler, they'll recall how happy they felt listening to Delia's lovely voice, and it'll cheer them up. That's as much of a gift to the world as moving souls in operatic tragedy. Different, but of equal benefit to her fellow beings.'

George was frowning. 'That is to suggest that mere enter-tainment is of equal value to . . .'

'Stuff,' said Marjorie. 'There's room for both. I don't – didn't – write highbrow stuff. I love to read it – well, some of it; there's nothing better than Shakespeare or Horace – but we need the cakes and ale as well. You need more cakes and ale in your life, George, then you mightn't be so sad.'

George's face lit up with the smile that transformed him from an ordinary-looking man into one of great charm. 'You are right. You are quite right.'

What a nice man he is, thought Jessica, and found herself yawning as widely as Delia had done.

'Time to cart Delia off,' said Lucius.

FOUR

Delia came drifting into Jessica's room early the next morning, her hand over her eyes, lamenting the state of her head. 'Be an angel, and close those shutters,' she said. 'The light's positively vicious.'

'Drink some water,' said Jessica. 'Lots of it. I knew you'd regret all that wine.'

'I don't regret it at all, it was delicious, every drop of it. Have you got an aspirin?'

'Yes, but have it after food.'

'Coffee would be good,' said Delia, wincing as she moved her head rather too quickly.

Downstairs, Lucius, clean-shaven and with the glowing virtue about him of one who had had an early morning swim, handed Delia a sinister-looking glass of red liquid.

'What's this?' she said suspiciously. 'It looks perfectly foul, and smells like cough mixture.'

'It's the Italian version of a prairie oyster,' said Lucius. 'I made do with what's in Benedetta's cupboards, but I think it will work. Knock it back in one go.'

Delia looked doubtfully at the glass, but obediently drank it. A horrified look came over her face, and she made a dart for the door. Then she stopped, a look of surprise on her face. 'Good heavens, what on earth was in that?'

'This and that,' said Lucius. 'Now, eat a hearty breakfast, go for a swim, then fall asleep in the shade somewhere, and you'll be fine by lunchtime.'

'What it is to be young,' murmured George, as he watched Delia eat.

'Did you over-indulge in your youth?' Delia asked.

'Rarely. During the war, of course . . .'

'Alcohol wasn't always easy to come by,' said Marjorie.

'I was still at school then,' Delia said. 'So I wouldn't remember.'

Delia took Lucius's advice, and lay prostrate under two umbrellas, a heap of books beside her, and a jug of iced water thoughtfully provided by Benedetta, who had also pressed a tiny glass of some fearsome-smelling brown liquid on her.

Delia took a sip of it. 'Poison,' she said. 'Benedetta is a Borgia in disguise, and she's doing away with me.'

Jessica sniffed it. 'It does smell a bit witchy. I'd knock it back if I were you. I expect Benedetta knows all about the morning after the night before. Not personally, of course, but I bet Beatrice Malaspina's arty guests were a merry lot.'

'Talk and wine and smoke far into the night,' said Delia. 'The artistic life.'

'Not smoke for you. You have a voice to look after.' Jessica unfolded a deckchair and settled into it with a book.

'What are you reading now?'

'One of Marjorie's books. I remember enjoying them, so I thought I'd read them again.'

'What's the point if you know whodunnit?'

'They're good stories on their own account. Not all detective stories are, you're quite right, but Marjorie's are witty and well written, and I bet I like them just as much second time round. We'll see.' She opened the book and smoothed the first page with her hand. Then she put the book down on her stomach. 'I can't believe Lucius is going to marry Elfrida. What a waste of a man! Can't we do anything about it?'

'Like reveal all? Try and tell him what Elfrida's really like?'

'I suppose you can't tell a man who's in love frightful things about his betrothed. He wouldn't believe us, for a start.'

'In love? Lucius isn't in love with Elfrida,' said Delia. How could he be? It was all part of his pointless self-sacrifice. 'He's what, in his thirties? His parents, especially his mother, will be nagging away at him to settle down and get married, and if he hasn't got anyone he's in love with, and probably can't fall in love with anyone, not with the distorted, bottled-up life he's leading, then why not Elfrida? Seemingly a perfect wife for a banker, and she's the type to be on the lookout for a rich husband. It's only surprising that she hasn't found one before now.'

'He'll be miserable married to her.'

But just as miserable even with no Elfrida in the frame, thought Delia, recalling his bitter words of self-blame. 'Only perhaps if he had chosen someone else – there must be suitable banker's brides who are kind and funny and – well, nice.'

'Not a class A bitch like Elfrida, you mean?'

Marjorie appeared at the door. 'May I join you?'

Jessica, to Delia's surprise, smiled at her. 'Do,' she said. And she looked as though she meant it, and not as though she were saying inwardly, Please don't, please take your abrasive self elsewhere and leave us in peace.

'You don't have to ask,' Delia said. 'Look, Jessica's got one of your books here.'

'I wish you hadn't,' said Marjorie, embarking on a dangerous wrestling match with a deckchair.

'Let me do that,' said Jessica. 'There's a knack to these damn things.'

'It's a reproach to me,' said Marjorie, settling herself in

the deckchair once it had been persuaded to do its duty. 'I find it hard to think that I ever wrote them. Did I hear you mention Elfrida? Do tell about Elfrida. I was intrigued and longing to know more yesterday, but I can see you didn't want to upset Lucius.'

'Where to begin?' said Jessica. She adjusted her sunglasses. 'She was in our class at school. We had to endure her for five long years.'

'Four,' said Delia. 'She left the year before we did, don't you remember?'

'Oh, yes, to go to finishing school in Switzerland.'

'I thought that was what all you posh girls did, when you left your boarding schools.'

'Not from Yorkshire Ladies, you didn't. Plenty of rich northern girls there, yes, that's true enough, but the school had – still has, I suppose – an ethos of dedication and duty. The headmistress wanted us to go on to university or training college.'

'Or to get married,' said Jessica. 'That was approved of, to the right kind of sober, sensible husband. Although old Mrs Radbert thought eighteen was too young to get married. "Live a little," she used to say to us. "Earn money of your own, because you never know when you may be glad of the training. Even the best regulated of households can go awry."'

'Not like her predecessor, who wouldn't have daughters of divorced parents in the school,' Delia said.

'Ah, the stigma of divorce.'

'It's different these days, isn't it?' said Jessica.

'Not if you're Princess Margaret, it isn't,' said Marjorie.

'Oh, the royal family. They have to live by other rules.'

'I used to love reading school stories,' said Marjorie, wistfully. 'Even long after I was that age. Angela Brazil, and girls called Pauline shooting the winning goal. Midnight feasts in the dorm, and everyone having such fun. Unless you were the class sneak, or didn't play up and play the game, of course. My school was mostly just boring. Large classes and sit still and pay attention and pass exams. I was never very good at exams; my mind was always off wool-gathering. I couldn't get out of there fast enough. Which is funny, when I think how much time I've spent since educating myself.'

'School was pretty beastly, actually,' said Delia.

'The last day of term was good,' Jessica said.

'There seemed to be more first days of term than last days.'

Delia had read some of those books, too, before she was sent away at the outbreak of war. She would, her father said, be safer at school, in the country, than she would be near a manufacturing town like Leeds, which was sure to be bombed flat within a few weeks. She had gone into the junior school at Yorkshire Ladies, a slightly friendlier place than the senior school set in its gaunt Gothic mansion high on the moors.

The girls had hoped that the school might be taken over; stories went the rounds of how first this and then that famous school – where many of the girls had brothers – was being forced to give up its premises for government departments, for the BBC, for the armed forces, to be hospitals. Lunatic asylums, even, one girl had said. They all agreed that Yorkshire Ladies would make a very good lunatic asylum.

'If they made a mistake,' Delia had said, 'and sent somebody who wasn't mad, it wouldn't matter, because after a few months here they would be.'

Camaraderie in the dorms? Not with Elfrida ruling the roost.

'She used to hold trials after lights out,' Delia said.

'Oh, God, yes she did,' said Jessica. 'Elfrida really was the rock bottom, Marjorie. She had her little clutch of cronies and hangers on – she was a terrific queen bee. If you crossed her, then she hauled you up before her, and issued punishments which her helpers saw to it were carried out.'

'Like what?' said Marjorie.

'Being made to stand outside the window in your pyjamas

in sub-zero temperatures. One girl caught pneumonia, so she stopped that.'

'Didn't the girl tell?'

'Didn't dare. But she got her parents to take her away. Burning the back of your hand with a match, that was another favourite.'

'Pity your brother didn't survive,' said Jessica. 'They'd have made a nice couple.'

'I remember being shut in the lav overnight.'

'And she had other tricks,' said Jessica. 'She and her gang used to hide your games kit, so you'd be in trouble. Or spill ink on your work. And when she became a prefect, my goodness, the younger girls paid for it, didn't they? No, Lucius has landed a right one there. Of course, she might have changed.'

'Pigs might fly.'

'Poor Lucius. He's for it, then.'

'I wonder what happened to Rose and Penny,' said Delia. 'They simply used to ignore Elfrida, and somehow they got away with it. They were lesbians.'

'Pashes on the teachers, you mean?' said Marjorie, after a pause.

'No, each other. In fact, they were man mad, from the time they were about twelve. They said what they did together was practising for the real thing. They used to huddle in bed under the eiderdown.'

'Tremendous squeals and so on,' said Jessica.

'I wonder what became of them.'

'I can tell you. Penny married an architect, and has five children. I saw her in London a couple of years ago. She was shopping with her husband. He looked completely exhausted, poor man. I expect she's always jumping on him. And Rose is a very expensive and high-class tart.'

'No! You're making it up. Rose, a tart?'

'She's making a fortune, apparently. We bumped into one

263

another in Harrods a little while back, and had tea. You would not believe what she charges a night. Loves her work, so she tells me, and gets given stacks of lovely prezzies as well.'

Marjorie was looking disconcerted. 'It doesn't sound at all as I'd imagined it. I wish you hadn't told me. I don't think I'll ever be able to read a girls' school story again.'

'What it chiefly was,' said Delia, 'was bitterly, unimaginably cold.'

'And we were always hungry. The food was so awful I can't bear to think of it. With all the stodge and starchy things we ate, we were pasty-faced and puffy and had bad complexions. People say the wartime diet was so wholesome and healthy, without all those nasty fats and practically no meat; well, it's rubbish.'

'Carrots,' said Marjorie. 'The government was always urging us to eat carrots. I never want to see a carrot again, although I used to like them. There was that pilot they kept on bringing out to say that he could see in the dark because of all the carrots he'd eaten.'

Lucius and George came up the steps to the terrace. 'Here you all are,' said Lucius. 'George and I have been doing a bit of tidying up at the top. I must say, it's a wonderfully watery world up there, now the pools are all full. You should come up and have a look.'

'Too hot to hike all the way up there, thank you,' said Delia. 'I'll take your word for it. As far as I'm concerned, as long as the fountains down here continue to flow or gush or trickle as appropriate, I'm happy.'

'We thought we should go and look at the next room in the tower,' said George. 'It has to be faced, and perhaps the codicil will be there.'

'I think the best thing to do with that tower,' said Delia, 'is to lock it and toss the key into the sea.'

'If we did that,' said Lucius, 'then Benedetta would buy a fat fish in the market, and guess what?'

'The key would be there in its stomach,' said Marjorie. 'Like in the legend. It's our destiny, and we can't escape from it. Let's get it over with. In fact, as long as there aren't any more pictures of me, I'll be curious to see what it's like.'

'I can't believe you didn't go and look at the other rooms,' said Jessica. 'What if the codicil is there just waiting for you to pick it up? Wouldn't you kick yourselves, not having found it at once?'

'We simply could not face it, not immediately,' said George. 'And our time is not so limited that some hours or days are of importance. Marjorie believes the next floor will be Purgatory and then Paradise at the top. I hope she is right, although I fear that Purgatory may also be unpleasant.'

'To find out that a perfect stranger knows so much about our private lives is unpleasant whatever she's got on the walls,' said Delia.

Benedetta came out with a basket of fruit and Lucius spoke to her in Italian. Marjorie watched his face. 'He's questioning her about the tower,' she said.

How did she know? It was uncanny the way Marjorie jumped to conclusions on no logical evidence, and odd how often she turned out to be right. Delia tried to distract her. 'You were right, Marjorie, about my mother hardly looking the picture of happiness.'

'What?' said Jessica. 'Is there a picture of Lady Saltford there, too?'

'In the photo of Felicity's wedding, you remember how sour she was, although I can't think why. Everyone said what a perfect couple they were.'

'You sound bitter,' said Marjorie. 'Don't you like your brother-in-law?'

Delia made a quick recovery; she had nearly given herself away there. 'The thing is, Marjorie, that my mother isn't exactly fond of me, and never has been. She doted on my

265

brother, so I suppose when he died she gave up motherliness. She's very attached to Felicity, though.'

George looked at her with concerned dark eyes. 'That is not a happy start in life,' he said. 'I wasn't brought up by my father, so I lacked any paternal affection, but I was greatly loved by my mother, and in that I was fortunate.'

'Your father is fond of you,' Jessica said to Delia. She was peeling an apple, watching the peel fall in a single coil to the plate.

'Is he? You could have fooled me.'

Benedetta had been voluble, although her flow of words was accompanied with much head shaking and many gestures of denial. 'Out with it,' Marjorie said to Lucius, as the door closed behind Benedetta.

'She clams up when you try to get anything out of her about Beatrice Malaspina,' said Lucius. 'However, what adorns the walls of the tower is all Beatrice Malaspina's own work. Unlike the fresco in the drawing room, which you can see was done by different hands. She began working in the tower just after the war, apparently, when she came back to the Villa Dante from England. She must have done all the background first, and the other things . . .' He paused. 'The photographs came later.'

'It's her testament,' said Marjorie. 'This is her real testament, not the one in the lawyer's office.'

Jessica turned to Lucius. 'Did Benedetta look for the codicil in the tower, when the lawyer told her to hunt for it?'

'She said that Beatrice Malaspina told her not to go into the tower on any account. She is convinced it's dangerous, and she's very alarmed that we've taken off the chains and gone inside.'

'Danger is right,' said Lucius. 'I'd rather never set foot in the place again. What an odd woman, to bring us here and offer us the delights of the Villa Dante, and then to smack us in the eyes with that lot.'

'Personally, I have absolutely no desire to see those terrible images on the ground floor ever again, nor to discover more pictures of myself,' said Delia. 'Why don't you and Lucius go, George, and report back?'

'Oh, but you have to go,' said Jessica. 'Otherwise you'll all be imagining things far worse than anything that's actually there. Take an oil lamp, torchlight is always creepy.'

FIVE

At the door to the tower, Delia hung back. 'You go in, and tell me what you find.'

George and Marjorie exchanged glances.

'No,' Lucius said. 'It's courage time for all of us.' He gave Delia a push, and followed her inside, holding the lamp aloft.

They stood at the bottom of the stone staircase in the semi-darkness.

'I'll go first,' said Lucius. 'One of you can catch me if I fall. Those steps look steep and perilous.'

'How old was Beatrice Malaspina? In her eighties,' said Marjorie. 'If she could go up and down, so can we.'

One by one they went up to the gallery on the first floor. They stood for a moment in silence before Lucius said, 'Here goes,' and grasped the iron ring, a more ornate one than downstairs, that hung from a lion's head. 'It's locked,' he said, standing back. 'And no flowerpots in the vicinity.'

'Oh, well,' said Delia, relieved. 'What a shame. Maybe the key will turn up some time.'

Marjorie was standing stock still.

'Come on,' Delia said. 'Back into the sunshine.'

'No,' said Marjorie. 'Let me think. Dante. How do Dante and Virgil get from the Inferno to Purgatory?' She answered the question herself. 'When they get down to the lowest circle of hell, which is all ice, they slide down Lucifer's legs and then go up on to the surface again. Through the centre of the earth and up and on to the next place. So the way to Purgatory is via Hell.'

'If you want to put it like that,' said Delia, impatient to get out of the tower. 'Only there's no way up here from downstairs. George shone his torch all over the ceiling down there, and it's nothing but horrible pictures.'

'I bet the key's down there,' said Lucius. 'Here, hold this and pass me the torch.' He handed the lamp to George and brushed past the others to run back down the stone steps. They heard the door below open, and then, a minute later, it closed with a thud and he was coming up the steps.

'Hanging on a hook beside a charming photo of prisoners in the frozen wastes of what I guess is Siberia,' he announced, holding up a large and ornate key, which he inserted into the lock. He turned the ring again, and this time the door opened.

He stood for a moment in the doorway, as the others hung back, all of them reluctant to see what was inside, then stepped over the threshold.

Delia looked down at the floor, visible even without the lamp. There was much more light in this room, coming from six wider slits in the stone walls, each one set with a slender window. The curls of the apple peel sliding through Jessica's fingers at lunchtime jogged at her mind. Then it came to her. 'The spiral on the floor on the ground floor went anti-clockwise,' she said. 'From left to right. On this floor, it goes the other way.'

'That's something positive, at least,' Marjorie said.

'These windows open,' said George, loosening the catch of the nearest one and letting in a welcome draught of fresh air.

Delia stood in the centre and turned round slowly. On the walls, images were piled on images just as they had been downstairs – but here the pictures were different.

'Daily life,' said Marjorie.

It was just that, a village street, a busy London road in the rain, people waiting at bus stops, an old man snoozing in a wheelchair, a child in a pushchair, a woman diving from a high board, a dog barking at the moon, a house, a cottage, a run-down warehouse; hundreds of overlapping images of life out and about in a bustling world.

'So this is Purgatory? Life?' said Lucius. 'It's a neat conceit.'

Delia wasn't listening. Her eyes had caught sight of a picture containing figures that were all too familiar. She went over to have a closer look.

Marjorie was standing beside her. 'Your sister's wedding day again.'

'Different shot,' said Lucius.

'Where was she married?' Marjorie asked.

It had been a big, fashionable wedding. Vulgar, Lord Saltford said with tart brevity. The venue had been a problem, with Theo insisting on a Church of England ceremony, and Delia's father blasting off about idolatry and popish practices. Theo had decided on the Temple church in London, a suitable venue for a lawyer. Felicity was ravishing, Delia had to admit it, in her Dior wedding dress.

'It was a sham,' she said in a whisper. 'All a sham. He didn't love her, and he doesn't love her now.'

Only Marjorie was close enough to hear, and she just gave Delia an appraising look before going closer to the picture. 'Lovely tiara,' she said.

'It belonged to my grandmother.'

'There's your mother again. You don't take after her, not at all.'

'No. My sister does. I look like my father.'

'Is he in this picture?'

'No.'

Of course, the father and mother of the bride had to enter the church together, and sit in the front so that he could give

270

Felicity away. They came out of the church together, greeting friends and relatives, put on an act for the camera. But this shot had been taken in a more private moment, when Lord and Lady Saltford, who hadn't spoken a word to each other in private for as long as Delia could remember, had separated and gone to join their own friends.

It was Lucius who spotted the photo of Marjorie, high up on a wall next to one of the windows. 'You look a bit bleary-eyed,' he said. 'Was it taken at a party?'

It was typical of Maria, with her casual cruelty, that she should have run off with that man on the day of Marjorie's book launch. They had been shopping and Maria had bought herself a green frock, very chic, very expensive and perfectly suited to her elfin looks. Marjorie had opted for wine velvet. 'I need to look the part,' she'd said. 'Now that they're dubbing me Queen of Crime.'

They were going off for a short holiday the day after the launch, that had been the plan. A few days in the country relaxing in a cottage that belonged to a friend of theirs. Marjorie was well into her new book, and intended to take her typewriter and do some work and gardening while Maria listened to the wireless and cooked delicious food, and in the evening they would play gramophone records while Maria stitched at her embroidery. Marjorie remembered her hands all too vividly, neat and delicate, and the needle stabbing in and out with exquisite precision.

'Who's the witchy little creature?' asked Delia. 'Her face looks familiar. Isn't she an actress? I'm sure I've seen her on television, and in films.'

'Maria Harkness,' said Marjorie, hardly able to bring herself to say the name. 'She was . . . a great friend of mine.'

'Of course. Her life's even more scandalous than Jessica's,' Delia said. 'She's always in the lurid newspapers because she's run away with someone, or someone's wife is accusing her of nameless orgies and breaking up the happy home.'

George had noticed Marjorie's distress. 'I think she was more than a mere friend,' he said to her, in a voice too low for the others to catch.

Marjorie nodded, tight-lipped. 'She tore up my new book before she left. The one I was writing. Into shreds. The top copy and the carbon copy which I hid away for safekeeping. Every page, and all my notes.'

Maria had left a note to her on her typewriter.

You cage me in, you're obsessed with your work, you don't accept that anyone but yourself has an artistic soul. I have to be free of you. I have to lead the life I really want to lead.

The life she wanted to lead. What kind of life had she been leading before she moved in with Marjorie? A bit part actress, rarely in work, eking out a miserable existence as a waitress. Resting, she called it, as actors did.

That was Max's main attraction, she supposed. Max was a producer, and certainly Maria's career had suddenly blossomed. Her kind of looks became fashionable; she was working, and becoming a name. Marjorie, hating herself for doing it, had gone to a performance of a play she was in in the West End, a silly, trivial drawing room piece, where she had played the maid, the soubrette. She would never be anything more than a soubrette; she had the soul of a soubrette. Marjorie had left after the interval and gone home to her flat, the flat which she had shared with Maria, where they had been so happy. A flat rapidly becoming denuded of its good furniture and nice things, as the money ran inexorably out.

Purgatory, not Hell? No. Just part and parcel of the general suffering of life, the price you paid for loving anyone. It had been her reaction to Maria's departure that truly belonged in Hell, as Beatrice Malaspina had, in her extraordinary way, known.

'Is there a picture of you here?' she said to George.

*　　*　　*

272

There were several pictures of George. A schoolboy in short trousers, baggy ones that came to his knees. A serious, dark-haired child, with owlish wire spectacles, staring uncertainly into the camera. In the background were blurred figures on the move, other boys, a man in a black soutane. Then another one with a serious expression, a studio portrait taken in Paris of him in academic robes, his roll of parchment held in his hand. There he was in Cambridge, riding his bicycle out of the gates of Trinity, still in owlish spectacles. It seemed to be raining, and the billowing gown was a testament to the bitter winds that howled into the city from the steppes. And that was a snapshot taken in his digs, in Richmond Terrace, a dingy little room, with a bed and a desk and a small window.

'How dismal,' Marjorie exclaimed, before she could help herself. After all, when she considered how shabby and depressing her recent abodes had been, who was she to cast stones?

'Appalling,' said George. 'And dreadful food. I do dislike English food. I am an exile, I think this is what these photographs say of me. Lost in the scientific life, with no joys beyond those of the intellect. Then, when those fail,' he said to himself, 'what is one left with?'

Lucius was looking at a set of photographs of himself. A graduation picture, Harvard, class of '50. A snapshot of him in a Norwegian pullover, leaning on crutches; that was the winter he came a cropper on the ski slopes. Going in through the doors of the marble-fronted building of the bank, dark-coated, indistinguishable from all the other men around him. At the White House, with his parents, in formal dress, a presidential reception for generous donors and fundraisers. His mother was a whizz at fundraising.

Purgatory? Just life. These photographs aroused no emotion in him. Unlike the photos in the room below.

SIX

Delia's eyes were dazzled.

Lucius had silently taken the key from its hook in the first-floor room, where it hung from a painted dovecote. This wasn't a heavy old key, but a gleaming modern brass one, which fitted smoothly into the polished lock on the floor above.

All their eyes were dazzled as the door swung back; that was the first, overwhelming impression as they one by one went through the narrow doorway into the top room of the tower: light. Sunlight came pouring through the windows placed all round the tower, not wide, but letting in the light to reflect and bounce off the glittering walls. Outside, a bird was singing its heart out, and as it paused another took up the song.

There were no collages here, no superimposed images. Instead, the uneven surface of the wall had been covered in pieces of ceramic tile, making a shifting brilliant mosaic of white and black and red and gold and orange.

'Like a Klimt,' said Lucius.

'It's breathtaking,' said Delia.

'However did she spend five minutes in here without going blind?' said Marjorie.

'The interplay of light and colour is extraordinary,' said George. He went over to one of the windows. 'And the view! It is indeed paradise.'

Delia joined Lucius at another window. Below them rolled a landscape out of time, green, full of the promise of spring, a tapestry of cypresses, fields, neat lines of vines, olive groves, each with its distinctive colour. The hills looked as though their curves could only have been made by a painter's hand, and beyond it all was the deep blue of the shining sea.

'This is straight out of Perugino, this landscape,' said Lucius, who seemed to have been holding his breath and now let it out in a long whistle.

'How beautiful,' said Marjorie. She had tears in her eyes. 'It is so beautiful that it hurts. All that misery and horror downstairs, and then this. How did she make a room like this?'

George was examining the walls. 'Every tile is different. It is not like a mosaic where all the tiles are ceramic squares. Here she has taken larger tiles and broken them up, and then found a piece to match every roughness and indentation of the wall. This was painstaking work, which must have taken a long time.'

'Maybe she wore glare glasses,' said Marjorie, who was still blinking from the brilliance of the light. 'Or maybe it was a winter room, or she worked in the evening, when there were shadows.'

'She certainly came up here at night,' said George. 'Here is a very fine and powerful telescope, she was a stargazer as well.'

'At least there are no pictures relating to any of us here,' said Delia with relief in her voice, a relief that was flooding over her, for although she hadn't known what to expect, she had been bracing herself for further revelations of a kind she would rather not have to face.

She spoke too soon. Marjorie had opened a leather-bound

book which lay on the table in the centre of the room, and she let out a little cry. 'That's what you think, is it? Just look at this photo album. I don't know who those are of, but since these are me, I expect all the others are of you three. What is this? What is she up to?'

Lucius was flicking through the pages of the album, a wry smile on his face. 'Marjorie's right, as she always is,' he said. 'This is a snapshot of me as a kid.'

Delia stood at his shoulder and looked at the picture of a little boy, no more than eight or nine. He was sitting on the bank of a river, wearing shorts and a floppy hat, and his knees were drawn up so that he could rest a pad on them. In his hand was a pencil. He was utterly absorbed.

'And completely happy,' said Delia softly.

'These are pictures of our happiness,' said Marjorie.

'Perhaps,' said Lucius. He turned a page. 'I fancy this is you, Delia.'

She couldn't believe her eyes. The photo was of a small girl of about five, in a bathing dress, holding a shrimping net in one hand and a bucket in the other. Beside her was a tall man wearing an old-fashioned bathing suit with a vest top. He was gazing down at the girl with a smiling fondness that brought a lump to Delia's throat. 'That's me, and my father. A summer holiday, 1935 or 6. I remember it so well. My mother couldn't come, and so just the four of us went off, my father and Felicity and me and Nanny. It was wonderful. I was so happy. Oh!' Her hand flew to her mouth. 'What a magician! How did she ever get hold of such a picture? You're right, Marjorie, that's what these are, our moments of happiness. Go on, Lucius, have a look at the other pictures.'

There was Marjorie, in another seaside snapshot of her as a lanky girl on a donkey. 'Margate, 1924,' said Marjorie at once. 'There's Pa, laughing at me, and Ma waving at the camera.'

'Here's George,' said Delia. 'I'd know those dark eyes of yours anywhere, George. Is that your mother?'

There was a long silence as George looked at the photograph, now a sepia colour, and not sharply in focus. 'Yes,' he said at last. 'That was taken one summer when I was about fourteen. That's my mother – that hat with the flowers was always her favourite hat. I loved that hat. And that man in the soutane is Father Xavier. This was taken at my school.'

'A Jesuit school?' said Lucius.

'Yes. My father was a Catholic, and he wanted me to be educated by the fathers.'

'Wasn't your mother Catholic?' Marjorie asked.

Another long silence.

'No, she was Lutheran, as are most Danes.' He gave a strange little sigh, and then the words began to tumble out, in a manner most uncharacteristic of him.

'My parents never married. I am illegitimate, a bastard,' he said, with a world of bitterness in his voice. 'My mother met my father when she was studying in Germany. He was German. They fell in love, but he was already married. Unhappily, but there was no question of a divorce, he was a very devout Catholic. It was impossible.'

Not devout enough to skip the adultery, thought Delia with a flash of anger at what men and women did so heedlessly and what pain it could cause their children.

'My mother went back to Denmark, and I was born there.' George turned and smiled at Delia. 'My family were very much as you say your father is, strait-laced, strict in their morals. I think my mother had a hard time of it, and they wanted me to be sent for adoption, or even to an orphanage, but she wouldn't have it. My father sent money, always, and sometimes, in the summer, we were able to be together.' He had been looking through the pages of the album as he spoke. 'There,' he said. 'There we are, on the boat on Lake Geneva. My father was a fine yachtsman.'

'And a very handsome man,' said Delia, looking at the smiling man at the tiller of the yacht, the white sail billowing out above the head of a woman in a floral frock and George, younger here, wearing white shorts. He had a solemn expression on his face as he clutched a rope. 'Why aren't you smiling, George?'

'Don't let that deceive you. It was a very happy day. I was only anxious lest I should let the halyard slip at the wrong moment. Here is another picture of us, some years later, in Berlin. That was just before Christmas, and very cold. My father had taken me into a toyshop, to buy me a Christmas present.'

'What did he give you?' Marjorie asked.

Now George laughed with real humour. 'Would you believe it? I'd wanted a microscope. They had them in the toyshop, but not good ones, only to play with. So my father at once took us to the shop that sold scientific instruments and bought me a really good microscope.' His face grew sombre again. 'I have it still.' He pointed at the photograph. 'That's it, in that package under my arm. You see how I'm hugging it.'

'Are your parents still alive?'

'My mother is. My father . . . My father died in the war.'

'Here you are, in academic cap and gown,' said Delia, hoping to move him away from what were obviously, now, far from happy memories. 'Isn't it odd,' she exclaimed, 'how looking at pictures of times when one was happy makes one sad in the present.'

'Sad that the happiness doesn't last?' said Lucius. 'Very true. That's an impressive gown, George. What were you getting?'

'Those are my doctoral robes, at Cambridge. A very proud day. There is my mother, you see, so pleased.'

'Who is the young woman beside her?' asked Marjorie.

'That is Marilyn.'

'Marilyn?'

'She was my wife. We married shortly after that day. Here we are, outside the register office. Another happy day.'

'I had no idea you were married,' said Delia, and then could have bitten her tongue off; George was so obviously not married at the moment. Whatever had happened to that smiling, pretty, curly-haired Marilyn?

'She died during the war,' George said, looking into a place that only he could see. 'Not from a bomb or anything like that. She had tuberculosis. And of course, at that time there was no question of travelling to Switzerland, to the mountain air that might have saved her. The English climate is not kind to TB patients; there isn't the sun or the dry air that heals the lungs. And that was in the days before antibiotics. So . . . she died. She was twenty-three.'

George straightened. 'This Beatrice Malaspina makes fools of us all. Like Marjorie, I have no understanding at all of how she obtained these pictures. Marjorie, this is you, in trousers. How can you look so very cheerful when you are clearly working so hard?'

'Digging for victory,' said Marjorie. 'That was in 1942. I'm always happy when I'm grubbing about in the ground or digging. How could one be happy in such dark times, you might say, but yet, at that moment, I was. Yes, I was tired, working so hard, with the ambulance driving and the digging and the sheer hassle of living – you'll remember that, George – but I had friendship, love even, and I was writing well, with precious moments snatched at my typewriter.'

'And here's another one of you,' Delia said.

Lucius laughed. 'I don't know who looks more startled, you or the horse.'

Marjorie was seated astride a gorgeously caparisoned horse, with a woman holding the bridle and smiling up at her. 'That was Polly. The girl, not the horse. The horse was called Jenkins, don't ask me why. She was a school friend, who ran away to join the circus. She loved horses. I wonder where she is now? Before the war, I used to go and help out. Touchy, private folk in the circus world, but once they get to know you they're very kind. She married a trapeze artist, and went to America.' She turned to Lucius, her face alight with pleasure at the memory. 'Perhaps you saw them when you were taken to the circus as a boy.'

'Perhaps I did,' said Lucius. 'I loved the trapeze acts. This is a very formal picture, Marjorie. Were you happy then?'

'Yes, because it was taken for the newspapers when my third book was published – that was the first one to be a bestseller. And this is a group photograph taken at the Detection Club. However did she obtain this? Everything about the Detection Club is private. There's Dorothy Sayers, and that's Margery Allingham.'

'And that man with the vast stomach has to be G.K. Chesterton,' said Lucius. 'Who's the guy with the moustache?'

'John Creasey. We did have such good times at the club dinners.'

'Is it still going?' said Delia.

'Oh, yes. It's an institution.'

'Do you still belong?'

'Once you're admitted, you're a member for life. Only I haven't been for some while. It's not the place to be, among your fellow writers when they're still being published and you haven't written a word for five years.'

'Who's this?' asked Lucius. It was a strange snapshot, of Marjorie taking a photograph of another woman. Marjorie was peering down intently into the glass of her camera, while the woman was peeking out from behind an ornate screen with a saucy expression on her face, displaying a shapely leg encased in a net stocking with a red satin slipper on her foot.

Marjorie's mouth tightened. 'It's just as Delia says. I was happy then, at that moment, but now . . . To look at that picture now brings me no happiness at all. That's Violet. She was dressing up for a panto we were both taking part in. She played Prince Charming. It was an Arts Club affair, for charity.'

'What were you?' said Delia.

'Not the Widow Twanky, in case you were wondering. That was played by John Neville, the actor. I was the Wicked Witch of the West.'

Delia was looking through the pictures of Lucius. 'Here you are in shorts and singlet, winning a race. What a triumphant look on your face.'

'The hundred yards at my prep school,' said Lucius. 'And that's me at college. I was Robin Oakapple in *Ruddigore*. Delia, do you know any Gilbert and Sullivan?'

Marjorie looked pleased. 'Are you a Gilbert and Sullivan fan? They put on terrible productions at the Savoy these days, but I do like the music and the humour.'

'I, too, have sung in Gilbert and Sullivan,' said George, even more surprisingly. 'I played the Chancellor in *Iolanthe*.'

They all looked at Delia. 'I love it,' said Delia. 'As it happens.'

'Well,' said Marjorie, 'according to this, Lucius, you haven't had a happy moment, at least not one Beatrice Malaspina could get her hands on, since that photo of the college production. No, I'm wrong. Who's this enchanting-looking woman?'

Lucius looked amazed, and then smiled. 'Now, that's a picture that causes me no sadness at all. That's my grand-mother. My maternal grandmother. Isn't she a honey? And can you see the portrait behind her head? That was my grand-father. Look at the twinkle in his eye.'

'You're very like him,' Marjorie said.

'I don't remember him so well, because he died when I was quite small. He was much older than Grandma. She loved him very much. Everyone did. Even my father, who rather disapproves of that side of the family, reckons they're raffish, said my grandfather was a man who had more charm and kindness than anyone he'd ever met.'

'Did your mother inherit the charm? Is that why your father fell in love with her?'

'She inherited her mother's looks, because my grandma was certainly a looker when she was young . . .'

'She's pretty good even in this picture,' said Marjorie. 'And she must be what, past seventy?'

'Yes. No, my mother doesn't have the charm.' Or the kindness, he added, under his breath.

'But you got the charm,' Marjorie said, equally quietly, but not so quietly that Delia didn't catch her words.

Charm! Yes, he did have charm, that elusive and inexplicable thing that outlasted looks and even sex appeal. Theo had sex appeal, and so did Richie, but neither of them had an ounce of charm.

'Charm can be very superficial,' she said, sounding priggish even to her own ears.

'Do you think so?' said Marjorie. 'I think it's one of the great gifts of the gods. Beatrice Malaspina had charm, no doubt about it.'

Delia had quickly turned over the pages which had to do with her and her moments of happiness. Up here in the tower, with the four of them bound together by the power of the strange Beatrice Malaspina, there was too much of the confessional in the air. George, that most reserved of men, had come out with all that about his mother, so very personal, and yet he didn't seem to mind. There was Lucius, revealing his affection for his grandmother, and Marjorie, quite open about her friendships with girls. But she wasn't going to fall into that trap. She was afraid of these photos. She didn't want to look at them herself, nor did she want the others to see them, and to ask when? and where? and who?

Lucius quietly but firmly took the album from her. He laid

it down, and opened it at the first page. 'Let's go through the pictures page by page, not just peeking here and there. Perhaps there's a clue here about how Beatrice Malaspina got hold of them.'

'And why. The why is more important than the how. One is a practical matter, the other is about motivation. What was – is – she up to? What does she want from us?'

'And what has it to do with the codicil?' While Delia and Lucius and Marjorie had their heads down over the album, George had been making a quiet but thorough search of the room. 'I am certain that the codicil is not here,' he said, pushing the final drawer back in.

'That's what Beatrice Malaspina meant us to do,' said Marjorie. 'Go through the album, remembering everything that's in the photos.'

'I think better not here, in this beautiful room,' said George. 'These pictures remind us all of times when we were happy, but, as Marjorie says, that brings pangs, that we no longer have such happiness in our lives. All of us have come to the Villa Dante with some degree of unhappiness. I think for all of us, this time marks a change in our lives, a decisive moment, when we may go one way or the other. And, although I am a private man and I do not care to have any element of my life exposed to the indifferent or curious gaze of other people, I think that Beatrice Malaspina intended us to share these moments she has selected for us to see. With one another, with no one else.'

'You're right,' said Marjorie. 'The other pictures are plastered to the walls, these aren't. So she meant these ones to be removed. Of course, George, it isn't just us. It's Jessica as well.'

'I do not in the least mind Jessica looking into my past,' said George at once. 'I should have included her. Beatrice Malaspina may not have invited her, as the rest of us, or intended her to be here, but . . .'

'Fate has brought her here at the same time as us, is what you won't say,' said Marjorie. 'Fate not being a suitable force for scientists to consider.'

'I am coming to believe that Beatrice Malaspina is not a force which can be explained by any scientific reasoning,' said George with a smile.

'Let's go,' said Lucius. 'And keep your views to yourself, George. They're just too unsettling for me. A week ago, I would have said that my life was proceeding in an orderly way and I wouldn't have said I was unhappy. Not happy, either, but getting along fine with things. Certainly no turning points or decisive moments on the horizon.'

'Marrying Elfrida will be a decisive moment all right,' Delia muttered to Marjorie as they followed the other two down the stone staircase and out into the sunshine.

'It doesn't seem as bright out here as it did up in that top room,' remarked Lucius. 'What an artist the woman was. I begin to wonder how much of the rest of the stuff around the house was done by her. Oh, not all of it. I recognise some very famous hands have been at work, but some of those frescoes . . .'

'I thought they were old.'

'Many of them are,' said Lucius. 'Some aren't. Anyhow, I'm going to have a closer look.'

'After we've gone through the album,' said Marjorie.

'No,' said Delia. 'I don't want to look at any more photos now. Enough is enough; one can't have all one's past exposed is so short a time. I need to adjust. And it's only fair, there are far more photos of me than of the rest of you.'

'Perhaps you have been happier than us,' said Marjorie.

'Perhaps I just had more photographs taken. Although I'd have thought there'd be more of you, Lucius. Don't they take photos all the time in snap-happy America?'

'My mother took most of the photos, and she prefers more formal shots. She doesn't care to have a record of any of us with mussed-up hair or squinting into the sun. Best of all are studio pictures, a perfect image to smile upon the world from a silver frame.'

'Who ever looked happy in a studio photo?' said Marjorie.

SEVEN

'How was the tower?' Jessica asked, coming out of the villa to meet them.

'Exquisite.'

'Enchanting.'

'So beautiful, you won't believe it.'

'Sensational.'

'You have to go and look.'

'Well, I shall, in due course, although I feel the tower is very much private property and no trespassers allowed. What's this? You haven't found the codicil slipped between the leaves of a book, have you?'

'It is a photograph album, from the top floor of the tower.'

'Our happy moments, would you believe it?' said Delia lightly. 'Although how Beatrice Malaspina knew that's what they were, heaven only knows. She seems to have been spot on, so far, but there are heaps of me which I don't especially want to look at.'

'You were happy, a lot,' said Jessica. 'Is it for your eyes only, or may I look too?'

'Not now, it's lunchtime,' said Delia. 'When was I happy?'

'Mostly when you weren't anywhere near your family.

When you were in those harum-scarum moods, not that I've noticed you in any of those recently. And I suspect the album may be fairly thin on the last three or four years.'

After a large lunch, Jessica expressed complete satisfaction and a thorough sense of well-being. 'Pythonesque, but feeling good,' she announced.

Lucius laughed at her, and followed her out to where her deckchair sat in the midst of a pile of books.

'Good stuff Marjorie writes,' she said. 'Gripping. Although I confess I did nod off once or twice, but that was sleepiness and the sun, not Marjorie's prose. Aren't the others coming out?'

'George has gone for a walk. I think he is in a reflective mood, as he seems to be quite a lot. Something's worrying him. He won't say what it is, so we can't help.'

'It's something to do with his work, Marjorie says.'

'It could be. She and Delia have gone upstairs so that Marjorie can try on a dress, one of those garments so mysteriously hanging in the cupboards.'

'Have a deckchair,' said Jessica. 'Benedetta's bringing coffee out.'

Lucius did some efficient work with a deckchair, earning a coo of admiration from Jessica. 'That's the stuff to give the troops, show it who's boss. Delia and I get tied up in knots with the horrid things, and Benedetta will insist on Pietro's putting them away every night.'

'I expect she thinks the dew will make the fabric shrink and rot,' said Lucius.

Jessica lay back and closed her eyes, only to open them again at Lucius's direct question. 'Is Delia in love with your brother Theo?'

'I didn't have you down as a gossip.'

'I'm not, but there's some mystery there, and I, well, I guess I'm just curious.'

To his fury, he found himself reddening, and hoped his tan was sufficient to hide it, but he was safe for the moment. Jessica was looking into the distance.

'Of course, if you feel it's betraying a friendship . . .'

'First, you tell me where you got that idea from.'

'The photographs. Why should her sister's wedding be down there in Hell? And from her reaction to the photo. That's hell, if you like, to be in love with your sister's husband.'

'She isn't,' Jessica said firmly.

They sat in silence for a few moments, until Jessica gave in. 'All right, she was in love with Theo. Very much so. She wanted to marry him. Only he met Felicity, and that was that.'

'He preferred that piece of perfection to Delia?'

'I like the incredulity in your voice. I will say one bitchy thing, although Theo is my brother: Felicity is due to inherit more than Delia.'

'That is a bitchy remark,' he said appreciatively. 'How do you get on with your brother?'

'So-so. He's a stuffed shirt, and he likes to lay down the law.'

'Whyever did Delia fall for him?'

'He's also handsome and has sex appeal. So my girlfriends tell me. He's great buddies with my husband, so we don't get along too well together at the moment.'

'Tell me about your husband.'

'You want to know what a shit I married? Are you sure? It's a tale to make those statues weep. But it might be good for you to hear it, after all, you're about to take the plunge with Elfrida, aren't you?'

Lucius was taken aback. 'I beg your pardon?'

'Sorry if my words offend you, but you asked.'

She put her sunglasses on. Lucius lay back in his deckchair and waited.

'Richie Meldon. Hmm, what can I say about Richie? Where and when did I meet him? When I was working for his father, Tom Meldon, who's as bad as his son, but more open about it. That was one job I really would have done better not to take. So, let me start with Richie as the world sees him, Richie the darling of the press. I'll give you the who's who, right? Born around 1920. Public school, can't remember which one, oh, yes I can, one of those tough northern ones, Barnard Castle, or was it Sedbergh? All rugger and team spirit and fostering male values. Funny choice, given that his father's so left wing.' She paused, thinking of the Meldons, father and son. 'Tom Meldon's a rags-to-riches man. Very ragged, lot of riches. Anyhow, back to Richie. He joined up as soon as war broke out; he'd already learned to fly, Daddy's money coming in handy again, and he went straight into the RAF as a pilot. He was an ace flyer, and came through the war without a scratch. There were always pictures of him in the papers, even then, with a white scarf round his neck, grinning all over his face, arm draped round a WAAF or the tea lady. Handsome, daring, successful.'

'You can't knock him for having a good war.'

'Only a man would call it a good war. I call it a violent and bloody war. Yes, I know it was a necessary war, but it still makes me shudder. After the war he was still always in the news, driving a fast car in some desert rally, riding in steeplechases, dipping about the country in his plane.'

'Good copy for the press men, I can see that.'

'He had to have a career, he couldn't just sit about looking pretty. So he decided to go into politics. He was instantly picked for a safe Tory seat – you know about Tories?'

'They're the Conservatives, is that right?'

'That's it. The right wing. Labour are the socialists, which you'll know if you're in banking, because naturally you bankers don't care for the socialists. Reds, don't you call them?'

'People do.'

'In England, we do if we don't like them. Richie's father's a red, although perhaps more of a pale pink these days. He was put in the Lords by the Attlee government. He gave a pot of money to the party, I expect; that's the usual thing.'

'So they're on opposite sides? Isn't that unusual? In America, when you get these political dynasties, it's like father, like son. The Republicans produce Republican sons and ditto the Democrats.'

'Richie joined the Tory party because he smelt defeat coming for Labour, and he wanted to go into Parliament on the winning side. If Labour had been in power, he'd have stood for them; it's in his nature to be among the rulers.'

She took her glasses off and rubbed her eyes. 'Honestly, I don't want to talk any more about Richie. If you want any further details, ask Delia. She saw through him straight away. If only I'd listened to her, I wouldn't be in this hole now.'

'So why did you marry him?'

Jessica looked out across the garden. She heard the lazy hum of a bee flying past, the sudden trill of a bird, the bark of a dog in the distance; saw the vibrant greens of the trees and plants and the brilliant colours of the May flowers, the great deep blue dome of the sky above her, and an honesty born of the moment compelled her to say what she hadn't admitted to herself or to anyone else. 'I married him because he was rich.'

EIGHT

Delia and Marjorie sat side by side on the sofa, looking through the photograph album.

'This is me when I was three, with my first tricycle,' said Delia. That had been a lovely day. Looking at the photo, it came sweeping back to her. 'I remember it so clearly.' The trike was red, although her father said black would have been a more practical colour. 'That's Nanny. She was my support and comfort. Far more of a mother to me than my actual mother.'

'It's odd how the richer and more upper class people are, the less time they want to spend with their children. You'd think it would be the other way round.'

Delia had flipped on to some photos of Marjorie. 'This is the one of you and the donkey again, and here's a pony with his ears jutting through a hat.'

'That's Codger, who pulled my father's cart. When I was little, we took our produce to market with a horse and cart.'

'Do you have copies of these photographs?' Delia asked.

Marjorie shook her head. 'I don't, and what's more I can't remember ever seeing them. Since both my parents are dead, I can't ask them, and nothing was left when their house was hit.'

'That's the real mystery – how Beatrice Malaspina got hold of all these. It's all very well to say press cuttings, but that can't be where she got some of these very personal ones.'

'Perhaps she employed a firm of private detectives.'

'Do you think so? It would explain some of them, I suppose.'

'The only explanation, but what an expense! They don't come cheap.'

'I don't think money was an object with Beatrice Malaspina.'

'No. And when she made up her mind she wanted something, that was it. Determination is a large part of her make-up.'

'I do like it the way you speak of her as though she's still here. I do wish she were, and we could ask her all our questions.'

'She isn't, so we just have to puzzle it out for ourselves. I like the look of your father. He has a kind face.'

Delia tilted her head to look at the photo. 'Kind? I wouldn't call him kind.'

'Would he kick a dog, or shoot a cat?'

'Oh, good Lord no, never, not in a thousand years.' Delia was laughing, then she grew abruptly serious. 'No, in my family we left all that kind of thing to my brother Boswell.' Whom did he inherit his vicious streak from? Her mother? Her father?

'So you'd agree that your father, if not kind, isn't unkind.'

'Marjorie, why are you harping on my father? What does it matter whether he's kind or unkind? He's an austere man, and a just man. He hates alcohol and tobacco, and lives what he would call a moral life. There's nothing more to say about him.'

'He has a fascinating face. Not the face of a narrow man at all. He doesn't look disapproving.'

'He doesn't have to. His own life is so perfect, he can

afford to look down on everyone else who fails to live up to his high standards with an air of sad detachment.'

Marjorie was riffling through the leaves of the album, looking for more pictures of Delia. 'There are none here of your parents together. Isn't it a happy marriage?'

What a joke. 'Is there any such thing as a happy marriage? My mother's an enchantress. She cast a spell over him, he married her, and then I suppose disillusionment set in. They are perfectly pleasant and civil to one another in public and never say a word if it's just family.'

'They don't quarrel?'

'Not as far as I know. They used to, when I was little. Not for years. If they don't speak, how can they quarrel?'

'Does their estrangement have anything to do with the death of your brother?'

Delia was remembering the first time she went home after hearing that Boswell had died in action.

'My father didn't care that my brother had been killed,' she said. 'That's odd, if you like. My mother was upset, although it was silent grief, not sobs and lamentations. She was English to her fingertips. My father didn't say a word about it, never showed that he minded in the slightest. A letter came later on from his commanding officer, saying that he had died gallantly, a wonderful officer, missed as a friend as well as an outstanding soldier. My father said, not so that my mother could hear, but I did, "What lies these men tell."'

'It must have been hard on your mother, if your father despised his only son. Why don't they divorce, if it's such a cold marriage?'

'You're very persistent. Do drop it.' For a moment, Delia was tempted to close the album, stand up, stretch, say she'd had enough of boring old photos and the past, and she was going to go down to the beach for a bathe. Only she didn't. There was something compelling about Marjorie and her probing questions. 'My father is implacably opposed to divorce. That vow you take in church is binding as far as he's concerned. His marriage has mostly been worse rather than better, but I expect he thinks that's just part of God's way of testing him.'

'Your mother could leave. She could get a divorce.'

'My mother's family don't divorce. They haven't ever, none of them, not in generations, ever had a divorce. Not a brother or a sister or even a cousin has ever sullied themselves by ending up in the divorce courts. It just isn't done.'

'How fascinating, in this day and age,' said Marjorie. 'So are they placid English squires, or do they simply take lovers, like those families in the days of the Regency who were all in and out of one another's beds?'

'I have no idea what my mother may or may not have done,' Delia said in a chilling voice. 'Really, it's no business of mine, and certainly none of yours.'

'Ah, up go the keep-off signs,' said Marjorie with perfect good humour.

'My father fell in love with a beautiful face and a fascinating personality,' said Delia stiffly. 'It's not an uncommon story, is it? I don't suppose Lucius is in love with Elfrida – I don't see how he could be. Yet he's going to marry her, and I dare say they'll rub along together as people do. Isn't that in the end what marriage is all about?'

'I wouldn't know,' said Marjorie.

'Do you regret never having married?'

'There was never the slightest possibility of my marrying,' said Marjorie. 'Who's this man you're with here? Now here you do really look happy.'

'I was in love,' said Delia, barely able to look at the photo. However had it come into Beatrice Malaspina's possession? Theo had given the camera to a passing stranger, who had snapped them, his arm round her shoulders, her laughing up at him, alive with affection and happiness. She had had three prints made, one for her, one for him and one for safekeeping, because she couldn't bear the thought of losing any image of him.

'I tore my copy of that photo up,' she said. 'That's Theo. Yes, the man who married my sister, before you ask. He was my lover and I was passionately in love with him.'

Marjorie's eyes gleamed. 'Now why did he marry your sister instead of you?'

Marjorie and her whys. 'Because she enchanted him, just as my mother did my father. Felicity has that kind of power; she beckons to men and they come.'

'A Circe,' said Marjorie. 'So he wasn't as much in love with you as you were with him?'

'Of course he was.'

'He must be a remarkable man if he could be so much in love with two people at the same time.'

'He wasn't in love with Felicity. I tell you, she's an enchantress, and she flattered him, and she's beautiful and glamorous. Stunning, actually. It was a momentary thing, that's all, only he woke up and found he was married to her.'

'He must be a very weak man, then, to let himself be pulled to and fro like that by a pair of women.'

Delia flared to his defence. 'He's a very purposeful man, he's a brilliant lawyer, he's not in the least bit weak. I would never fall in love with a weak man, I'd simply despise him if he were like that. Don't forget, Felicity has money, or will have money. She's the older sister; she thinks she'll get the lion's share of any inheritance from my father, and I know she'll get the money my mother was going to leave to Boswell.'

'How do you know?'

'She told me so.'

She'd done so quite casually. 'Oh, Mummy isn't going to leave you anything more than a string of pearls. The lawyers explained it all to me. She made a new will when Boswell died. She says Daddy will provide for you. The money that she inherited from her father will come to me.'

That had stung Delia. No, stung was too mild a word. Yet it wasn't as though she didn't know how little her mother cared for her, in comparison to Felicity, whom she adored. 'So Felicity will be much richer than me.'

'Are you still in love with him?'

Delia's answer was evasive. 'I hardly ever see him.'

'It's a good basis for murder.'

'I don't want to murder Theo.'

'No, but perhaps you think, in the deepest recesses of your heart, that life might be better for you if Felicity weren't there.'

Delia shook her head. 'I don't want Felicity dead, I just wish she'd stayed in America, never met Theo, never married him. It's rather beastly to start making up murder plots around me.'

'We novelists make up stories all the time, that's our job, and we put them down on paper. We make patterns to lives. That's why people like stories, whether they're told them at their mother's knee or they read a detective novel on the train going to work. That's what everyone wants, a pattern.'

Delia sat back, and pushed the album away. 'Happy moments,' she said bitterly. 'If Beatrice Malaspina had meant us to recall happy moments, she hadn't bargained on having you around, had she?' She got up, and stretched, and said she was going for a swim.

Marjorie didn't offer to accompany her. 'I'm going back to the tower,' she said, closing the album and laying it on the table, not casually, Delia noticed, but with care, as though it were a precious object. 'The light was so bright that I was half blinded. I'm going to put on my sunglasses and have another look round. And then sit and drink in the view. I shall wave to you, if I see you in the sea.'

Delia escaped, and went to get into her bathing things. She was about to put on her usual swimsuit, when she hesitated. She'd brought another one with her as a spare, a costume in kingfisher blue speckled with the other colours of a kingfisher's wing, a jewel of a bathing suit. She'd bought it on an impulse, suddenly drawn by the vivid colours, and then had never worn it. Now she put it on, and took up her robe and towel. Marjorie and her stories; the woman really is half mad, with all her voices and wild theories. No wonder she can't write any more if she's got a head full of all that pseudo-psychological stuff.

NINE

They had put the key to the tower back under the flowerpot.
Why, Marjorie asked herself as she bent to pick it up. Who
was it locked against? Benedetta? She was prepared to bet
that Benedetta knew exactly what was in the tower, and
wasn't in the least interested in it. Or probably still thought
that it was indeed dangerous. *Pericoloso!* 'Well, Beatrice
Malaspina,' she said aloud as she let herself in, 'your notice
was spot on. Dangerous is precisely what this tower is. Not
crumbling stones, but a lot of other crumbling going on.'

She had no intention of looking at the ground floor room;
who could want to be reminded of the horrors of war in
such a powerful and dramatic way? Maybe it didn't have the
same impact on Delia, but she had lived through the Blitz
and all she wanted to do was forget it. Nor did she care to
linger on the Purgatory floor. No, it was the top room, with
its shimmering light and beauty, that drew her. She climbed
the final flight of stairs and opened the door into the round
chamber. She had been holding her breath, apprehensive that
it might not be as magical as she remembered it.

She went slowly round the windows, looking out each time
at the fragment of view stretched out before her, a close one
of the olive groves, a distant one of the sea, a more distant

one still of undulating hills, rolling away for ever, dotted with farmhouses and cypress trees.

She went to the table. There was a wooden box lying there, which she opened. Paints. Not surprising; she would be happy to paint up here herself if she were an artist. Had Beatrice Malaspina sat up here, making those drawings for the notebook they had found? Self-contained, self-motivated, had she been a happy woman? There was a relish and an exuberance to the sketches and the notes that made it seem so.

Then the notebook was forgotten, as she saw what she was looking for on the floor, under a chair. Something she had noticed from the corner of her eye, just before the astonishing revelations of the photo album. She crouched down and drew out a small portable typewriter, in a zip case. She looked down at it for a moment, then took it over to the table. She unzipped the case and took out the machine. A modern one, and, it seemed, in excellent condition. Had it been used for typing letters? Would a woman of Beatrice Malaspina's generation ever have typed letters? Business letters, perhaps. To her lawyer.

Codicils, for example. She could try it out, if there were any paper. On an impulse, she pulled at the handle of one of the drawers in the table. It opened easily, and inside was a boxed ream of typing paper, a fresh typewriter ribbon, still in its cellophane wrapping, a typing eraser and a selection of pencils.

Thank you, she said aloud. She had no hesitation now. She took everything out and closed the drawer. Then she zipped the typewriter up in its case again. Why? Was there any hope of her writing again? Probably not, but just to have the typewriter gave her a feeling of warmth, of familiarity. These were her tools, this was a gift to her from Beatrice Malaspina, and presents, she had been brought up to believe, must always be accepted with a good grace.

She lifted the typewriter by its handle. There was a table in her room that would be just right.

* * *

Ten minutes after Marjorie had gone, George was climbing the stairs. The light drew him, the light and the circular room and the views had given him a feeling of comfort and serenity which was a rare sensation these days. It was almost like a chapel, a place where one was in the presence of – what? God? No. Of a breathing, living harmonious universe. Where there were no discordant notes, no irreconcilable differences with your conscience.

Once in the tower room, he took a deep breath, and did exactly what Marjorie had done, going slowly round in a circuit of the windows, letting the greens and greys and blues and the light itself soothe his heart and his mind. There was a crystal hanging on a thread from a hook in the centre of the room; he hadn't noticed that before. Now it caught the light as it moved gently in a slight breeze, and set a kaleidoscope of colours dancing over the walls and ceiling of the room. George watched, like a child, not present except in that iridescent rainbow, unaware of himself or the tower or the time or anything but the light.

What an artist, to create this room. What patience, to place each one of these tiny tiles just as she wanted it. Nothing by chance, he was sure, with Beatrice Malaspina. Like the notebook, those artfully artless drawings, snapshots of a life; what did they signify? Why take such pains to hide the revelations of the tower from them? Did the drawings and writing in her notebook have any further, deeper meaning? They would probably never know.

He came to with a sigh, a sigh that took some of the tension out of his shoulders. Marjorie's impulse had led her to find the typewriter. George's led him to think that there must be another room on this floor, in the space that was taken up on the other floors by the stairs.

He found the way in only by chance, running his hand over the smoothness of the tiles, and hearing a click as the pressure of his fingers on one small piece released the catch of a door which had been invisible among the surrounding mosaic, covered as it was with the gleaming pieces of tile.

The door swung open on smooth hinges, and he stepped through it to find himself in a library, a small room lined from floor to ceiling with leather-bound books. Some very large, some the size of a hand.

And every one of them, George realised as he carefully and reverently took down first one and then another, a treasure.

There was a round table in the centre of the room, with a lamp on it – so there was electricity here, but not in the rest of the tower, only in this room. George was not a collector of fine books; he had no idea of what such volumes might be worth, but the names alone were beyond price: a sixteenth-century copy of Dante – of course – a very old illuminated prayer book, and some surprises, a first edition of *Clarissa*, a book that George had never read, an illustrated Virgil, and, to his joy, several scientific treatises.

He had no idea how long he was there, absorbed in books and pictures, the soft smell of the leather, the perfect peace of the room. It could have been minutes, but he realised it was much longer than that when he was brought back to startled awareness of time and place by the clamour of Benedetta's gong. Good heavens, it couldn't be dinner time already. He looked at his watch. It was.

He replaced the book he had been reading on the shelf, and was about to hurry out when a book lying on the floor by the door caught his eye. He rebuked himself for his clumsiness – what carelessness to let any of these precious volumes fall. It might have been damaged. What was it? He hadn't noticed it when he came in; his eyes had been on the shelves. He stooped and picked it up.

It wasn't old, although it had a fine binding. There was the familiar symbol of his youth on the cover, and before he opened the book he knew what it would say on the title page.

TEN

Delia ran the last few yards to the water's edge and plunged in, swimming energetically out into the deeper water with as much vigour as if a shark had been on her tail. She wanted to shake the fidgets out of her system, to be free of those bloody photographs, just to live in the present moment, what Nanny used to call the joyous present. 'The present moment's the only one you ever have,' she would say, 'so don't wish it away or lose yourself in yesterday or tomorrow. Yesterday's gone and by the time tomorrow's come it's today.'

Like in *Alice*, with the Red Queen and her impossible statements. Beatrice Malaspina was a bit of a red queen. Powerful, self-willed, unexpected, manipulative. Perhaps the girl Alice – what was her name, the real Alice? Alice Liddell – maybe that Alice had had an aunt or a grandmother or even a governess who was like the Red Queen. Maybe Marjorie should write a children's book with Beatrice Malaspina as the central character, a bogey to scare the little ones to sleep with.

Bother Marjorie, with her remorseless interest in other people's lives. Not that she'd passed any comments, not really, but her questions had driven Delia to a self-examination that she'd rather not have made.

Theo – the mere thought of him took the sun out of the day. What a pity, she said savagely to herself, as she flipped over and dived down to the sandy seabed, swirling her hands among the shells, that Boswell hadn't throttled Felicity that day when she'd found him with his hands round her sister's neck.

Felicity had passed out; what would have happened if she hadn't gone back to the drawing room to retrieve a book?

'Just a joke,' her mother had said.

And her own voice, the clear voice of an eight-year-old, 'I don't like Boswell's jokes.'

She surfaced, gasping from a gulp of air that turned out to be a wave. She shook the salty water out of her eyes, and as her blurred vision cleared she made out a figure on the shore.

Lucius waved, and she swam towards him in a leisurely crawl. 'What's up?' she called.

'I'm going into town, to make a telephone call. Want to come?'

'There won't be time. It's half an hour each way.'

'There will be time, if we walk quickly.'

She considered. 'All right. Only I have to change.'

'I like the swimsuit,' he said as she came out of the water. He handed her her towel and then her robe. 'I've not seen you in that one before. It suits you, those are your colours.'

'Thank you.' Odd that he noticed. Most men wouldn't.

'Share the joke?' he said as they walked up the beach towards the path.

'What joke?'

'You smiled.'

'Oh, nothing.' She broke into a run. 'Give me ten minutes.'

When she came downstairs Benedetta was remonstrating with Lucius. 'She says we'll be late back, her pasta will be ruined, her fish overcooked, she won't bother any more, nothing but grated turnips for every meal.'

'You made that up,' said Delia, flushed after her brisk run into the house and a swift change. 'She eats out of your hand. Besides, you don't know the Italian word for turnips, let alone grated ones.'

'Turnip is *rapa*. I'm not sure about grated, I grant you, but I'll look it up when we get back.' Lucius was overflowing with the energy that seemed such a part of him.

'Do you burst out all over when you're in the bank or on the floor of the stock exchange or whatever it is you do?' she asked, breathless at keeping up with his swift strides.

'I'm not a stockbroker. No, daily life on Wall Street has a subduing effect, but here, with all the scents and sights of Italy around me, I feel kind of buoyant.'

'Half an hour trying to make a phone connection will subdue you,' said Delia. 'Who are you telephoning? Do you have to keep in touch over deals and mergers and funding for huge projects? Or shouldn't I ask?'

'I'm ringing the London office to say I'm delayed. Again. They'll be getting fretful at my continued absence, but that's just too bad.'

'You could ring Elfrida and have a loving chat.'

The piazza seemed livelier today. The shutters were up, but there was an expectancy in the air. Outside the hotel, an elderly man in a long apron and a boy were arguing over the exact positioning of a pair of bay trees in terracotta pots. A woman in black was burnishing the brasswork on the door and a small girl was shaking out the mat.

Domenico skipped up to them. 'She is here, ready for you!' he said to Lucius in careful English before switching into rapid Italian.

'What's he saying?' asked Delia.

'That visitors are coming to the hotel. From England. Three separate visitors, and they all made reservations by telegram. One arrives tomorrow and the other two the day after.

304

They're not related, but they will surely be friends of ours, so Domenico says.'

'I sincerely hope not,' said Delia, alarmed for a moment. 'Fortunately, nobody knows where I am, except an old tight-lip of a lawyer. Ditto for Jessica.'

'No forwarding address for your loving family?'

He disappeared into the bar, and Delia sat down at the little table which had been set outside, under a faded striped awning. A lean cat slunk past, pausing to gaze at her with huge knowing eyes. A window was flung open above her head and a volley of what sounded like abuse was shouted across the square to where the plant movers were now enjoying a cigarette and surveying the results of their labours.

Signora Ricci came out with an ice in a glass dish, which she put down in front of Delia. She had finished it by the time Lucius came out. 'All done,' he said. 'Ready?'

'Aren't you having an ice?'

'I had a coffee inside. Domenico!'

Domenico appeared beside them out of nowhere, and then hurtled off across the square, beckoning dramatically for them to follow him.

'What's he up to?'

'Wait and see.'

'Somehow,' said Delia, as she climbed on to the scooter behind Lucius, 'I didn't see you as a Vespa man.'

'I've always longed to ride one of these,' he said. 'I've hired it for a week with an option to extend.' He twiddled a knob under the handlebar. 'Hell, what's this do?'

Domenico leapt forward to elucidate, the machine roared into life, and they were off, bumping over the cobbles.

Delia, caught unawares by the violent start, just managed to hold on and clasped her hands around Lucius's waist. 'You should be riding side-saddle,' he shouted back to her, 'the

305

way the Italian girls do. You'll scandalise the good inhabitants of San Silvestro.'

Halfway back, she jabbed him in the back, and the scooter came scudding to a standstill.

'What's up? Travel sickness?'

'No, I want a go driving it. Get off and let me try.'

'Okay.'

He got off, and showed her how to start and control the Vespa. Then he climbed on behind her, and, somewhat jerkily at first, they were off again.

'It's exhilarating!' she cried. 'Can't we hire another one?'

'Good idea,' he shouted into her ear. Was he holding her rather tighter than was necessary, she wondered. As men always did when they got the chance.

'Are you afraid of falling off, or do you think I'm going to come a cropper?' she said, turning her head so that he could hear her. He loosened his grip.

'I should love to see Marjorie and George on one of these,' he said.

Which nearly unseated her, and she took the turn in through the half-open gate with only inches to spare.

'Jessica will love it,' she said as she applied the brakes. 'What's an MG compared to this? And, moreover, we're just in time for dinner. Look, there's George, looking positively ruffled. I wonder who rattled his cage?'

ELEVEN

Jessica was curled up on a sofa with one of Marjorie's books. Marjorie was sitting in a dark part of the drawing room, smoking a cigarette and wrapped in thought, while in a nearby chair, George was enjoying a pipe. Lucius was sitting near a lamp, his fingers tapping on the arm of the chair. Coiled, thought Delia. Tense. Not relaxed, not at ease.

She slipped out of the room.

She would need the torch. There it was, by the side door. George would have put it there, George with his methodical ways. George the most secretive of them. It had cost him an effort to reveal his birth, but that wasn't what was preying on his mind. Well, if Beatrice Malaspina and the Villa Dante went on working their magic on them all, perhaps he'd come out with it. It couldn't be anything very shocking. What could George have done to weigh on his conscience? The bomb. Yes, there was that; he seemed almost to take personal responsibility for the bomb. She'd challenged him on that. 'Science is to blame,' he'd said quietly. 'Science and humanity, the unceasing desire of mankind to know more than is good for us as a species.'

She could see, though, that it would be a burden, having had even a small part in creating the monstrous weapon that

307

now overshadowed all their lives and would no doubt continue to do so for as long as the human race survived.

'It's never the knowledge that is dangerous,' George had said sadly. 'It's the use to which that knowledge is put. Nuclear fission can bring blessings to the world.'

'Or blow us all up,' Marjorie had said. 'Which given the stupidity of politicians is much the most likely outcome.'

Delia lifted the flowerpot, carefully, in case its former occupant had taken up residence again, and picked up the key to the tower. For a moment, once inside, she had an urge to go into the bottom room, just to remind herself how ghastly life was, but she resisted the temptation. 'That isn't why you created that room, is it?' she said aloud, addressing the absent Beatrice Malaspina. 'You old witch, you knew exactly what you were doing.' She went on up the stairs. 'If I believed in ghosts, which I don't, then I'd say your spirit was still here, haunting the Villa Dante, watching us. Laughing at us. Is that what spirits do, mock the mere mortals who are left behind? At least,' she went on, still speaking out loud, 'you aren't doing what that poltergeist did at school, throwing things and turning taps on and off and giving everyone the frights.'

Adolescent energy, they'd said, finally, when all attempts to find a culprit among the girls had failed. An unusual but not an unknown phenomenon. In the end, a friend of the school chaplain had come to stay, a merry little man in a shabby cassock, with a huge cross about his neck. He'd gone round the whole school, sprinkling holy water and blessing every single room, every nook and cranny, every cupboard, anywhere he could find. He'd even gone up into the roof and trotted to and fro among the eaves. After that there'd been no more trouble.

George reminded her of the little priest in the cassock. Only George was so often sombre, and that priest had been bubbling with good humour.

In fact, she said to herself, as she opened the door into the top room, I think George was meant to bubble a bit. I wonder what happened. Life, I suppose.

She stood in the centre of the room and revolved, letting the beam of the torch lie on the walls, bouncing back patterns of light and colour. She sang a few bars from *Rheingold*, not a good acoustic in here with the tiled surface, but interesting echoes. That was something she shared with Beatrice Malaspina, a love of Wagner, if the picture of her at the opera in the notebook was anything to go by.

Come on, she wasn't here to flash lights around and think about Wagner. She was here for a purpose. There it was, on the table, a wooden box. She turned the two brass clasps and lifted the lid. On top, forming a second lid, was an artist's palette. She put her finger in the thumb hole and lifted it. Paints. By the look of it unopened paints. So not paints that Beatrice Malaspina had used. Had she bought this handsome new box, and then set off to Rome, never to return to her tower and her paints?

Hooey, Delia said to the still air. She'd put it there for a reason. She laid the wooden palette back in place, closed the lid, did a last whisk round the tiles with her torch, and left.

'This is for you,' Delia said, handing the box to Lucius.

He looked down at the wooden box she had plonked on his knees.

'Courtesy of the late Beatrice Malaspina.' She turned to Marjorie. 'Your habits are catching. I found myself talking out loud to Beatrice Malaspina, just now in the tower.'

Jessica and George got up and came over to where Lucius was sitting.

'What is it?' Jessica asked.

'Paints,' said Marjorie. 'Left by Beatrice Malaspina as a present for Lucius. Brand new, I expect.'

'Yes,' said Delia. 'Go on, Lucius. Open it. See if they're the kind of paints you use.'

'Since I don't these days use any paints . . .' he began, but couldn't resist opening the box and lifting the lid. He took out the palette and looked down into the box, the fat little tubes laid out in neat rows.

'There's something about a paint box,' said Jessica. 'I could never draw or paint for toffee, but I always wanted to have crayons and paints in my Christmas stocking.'

'I won a large box of Cumberland coloured pencils when I was a girl,' said Marjorie unexpectedly. 'At a fête. It was my most treasured possession for years and years. I couldn't bear to use them, and then they went up in a puff of smoke when our house got hit. I can see them now.'

'There's something beneath the paints,' George said. 'They are on a tray that lifts out.'

They were, and at the bottom of the box was a dipper, several brushes, and a photograph.

'Go on,' said Delia. 'You have to see what it is. Another greeting card from Beatrice Malaspina, bound to be.'

The photo was a snapshot of the room they were in, a close-up of a section of the frieze of pilgrims, as Marjorie had christened it. On the photograph, neatly drawn in Indian ink, were the cartoon outlines of four figures.

Lucius wrinkled his brows. Then his face cleared, and he began to laugh.

'It's us,' said Marjorie. 'Her last visitors.'

Benedetta came into the room with her tray of golden wine and biscuits. Lucius put down the box and stood up. He took Benedetta over to the wall, where the line of people streaming towards the Villa Dante tailed off, the last figure, of a woman, looking round and offering an encouraging hand as though to those coming along behind – only there was nothing but the pale green of the grass.

He spoke to her in Italian, and she was nodding her head in agreement. She pointed to the last figure, and said, quite distinctly, 'Signora Beatrice'. Then she almost dragged Lucius along, pointing to figures, naming them, her face clearly showing what she thought of them. She gestured to a little figure in black with great pride. 'Picasso,' she said, jabbing her plump bosom and laughing.

'Phew,' said Lucius when he had disentangled himself and had a glass of wine in his hand. 'That certainly popped the cork out of the bottle. Yes, these people are all visitors who have stayed here over the years. Some of them were painted by Beatrice Malaspina herself, others weren't, and since she had a very distinguished set of artistic friends, there are some amazing portraits.'

'And the figure at the end, of course that's her. Why didn't we notice it?'

'We weren't looking.'

'She wants you to go on with it,' said Delia. 'She wants you to draw us.'

'Oh, sure,' said Lucius. 'Me and Picasso.'

'I went up to the tower earlier today,' Marjorie said. 'I found a typewriter and ribbon and paper, just as though it had been left for me. So I took it.'

'I, too, went up to the tower,' said George. 'I was intending to tell you. Next to the round room there is another room, a small library, filled with such a collection of books – I can't describe it, you must see for yourselves. Among them – no, not among them, left on the floor for me to trip over – was a particular volume. I feel sure, given how much Beatrice Malaspina seems to have known about us, not merely our lives, which facts are to an extent recorded and can be found out with expense and time, but also our natures and dreams and failures – given this, I am sure that the book was left there deliberately as a message to me.'

'Go on,' said Delia.

He looked surprised. 'Go on? There is nothing more to tell.'

'Yes there is,' said Lucius. 'Out with it. What's the book?'

'A Bible?' said Marjorie.

'Close,' said George, 'but no. It is a copy of the *Spiritual Exercises* of St Ignatius Loyola, founder of the Jesuits.' He paused. 'You might say it is a systematic scheme of prayer and examination of the soul to bring you closer to God.'

'If one has a soul,' said Delia. 'Which, being a man of science, you'd say is all rot.'

'Who am I to argue with a man such as St Ignatius?' said George.

'What's the message, then?' said Jessica. 'Is she telling you to pray, or to go to church?'

'No, she is telling me that there are always several ways to look at the same thing. It is the eye and mind of the beholder that determines what we see and believe, not the object of our contemplation in itself.'

'I went to the tower, too,' said Lucius, breaking the slight uneasiness that followed George's words. He dived into a corner of the room, and dragged out a portable record player. 'It was sitting under the table with a pile of records, including, I'm glad to say, some Gilbert and Sullivan. This, Delia, is for you, the gift that Beatrice Malaspina left in the tower for you. An uncanny choice, if you ask me.'

'How could she know?'

'Come on, George, plug it in,' Jessica said. 'Here's *Ruddigore*.'

Lucius was examining his paints. 'Gouache,' he said. 'I suppose that would work. One would have to do something to fix it, but yes, it would work; it was probably what she used. Good paints, too, by the look of them.'

'You'll need a sketch book,' Marjorie said. 'You can have mine.'

'Don't you want it?'

'Not at present,' she said with one of the smiles that so transformed her angular face. 'I have other fish to fry.'

TWELVE

The May mornings were hotter than the days when they had first arrived, the early swift dawns of yellow and turquoise and pink giving way to skies of endless blue and a warmth that worked through one's bones, as Marjorie put it.

From an upstairs window came the steady tapping of a typewriter.

'I don't like to mention it,' Jessica said, as she came into the drawing room from the terrace, 'but Marjorie seems to be writing.'

'Hooray,' said Delia. She was looking through her pile of records. 'It could just be letters, of course.'

Lucius was on his knees beside the fresco. On the sketch pad he had drawn the outline of a group of figures. 'I wish the light were better in here. I tried opening the shutters, but the sun bounces off the wall and you can't see the figures any more clearly.'

Jessica peered over his shoulder. 'You've drawn two more figures.'

'We've got to include you, and I fancy another drawing of Benedetta. I can hardly hope to match the earlier one,' he said with a grin, 'but she was young then; I think we need one of her in her full power of age.'

'Don't you think you should follow Beatrice Malaspina's instructions to the letter? She drew four figures on the photo.'

Lucius sat back on his heels to look at his work. 'I think mine kind of match. She could certainly draw; well, that was clear from the scenes in her notebook.'

'Yours are fine, but you're still not following her orders. I don't mind if you leave me out, and Benedetta will hardly be bothered, will she?'

'You think Beatrice Malaspina will come back and put a curse on me? No, if I'm going to have a go at it, I'll do it my way. All of us, or none.' He raised his head and called across to Delia. 'Will you sing some Gilbert and Sullivan for me?'

'Maybe,' said Delia, going to the piano. She flexed her fingers, and then began to play soft deliberate notes.

Lucius looked up. 'Bach,' he said.

'Morning prayers,' said Delia. 'There's an old girl from our school, Perdita Richardson, who's a famous pianist. She told me, when she came to speech day, that she starts every day with Bach. I thought it was a good idea, and so I do the same. Sometimes I sing, and sometimes I play. Now, be quiet and get on with your drawing.'

The tranquillity of the morning's endeavours carried over into a long leisurely lunch outside under the pattern of vines, which were growing more luxuriant by the day.

At four o'clock, Jessica, who had been reading and digesting her lunch, found Delia, deep in a score. 'Fancy a dip? I'm off to the beach.'

All five of them swam, not talking much.

'Busy bees aren't in it,' Marjorie said, lying motionless on her back. 'And yes, since you're all too polite to ask, I'm writing.'

'And I,' said George, 'am reading, and remembering the days of my youth, and the fathers.'

'Good memories, I hope,' said Lucius, who was swimming in lazy circles round Delia.

'Mostly, but the fathers were as one would expect, of all kinds. Some almost saintly, others quite the contrary.'

'Teachers are all the same,' said Jessica. 'Whether they're wearing long black frocks and are men, or tweed suits and pince nez and are women.'

'This is a perfect day,' said Delia. 'Here in the sea, I feel cleansed. It is totally peaceful and achingly beautiful, and a day like a jewel, one that I want to last for ever.'

'Why not?' said Lucius. 'At least for a few hours more. Benedetta is preparing a feast, and we shall eat under the dusky sky brimful of stars, and Delia will play us soft melodies under the moon.'

'There's just one thing missing,' said Marjorie.

'What's that?' said Jessica.

'Love. All this is such a perfect setting for love.'

'Oh, love,' said Delia, closing her eyes and blowing a little spout of water into the air. 'I've done with love.'

Lucius grabbed her legs and pulled her under the water.

They went back to the house after a long swim, hot, salty, tangle-haired – except for George, who, as he ruefully remarked, smoothing his receding hairline and balding head, had very little hair to tangle.

Marjorie was planning a new and exciting cocktail, Delia was longing for a shower, George was going upstairs to shave, and Lucius wanted to change in double quick time and get back to his sketches. His fingers tingled with the delight of holding a pencil and the prospect of painting made him almost dizzy.

'All of which,' said Delia, 'will lead to a wonderful dinner under the stars, and the end to a perfect day.'

The roar of a powerful engine rent the air.

'Lord, surely not the *avvocato* back with the codicil in his hand,' said Lucius.

'Oh, my God,' said Jessica, as a sleek red Jaguar swung through the gates. 'I know that car.'

Delia had gone white under her tan. 'So do I.'

Arrivals & Departures

ONE

Delia's heart had taken over her body; thump, thump, thump. Her mouth was dry and sour and her stomach felt as though she had fallen abruptly from a great height. Speechless and motionless, she stood frozen, her towel dangling from one hand.

In what seemed an infinity of time, the car came to a halt, the driver got out, gave a cheery wave and went round to the passenger side.

Lucius was beside Delia, and she came to with a kind of shiver.

'Your sister, I assume,' he said. 'I recognise her from the photos. What a stunner,' he added.

Lucius too, Delia thought. Every man's reaction to Felicity.

She ran her tongue over dry lips. 'I told you she was attractive.'

'Definitely a looker. Not my style, but one just has to admire anyone so lovely. Is that Theo?'

'Yes, that's Theo.'

And there they were, the two of them, loud, delighted to have found the villa.

'What an amazing place,' said Theo. 'My word, this is a pleasant spot.' He came forward to kiss Delia on the cheek, and she felt faint at the familiar smell of him: the slight perspiration, the lingering note of his cologne, discreet, expensive, suitable, and utterly part of him.

Her longing for him was so acute that it hurt. She forced a smile. 'Hello, Flicka,' she said to her sister. 'What on earth are you doing here?'

Felicity was standing with her eyes shut. 'Just feel the warmth, oh, what heaven. Isn't it heavenly, darling?' This to Theo. 'Clever Delia to have a friend who owns a house like this. Aren't you going to introduce us? And Jessica, hello, darling.' She blew Jessica a kiss. 'Haven't seen you in ages.'

There was a long silence. Then Delia, stiffly, introduced the others. 'This is Marjorie Swift. George Helsinger, and Lucius Wilde.'

Felicity bestowed a dazzling smile on them all. Then she took a gold and diamond compact out of her handbag, and checked her lips in the mirror. George, Delia noticed, was eyeing her with a look of astonishment. Delia had a feeling that few women quite like Felicity had ever come George's way.

Theo was frowning. 'Lucius Wilde . . . Lucius Wilde . . . I know that name.' His face cleared. 'Of course, the banker. You're engaged to Elfrida, terrific girl, lucky you.'

There was a note of relief in Theo's voice, gratitude for finding at least one of the right sort here. Delia knew him too well. George he would dismiss at once as a don; clever, but not within his sphere. And Marjorie, with her south London accent and ungainly stance? Little does he know, Delia thought, that Marjorie is probably summing him up in one glance, and some part of him will appear in her book.

'Who's your host, or hostess?' said Theo, looking enquiringly at the other three.

'Beatrice Malaspina,' said Marjorie.

'Is she around? We hoped we might trespass on her hospitality for a few days. It looks as though she's got plenty of

room. Do you think she'd squeeze Flicka and me in somewhere, Delia?'

'Actually, she's dead,' said Delia, 'so it would be a bit difficult to ask her. I think you'd be much better off in the town.
There's a hotel there.'

Felicity gave a little scream. 'Delia, don't be so horrid. We
drove through the town; we had to stop and ask the way,
and there's only one hotel, not suitable at all. You know what
Italian hotels are like.'

'No, I don't.'

'Of course they must stay here,' said Lucius.

Delia glared at him. How could anyone be so insensitive?
How could she bear having Theo in the same house, here at
the Villa Dante, for breakfast, lunch and dinner, swimming,
sitting on the terrace, just being there, tugging at her heart?

Theo gave her a smile, the smile that melted her resist-
ance. 'Oh, I suppose Benedetta can make up a room,' she
said ungraciously.

Theo opened the boot of the car and began to unload the
luggage. There seemed to be enough for a stay of a month,
never mind a few days, but that had always been Felicity's
way; she had no notion of what it meant to travel light.

George went to give him a hand. 'Thanks, old chap,' said
Theo. 'I thought these Italian houses were teeming with staff.'

'It is hardly necessary, since the house is not at present
inhabited, except by the five of us, who are merely here en
passant,' said George. 'There is Benedetta, and Pietro, the
only manservant, who is hardly of an age to haul suitcases
about. He looks after the garden, but is very lame.'

'Well, well,' said Theo as they went into the hall. 'This is
all very pretty, I must say. Don't you think so, darling?'

'Oh, if you like that sort of thing,' said Felicity. 'It's all a
bit old-fashioned, though. Is there a swimming pool?'

'No,' said Delia. Felicity probably thought villa meant a
house with a pool. 'There's a beach if you want to swim.'

'And come out looking like you, a perfect fright? Delia, do you have any idea what's happened to your hair? Nice swimsuit,' she added, as Delia's robe fell open. 'Can I borrow it? I've only got a plain white one, and that's hopeless until one has a tan.'

'No, you can't,' said Delia, who knew that if she let Felicity get her hands on any item of clothing she fancied, she would never see it again. 'Put on fake tan lotion if you're bothered about looking white.'

White skin, her skin white, next to Theo's dark skin; he was so dark that she used to call him her gypsy, with black hairs on his chest.

He had never liked that. 'Hardly a gypsy,' he protested. 'I think I can safely say that I can trace my family for centuries, back to the Conquest, and I assure you, there's no gypsy blood there. I owe my colouring to my great-great-grand-mother, who was Spanish. With sixteen quarterings, so no gypsy blood there either.'

'I'd like gypsy blood,' Delia had said. 'Wild and romantic.'

'I can be that without gypsy blood,' he'd replied, seizing her and pulling her down against his chest.

The memory stung, it was vivid and painful, like all her memories of being so ecstatically in love.

She had hoped she was getting over him, here, in the extraordinary surroundings of the Villa Dante. She thought that the pain had dulled, and so, for a while, it had. Only now that he was here, she knew that nothing had changed. In London, in company, with her work to keep her busy, she had told herself that feelings faded, that as time went on the agony of remembered love and the sharp pain of the end of their affair would lessen and vanish.

One grew out of old loves, everyone said so. 'Goodness,' Jessica had remarked, 'there's nothing more appalling than running into a man you were in love with five years ago, and wondering what on earth you ever saw in him.'

Benedetta seemed pleased to have new guests. She looked approvingly at the expensive leather luggage, and with rapture at Felicity's lovely face. 'La bella signora,' she said to Delia. Then she said something in Italian to Lucius.

'She thinks the bella signora and the handsome English gentleman should have the room you're in. Such a comfortable bed, so suitable for a married couple.'

'Forget it,' said Delia. 'There are other rooms for two people. They can have one of those.'

She would have given up room, bed, balcony, view, anything to Theo, but she was damned if Felicity was going to revel voluptuously with him in what she had come to think of as her bed.

'I mean, it's a lot of trouble for me to move. Much quicker and easier to put them somewhere else. And they aren't staying long.' I hope, I hope, she added under her breath. They were putting up a good show, she said to herself, quite the happy young couple. But it was all show, of course. It was a marriage like her parents', based on convenience and money and ambition, not on deep and lasting affection, let alone love.

Delia came early into the drawing room, wanting to down a strong cocktail before she had to face Theo and Felicity again. If only she could get Theo to herself, if only she could let him know that her feelings hadn't changed. She frowned.

Marjorie handed her a drink. 'I made it a stiff one. You look as though you could do with some bucking up. Quite a girl, your sister.'

'Yes, she is.'

'Why are they here?' went on Marjorie. 'Is this a courtesy call? Your Theo doesn't strike me as a man who does anything without a reason.'

'I don't know,' said Delia. She had been so surprised to see them, so overwhelmed at Theo's arrival, so filled with her ancient dislike of her sister that she hadn't given the reason for their presence a second thought. 'Come to that, however did they know I was here?'

'Surely you left a forwarding address?'

'I did not. The only person who knew I was here was Mr Winthrop.'

'What does your brother-in-law do for a living?'

'Oh, he's a barrister . . . You don't think . . . ?'

'All these lawyers are thick as thieves. What kind of barrister? Not criminal law. I know all the London criminal barristers – not to know personally, but who they are. Professional interest,' she added, seeing Delia looking puzzled. 'Crime, detective stories. I spend quite a lot of time in the courts. Good for plots if you catch the right trial.'

'No, that's not what Theo does. He's to do with money. Tax, trusts, that kind of thing.'

'Chancery,' said Marjorie, nodding her head. 'That's where the money is.'

'Theo likes money.' The drink was already going to Delia's head. 'He and Jessica come from a very old but impoverished family, and he's determined to restore the family fortunes. I told you, that's why he married Felicity. For her money.'

'Is it?' said Marjorie.

Lucius came in, and Delia noticed with the part of her mind that wasn't waiting for Theo to appear that he was dressed very dashingly. 'I haven't seen that suit before,' she said.

'One of the special efforts in the cupboard. Adds a period feel that goes with the house, don't you think? Quite out of style, naturally, trousers too wide, jacket cut all wrong, lapels not at all the thing. Your sister will say I'm old-fashioned.'

'It suits you,' said Marjorie. 'It has an elegance that modern suits lack.'

'Just what I thought. Pour me one of your corkers, Marjorie. The others not down yet?'

'Jessica's putting on her face. She says Felicity always makes her feel like a dowdy provincial, so she's decided to go for the war paint. I don't know about George.'

'George is here,' he said, coming into the room. 'So much for our perfect day. I do not think it has ended so very perfectly.'

'Not for Delia, at least,' said Marjorie. 'I never saw anyone less pleased to see their relations.'

'On the contrary,' said Delia. 'It makes me very happy.' To see Theo, she added to herself. But did it? Was happiness the word? Why, oh why did he have this effect on her? Because she was still in love with him, and that was the way of love, she told herself.

Dinner was long over. Felicity, with extravagant yawns, had announced she was going to bed. She told Theo not to be too long, flashed a smile round at the other mortals, a smile that held warmth only for Lucius, and left the room, her scent lingering on the air behind her. George went up soon afterwards, and Marjorie said gruffly that she was going up to do a spot of work. She had something she wanted to get down on paper.

Go to bed, go to bed, Delia willed Jessica and Lucius. But instead, Jessica went over to the gramophone and Lucius joined her.

This was her chance. Theo came and sat beside her, opening his cigarette case and offering it to her. She shook her head.

'I forgot, you don't like this sort.'

'Come and see the fountains. There's still a moon, and they look amazing at night.'

Theo glanced over to the piano, where Jessica and Lucius were sharing a joke.

'Why not?' he said, getting to his feet.

'This way,' said Delia, anxious to get him out of the room before the others noticed that they were leaving together. She

didn't see Lucius's eyes follow her out of the room, a troubled expression in them, nor Jessica's faint shrug of the shoulders as she watched them go.

The night was balmy, with only the hint of a breeze to stir
the leaves above their heads. Theo's cigarette glowed in the
dark. 'What are all those twinkling lights?'

'Fireflies,' she said. He had hooked his arm in hers; she
was breathless at the closeness of him.

'Good chance to talk,' he said. 'What a crowd of people.
What on earth are you doing here, Delia? Old Winthrop,
who gave me your address' – so Marjorie was right – 'said
you'd inherited something. Not this place, by any lucky
chance?'

His voice was light, but Delia could sense the keenness of
the question.

'Terrific upkeep, of course, but you could sell it to an
American for quite a tidy sum.'

'I haven't inherited any house,' said Delia. Some instinct
for self-preservation came to her aid: it would be better, much
better, if he knew nothing about the codicil. She could see
him getting in touch with Dr Calderini, talking about legal
steps that could be taken . . . 'It's a small bequest. The lawyers
are letting us stay here while it's sorted out. Italian legal
bureaucracy, you know.'

'A valuable bequest?'

'No, no. Just a brooch – a cameo,' she said, improvising
hastily.

'Who is this Beatrice Malaspina? An Italian by the sound
of her.'

'She was English. The house has belonged to her family
for several generations.'

'Was she your godmother, something like that?'

'No. I never knew her, or had even heard of her before I
got the letter from the lawyer.'

'What, named in the will of a total stranger?'

'She was an opera lover,' Delia said. That at least was true.

'Oh, I see. It's still odd, but it must be above board if Winthrop and Jarvis are handling it. They're sticklers for that. Very careful about who they take on.'

'They won't handle Jessica's divorce.'

Theo dropped his cigarette and ground it out with his shoe, a gesture that irritated Delia. 'No, well, they wouldn't. Not at all their kind of thing.'

'What's a divorce these days? Everyone does it. Just think how much happier Mother would be if she didn't have to stick with my father, because of his rigid ways.'

'Steady on,' said Theo. 'Divorce isn't quite so easy as all that. It still carries a stigma.'

'I don't give a button for that. Do you?'

'Me? I wouldn't go around casting stones at my friends who've got a divorce, but really, Delia, Jessica knows it isn't a step to be taken so lightly. She's only been married two or three years; marriages are often stormy at first, and then you settle down.'

'With Richie? I doubt it.' She turned and drew closer to him. 'We make mistakes. Jessica made a mistake. You made a mistake, but mistakes can be put right. Theo, I understand how you felt about Felicity. I know she swept you off your feet, but—'

'She did, rather, didn't she?' said Theo ruefully. 'You took it hard at first, didn't you? I didn't behave very well, I admit.' He laughed. 'We even considered an elopement, so as not to make it all too painful for you, wedding, brides-maids and so on. Only it seemed a bit rash. Can't say the others in my chambers would have been very happy about it, although they'd have understood, once they met Felicity.' He laughed.

Why was he being so obtuse? 'What I mean is,' she went on, 'that divorce is possible, easy even. If you were divorced, we—'

'We?'

'You and me.'

'Stop there,' said Theo in quite a different voice. 'Stop right there, Delia. Listen, there is no we. The we is me and Felicity. We're married and we stay married. I can't imagine how you could get any other idea in your head.'

'Theo, I'm still in love with you.'

'Oh, damn it,' he cried. 'What are you talking about? Look, we had an affair, three years ago. An affair is something that lasts a certain while and then comes to an end. We had good times together. But then I met Felicity and I fell in love – and, well, that's that.'

'How can it be, when I feel like this about you?'

'Delia, pull yourself together. You're drunk. You were drinking far too much wine at dinner, I noticed.'

'Why are you here? Why did you come?'

'Delia, if I'd imagined for one moment . . . All this is simple dramatising. You've been cherishing feelings for me . . . I'd no idea. You live by your emotions, Delia, and it's very wearing. It always was wearing. Because there isn't a man in your life at present, you're casting around for someone to get emotional about, and with immense stupidity you've decided to rake up all those old feelings you had for me. It's over, Delia. Finished. Now pull yourself together. We'd better go back in. Asking me to look at the fountains, and then coming out with all this stuff. It's excruciatingly embarrassing for me, don't you see that?'

'Embarrassing? Embarrassing for you?' She let out a kind of wail, and, turning away, ran into the house, his words ringing in her ears. She cannoned into Lucius, who had come out of the door.

'Delia, what—'

'Oh, go away,' she shouted at him, and headed blindly for the stairs. As she fled, she heard Lucius ask, 'What have you been saying to her?'

And Theo's stiff reply, 'Just a private matter, a family matter. She's overwrought, that's all. Fancy a cigar before we turn in?'

TWO

Jessica came into Delia's room, carefully carrying a cup in her hands. Delia was in bed, her hair smoothed down, looking, Jessica thought, like a child at the end of her first day up after measles. Distressed and drained.

'What's that?'

'Hot milk.'

'I never drink hot milk.'

'Tonight you do. It's got a dash of brandy in it, to help you sleep.'

'Oh, for God's sake, don't come mothering me, Jessica.'

'It's no good being nasty to me, is it? It's been a shock to you, the relatives turning up uninvited. You don't get on with Felicity, and you're still carrying a torch for Theo. That's a strain on anyone.'

'I am not carrying a torch for Theo.'

'No, but you think you are which is almost as bad as if you were. It's beyond me how an Englishman of the most ordinary and dullest kind, conventional, not very perceptive, can have sex appeal, but Theo has. It'll probably help him make a fortune at the bar.'

Delia said, 'Whenever Theo talks about the bar, I always

imagine a pub in the City, full of black-jacketed lawyers with their elbows on it.'

'Go on thinking of it like that. Seriously, Delia, Theo's not worth it. He's a nice enough man, and I'm fond of him, but I don't have any illusions about him. He's not someone to wreck your life over. I shan't forgive him for appearing like this; I do wonder why they've come.'

'They said they were in Italy, touring.'

'And just happened to be passing the Villa Dante which is in the middle of no one's tour, and thought they'd drop in. Hardly convincing.' She sat on the bed, and waited for Delia to finish her drink. 'I have a horrible feeling he's come to talk me out of trying to divorce Richie. I can't believe those lawyers gave him the address of the Villa Dante. Discretion, ha, ha, ha.'

'The sooner they come out with the real reason for their presence here, the better. They can say whatever it is they've come to say, and leave.'

'I don't think they'll find our company too congenial, so maybe they'll buzz off tomorrow.'

'They might. Theo finds me an embarrassment.'

'Is that what he said? Pompous ass.'

'But how can I stop being in love with him? How can I help how I feel when he's there, in front of me, across the table, sitting next to me?'

'You aren't in love with him. You were, and the traces remain. The best remedy is falling in love with someone else, of course. That can work a pretty miraculous cure. For God's sake, Delia, you aren't eighteen, you aren't full of adolescent hormones any more. Stop thinking about him, stop dwelling on it and feeding the flames. Now drink this up and go to sleep.'

'Easy to say, hard to do, to stop thinking about it. About him.'

'Do you know what? Grown-ups do it all the time. It's how we get through life, ducks.'

'It would be different if he really loved Felicity.'

'Oh, would it?'

'Yes. But he doesn't.'

'Pack it in. Finished? Then give me the cup. Turn the light out, and nothing will seem so dire in the morning.'

'Thanks for the drink, Jessica. I shan't sleep, but it was a kind thought.'

Marjorie was waiting outside the door. 'Did she drink it?'

Jessica put a finger on her lips and walked towards her room. She opened the door, and gestured to Marjorie to go in. 'I don't want her to hear us whispering. She'll think we're plotting. Yes, she drank it all. What a pair of schemers we are. How strong was that bromide you put in her milk?'

'It'll knock her out until the morning.'

'If she wakes up groggy, she'll suspect something, won't she?'

'No, she won't. Wake up groggy or suspect anything. She'll just think she drank too much last night, which she did. Why is she in such a state? Is it just Theo being here?'

'You know about her and Theo, do you? I think he must have had rather a go at her.'

'Hard for him, to have his wife's younger sister yearning for him as she does. He doesn't care tuppence for her, except out of family duty, you can see that.'

'You can, and I can, but she can't.'

'He's totally wrong for her, so it's a good thing he did marry that sister, who's a remarkably silly woman.'

'Not silly. Not much brain of your or Delia's kind, but shrewd as they come, don't you think, under the fluff?'

'Does Lucius realise what's going on?'

'I'm not sure.'

'I expect he does; he's a man who doesn't miss much. A bit of a blow for him, in that case.'

'You've noticed, have you?'

'It's fairly obvious.'

'Delia says he's not her type.'

'Oh, types!'

'Women do go for the same kind of man. I do, which is partly why I ended up with Richie, God help me.'

They went downstairs, neither of them ready to go to bed.

'Where are the men?' Jessica said, when they were in the hall. 'In the drawing room? Let's go and sit outside. We'll be bitten to pieces, I dare say, but I don't feel like masculinity and smoke. It's odd how Theo's arrival has turned the drawing room into feeling like a men-only area. Of course, he's the sort of man who's most at home in his club.'

'We'll have to put a stop to that,' said Marjorie. 'I'm not going to let the drawing room become his territory. But for now, let's go and sit under the stars.'

'I'm afraid,' said Jessica, when they were installed on a marble bench, 'that if Mr Winthrop told Theo where I am, then the newspapers may find out. Oh, God, I do wish the press hadn't gone over to tittle-tattle and gossip and innuendo. When did that happen? They didn't used to be like that.'

'They got intrusive after those magazines started up in America, telling all about the lives of Hollywood stars,' said Marjorie. 'And other famous people. The English papers realised that there was a vast readership eager for all the dirt on people in the news, and so they obliged. Look at the stuff that Giles Slattery writes in his gossip column.'

'Giles Slattery? Dreadful man, he's the bane of my life.'

'He has a reputation for never letting go of a story until he's got to the bottom of it.'

'It's extraordinary how people can be interested in me and my life, when they've never met me, or any of the people in the stories, and never will. Why don't they keep their eyes on what's happening next door or what Auntie

Flo's up to with the milkman? Probably far more interesting in any case.'

'It's the way of the world,' said Marjorie. 'In books, characters don't work if they're just ordinary, they have to be more alive, more vigorous, more wicked, more sly than the person next door or your boss at work. That's why readers get absorbed. Daily papers are the same, they look for the story. Your mistake was marrying a man in the news like Richie Meldon. If you'd gone off to teach in a girls' school on the south coast, you'd never have seen your name in the papers from one year's end to the next.'

True, thought Jessica, and for a moment she wished with all her heart that that was what she had done. That she was concerned only with whether Jemima in the sixth was going to get her scholarship, and how well little Hetty was coming on after a bad start, and did you hear what Miss Hopkins said to Miss Frederickson yesterday? She laughed. 'I dare say the common room of any school is as much a hotbed of gossip as anywhere else. We're all keen to know more about our fellow men, aren't we?'

'I'm endlessly inquisitive about people, and every detail I can find out about them, but not out of sheer nosiness, just because it's my stock in trade.'

'But didn't you say you don't base your characters on actual people?'

'Elements are what one uses, facets of characters, snatches of incidents. It all goes into one's brain in a kind of porridge, and then comes out in a thousand different shapes.'

Jessica stretched and yawned. 'We need a bit of colour in books, now we're all existentialists and life is totally without meaning, nothing but an absurd and random sequence of events that happen to us. We don't cause them, we can't change them, it's just the way things are. We live lives without meaning, and then we die, and who cares?'

'Beatrice Malaspina wouldn't have shared that view.'

'She was of another generation. They believed in things then.'

'Things?'

'God. Truth, Progress. Control of one's life. Now we know better.'

'Rubbish. Plato said the unexamined life is not worth living. That's what Socrates spent his time doing.'

'Socrates has been dead a long time. And I bet Socrates never knew a man like Richie, who's a class A bastard.'

'Knowing that, you married him?'

'I didn't know it when I married him. He was forceful and good in bed, if that means anything to you, and he comforted me when I was a bit desperate. And he was rich.'

Delia didn't wake up feeling at all groggy. She woke up with a clear head and a sense of peace. She lay in bed, watching the play of light at the shuttered windows. In a moment she would go over and open them and let in the brilliant light, and look out at the sea. One could be very happy here, she said to herself. Then it all came flooding back, and she remembered how unhappy she was.

'You live by your emotions, Delia.' Theo's words echoed in her head. And Jessica, telling her to grow up, to use her brain, not think with her hormones. She winced at both memories, and it was as if a cloud had passed over the sun.

Only, glancing at the windows, it hadn't. The cloud was in her mind, blotting out the world around her; in this case, here and now, a world full of beauty.

Thoughtful now, she got out of bed and opened the shutters. She went out on to the balcony, and breathed in the air, so fresh and clear that it almost hurt. She blinked, and watched a lizard on the wall below make its curious scuttling journey to the ground.

The birdsong. Such an amazing sound when one stopped to listen, to really listen, the songs and chirrups and swooping sounds that matched the soaring flight of a swallow far over-head in the already blazingly blue sky. She sang a blackbird's notes back to it, and laughed when it responded with a further stream of song.

She went to the table and picked up the music that was lying there. She took a chair out on to the balcony, and then, with her feet propped on the lower ledge of the balustrade, opened the score and began to hum. Odd how well she'd slept last night. She'd been prepared for a night of wakeful misery, and in fact she had slept as soundly as a child.

She was almost the last down to breakfast, a deliberate move, lest she should find herself alone with Theo, a noto-riously early riser. All the others were there except her sister.

She reached for one of Benedetta's little rolls. 'Where's Flicka?' she said, to the table in general.

'Not up yet,' said Theo. 'She's feeling a bit ropy, after the journey and so on.'

Marjorie was filling Delia's cup with coffee. 'She's preg-nant, isn't she?' she said, just as though she'd been saying that it was nine o'clock.

Delia's hand with the coffee cup hung suspended in mid-air. Jessica was looking at her; Lucius, who was standing at the window, whipped round to stare at Theo.

He doesn't like Theo, Delia thought. You'd think, banker and lawyer, Boston and Gloucestershire, Harvard and Cambridge, they'd have a lot in common. But they couldn't be more different, and Lucius doesn't like Theo at all. These thoughts rushed through her mind in a flash, and she found herself putting her cup carefully down in its saucer and saying, 'Is she?'

'How the devil . . .' began Theo.

He looked like a turkey, fluffing his feathers in masculine temper. 'Marjorie knows everything,' Delia said. 'So, is Flicka expecting a baby?'

The words came neatly out of her mouth, but it was as

though they were spoken by someone else, not the raging, desperate Delia who was actually sitting at the table.

'As it happens,' said Theo, still glaring at Marjorie, 'she is. We were going to tell you, of course, Delia, and Jessica, being family. But it's hardly . . . well, it's not something to be broadcast to all and sundry.'

There was that voice again, calm, normal. 'Don't be so Victorian, Theo. That means I shall be an aunt. I'll like that.'

Theo was looking at her now, with some perplexity. 'We hope you'll be a godmother.'

'Certainly I will. I shall go along to Mappin and Webb as soon as I'm back in England and buy a silver cup. Although, if it's a girl, I might find something more useful, like pearls. I've got three silver cups, and I've never used any of them.'

It was as though the others had let out a collective sigh of relief, and they broke into a clamour of conversation about totally useless christening presents. And Delia found herself joining in, laughing, swapping anecdotes about frightful and inappropriate presents in general. As though Theo weren't there. As though he were there, and it didn't matter. As though he were just her sister's husband, just one of the family.

Which was exactly what he was.

Her sense of unreality carried her through the morning. Lucius was working at the fresco, not put off by Theo's comments and advice. 'I envy you, having a hobby like that. I often thought I might take up sketching myself, to help one unwind after a busy day.'

'A cocktail's more effective, don't you think?' Delia said.

Theo was in earnest. 'I know a fellow, a solicitor, London man, one of the top boys, who does embroidery. Intricate work, but I'm not sure about that.' He looked down at his thick fingers with some complacency. 'I think you need a woman's hand for that kind of delicate stuff.'

For the first time since she'd met Theo, Delia wanted to

laugh at him. She must control herself. 'Marjorie sketches,' she said. 'Strictly amateur, though, she says.'

'Delia, I wanted to ask you about her.' Theo lowered his voice. He seemed to be wanting to make an effort to be friendly with her. 'Oh, and by the way,' in an even lower voice, 'no hard feelings about last night?'

Lucius had sharp ears, and she saw that he had heard Theo's words. His shoulders were taut and expressive, and he clenched his fist, then deliberately released it, flexing his fingers before taking up a brush.

'I was a bit tipsy,' she said. 'Forget it.'

'Oh, good, that's all right then. But this Marjorie, who is she? I mean, she doesn't seem quite your sort of person. A bit common, wouldn't you say?'

'Knock it off, Theo,' said Lucius, looking up from his wall. 'Marjorie's got plenty of class, just not the Eton and Oxford sort. She's a distinguished author, as it happens, and someone whose acquaintance I'm glad to have made.'

'If you say so,' said Theo doubtfully. And then, 'Is George another writer?'

'He's a scientist,' said Delia. 'A brilliant one. Cambridge, America. A physicist.' As the words left her mouth, she knew what Theo was going to say.

He said it. 'Oh, a boffin! One of the backroom boys. Excellent.'

'I think,' Marjorie said to Jessica, 'that perhaps the scales have fallen from Delia's eyes.'

'Do you think so? Can it happen so quickly? They obviously had a bit of a scene last night. Delia more or less dragged him out into the moonlight. Lucius was seething.'

'Did he say anything?'

'No, he's so very good at hiding his feelings, but I could tell. He just muttered a bit, and then we went on with the music.'

They were on the beach, having ascertained that Felicity was planning to lie on the terrace under an umbrella, and that George was going to show Theo the grounds. Theo was keen on grounds.

Jessica sat up and applied some more lotion to her knees. 'Why do knees get browner than the rest of one's legs?' she said.

'One of nature's little foibles. Now,' Marjorie went on, leaning back with her hands clasped behind her neck, 'we have to make Delia fall in love with Lucius.'

'Can't be done,' said Jessica. 'Off with the old love before you're on with the new. Delia will be feeling sore about Theo for quite a while, won't she?'

'Time isn't on our side. In the near future, Lucius will be off to England, and wedding bells will chime for him and Elfrida.'

'Why is it that the nicest men always end up in the hands of ghastly women? Lucius must do his own wooing.'

'Too much the gentleman to pester Delia. I can see in days of old he'd be running a sword through Theo, but as it is, in the middle of the twentieth century, he can do nothing but simmer and brood with jealous brow on the folly of woman.'

'If Lucius has fallen in love with Delia, then he must break off his engagement to Elfrida. A letter would be good. Don't you find it's hard to argue with a letter?'

'He may think that Delia won't ever care for him, in which case he might as well be married to Elfrida as not.'

Jessica rolled over on to her stomach. 'He's not the lie down and take what fate dishes out type. He's a mover and shaker.'

'He needs to shake some sense into Delia.'

'That would do her good, I dare say, but it won't make her fall in love with him. That's the X factor, isn't it? The chemistry or magic that makes people fall in love.'

'Perhaps Beatrice Malaspina will take a hand.'

Jessica snorted. 'Ghostly emanations?'

'I think she had it all planned. I think she wants Delia to fall in love with Lucius.'

'I think she was a most peculiar woman, and certainly an interfering one. Lord, all this influence from beyond the grave! You don't need ghosts, do you, just a passion for getting your way and a lot of money to make sure people dance to your tune even when you're no longer there. It's eerie.'

'But effective.'

THREE

Delia saw the man walking along the road that led to the house. She was standing at an upstairs window, lost in thought, when the erect military figure caught her eye. English, of course, in that jacket and panama. And no one she knew, thank God. He must be one of the visitors from the hotel, had no doubt heard of the English people staying at the Villa Dante, had decided to pay a call.

She sped down the stairs, ran through the hall and took the steps down from the front door in flying leaps. But by the time she got to the gates, he'd let himself in; a bit of a nerve, that, not bothering to ring or wait. She stood there, as though blocking his way to the house, her hands on her hips. He came up to her and removed his hat.

'You must forgive the intrusion, but I understand a Dr Helsinger is staying here.'

Lucius appeared at her side. 'Do you know this man?'

Delia shook her head, and after a momentary hesitation, the man introduced himself. 'Mr Grimond,' he said.

'A friend of George's?'

'Not exactly. Is he here?'

'Did I hear my name?' George had been among the olive trees with Marjorie. 'Far too late to prune, of course,' she had said, 'but the trees have been neglected. We can't do any harm if we tidy them up a bit and remove the straggling bits.'

There was something endearing about George, walking up to them with a sprig of olive in his hand.

'Dr Helsinger? Rodney Grimond. I wonder if I could have a word. In private.'

George had gone an ashen shade, and for a dreadful moment Delia wondered if he was going to pass out. He made an effort to recover himself. 'I do not know you,' he said.

'It's official business. If there's somewhere we can go . . . ?'

Delia saw the look of appeal in George's eye, but before she could say anything, Lucius had stepped forward to stand beside George. 'I'll stay with you if you like,' he offered.

'I think it would be better if I speak to Dr Helsinger alone.' Mr Grimond's voice showed that he was used to getting his own way.

'Yes, but if he doesn't, if he wants a friend standing by, then here I am.'

'I would prefer it, thank you,' said George. 'Perhaps we could go into the dining room?'

Delia watched them go, and then, running again, set off for the olive grove to find Marjorie and tell her about the arrival of Mr Grimond.

In the dining room, the three men grouped themselves at one end of the table. Mr Grimond placed a battered leather brief-case on the table and snapped open the lock.

'Just who are you?' Lucius asked. All his senses were on edge. He knew this kind of person; he'd had dealings with just such people in the States, purposeful men from the CIA setting about the government's business with quiet persistence. What had George to do with anyone of this kind? Secrets? Atom scientists had access to secrets, and with one spy revelation after another, perhaps this Grimond was here as a matter of routine security. But would the British government send a man all the way to Italy on a routine matter?'

'Do you have some identification?' he asked.

Mr Grimond reached into his inner pocket and pulled out some papers. He handed a card emblazoned with a crest to George, who passed it to Lucius.

'All very official and correct-looking, but I could run one of these up for a couple dollars any day of the week.'

George raised his hand in a weary gesture. 'I think we can assume that Mr Grimond is who he says he is.'

'If I can cover a few preliminary points. You are George Augustus Helsinger, born 1913 in Denmark. You are still a Danish citizen, although you have worked in England since 1932.'

'Mostly.'

'Mostly?'

'I was abroad from 1943 to 1945. In America.'

'Yes, you were a member of the team of scientists who went out from Britain to work on the development of the atomic bomb at Los Alamos.' George said nothing, and Mr Grimond went on. 'You knew Klaus Fuchs?'

'I knew most of the physicists there. We were a small community.'

'Come, come, there were several thousand personnel on the site.'

'But not several thousand physicists.'

'Did you know him well?'

'We were working on entirely different problems. We saw very little of one another.'

'Did you suspect he was passing secrets to the Soviets?'

'Of course I didn't.'

'Were you surprised when he was arrested?'

'I was appalled.'

'And yet many of his fellow physicists, Mr Oppenheimer

343

not least among them, expressed concern about the bomb and how the project would be handled by the politicians after the war.'

'I expressed concern about the bomb being dropped on Japan. Many of us did. For some, that concern extended to worrying about the dangers inherent in non-scientists' having control of anything so – so enormously lethal. That does not mean I knew what Klaus Fuchs was doing, or that I condoned his actions when I heard of them, nor that I myself would ever, under any circumstances, do such a thing.'

He paused, and Lucius broke in. George had himself well in hand, but Lucius could see the line of perspiration on his upper lip and the rigidity of his shoulders. 'Fuchs was tried and imprisoned nearly ten years ago. Isn't this rather scraping around in the dead ashes?'

'We have reason to believe, from information that has recently come to light, that Fuchs was not the only traitor. The reason this is of concern is not only that there is no statute of limitations on treason, but that so many of the scientists are still working in highly sensitive areas. You included, Dr Helsinger. And I would like to know why you are in Italy. We did issue instructions to your laboratory in Cambridge that none of the staff who had any connection with Fuchs should leave the country without telling us.'

'I have been away from work for some time. I was ill. I heard of no such request, and if I had, I would have ignored it. I do not think you can keep people in England on the grounds that they once knew Klaus Fuchs.'

Mr Grimond took some papers out of his briefcase and laid them on the table. He selected one, and laid it on top of the others. He straightened the papers into precise order. 'Let us return to the war years at Los Alamos. Among your team was one Dr Jamieson, is that so?'

George nodded. 'She died in 1945, of radiation burns, the result of a most tragic accident in the lab.'

344

'Dr Jamieson was invited to join the team at your request. One of only a tiny number of women scientists working on the project, is that not correct?'

'I fail to see—'

'Why did you ask for Dr Jamieson rather than anyone else?'

George was beginning to lose his temper. 'What an infinitely stupid question. There is only one reason you request a particular scientist, and that is because he, or in this case she, has something unique to offer. Dr Jamieson was outstanding in her field. Women physicists are rare, but physicists of the ability of Dr Jamieson are even rarer. She had met with prejudice in her career; I do not have a problem with women colleagues. However, I would not have asked for her had she not been one of only two physicists in the world at that time who had that particular expertise.'

'Why didn't you choose the other one?'

'Because he was in Berlin, working for the Nazis.'

Lucius intervened. 'Speaking as an outsider on this cosy conversation, isn't this history, Mr Grimond? Dr Jamieson is dead.'

'We are not at the moment interested in Dr Jamieson in as much as she is, as you say, no longer with us. We are very interested in the reasons for Dr Helsinger's choosing her as a member of his team, given her antecedents.'

'Are you now or have you ever been a member of the Communist Party?' said George with a sigh. 'Before you ask, I never, on any single occasion, discussed politics with Miranda. She was an American, working at Berkeley before she came to Los Alamos. She must have been cleared for security, as we all were. Was she left wing? She may have been. It's no crime. And, as Lucius says, it can't matter now.'

'Were you aware that Jamieson was her married name?'

'I knew she had been married, yes.'

'And divorced.'

'Yes.'

'Were you aware that she was Italian by birth, and that her father, the late Guido Malaspina, was . . .'

'What did you say her name was?' Lucius exclaimed.

'Malaspina. Ah, I can see that means something to you, as indeed it should, for it is in his house that you are currently staying.'

'His wife's house, to be strictly accurate,' said Lucius, exchanging a quick glance with George, who was looking thunderstruck.

At that moment the door opened and Theo came in. He looked larger than normal, and had a frown on his face. 'I thought you might need a hand, George,' he said. 'Delia filled me in on a few details.' He turned to Grimond. 'You are?'

'I see no reason . . . Very well.' He produced his card once more, the crown of a government document clearly visible.

'I'll sit in on your little talk, I think. I'm a lawyer.' Theo pulled out a chair and sat down. He had a notepad and pencil in his hand, which he laid on the table. 'You work for a government department, and you have some questions you want to ask Dr Helsinger. Carry on.'

'Mr Grimond was about to tell us about Mr Malaspina,' Lucius said. 'Judging by the distaste in your voice, Mr Grimond, he must have been a master criminal, a member of the Mafia.'

'Worse. He was a left-winger, with strong connections to the Communist Party in the nineteen twenties.'

'Anyone who was anti-fascist in the twenties had links to the Communist Party,' Lucius said. 'Does that make his daughter, an eminent scientist by all accounts, a fellow traveller? A spy? You should have more respect for people's reputations, Mr Grimond.'

'I have no respect for traitors,' he said severely.

'I think this conversation should finish right now,' said Lucius.

'This conversation will finish when I say it will, and I think it would be helpful if I spoke to Dr Helsinger alone, as I requested.'

'No,' said Theo. 'Not if Dr Helsinger wants us to stay.'

'Which I do,' said George.

Mr Grimond got to his feet. 'Dr Helsinger should not have left England without informing the authorities that he was doing so. In the circumstances, and given that his replies have not been helpful – in fact, he has not responded in a cooperative spirit – I must request that you return to England immediately, Dr Helsinger, for further questioning, under Section 2 of the—'

'Hold on,' said Lucius. 'Are you arresting George? Because I'm not sure you can do that.'

'You seem to have little notion of just how far my powers extend, Mr . . . ?'

'Wilde.'

'Of the banking family, I assume. You've recently applied for permission to stay and work in England. In view of your obstruction, and given what occurred during the war, I must warn you that you may be denied residence in the United Kingdom.'

'Save your breath. I'm an American citizen, on Italian soil. Whoever I may be answerable to, it's not you. And I don't like ex-military men who threaten me. In fact, I don't like military men at all. As to residence in England, I'm going to marry an Englishwoman, and I believe that gives me certain rights of abode. Does it, Theo?'

Theo was nodding in agreement. 'Under certain conditions, but I doubt if Mr Grimond is issuing more than an empty threat. Isn't the current American ambassador your uncle?'

'He is.'

'The CIA won't let that prejudice them, and once I pass your name to them . . .'

'The CIA wouldn't believe an Englishman who told them the sun was going to rise tomorrow.'

'As to Dr Helsinger,' said Theo, 'you are mistaken if you think you can compel him to return to England. I understand he holds a Danish passport, and he is on Italian soil. Should he not wish to return, you would have to apply for extradition, and given the law as it stands, although I confess it's not my field, I would say you haven't an earthly.'

'I intend to return to England,' said George with dignity. 'It is my home. And where I work. But in my own good time, and not under duress.'

'It may be your home, but you might find you no longer have a job to go to,' said Mr Grimond. 'Security with regard to anyone working in atomic science is being tightened every day, and I doubt very much if you would be given the clearance you need to continue in your present position.'

'I think you've said enough,' said Theo.

'More than enough,' said Lucius. 'God, I thought the days of McCarthy and his ilk were over, but it looks as though you Britons are just getting there. If you start seeing Reds under the beds, then you'll come to regret it.'

Theo saw Mr Grimond off the premises in silence.

'He's seething under that stiff upper lip,' said Lucius to George. 'Do you want a drink? This must all be very shocking for you.'

'No,' said George wearily. 'I have been expecting it. It explains several things that worried me before I left England. At work. Remarks made, uncertainty about funding. I think that Mr Grimond is right, and that my time at Cambridge may have come to an end.'

'Cambridge University isn't going to let itself be bullied by men like Grimond.'

'Men like Grimond hold the purse strings, or have a great deal of influence with those who do,' said George. 'No, what has shocked me is the revelation that Miranda was Beatrice Malaspina's daughter.'

'What is all this about the Malaspinas?' said Theo. 'I don't

348

like to see a man badgered, but face it, George, this Malaspina sounds as though he may have been mixed up in some rather undesirable activities.'

'I think I hear Felicity calling for you,' said Lucius mendaciously, and then, as Theo hurried out of the room, 'Come on, George. This is big news. Let's go find the others.'

'You worked with Beatrice Malaspina's daughter in America?' cried Delia. 'And you never said?'

'He didn't know,' said Marjorie.

'Didn't you recognise her from the portrait of her mother?'

'She does not seem to have taken after her mother, and you know, I am not so very good at faces and likenesses. Miranda was very American, very modern, her hair, her clothes; in Los Alamos we all dressed casually. She wore jeans, I remember, as most of us did.' He went over to the painting. 'Now, I can see a resemblance, in the eyes, the nose, that very distinctive nose, but plenty of people have a nose with that profile, like a Roman. You have an aquiline nose, Delia, and so do half the people in San Silvestro. And here Beatrice Malaspina is wearing her hair swept up, a formal frock . . . you can see why I would make no connection.'

'Odd,' said Lucius, 'that there are no photographs of Miranda Malaspina in the house. Nor of Guido Malaspina, if it comes to that. I think maybe we should have a word with Benedetta.'

Benedetta was not pleased to be summoned from the kitchen.

'She's asking if the other Englishman is staying to lunch,' Delia said, concentrating hard. 'I wish she wouldn't speak so fast.'

'And that's all we're going to get out of her on the subject, I reckon,' said Lucius, reporting the gist of the conversation as Benedetta hurried back to her steaming pan of pasta, muttering imprecations as she went. 'Miranda Malaspina married an American, which we know, and died, tragically, in America, which we also know. She and the heathen American were divorced, and there were no children from the marriage.'

'Well, it's a quarter of the mystery solved, at least,' said Jessica. 'Now you know what the connection is between George and Beatrice Malaspina.'

'What was Miranda like?' Delia asked George.

'A very fine mind, a brilliant scientist. Had she been a man . . . It is still very hard for a woman to gain the recognition she deserves. The scientific world is a very masculine one.'

'How did she die?'

'From radiation burns, which is a slow and painful death; she suffered greatly and bore it with great courage. She was in the hospital in Santa Fe, but there was nothing that any doctor could do for her. I spent as much time with her as I was able. We had become good friends.' His eyes were dark with sadness at the memory. 'It was a tragedy, for her to die like that, so painfully, from the radiation.' His voice faltered and he fell silent.

'It sounds simply horrible,' said Jessica.

Delia's blood was running cold. 'That's what will happen to us if someone drops the bomb.'

George turned a sombre face to her. 'It is how so many perished, miserably and without help, after we bombed Japan. It is why . . .'

'Why you've been haunted ever since by guilt at having had anything to do with it.'

'Yes,' said George. 'And I have gone on working in the same field, contributing by my work to ever more terrible possibilities . . .' He shook his head. 'Perhaps it is for the best. Perhaps Mr Grimond has done me a kindness.'

'How?' said Delia. 'By telling you Miranda's name?'

'He means,' Lucius said, 'that he may not be able to go on with his work in Cambridge.'

'What would you do if you couldn't do that?' said Marjorie. 'Are there other places – no, that's stupid. Not in your field.'

'For now,' said George with an effort, 'I shall not think about it. Here we are, let us all make the most of our time here. And I am even more grateful to be here now that I know it was the home of Miranda Jamieson. She was a remarkable woman, and I only regret that I never knew her mother.'

'You didn't know her, but she seems to have known a lot about you,' Delia pointed out. 'Including how you felt when the test on the A bomb was a success.'

'Which was after Miranda had died. So how did she find that out?'

FOUR

Lucius's figures were taking shape. Jessica and Delia were enchanted to see themselves in flowing robes. 'How do you know if they're accurate?' said Marjorie. 'Or is it just Hollywood mediaeval?'

'Definitely not,' said Lucius. 'You may have noticed that there are a lot of art books here, some even with colour plates. I've lifted the frocks from the paintings of Giotto, who was a contemporary of Dante's. All the pilgrims are dressed in the clothes of that period.'

'Yes, but most of them still look more modern. It's only the pose and the clothes that look like something out of the middle ages, and the landscapes, with that funny perspective. Yours is modern, too.'

'So I should hope. I'm here and now in the fifties, not doing a pastiche of an old master. Now, I noticed an art shop in San Silvestro, and I'm short of a couple of things, so I shall take a trip into town on my little Vespa this afternoon.'

'The shops don't open until after four,' Marjorie reminded him.

'No, of course not. That takes some getting used to, these shop hours.'

'Are you sure it isn't early closing?' said Delia.

They thought about that. 'Monday morning for almost everything, Wednesday afternoon for food, Saturday afternoon for . . .'

'Well, it's Tuesday, and Tuesday everything's open,' said Lucius. 'Anyone want a lift into town?'

'I'm going to take George shrimping,' said Jessica. 'I found a shrimping net in the stable. It will do you good, George, to dabble about in the rock pools in the sun. Your pate is nicely bronzed now, so you can keep up the tan.'

George laughed. 'I have not been shrimping since I was a small boy. I should enjoy that very much.'

'I'm writing,' said Marjorie.

'Delia?'

'No thanks.' Delia couldn't have said why she was disinclined to go with Lucius. She enjoyed zipping about on the Vespa, but she wanted some time to herself. 'I've got some postcards to write,' she said. She would find a place away from the others, and away from Theo and Felicity, just to do some thinking. She had a lot to think about, and at the back of her mind was still the nagging question, why were Theo and Felicity here? Was it to have a go at Jessica, to try to make her go back to Richie? Or was there something else?

After lunch, she took herself to the olive grove, but realising that she would be eaten alive by insects there, and hearing Felicity calling her name, she slipped round the house and let herself into the tower. There could not be a better place for putting her thoughts in order than in the brilliance and serenity of the top of the tower. And since Lucius had thoughtfully tied up the chain and put the *pericoloso* notice up again, she knew that neither Theo nor Felicity would look for her there. Both of them were the kind who took heed of warning notices.

* * *

353

It was past six o'clock, and the heat of the day had mellowed into a comfortable warmth, with the walls of the house smelling of hot stone, and letting off their own gentle radiance, before Marjorie heard the sound of the Vespa, and knew that Lucius was back. She rolled the page she had just finished out of the typewriter, got up, stretched, and went to her window. There was Lucius, just coming through the gate.

He had a passenger on the pillion. A woman.

A woman whom Marjorie knew by sight; what on earth was she doing here, with her arms clasped round Lucius's waist?

'More visitors,' said Jessica, who had come back from a happy time on the beach with George. Delia, who had seen them arriving from her vantage point in the tower, came out on to the doorstep to join her.

'This is turning into Piccadilly Circus,' she said. 'A guest from the hotel, I suppose. Why on earth has Lucius brought her here?'

'A girlfriend?' said Jessica, and they both laughed, for the woman who had slid off her seat was certainly not Lucius's girlfriend. She was in her fifties, with short and very elegant grey hair. She was wearing a linen suit, had a lean and interesting face, and was looking very amused at whatever Lucius was saying to her.

'I don't believe it!' said Marjorie. 'What can she be doing here?'

'Who is she?'

'Olivia Hawkins, the publisher. She's a partner at Hawkins & Hallett.'

'Are they your publishers?'

'No, but it's a small world, and I've met her once or twice. She has quite a reputation in the book world.'

'She looks what Lucius might call a tough cookie.'

'She has a very good name, and works with some first class authors.'

354

Marjorie felt a pang as she said this. Once, she would have been called a first class author. She was writing again, yes, but after a gap of more than five years her name would have faded from public notice. Other, fresher faces, new writers, had taken centre stage.

Although to be fair to herself, she had a better chance of making a comeback than an actress like Maria; those extra years mattered to an actress. No one cared very much how young a writer of detective stories was; in fact, they admired the older ones. Look at Agatha Christie, going from strength to strength. Not that Marjorie was in that league, but the very title Queen of Crime was one that went with age and experience.

'Did you tell her you were here?' Delia asked, as the woman and Lucius came towards them, sharing a joke; it was clear that Lucius liked her.

'No, why should I?' said Marjorie. 'I told you, she's no more than a slight acquaintance.'

'I ran into Olivia in the Piazza,' said Lucius. 'She had been asking for a taxi to take her to the Villa Dante, and so Domenico brought her to me.'

'Like a grouse in a dog's mouth,' said Olivia. She held out her hand to Marjorie. 'I don't expect you'll remember me. I'm Olivia Hawkins, and I'm very glad to meet up with you.'

'Me?'

'Petronella told me your whereabouts, and since I was coming to Italy, I decided to make a detour and see if I could find you.'

Petronella was Marjorie's agent, a fair-weather friend, who never returned her phone calls and never wrote to her. Marjorie had given the address of the Villa Dante to her secretary before leaving for Paris, because from time to time, just occasionally, dribs and drabs of money came in, from a reprint, or a foreign edition, and ever dwindling royalties from her English and American publishers.

'You need to find a new agent,' Olivia was saying briskly. 'Petronella's no use to you, she's a perfect fool of a woman. Fine when everything's hunky-dory, but useless when the going gets tough. Now, tell me at once, are you working on anything?'

They all liked Olivia Hawkins, except for Theo, who could be heard muttering that Delia was getting herself involved with a very peculiar set of people; he clearly found the formidable Olivia rather terrifying.

Felicity admired the cut of her suit. 'Celestine?' she asked after a swift glance, and then took no further notice of a woman who was clearly not of her world.

'One extra for dinner, if you can manage it,' Lucius told Benedetta. She, too, seemed to approve of the new arrival, the English signora, who spoke beautiful Italian, she told Lucius. 'Pure Tuscan, I gather,' said Lucius with a grin. 'My Roman accent doesn't meet with such favour, although I have to say, when I hear Benedetta and Pietro bickering, they seem to be speaking an entirely different language altogether. Etruscan, perhaps.'

Marjorie was in a daze. She couldn't believe that Olivia had come to San Silvestro expressly to find her. 'I have business in Rome, and so it seemed too good a chance to miss, you being here,' she said. 'Do I see crostini? How delicious. Lucius, watch what you drink, because I can see I shall be in no state to take the handlebars of your Vespa. What a wonderful vehicle; I've been fascinated watching all the young people whizzing around on their scooters in Rome. I plan to buy one the minute I get back to England. Just the thing for London traffic.'

She popped the morsel into her mouth and cooed with pleasure. 'Anchovy and *sticchino*, quite exquisite. Marjorie, remind me who you're with.'

'I'm published by Philberts. Or was. Most of my books are out of print now.'

'And let's hope that any option on your next book will have expired,' Olivia said. 'A good agent is what you need, and I shall put you in touch with Gregory Silkin, just the man for you. Now that you've started writing again, you need a publisher, and we'll do better for you than Philberts, I promise you.'

'Started isn't finishing,' said Marjorie, who felt that the ground was being cut from under her feet.

'I know, you'd rather spend the next year or so writing and rewriting and then scrapping it all, and never finishing so that you don't have to show it to anyone – oh, I know all the authors' tricks, I assure you. It's not surprising you've had a lull after that dreadful accident. An electric fire falling into the bath! What a miracle you survived.'

Marjorie braced herself, and the words were out before she could stop them.

'It wasn't an accident. It was suicide. Unsuccessful suicide.'

Around the table there was a sudden silence. Jessica, shocked, was shaking her head in disbelief. George's dark eyes were full of sympathy, and Lucius sat back, watching Delia watching Marjorie.

'I guessed as much,' Olivia said matter-of-factly. 'You tried to kill yourself because your lover ran off with that ridiculous man.'

'I told you she was a liz,' Theo said in an aside to Felicity, who was looking at Marjorie as though she were some creature in the zoo.

Delia heard him. 'Shut up, Theo. Marjorie had a girlfriend. So what? Most of the men you were at school with went to bed with one another and I expect lots of them still do. And aren't half the bench of judges as queer as coots? Anyhow, it's none of your business whether Marjorie's lover was a man or a woman.'

Theo subsided, Felicity cast a reproachful look at her sister, and George spoke.

'Forgive me, Marjorie, but is that not an extremely bizarre and unreliable way to attempt to take your life? Jumping into the bath holding an electric fire?'

'Effective, I would have thought,' said Lucius, 'but clearly not.'

'The electricity where I was living was not very reliable. The wiring was old, and it used to go off. As it happened, at precisely that moment the woman in the room above plugged in her iron and fused the system. So I had nothing more than a tremendous shock.'

'Which left you with your voices?' said Jessica.

'That's a well-documented consequence of a severe electric shock,' said Olivia. 'It can happen, so I've read, when a person is struck by lightning.'

'Perhaps,' said George, in his kindly way, 'the voices were always there, but they kept themselves on the page when you were writing. However, when you couldn't turn to the type-writer, they spoke inside your head, instead.'

'It doesn't explain her uncanny knowledge about what Beatrice Malaspina's been up to,' said Jessica in Delia's ear.

'Attempted suicide is a crime,' said Theo, coming back into the fray.

'Yes, and when I finally came to, the first thing I looked for was a constable sitting at the end of my hospital bed. Isn't that what happens? You'd think they'd have more important crimes to deal with. Anyhow, since people thought like George here that it would be a daft thing to do deliberately, it was taken for granted that it was an accident, that I slipped on the lino . . .'

'Forget it,' said Olivia. 'Forget it and move on. Now, Dr Helsinger, Marjorie tells me that you are an atom scientist, and that you had a visit from a Mr Grimond today.'

'A highly unpleasant man,' said Lucius. 'Definitely one to put top of the Not at Home list.'

'He's staying at the same hotel as me, or he was, since I

understand he's left. I should say he's out for your blood, Dr Helsinger, and I advise you to be careful.'

'George, if you please. Do you know this man?'

'I most certainly do. I had the misfortune to work with him during the war, when he was Colonel Grimond. I see he's dropped the military title. We were in MI5,' she added. 'I left after the war to go back to publishing; he stayed on to become a big cheese. He is an unforgiving man, George, a terrier when he scents even a whiff of Reds. And no doubt, as far as he's concerned, all atom scientists ought to be kept under constant surveillance, their passports held under lock and key, and they themselves preferably curfewed in a guarded hostel at nights and weekends.'

That made George laugh. 'I have come across some of these people. We had them in America during the war, at Los Alamos.'

'You were there?' Olivia's eyes were bright with interest. 'Have you ever thought of writing a book? Atom science for the layman? We're planning a series of books on modern science, and such a book would be perfect for us.'

'No, you can't have the typewriter,' Marjorie said. 'Go on, George, you could do it. I heard you explaining about isotopes to Delia, and even a child could have understood it. You're a born teacher, and if you can write in the same way, you'll earn the undying gratitude of a bewildered world.'

'Isotopes?' said Olivia, pleased. 'I think our readers would be very keen to have the low-down on isotopes. If we're all going to be blown to kingdom come, the intelligent citizen would at least like to understand how it happens.'

Felicity let out a squeak of dismay. 'Of all the things to talk about at dinner, bombs and blowing people up! How horrid!'

'One has to face facts,' said Olivia cheerfully. 'People like George have opened that particular Pandora's box, so we have to learn to live in the new atomic age. Now enough of bombs. This is far too glorious a house to mar the atmosphere with any more talk of weapons or war. I understand from Lucius that your hostess is the late Beatrice Malaspina, who invited you all here in her unavoidable absence, although none of you knew her. Is this true? Do none of you have any idea why you're here?'

'The only link any of us has discovered to Beatrice Malaspina is that George knew her daughter,' Lucius said.

'Why did you blurt it out like that, Marjorie, about trying to commit suicide?' Delia said as they went upstairs. The sound of the Vespa faded into the distance; Lucius was taking a decidedly merry Olivia back to her hotel.

'It seemed time.'

'Aren't you afraid that Olivia will bruit it abroad? Aren't publishers terrific gossips?'

'Do you think she will? I'm not sure that I care very much, unless it means the police knocking on my door one morning.'

'If she was in MI5, she'll know how to keep her mouth shut. Is she married?'

'Not that I ever heard,' said Marjorie. 'I imagine that, like me, she's not the marrying kind.'

'I like her,' said Delia. 'I like her a lot.'

'So do I,' said Marjorie.

FIVE

They had asked Olivia to spend the next day at the villa. Only Theo, who still felt uncomfortable in her presence, had objected, but Delia told him that he, as a guest in the house, could hardly lay down the law as to whom she and the others might invite. 'After all, we've asked Olivia, and no one invited you and Felicity.'

Delia was becoming hourly more irritated with Theo and his uxoriousness. Where had those passionate feelings of only a day ago gone to? Faded with the moonlight, flown away with the wind and the bats. Her lingering passion for him was a chimera, a mere ghostly echo of feeling she had once truly had, but which had, she now admitted to herself, vanished a long while ago.

And, with her new sense of clarity, she could see that Theo did indeed dote on Felicity. Delia had taken it for granted, given Felicity's likeness to their mother, that her sister was of the same kind as Fay Saltford. But now she suspected that the likeness was merely a thing of flesh and bone, and that Felicity's hankering for glamour and excitement was only skin deep; that with motherhood she would become, always beautiful, but attached to her home and husband in a way that their mother never had been.

The difference was that Felicity did love Theo. She hadn't snatched him away from Delia in a fit of power and pique at Delia's having such an attractive man in tow. Theo had fallen in love with her and she with Theo, and their mother had possibly never had that kind of affection for her father. That was uncharted territory, that was the area where no child could ever go, into those years when parents met and wooed and married, and lived together before you were born.

Happy families, she said to herself. One doesn't know the half of it.

Olivia walked up to the villa, arriving after breakfast. She was clad in white knee-length shorts, which made Theo frown and mutter to Felicity about women of a certain age, but Delia could only admire her lean brown legs. Lucius was back at his paints, but he instantly put down his brushes and allowed her to admire his handiwork, which was, no question about it, extremely good, although it gave Delia a shock to see her modern face looking out at her from that timeless Italian landscape.

'The sunglasses add a surreal note,' said Olivia.

'Yes, why have you put them in?'

'Humour,' said Lucius. 'Beatrice Malaspina was a woman who dearly loved a joke, one can see that. Besides, your eyes are far too full of fire and colour for me to capture in this small space. You demand a bigger canvas. Anyhow, I see you this summer in those sunglasses, so there you are.' He got up, and brushed his knees. 'Do you think Olivia would like to see the tower?'

'Yes, she would,' said Marjorie, appearing at the door. 'I was planning to show it to you, Olivia. Be prepared; it's not for the faint-hearted. It will remind you of everything you've come to Italy to get away from.'

'You mean it's a gallery of my fellow publishers and agents bearing pitchforks? Lead me to it.'

Alone with Lucius, who looked slightly nonplussed at having his role as cicerone taken away from him, Delia examined his painting. 'You've got George to a T, only he doesn't look so unhappy as he does in life. He is such a grave man, and I don't think he's meant to be that way. You've made him look almost monkish.'

'That was Marjorie's doing. She said she saw him as a priest, so that's what he is, a preacher of science.'

'Not for much longer if they take his job away from him. Where is he? I haven't seen him this morning.'

'In San Silvestro. He went to early morning Mass.'

'It isn't Sunday.'

'He may need the ritual after the shocking attack from the Grimond man. We should never have let him set foot in the villa. I'd rather have cockroaches.'

'Benedetta wouldn't. Those kind of people are like cockroaches, though, I do agree. Sinister and unstoppable, and with no concern for the world they invade.'

'Like tax inspectors.'

'And the men from the ministry of food who came round after the war to check up that you weren't eating your own eggs. We had one at Saltford Hall, and my father nearly came to blows with him. I've never known him so angry. He isn't usually an angry man.'

'I should like to meet your father.'

'Do you think so? I don't think you'd have anything in common. He lives such a moral and righteous life that he's barely human.'

'If he were barely human, you wouldn't be up in arms against him all the time.'

Delia considered that. 'He infuriates me. He's silently criticising me all the time. He thinks that whatever I do is wrong.'

'Isn't he proud of you?'

'What's there to be proud of?' And then, quickly, 'No, I'm not fishing, nor indulging in little Miss Self-Pity. It's simply that so much I've done is the kind of thing he hates. Spending all my time at Cambridge doing music instead of concentrating on my languages, then going in for singing and opera when I came down.'

'Yes, it sounds like a stiff pa's nightmare,' Lucius said, all his attention focused on the figure of Marjorie, whom he'd painted with a swagger and a keen eye.

'My father wanted me to go into the family business. Put in a good day's work for a modest salary.'

'If you weren't working, and your father was keeping the purse strings closed, how could you afford to eat, let alone do the operatic training?'

'My godmother left me some money. She died just before I finished at university.'

'So you blued the poor old thing's life savings to embark on a career on the stage.'

'Poor old thing nothing. She was even older than Beatrice Malaspina, she was rich in a big way, and what she left me was small change to her.'

'Who scooped the rest?'

'A cats' home.'

'As a banker, I wince. As as human being, I applaud. I like cats.'

'She was my great-aunt, my father's aunt, and very like him: no doubts about what was right and what was wrong.'

'So she hadn't heard about your bohemian longings, one supposes.'

'She had. That's why I got enough to keep me in cat food . . .'

'And the moggies scooped the pool. Well, if that didn't teach you a lesson, I don't know what will. Why is your father so against opera, by the way? It seems very Victorian.'

'He's a puritan. A killjoy. He doesn't want anyone to be happy. Music makes people happy, and it's colourful and all the things he hates.'

'Really?'

Lucius wasn't looking at her; he was stirring a drop of white into a patch of green that he'd spread on his palette. Did her father not want people to be happy? Wouldn't that mean he actively wanted people to be unhappy, and was that the case?

She remembered him standing on the platform, seeing her off on the train back to school. Taking his hat off to her, as the train pulled out, a politeness to a lump of an eleven-year-old schoolgirl. She remembered getting his letters; every single week, without fail, she knew that she would get at least one letter. Her mother never wrote to her. Her father wrote about the house and the weather, and about the business, and never forgot to ask how she was, how the term was going.

And she wrote back, as school rules obliged her to: Sunday afternoon, after lunch, one hour set aside for writing a letter home. A letter that had to be put inside an unsealed addressed and stamped envelope for the duty mistress to read before it was sealed and posted on Monday morning. She told her father of her childish and adolescent successes, and also of her disappointments and failures, and he wrote back always with praise for her achievements and sympathy for what had gone wrong.

She remembered him looking out things from home for her to take to Cambridge, to cheer up a bare college room: cushions, a rug, pictures. And arriving, uncommunicative and reserved, to talk the college authorities round into rusticating her for a fortnight instead of sending her down.

She'd sailed very close to the wind then. She'd bragged to her friends that she didn't give a hoot if she left Cambridge without a degree, but she did mind, and she knew her father would mind.

He'd had a brief interview with her before he'd left.

'You won't get a decent degree now, nothing like you might have been capable of if you'd worked. But at least get some kind of degree. There's nothing worse in life than a lost opportunity.'

He'd even asked her, when she went to live in London, if she were happy. 'I can understand why you don't care to live at home,' he'd said.

Then they'd begun to argue. She'd flung her antics in his face, trying to provoke him, so that she could fly at him and tell him what she thought of his stuffy out-of-date morality.

'I'm not sure I'm very good at men,' she said. 'I didn't get on with my brother at all. In fact I loathed him, and things have always been difficult with my father.'

'Not to mention Theo,' said Lucius, applying a tiny drop of green to the end of Marjorie's nose.

Delia flushed. How much did he know about Theo? Had Jessica, or Marjorie . . . ? No, it must be nothing more than conjecture, guesswork.

'He's changed,' she said defensively.

'No, he hasn't. You have.'

'That tower!' said Olivia, coming through the door with Marjorie. 'What an extraordinary thing for Beatrice Malaspina to have done.'

'She seemed more interested in holding a mirror up to our lives than in revealing hers,' said Lucius. 'I hope you passed a comfortable night at the hotel, by the way. I forgot to ask.'

'I did, even though my slumbers were disturbed by an uncouth guest who turned up at two in the morning and roused the house wanting to be let in.'

'So you have an annoyed Signora Lucci this morning.'

'Not at all. She is overwhelmed by the sudden popularity of her hotel with the English; I caught her at the desk this morning with an English phrase book. Which seemed to date from the time of the Great War, so that will be dandy if any veterans turn up. She can have a nice chat about the trenches.'

'Another English guest?' said Lucius. 'Who is it this time?'

'He's a newspaper man, a reporter. Interested in the Villa Dante, as it happens. He was asking if Mrs Meldon was staying here.'

'Dear God, does he look like a ferret?' said Jessica.

'He does.'

'You didn't tell him I was here?'

'I wouldn't tell a reporter anyone was anywhere, especially not this man. It's Slattery, of the *Sketch*.'

'I knew it, when you said he was a ferret,' said Jessica. 'Hell and damnation, however did he find me?'

'It seems quite easy for people to find those of us staying at the Villa Dante,' said Lucius. 'I live in hourly fear of finding Elfrida on the doorstep.'

'Serve you right if you did,' said Delia.

'I'll go and shut the gates,' said Marjorie. 'And warn Benedetta and Pietro to keep strangers out and their mouths buttoned, or I will if you'll come and translate, Olivia.'

'What's a ferret?' said Lucius.

'Don't you have them in America? It's like a weasel. Only white. And vicious.'

Which was a very apt description of Giles Slattery. And if he had found her address, what were the chances of Richie's not knowing where she was? Still, there was no danger of Richie coming all the way to Italy to find her. He'd bide his time until she was back in England.

'Where are you going?' said Lucius.

'Upstairs, out of sight.'

It occurred to Jessica, as she scanned the landscape from the window for signs of the ferret, that she still didn't know why Theo and Felicity had come to the Villa Dante. Theo wasn't the sort of man to set off on a jaunt abroad, and, come to think of it, weren't the courts still sitting? Which meant that he'd left work to come to Italy. Why? Just because of her desire to get a divorce? Theo didn't like to see her picture splashed all over the pages of the popular press. He probably thought it reflected badly on him, being so closely connected to her, but there must be more to it than that. Had Richie got at him, persuaded him to come?

He seemed on edge, but she'd put it down to the fact that Felicity clearly wasn't feeling too well. Who would, throwing up every morning? It was typical of Felicity to wake up feeling ghastly and then to come down mid-morning looking ravishing in an exquisite summer outfit.

Theo had said they needed to have a word with her about a few things, and she had avoided him and Felicity and any chance of a tête-à-tête, in case the vexed matter of her and Richie came up.

Yet her curiosity was aroused. She would get them alone, make them come clean about just what exactly they were doing in Italy, why they had gone to such lengths to find her address. What had to be said, moreover, that couldn't have been put in a letter?

Her attention was caught by a familiar figure coming along the road to the villa. She'd have known the wretched man anywhere, even though he had swapped his trilby for a panama, and his baggy suit for an equally misshapen affair in crumpled linen. There he was, with a camera strung round his neck, walking up to the gates as bold as brass.

Never one for the niceties, he rattled at the bars before turning to see if there was a bell. When he found it, he rang it, and Jessica saw with satisfaction that he was having to wait. Who would come out? Had Marjorie managed to convey to Benedetta that she must on no account admit him to the villa?

It seemed that she had, for it was Lucius who came out. A Lucius changed from the casually dressed man with a palette in his hand. This was a dapper Lucius, dressed *à point* in white flannels and a crisp short-sleeved shirt. His hair was sleek, his bearing easy and confident. He went up to the gates. Who was on which side of the bars? Lucius representing her looking out, or the ferret looking in?

She longed to be able to hear what Lucius was saying. Not that it mattered; nothing short of brute force would keep Slattery from his prey. Yet he had taken a step back from the gate, as though surprised.

Not as surprised as she was to see Delia drifting towards the gate, wearing a silk frock and an enormous straw hat. Sunglasses and high-heeled sandals completed the picture of elegance, and she slid her hand through Lucius's arm as she joined him at the gate. She was talking, at length, turning to Lucius as though for corroboration, gesturing, shrugging.

What on earth was going on? What had the pair of them said to persuade Slattery to leave, for leave he had, setting off down the road at a cracking pace.

She ran downstairs and arrived breathless as Lucius and Delia came in from the terrace.

'Well,' drawled Delia. 'Didn't we just see that little creep off, honey?'

'Your accent is impeccable,' said Lucius. 'How did you learn to do that?'

'I've spent quite a lot of time in America. And I'm a good actress, though I say it myself.'

'Where's he gone?' said Jessica.

'To catch a train to La Spezia, and then to make his way to the Villa Lante,' said Delia.

'To where?'

Lucius and Delia had hoodwinked him good and proper, but it wouldn't have bought them more than a couple of days' grace. With the resources of his paper behind him, eager for a muckraking scoop, he'd not be long gone, Jessica told them. 'But I am grateful. How did you manage to persuade him I wasn't here but might be there?'

'We're Americans, renting this villa from the owner,' said Delia. 'No, we'd never heard of you. No, you weren't staying here. Then Lucius asked to see the address he had written down and said no doubt there was a mistake, and he'd find that this Mrs Meldon was in fact at the Villa Lante, at San Sebastiano, quite a way further south. He knew for a fact that English people were staying there, but he'd have to be wary, because he'd heard that they were fanatical about privacy. Rumour had it that one of the group was a film star, incognito, keeps herself to herself behind dark glasses.

'So off he trotted,' finished Lucius, 'like a good little newshound.'

'He'll find out you lied, and he'll be more persistent than ever. He'll be back like a shot when he finds you've been leading him up the garden path,' said Jessica.

'He won't be back soon,' said Lucius. 'As it happens, there is a film star staying at the Villa Lante, and she is very, very concerned about her privacy, for reasons which I won't go into, and they are so sensitive about snoopers and news-papermen that they have guards and the ear of the local police chief. I think your ferret friend may have bitten off more than he can chew, given that he's off his familiar beat.'

'How do you know about the film star?' said Delia suspiciously.

'She's my cousin.'

That evening, they were back to their original group. Olivia had returned to the hotel, to change and dine out with friends who had a house a few miles on the other side of San Silvestro. And Theo had declared his intention of taking Felicity to dine in the town. 'Miss Hawkins tells us that there's a very attractive-looking restaurant in the main square there. We thought we'd try it.'

He was put out when the Jaguar wouldn't start. 'Damn those spark plugs, they were supposed to fix them.'

Jessica refused to lend him her car.

'Sorry, Theo, no can do. The foreign insurance is awfully complicated, and it doesn't include you. It doesn't take long to walk.'

'Walk!' Felicity wasn't walking anywhere. 'When it's so hot and dusty on that road? What would I look like? Besides, I don't have shoes for walking along that kind of surface.'

'Take the Vespa,' said Lucius, and they had the pleasure of seeing Theo, bolt upright, with Felicity sitting side-saddle behind him, phutting gingerly off through the gates.

George had spent most of the day in San Silvestro, and now, as the sun sank in a glowing ball into the sea, making the silvery water red, he demanded to be told what had been going on. 'I met Miss Hawkins, and she said a reporter had been here. Why was this?'

Delia didn't ask what he'd been doing in San Silvestro and he didn't say, but he had a strangely peaceful air about him this evening, as though he had come to some decision which relieved him of the burden that had been troubling him so much.

The observation surprised her. She wouldn't have noticed any difference in him only a few days earlier. Could it be that by facing up to truths about oneself, one became less not more self-centred, and therefore more aware of how other people were feeling and thinking?

Marjorie was another one who looked altogether more relaxed and happy. But Delia knew the reason for that: she was out of her slump, she was writing again, and Olivia Hawkins had brought the prospect of a new start to her stalled career. And more than that, for it was likely that the two women were going to be friends. At least.

Lucky Marjorie.

George was laughing now, as Delia adopted her American persona to show him how they'd managed to get rid of Slattery. 'You remind me exactly of certain women I knew in America,' he said.

They talked about Lucius's painting, and Marjorie's writing. It was going to be a tough book, she said. Not tough to write, that went without saying, but tough in substance

371

and subject matter. Teddy boys and the underlife of London. Gangs.

'What do you know about gangs?' Lucius said.

'There was a gang down my way when I was a girl. Gangs are gangs, and the public like gangs just now. Readers want to be scared. Life's good, there are jobs. The great fear is the bomb, but that's too big and alarming a fear to take to bed with you. Gangs, wickedness in a seedy part of the town, gives you a thrill and makes you glad to be snug by the fire in your cosy suburban house.'

After dinner, Delia played and sang, and the others sat on the terrace, with Benedetta's yellow candles keeping the insects at bay, and the music blending with the endless raucous sound of the cicadas, the soft hooting of an owl, the distant sound of the sea.

'I wish this could go on for ever,' Jessica said. 'I wish that summer had no end, that the stars were never hidden behind clouds, that the air was always balmy and the world didn't exist beyond our gates.'

'Heaven, in fact,' said George. 'Plenty of time for that in due course, Jessica. Meanwhile, think of the calm after storm, the harbour after a perilous journey . . .'

'Who's that from?' said Jessica. 'Dante again?'

'Ariosto,' said Marjorie. 'He was translated into English by John Harington, to whom we owe the invention of the water closet. Which is why we call it the jakes. He was one of the many Elizabethans who had a love affair with Italy and Italian.'

'This is a country that casts a spell on the English, I think,' said George.

'I think,' said Jessica, lighting a cigarette, 'that anywhere that isn't a land of fog and drizzle casts a spell over the English. Now, while it's just us, do you realise you haven't done a thing to find that codicil since Theo and Felicity arrived? Pretty soon, *il dottore* is going to be tripping up to the door, and you're going to have to admit defeat.'

'I expect it's staring us in the face,' said Delia sleepily.

'Defeat?' said Lucius.

'The codicil. Either that, or it doesn't exist. Perhaps what she left us are these days here. In which case, our inheritance is nearly spent.'

'That is a possibility,' said George. 'And the gift of a tranquil spirit is not to be sneezed at.'

'No,' said Marjorie, giving way to a yawn. 'She left a codicil all right. We're just too dim to find it.'

'I shall say a prayer to the great St Antony of Padua, who finds what is lost,' said George. 'And I have looked, Jessica. I searched in every one of the books in the tower, and there are treasures there indeed, but no documents, no legal paper.'

'You could try St Jude,' said Lucius with a smile.

'Jude?' said Delia, thinking how much she liked that smile.

'The patron saint of lost causes.'

SIX

Marjorie came out with it in her direct way at breakfast the next day; how did she know that was what they had been talking about first thing that morning?

'Tell me about your father's business, Delia. You never said much about it. Textiles, isn't it? Mills up in the north, grinding the faces of the poor as they labour at their looms.'

Theo choked on a piece of apple which he had carefully peeled and quartered.

'Not much grinding these days, unfortunately for your Dickensian visions,' Delia said. 'The unions don't like it. As it happens, my father has always been one of your enlightened employers, and he values his workers far too much to oppress them.'

'Isn't the textile industry being wiped out by cheap imports flooding into the country?'

'Yes, but my father's canny. He did very well in the war, out of making artificial silk for parachutes.' While she was still at school, she had begged her father for some parachute silk, just a few scraps to make some underwear. He had flatly refused, but then two yards of the stuff arrived in a parcel. It was a miracle that it had survived the post office pilfering. Flawed fabric, he said in his curt note. Flawed it might be, but to Delia it could have been silk threaded with gold for its value to her. 'Do you remember that, Jessica?'

'Yes. You divided it into six, and gave all your friends enough to make knickers and a camisole. Not just friends; you gave some to Regula, and I've never seen anyone so happy. Regula was a refugee,' she said to Marjorie. 'The school gave several scholarships to daughters of eminent refugees.'

'I wonder what happened to Regula,' said Delia. 'I lost touch with her.'

'Your trouble is, you've lost touch with all your friends. We'll go to one of those grim cocktails they do in London for old girls, and then you can meet up with some of them. Hadn't you heard that Regula became a doctor, working in the Midlands?'

'Really, Delia.' Theo had recovered from his tussle with the apple. 'It's hardly appropriate for you to talk about Saltford's in those terms. I don't know' – with a glare at Marjorie – 'why the subject has come up.'

He thinks Marjorie was listening at the door, Delia said inwardly. He doesn't know Marjorie's knack of picking up what's in the air.

And there had been a good deal in the air during the conversation she had had with Theo before breakfast. He and Felicity, not sick for once, but looking quite radiant. How unfair that being pregnant should make her sister look even more beautiful, while less favoured women got to be puffy and podgy-faced.

They had cornered Delia as she was coming light-footed down the stairs. 'Good morning, Flicka. Feeling better this morning? What a heavenly day. I'm going to swim straight after breakfast.'

'You'll get cramp if you do,' said Felicity, sounding so like their old nanny that it made Delia laugh.

'A word, if you please,' said Theo, ushering her into the

drawing room, which smelt of beeswax and the roses which Benedetta had arranged in a huge china bowl. 'We need to have a serious talk.'

'On a day like this?' Delia was wary, although her tone was flippant.

'About Daddy,' said Felicity.

'Why? What's up? There's nothing wrong with him, is there?' No, there couldn't be; they would have said at once if he were ill, or . . .

'Nothing's the matter with him, except anno domini,' said Theo.

It took her a minute to grasp what he was saying. 'You mean he's getting frail?' That was nonsense; tough wiry lean men like her father didn't get frail, just more knotty and gnarled and unyielding.

'No, he's in perfect health, as far as I know, but he isn't getting any younger. He's nearly seventy, as you know, and he's been giving serious thought about what is to become of the business. He feels it's time to hand it over to younger hands.'

'He's got some good managers, hasn't he? What's the problem?'

As far as Delia knew, her father intended to divide his shares in the company between her and Felicity. The business would be looked after by the men he had appointed over the years, and they would draw dividends.

'The problem is,' said Theo, irritation showing in his voice, 'that he's got a bee in his bonnet about wanting to keep the business in the family.'

'Isn't that what he's always planned to do?'

'You don't understand. We're not talking about shares here, but hands-on day to day running of the business.'

'He's off his rocker,' said Delia flatly. 'He can't want Felicity to have anything to do with that. How can she, now that there's a baby on the way?' Besides, she might have added, you wouldn't trust Felicity to run anything more demanding than a stall at a charity sale, and she'd probably be bored with that after half an hour.

'Delia, try not to be dense. He wants you.'

'To work for him?' Hadn't she and her father been over this old ground over and over again?

'Not precisely work for him. He wants you to take over, to run the whole concern,' Theo said baldly.

Delia was speechless, but Theo still had plenty to say. 'I know. It is a ludicrous idea, and I've told him so. He won't listen to me, you know what he's like.'

A thought occurred to her for the first time. Did Theo want to be in charge at Saltford's?

'I haven't offered to step in, because I value my career as a lawyer, and I'm standing for Parliament at the next election. I can't possibly run a big outfit like Saltford's without giving all that up.'

'Besides,' said Felicity, 'he doesn't want you to.'

'It's you he wants,' Theo said to Delia.

'Well, that's out of the question too. Come on, Theo. I've no experience, I never have had an office job of any kind, what I know about the business is only odds and ends I've picked up from listening to him talk about it over the years. I wouldn't know where to begin, and I don't intend to try. My life is music. I made that decision, and I'm sticking to it.'

'Oh, you and music,' said Felicity crossly. 'Music's what people do who can't do anything else. It isn't a serious career. You go on about a vocation, but honestly, Delia, it's not like being a doctor or anything useful, is it?'

'You don't have any idea what you're talking about.'

'If you won't agree,' said Felicity, her lipsticked mouth quivering with either temper or concern, it was difficult to tell which, 'then he says he's going to make a trust and all the money will go to a charity.'

'What?'

'You and Flicka would get ten per cent, that's all,' said Theo.

'What charity?'

'It's something to do with vice.'

'Vice?'

'An offshoot of moral rearmament. Improving the moral well-being of our nation.'

'You're making this up.' For her father, business was business, and his moral views, although they influenced the enlightened way he ran his factories, had never, she was sure, influenced that side of his life.

'Ten per cent,' wailed Felicity.

'And we'd have no say at all; should the trustees at some point decide to sell the business, then that would be that. Your shares might become totally worthless.'

'And what do you think any shares would be worth if an ignoramus like me took over?' snapped Delia. She was full of rage against her father. If he couldn't control her life in one way, then he'd try to do it in another. How typical of him.

'Calm down,' said Theo. 'Look, I'm not putting this very well. I do think there's more to this than Lord Saltford enacting some kind of revenge on you for your frippery ways, which is what you imagine he's doing. He genuinely wants the business to continue, he wants it to stay in the family. He has two daughters, you and Flicka. You've inherited his brains, Flicka hasn't.'

'Brains! It doesn't take brains. It takes business know-how and acumen and understanding about money . . .'

'You went to Cambridge,' said Felicity. 'You've got bags of energy. You always organised things at school – that's why you got into so much trouble. I don't see why you can't do it. Or at least try.'

'Forget it,' Delia said. 'My answer's no.'

'Delia, really.'

'Really, nothing,' said Delia, racing for the door. 'Not another word, not one single word more on this subject.'

'But now there are no more parachutes needed,' Marjorie was saying, 'how is he managing?'

'Don't ask me, but the factories are still open, and he's still employing people, although not so many. There isn't the work there was in the war.'

'I suppose the women lost their jobs.'

'Some of them didn't want to go on working after the war. They wanted to go back to being housewives. I think he kept on most of those who wanted jobs. Women are better than men at a lot of the work.' Delia got up from the table. 'I really don't know why we're talking about the mills, on a glorious day like this. Who's coming for a bathe?'

'How old is your father?' Lucius asked as they walked through the olive groves to the beach. He stopped and looked up into the leafy kingdom above his head. 'Don't you love olive trees? The colour of the leaves, dozens of colours in there, and the gnarled trunks. These are very old, Pietro was telling me. Do you know that olive trees can live for centuries? I'm going to come out here and paint one, a portrait of a tree.'

'Nearly seventy.'

'Isn't he going to retire sometime soon, or is he one of those guys who'll go on until he drops?'

Delia's mind was still on the trees, which she was seeing as though for the first time, through Lucius's eyes, with attention, and a kind of awe.

'My father? Oh, God knows, Lucius. I'm not sure I want to talk about it. Theo's already managed to ruin what was a gorgeous day by bringing up that subject.'

'If you let Theo spoil a day like this, you're just being defeatist. Want to talk about it?'

379

And Delia, to her surprise, found she did. She told him about Saltford's, and the bombshell just dropped by Theo.

Lucius took her towel and laid it on the sand for her. Then he rolled out his own towel and sat on it. 'I reckon your dad thinks you're a chip off the old block. I can see where he's coming from. He'd have liked to hand over to a son, but the poor guy stopped one in the war. That leaves you and your sister, and while Felicity is a looker, she's not exactly the kind to make a captain of industry.'

'Nor am I.' She thought about her brother. 'I think it's just as well Boswell isn't around to take over. He'd have run the company like that weirdo in the Tolkien story.'

'*The Lord of the Rings*? Are you talking about the mines of Mordor?'

'If that's the burning earth and orcs, yes. Boswell would have liked to have an army of orcs working for him. Ruthless doesn't begin to describe him. Compared to my father, who's a humane person, and a humane employer, keen on safety and caring for his personnel and all that – well, the workers wouldn't have known what had hit them. Anyhow, he was killed in the war, and that's that. As you say, my father's left with me and Flicka. And talking of orcs, who's got Beatrice Malaspina's notebook? I want to have another look at those drawings. It's funny to think that those and the tower are the closest we've got to her; she remains as enigmatic as ever.'

She watched the gentle ripple of the waves as they broke on the shore. Why was the ever-moving sea so soothing, so endlessly fascinating?

'It's the light and restlessness and the patterns,' said Lucius, watching her. His heart went out to her, sitting there with her arms clasped round her legs and her chin resting on her knees.

She turned to him, and in a rare gesture of confidence lifted her sunglasses on to her forehead and looked straight at him. Her eyes were flecked with gold. Tawny, eagle's eyes to go with her aquiline nose.

'I can't do it, Lucius. Even if I wanted to. It's not for me. I'm not going to go on with opera, I've made that decision, but music's still my life. Can you understand that? Or has banking so eaten into your soul that you've forgotten art's a vocation, not a choice?'

'That was below the belt,' said Lucius. 'Leave me out of this. Your dad thinks you could do it. Isn't he a mean judge of character? I'd take it as a compliment, especially since you spend a lot of time and energy scrapping with him, don't you?'

'He's trying to control me.'

'No, he isn't.'

'Your parents pushed you into banking. Mine's pushing me into Saltford's. What's the difference? Except that you went along with it, and I don't intend to.' She was silent again, and then burst out, 'It's too late. I'm twenty-seven. I can't change the way I am.'

She got up and walked down and into the sea. Lucius followed her, plunging in and swimming beside her. 'Twenty-seven! How old was Winston Churchill when he took over in Britain's darkest hour? In his sixties.' He was stung by her assumption that life was fixed by twenty-seven, for if it were, then he, at thirty-five, had no future except as a banker and Mrs Elfrida. 'Let's do some logic on this. You've run through Auntie's money, okay, and at present your dad doesn't give you anything. How long will your savings last you?'

'Savings?'

'Thought as much. So, if the opera work dries up, you'll be skint.'

'There is other singing work. Musicals, that kind of thing. That's what I want to do.'

'It will take time to build a new career, and what guarantee have you that you'll be successful?'

'Life isn't about guarantees. Music's a risky profession, however talented or lucky you are. Don't I know it. You wake up one day with a sore throat, and you think, what if I lose my voice for good?'

'You have an apartment?'

'I rent a flat.'

'You could be in trouble. You're going to have to get a job, or find a rich husband.'

'No, thank you.'

'In due course, when your father dies, you'll get dividends with your ten per cent of the Saltford shares. If the company is still going, of course, and if your father doesn't change his mind.'

He could see that Delia hadn't thought this through. She had her sunglasses back on. Damn those glasses, you really couldn't tell what she was thinking.

'I'll have to find a job then. It's what out of work actors and musicians do.' She sounded so troubled that he longed to take her in his arms and say, no, no, marry me, then you won't ever have to take a job. But he couldn't, because Lucius the banker was going to marry Elfrida, and if Lucius the banker became Lucius the painter, how the hell could he support a wife?

'I expect you can teach. Train for something else. Wait on tables, become a tourist guide. I don't know.'

Delia was surging through the water towards the beach.

'Has Theo got any figures for your dad's company?' he asked, as he caught up with her at the water's edge.

'He pressed an envelope at me, but I haven't a clue how to understand company accounts.'

'Company accounts are easy. Anyone with half their wits in order can learn to read company accounts. When we've bathed and you've come out of the sulks, we'll go look through them. With Jessica, if you like; she's got a head for figures. She'll make you see sense.'

'I'm not in the sulks.'

'Smile, then, prove it.'

She swam back out a few feet, then turned on her back and kicked a spray of water at him.

He was right, Delia reflected. The figures weren't difficult to understand; she wished she had Jessica's quickness with figures, though. She'd found them absorbing. Delia finally understood them, but they still didn't catch her imagination.

'He's doing awfully well, isn't he?' Jessica said to Lucius.

'I'd say. Wish we were his bankers.'

'You think I'm nuts to even consider throwing all this away,' said Delia.

'I think you'd make your father a melancholy man, seeing his company pass into other people's hands.'

Felicity, exquisite in her white swimsuit, came sauntering across the terrace. She was still as slim as ever, and Delia knew that even when she was eight months on she'd still look wonderful.

'Delia, you are mean. You get cross with Theo every time he opens his mouth. He's only trying to help.'

'Yes, help you to Father's money.'

'Why not? Why should those ghastly preachy people get their hands on it?'

That was the rub. Clever, foxy old father, Delia thought. If he'd said he was going to leave the shares to some charity she cared about, it might be different. But lining the pockets of preachy people, as Flicka put it, for Delia felt sure that moral support in this case would start and finish at the pockets of those who ran the moral awakening league, was not an idea that pleased her.

Flicka turned her lovely smile on Lucius. 'Theo says you're a banker. You tell Delia how stupid and selfish she's being.'

'I make it a point never to get involved in family arguments.'

'Ha, wait until you're married to Elfrida. Do you have any idea what her family are like?'

'Felicity, shut up,' said Delia. 'Put on your wrap; it's lunchtime.'

'More pasta,' said Felicity. 'Terrible for the figure.'

Delia piled her plate high.

Felicity was in a complaining mood, and despite warning looks from Theo, indicating that there were others at the table, she was going to have her say.

'Honestly, you and Jessica are so tiresome. Take this wretched divorce. You're so obstinate, Jessica. It's not good for Theo to be associated with it, and it puts everybody's backs up, with Richie being a war hero, and such a pin-up boy with the public. Theo says the PM won't like it.'

'The Prime Minister can mind his own damn business,' said Jessica.

'It's all very well, but even if you do get a divorce you'll go round getting in trouble, as you always have, and then your name will be all over the papers again, which really isn't good for Richie's career. No, Theo, it's time someone made Jessica see the consequences of what she's doing.'

'That's all right, she can do what I did, and change her name by deed poll,' Delia said. 'Then it won't be Richie's name. There's nothing to it. I just signed a few papers, and hey presto! Vaughan instead of Thirsk.'

Lucius let his knife fall with a clatter. 'Thirsk? Your name is Saltford.'

'No,' said Felicity. 'That's Father's title. The family name is Thirsk. I was the Honourable Felicity Thirsk before I married Theo, and Delia was the Honourable Delia Thirsk.'

'Your brother! What was your brother's name?'

'Gerald Thirsk.'

'You call him Boswell.'

'That was one of his middle names. The family called him

Boswell, don't ask me why. Everybody else called him Gerry or Gerald.'

Lucius had gone as white as a sheet. 'Gerald Thirsk?'

The others were staring at him.

'Did you know him?' Theo asked.

'I killed him,' said Lucius. 'I shot him, during the war.'

Delia went cold. It couldn't possibly be true. Boswell had died in action . . . Dear God, yes, in Italy.

Felicity was puzzled. 'But you Americans were on the same side as us.'

'It was an accident,' said Delia urgently, her attention entirely on Lucius. 'You faced a court martial and were acquitted; the verdict was that it was an accident.'

Lucius began to speak, but Delia jumped in. He mustn't say what really happened. Not here. Not now.

'There's no blame attached to you,' she said swiftly. 'These things happen in wartime. Even if he was my brother . . .'

'Half-brother, actually,' said Felicity. 'You look quite pale, Lucius. There's no need; we don't really care how Boswell died.' She flashed him one of her lovely smiles, and then turned serious. 'You see, he wasn't a very nice man.'

'Half-brother?' Now it was Delia's turn to stare. 'What are you talking about?'

'Didn't you know? Oh, I thought you did. Mummy told me all about it ages ago, when I married Theo. I don't know why, because it was all ancient history, and by then Boswell was dead.'

'Felicity,' said Theo. 'Stop it.'

Felicity took no notice. 'She was pregnant when she married – well, we knew Boswell was born only seven months after the wedding, and it always seemed a bit odd that someone as moral as Daddy could have jumped the gun. Which he must have, now I come to think of it, because otherwise he'd have made a fuss at the time. And he didn't.'

Mother says he found out when Boswell had his appendix out, because of the blood.'

'Blood groups,' said Delia. 'So Father knew?'

'Well, yes. That's probably why they don't talk to each other.'

Theo had had enough. 'Felicity, must you wash your family's dirty linen in public? For heaven's sake, hold your tongue.'

'Everyone's family has murky bits, Theo. Don't make such a fuss. I thought Delia knew. I thought Mummy had told her.'

Delia could see that, brother or half-brother, it made little difference to Lucius.

'Actually,' she said, 'Boswell was about to commit mass murder when he met his timely end, Felicity, which won't surprise you at all.'

'No,' Felicity said. 'Daddy once said that if Boswell had come back from the war, it would only have been a matter of time before he murdered someone. He liked killing things, it was what he liked best. If he'd got used to doing it in the war, he wouldn't have wanted to stop, would he?' She forked a piece of lettuce into her mouth.

'Did Mother happen to tell you who Boswell's father was?'

'Oh, yes. Can't you guess? Tom Meldon. Jessica's father-in-law.'

It explained a great deal, Delia thought, as she sank back in her seat, now as white as Jessica and Lucius.

Jessica was speaking, in an unnaturally calm voice. 'Let's get this clear. Are you saying that Lady Saltford, before her marriage, had an affair with Tom Meldon, and was pregnant with Boswell when she married Lord Saltford?'

'Yes,' said Felicity. 'So Boswell was Richie's half-brother as well. It's odd, isn't it, that I married Theo, and Jessica married Boswell's half-brother? All in the family, you might say. No wonder Richie and Mummy have always got on so well together.'

'Excuse me . . .' Jessica began, and bolted for the door.

'That bad?' said Marjorie. 'I've brought you a stomach settler.'

Jessica was standing at the window, looking out towards the sea. 'I'm not ill,' she said. 'It's stupid of me to react like this. What does it matter whose half-brother Richie is? Is Delia okay? And what about Lucius?'

'Don't worry about him,' said Marjorie. 'I expect, when he thinks it over, it will make it easier for him to know that Boswell had a psychopathic personality. Such men are exceedingly dangerous, although they often thrive and do brilliantly well in a war. Felicity and her father are right; he'd never have come home and settled down to a quiet life.'

'No,' said Jessica. 'But I do feel sorry for him, and for his mother and Lord Saltford, who's a good man, however much Delia resents him. And for Delia herself, trust Felicity to blurt out about her mother almost in passing.' She felt a chill as she thought about Lady Saltford.

'It isn't easy for any of them. Lucius is between a rock and a hard place all right. He's in love with Delia, but he killed her half-brother. It's a nasty one.'

'And Delia will start worrying that since she's related to a man who was about to commit murder when he died, what happens if she's the same, deep down? Or if one of her children turns out to be like Boswell? I mean, Richie has a brutal streak in him.'

'It looks as though Lucius is stuck with Elfrida, poor sap.'

'I do wonder how much of this Beatrice Malaspina knew,' Jessica said. 'About Delia's family. That photo of Felicity's wedding in the ghastly tower room, for instance; that says it all. But how could she have known about Boswell, when even Delia didn't?'

'That brings us back to the journalist's mantra: who, what, where, when, why and how. Who was Beatrice Malaspina? What was she up to? Where did she get all her information from? When did she decide to weave her web? How did she manage it? And the big one, why?'

'Lots of questions and not many answers. I wish that codicil would turn up; what if it doesn't, and time runs out, and we all leave the Villa Dante without ever knowing the answers?'

SEVEN

Lucius was in the drawing room, painting, soon after dawn. It was the only way he knew to keep the teeming thoughts at bay; once he had a paintbrush in his hand, he could close off his mind and simply let the shapes and forms and colours take over. He could, in fact, stop thinking, and he had come to the conclusion, in the course of a grim night, that he did more thinking than was good for him.

He worked on Marjorie, wanting to give the green robe he'd put her in a more gothic look in the way it fell and draped. He saw Marjorie as one of the fourteenth-century statues gazing out from mediaeval cathedrals, looking in their elongated forms like aliens, beings from another world. If you took away the lines of despair and worry that time had etched on Marjorie's face, and worked down to the bones, then the spare, strong lines of those figures represented the essence of her.

After more than a hour, finally satisfied that he had laid every fold just as he wanted it, he put his brush down, stretched vigorously and yawned.

The door opened, and there was Delia. She had a bleakness about her eyes, and she stiffened when she saw him, and hesitated in the doorway. 'I don't want to disturb you while you're painting,' she said.

His heart turned over at the sight of her, and he wanted to wrap her in his arms and kiss away the strain and stress so visible round her eyes. 'Come on in,' he said. 'I was just having what you English call a tea break. I've been working on Marjorie.'

'May I look?'

'Do.'

She came over and looked intently at the figure, the paint still gleaming where he'd been at work. 'Awfully austere, but very like her. You've made her look, oh, I don't know. Independent. A force to be reckoned with.'

'Have you ever seen the work of Piero della Francesca?'

'Yes.'

'He's a favourite of mine. In particular, I love his pictures of Mary.'

'As in the Virgin Mary?'

'Yes. But forget sad-eyed icons, he painted powerful Marys. More Athene than Madonna, serene, straight-browed, intelligent, wide-armed, strong.'

'Not the conventional view of motherhood, then. Do you mind if I stay in here for a bit? I'll just sit down and be quiet. I don't want to talk, especially not about mothers, but I feel like company.'

It was as though a hawk had condescended to come down and fold its wings and perch nearby, and a sense of enormous gratitude swept over Lucius. All that, just for a few minutes of her presence; God, he'd got it badly.

He busied himself with mixing paints, although there was no way he could use the resulting pinky shade. 'Talk away,' he said lightly. 'It won't bother me.'

'You look quite different when you're painting,' said Delia. 'That's how I am with music, and I expect Marjorie's the same when she's writing.'

'You're professionals. I'm not.'

'You could be. Surely you're good enough.'

'Most often it isn't talent, it's circumstances that define an artistic career.'

'Circumstances can change. Or be changed.'

Yes, he said inwardly. But memories and the past can't; that's something you can never change. What you had done you had done, and among the things that he had done was the little matter of shooting a man. Who just happened to be Delia's brother.

As though she could read his thoughts, she said abruptly, 'It's true about Boswell.'

'What's true?'

'Everything. What a vicious man he was. What those people said at the court martial, about his being a monster and a menace. Listen, Lucius, if he hadn't died, if he'd come back to peacetime England, after six years of killing and God knows what else, he would have been the most dangerous man in the country. He wouldn't have given it up. The war wouldn't have satisfied his killing streak.'

'He might have stayed in the army, made a career as a professional soldier.'

'They wouldn't have had him, they don't want men like that as officers. They might put up with them during a war, but not afterwards. Knowing what he was like, they'd have shunted him out of the army the second the war was over.'

'Look, maybe it is better that he's dead. It just wasn't for me to do the job. An enemy bullet, fine; an accident, even a trial and an execution. What I did was murder, and the fact that the man I shot was a bad lot doesn't change that.'

'You mind more, though, now you know he was my brother. My half-brother.'

'It makes him more of a person. A man you grew up with, that your mother loved. He's no longer just a name and a rank. Yes, you're right. Knowing more about him and knowing he was your brother makes it worse. Much worse.'

'It's nonsense.'

'Maybe, but that's the way it is.'

The silence that fell was uncomfortable. Lucius was angry with himself and with her. The sense of equilibrium that painting had brought him had vanished and all the unwanted thoughts were crowding back. Why did she have to talk about Boswell?

'You have to come to terms with killing him; I have to come to terms with the knowledge that a person I'm closely related to was mad. Full of wickedness. George would say, evil. What if I'm the same, deep down? Or if I have a son, and he turns out to be just like Boswell?'

Lucius still wasn't clear in his mind about Boswell's family connections; he had been too stunned the previous night to take in the details.

He went over and sat down opposite Delia. 'Let me get this straight. Your father isn't Boswell's pa?'

'No.'

'Your mother cheated on your father? Boswell was the eldest of you, wasn't he?'

'My mother was pregnant with Boswell when she married my father. Her lover, and Boswell's father, was a man called Tom Meldon. He got married about two years later, and had another son, Richard. Richie Meldon, Jessica's husband.'

'So you and Boswell were half-brother and -sister, and Richie and Boswell were half-brothers.'

'That's it.'

'Is Richie violent? Does he have a psychopathic personality? Isn't he a member of Parliament?'

'He is an MP, although I don't know if that rules out violence. I wouldn't think so. And while he may not go round burning people, he's pretty ruthless. So is his father. I can't ever know, you see, whether Boswell got his violence from his mother, who is also my mother, or from his father, who's no relation of mine, thank God. Genes are funny things, aren't they?'

'Felicity seems sane enough. In fact, totally normal, I'd say. And she doesn't seem to be bothered that the baby who's due might turn out to be another Boswell.'

'She doesn't have the imagination to worry about that kind of thing. In Felicity's world, everything is always fine. She knows her baby will be perfect, she knows that she and Theo are going to be happy together for ever and ever, and they'll always have enough money . . . Felicity lives on the sunny side of the street.'

'Lucky girl,' said Lucius. 'A temperament like that is a blessing.'

'You aren't happy, are you?' said Delia. 'When were you last utterly and completely happy?'

'I've had some happy days here at the Villa Dante,' he said.

'Yes, I suppose I have, as well. It's a happy place, or at least a place where one could be very happy. It's a funny word, happy. An abrupt little word, pop, pop. And yet so huge in what it means.'

'The pursuit of happiness is written into the American Constitution, did you know that?'

'How can you legislate for happiness?'

'You can't, but you can give people the right to pursue it.'

'Not much good in your case, if you're eaten up with guilt over Boswell's death, and doing a job you dislike, instead of doing what you want to do, which is painting. Not to mention going to get hitched to Elfrida.'

Lucius blinked, as though she had struck him a physical blow.

Her hand flew to her mouth. 'Oh, my God, I'm sorry. Forget it. I shouldn't have said any of that.'

He got up and went over to the window. 'No, but you did say it, didn't you? Not for the first time, either. You came out with a few remarks when you got drunk the other night. In vino veritas, perhaps. I think I'll go for a stroll down to the sea before breakfast.'

He hoped for a brief moment that she might get up, say she'd go with him, a longing for her not to go away fighting inside him with his own desire to get away from her. Was that how she felt about him? He felt chilled at the thought of it.

'I'll see you at breakfast,' she said, making no move to get up until he had gone out of the room and on to the terrace. Then she did get up and watched him until he was lost among the olive groves. What a load of troubles he carried on his lean frame; even the muscles of an Atlas wouldn't support that lot.

She felt at a loss, and wandered around the room, pausing in front of the picture of the cardinal, and then looking up into the face of Beatrice Malaspina as though expecting her to speak. It was time for this to finish, time that damned codicil was found, time for them all to get back to the real world. The arrival of Grimond, Olivia and Slattery, hot on one another's heels, had brought the chill air of reality into the closed serenity of the villa. And Felicity's throwaway remarks, so casually informing her that her mother . . . No, she wasn't going to let that get to her.

That was a raw deal for her father. How had he coped with knowing that his son and heir wasn't his? He could have taken it all to court, but he would never do that. To have his name dragged in the gutter, people laughing at him for being a cuckold even before he was a husband, to have his wife's reputation destroyed. Would Tom Meldon have minded? Probably not; he was the one who came out on top in those virility stakes.

No wonder her father hadn't minded about Boswell's death. It wasn't heartlessness, or reserve, with grief felt but never shown. He had probably felt nothing but relief. Men did raise other men's sons as their own. She had heard of men who had come back from the war to find a baby on the way or a sturdy toddler in the nursery that couldn't possibly be theirs.

Which led to divorce, or, under a cruel law, to the compulsory sending of the child for adoption, whether its mother agreed or not, or, in the case of some men, just accepting the child as their own.

And that could forge bonds of affection, only not when the cuckoo in the nest was a Boswell, and the surrogate father was as perceptive as her father was. He'd had no illusions about Boswell, she realised. It was a pity he couldn't meet Lucius and hear his story. Lucius would find no hostility or disapproval there. There could be no question of whose side her father would be on; what Boswell had been about to do, in Italy in 1945, would be condemned without hesitation.

She stopped by the painting of the villa, with its welcoming poet in his funny hat. Then she followed the line of figures round, wondering who they all were, why they had come to the villa, how they knew Beatrice Malaspina, what it would have been like on a May day at the villa in the 1890s: long dresses, parasols, men in linen suits. Or the twenties and thirties, these people talking and laughing, drifting out on to the terrace, drinks in hand, light summer clothes, cigarette smoke rising in the air, gossiping, discussing books and artists and science, falling in love, starting affairs . . .

All gone, and just this two dimensional procession left, walking through time along the wall in a cheerful line towards the house. Blast that venetian blind, why wouldn't it open? With a sudden burst of irritation, she gave the pull a violent tug, and with a crash the whole blind came down, nearly crowning her.

The room was transformed as light flooded into the dark corner. She stiffened, suddenly, the accident with the blind forgotten. She stepped over it and went closer to the wall. What had Lucius been up to? Why had he put his self-portrait in here, so much further up the line than the rest of them, almost at the head of the column? Her eyes went to the other end; no, there he was in his grey suit and hat. Ego getting the better of him, to paint himself in twice? But how could he have fitted another figure in without obliterating one that was already there?

She put her head on one side, narrowing her eyes to get a better look. It was chance, that was all. It was another man, very like Lucius, a much earlier visitor to the Villa Dante. Had he noticed? She would point it out to him.

'Good morning,' said Marjorie. 'You're up early.'

'Look at this,' Delia said. 'Who's that?'

'Whatever did you do to the blind? Goodness, what a difference the extra light makes. That's Lucius. It's the image of him. I'd call it a striking likeness. Good heavens, though, it can't be, not there. Besides, look at what he's wearing. He hasn't got a cream suit like that nor could he have any time this century. Where is Lucius?'

'He sloped off to the beach. I'm afraid I rather went for him.'

'He'll live,' said Marjorie. 'He'll be back for breakfast; ruffled feelings never yet put a man off his food. Then we'll show him what we've found. I wonder he didn't notice it, he must have studied all these people before he started to paint.'

'Yes, but this part of the room has always been dim, and sometimes the last thing you recognise is a picture of yourself.'

'True, and it isn't just the features, is it? It's the way that man is standing, and Lucius raises his hand in that identical way.'

'It's uncanny.'

'What is uncanny?' said George. 'I heard voices. I hope I don't intrude.'

'How could you?' said Delia. 'Look what we've found.'

George's reaction was immediate. 'There is nothing uncanny about it at all. It is perfectly logical. I think we may have discovered another link between us and Beatrice

Malaspina. This man is related to Lucius, I am sure. It could be his grandfather, and so there is a connection between Lucius's family and the villa. He came as a guest, long ago, and had his picture painted on to the wall while he was here. Where is Lucius? This is an exciting discovery.'

Lucius stood and stared at the man on the wall. 'Well, I will be damned. How did I get to miss that?'

'Do you recognise him?'

'Sure I do. It's my grandpa Wolfson. My mother's father.'

'Is he still alive?'

'Lord, no. He was somewhat older than my grandmother, who's in her seventies. He died some years back. It doesn't make sense, though. When I was contacted by the lawyers, I asked her if she'd known Beatrice Malaspina, and she said, no, she hadn't.'

'Maybe this was painted before your grandfather knew your grandmother.'

Lucius wasn't listening. He was thinking back to his last visit to Miffy, before he set off for Europe. What were her exact words? 'I asked my grandmother if she had ever heard of Beatrice Malaspina, and she said she had never met a Beatrice Malaspina. Ultra subtle, my grandma. She didn't lie, but she didn't answer my question.'

'A pity you didn't press her,' said Marjorie. 'Perhaps she could have told you all about Beatrice Malaspina.'

'It kind of figures,' Lucius said. 'Edgar Wolfson, that was his name, was into art in a big way. And he spent a lot of time in Europe, looking at pictures, buying works by unknown artists. He had what they call an eye. So it's more than likely he'd get to meet someone like Beatrice Malaspina who moved in artistic circles, and had all these artists come to stay at the Villa Dante over the years.'

* * *

The discovery of a second link with Beatrice Malaspina was satisfying, but frustrating, as Delia pointed out. 'It doesn't help us find that damned codicil or even know why she asked Lucius here so many years later, when she isn't around to see him. Everything we find out just deepens the mystery. Come on, Marjorie, where are your voices when we need them?' she added, only half in jest.

Jessica, intrigued by the news, went and looked at the frieze again. 'Who knows, maybe your Auntie Gertrude is here, Delia. Or some relation of yours, Marjorie.'

'I can tell you one thing for certain,' said Marjorie. 'No one related to me has ever been to Italy. Neither of my parents ever set foot out of England. My father spent the First World War in England; he worked on the railways then. As did both my grandfathers, and they never went abroad, either. I don't have any uncles or aunts.'

'Then you must have met Beatrice Malaspina when she was in England.'

'Do you think I wouldn't remember a woman who looked like the one in the picture?' said Marjorie.

'She wouldn't have looked like that when she was older.'

'She'd still have had those eyes and that expression. Wrinkles wouldn't have changed that.'

'Nor her bones,' said Lucius. 'No, I'm amazed to see Grandpa Wolfson on the wall, but it doesn't solve the mystery.'

'Marjorie has that faraway look in her eyes,' said Jessica suddenly. 'What's up? Have you had a blinding revelation?'

'No, I just heard a car engine.'

'Oh, God, I bet it's Slattery in a taxi,' cried Delia, hurrying out of the room.

EIGHT

It was a taxi, but the man who got out wasn't Giles Slattery.

Jessica had never imagined that she would ever want to see Slattery, but she would have welcomed him with open arms in comparison.

Theo was out at the car, smiling, welcoming – how dare he? And he must be responsible for this, the traitor.

'Darling,' said Richie, catching sight of her before she could duck inside. He came towards her, relaxed, confident . . . Didn't he remember the suits? The golf clubs?

'What the hell are you doing here?' she said.

'That's not a very friendly greeting.'

The taxi was turning round. Delia flew down the steps, waving at the driver to stop. He looked enquiringly out of the window at her. 'Stop,' she cried. She gestured at the man, calling out to Lucius to tell her the Italian for 'Stay here'.

In a second, Lucius was beside here. 'Is that man—'

'Yes, that's Richie Meldon. Please can you tell the taxi not to go, not without Richie. He mustn't be allowed to stay. Jessica will be distraught.'

Lucius spoke to the driver, who gave an eloquent shrug and turned off the engine, then turned back to Delia. 'Richie doesn't look like he's planning to go anywhere,' he said.

'If he doesn't go, then I'm off in that taxi,' Jessica said. 'I refuse, I absolutely refuse, to stay under the same roof as that man.'

'How did he . . . ?' Delia began. 'Oh, don't tell me. Theo?'

'Theo. Who needs enemies when you've got relations?'

Marjorie came round from the other side of the house, took one look at Richie who was deep in conversation with Theo, and came over to the others.

'I see Jessica's husband has arrived. I recognise him from his photos.'

'He isn't staying,' said Jessica and Delia together.

'He looks to me like a man who'll do exactly what he wants.'

'This is private property, he has no right to come barging in,' Delia said. 'Nor has Theo any right to ask him here.'

'Guys like Theo and Richie aren't much bothered by that kind of nicety, I reckon,' said Lucius.

Jessica walked over to Richie. 'Pick up that suitcase and get right back in the taxi. You aren't staying here. There isn't room for you, and we don't want you. I can't imagine why you're here.'

'Don't work yourself into such a state,' said Richie. 'Can we go somewhere to talk? There seem to be rather too many people around for any private conversation. Oh, hello, Felicity. Looking lovely as always.'

Felicity brushed cheeks with Richie, giving him an automatic smouldering look, Delia noticed with growing irritation. Somehow, Theo and Felicity had taken on the appearance of host and hostess, welcoming Richie, excluding Lucius and George, who had every right to be here. Theo and co. were the intruders, uninvited and now definitely unwanted.

Richie laid a possessive hand on Jessica's arm. 'Come on, Jekky, let's not have a scene in public.'

She shook herself free. 'Don't you dare call me Jekky. And

I'll make all the scenes I want. This isn't in public as it happens. These are my friends, and we're guests here at the villa, invited guests, and you aren't.'

'From what I heard, you weren't invited, either. You tagged along with Delia, who was summoned here by a dead woman whom, I understand, she never knew. Nice place, though,' he added, looking up at the façade. 'It has possibilities.'

'Not for you it doesn't.'

How could Jessica have married a man like that?

'A tough in toff's clothes,' Marjorie said.

'She's doing her best to get rid of him,' Lucius said.

'She won't succeed. You can't argue with a man like that.'

'We can refuse to find him a bed.'

'Then he'll end up in hers.'

'Brute force might work,' he said. 'Or low cunning.'

'Is he like Boswell?'

Lucius stared at her, uncomprehending for a moment. Good God, of course, this sandy-haired man with the cold blue eyes was Boswell's brother. Half-brother. And perhaps that was the reason for his instant dislike: the voice was the same as the one he had heard on that Italian hillside, loud and imperious and used to command, used to being obeyed.

'Unfortunately, yes. He doesn't look like him, but he does sound like him. I hadn't noticed, but . . . Yes.'

Jessica looked like a cornered animal. She loathed him, Lucius could see that. Actually loathed him in a visceral way, not the hatred that was the flip side of love and could switch so easily to passion, but a deep hostility and rejection. Contempt. What had he done to make her feel like that?

She was going inside with him, arguing every inch of the way. And the taxi driver was still here, leaning back in his seat, eyelids drooping in that peaceful relaxed way that was so typically Italian.

'Should we tell him to stay?' Marjorie said.

'No,' said Lucius, after a moment's thought. 'Theo can drive Richie back to the station if Jessica manages to get rid of him.'

'There's nothing to discuss, and it isn't a question of negotiation,' Jessica said. She had taken Richie into the dining room and shut the door. She stood on the other side of the table from him, glad of the solid barrier. 'Our marriage is over. Finished. Kaput. Why can't you accept that? It was pretty worthless from the start. What did we have in common, what basis was there ever going to be for a lasting marriage, even if you hadn't turned out to have the morals of a Nero?'

'Sex,' said Richie. 'You like the sex, and isn't that where it's all based, in bed? Isn't that why people stay married?'

'That isn't why you married me,' Jessica flashed back. 'You got – sorry, get – plenty of sex in other women's beds without needing to exchange vows.'

'Sex is the start of it; it's a bond. Then there's the social side. You make a good MP's wife. And I can give you the things you want. Apart from the sex. A house, clothes, spending money.' He was smiling, the complacent, self-satisfied smile of a winner. 'Face it, Jessica, I hold all the cards. I won't give you a divorce, and I'll make damn sure you don't get a whisper of wrongdoing on my part, at least nothing that you can use as grounds for divorce. Give in. I'm stronger and cleverer than you, and whatever move you make, I'll counter it.'

Jessica wanted to lash out at him physically, to pummel him with her fists. And that, she realised, was exactly what he wanted her to do. She took a deep breath and looked away from him, up at the gods and goddesses cavorting across the ceiling.

'Fuck off, Richie.'

* * *

It was an impasse, and one that made them all feel acutely uncomfortable, with the exception of Felicity, who was wrapped in her usual cloud of contentment and Panglossian goodwill, and Marjorie, who had flung herself at her type-writer, struck with a rush of inspiration.

'How the hell do we get rid of him?' Delia whispered to George. 'Come on, use those brains of yours.'

'He cannot stay the night if there is not a room for him.'

'Then he'll simply go to the hotel and be back in the morning. The wretched man is ruthless, and he has the persist-ence of a limpet. He won't give up; he won't leave until he's forced Jessica to do what he wants.'

'Jessica may be stronger than you think.'

'If so, why did she ever marry Richie? He knows her weak-nesses, he'll play on them. Perhaps it would be best if she left. Could we sneak her away? We could be packed and ready in no time, and there's petrol in her car.'

'It might work,' said George, considering. 'Or it might not. I expect he will keep a close eye on her. And Theo has a powerful car, please remember that, which is now in good order. He might try to follow you.'

'Oh, that's far too melodramatic for Theo.'

'But not for Richie. And where will you go? Jessica can run all she wants, but in the end, it is not a solution to her problem.'

'That's the trouble, there isn't a solution, or not an easy one. It's maddening, she has something on Richie, but she can't or won't use it against him. I do wonder what it is.'

'If she doesn't want you, her best friend, to know about it, then I think it remains a secret known only to her and Richie.'

'We've got to do something, George.'

'I intend to pray.'

'Pray? George, what's come over you?'

'Old habits do not die quite as completely as one imagines

they have. Since I came to the Villa Dante, and in particular since I have been reading St Ignatius Loyola, I have often found myself saying a prayer.'

'Well, we all pray at times – the devil was ill and so on. But it's really the last gasp of desperation, don't you think, in a situation like this? It's a worldly problem that needs a worldly solution.'

'What has the devil to do with it?'

'Don't you know the old rhyme? The devil was ill, the devil a monk would be; the devil was well, the devil a monk was he.'

George laughed. 'I like that. I shall remember that. And prayer does work, although our prayers are mostly answered in ways we do not foresee.'

Delia stood on her balcony, watching Theo and Richie walk past the fountain, deep in conversation. Theo was showing Richie the house and grounds. He should have been an estate agent, she thought as his words floated up to her. 'At least five acres round the house, and I dare say the estate is much larger – these old houses usually come with a lot of land.'

She released her fists, which she had bunched so tightly that they hurt. Whatever Beatrice Malaspina had planned, it didn't include all this. She would never have wanted Theo and Richie strolling up and down outside her house. Polluting it with their pedestrian schemes. Nor would she have wanted Felicity, who was lying, exquisite in her bathing suit, on the terrace, although Felicity was more in keeping with her surroundings than the two men. She could be wearing a wisp of drapery and standing provocatively in a niche inside the hall or outside by the fountains, and she would fit in perfectly. And there was her fecundity, a sign of new life; Delia had a feeling Beatrice Malaspina would have smiled at Felicity, understood her, accepted her for what she was.

Which was more than she, her sister, was able to do.

* * *

Marjorie looked up from her typewriter, blinking. She rolled the paper out, and laid it on the pile on the table. Beside the typed pages was Beatrice Malaspina's slender notebook; Marjorie picked it up, and opened it at the first page. 'Come on, Beatrice Malaspina,' she said out loud. 'What's the message? Where's a clue?'

Lucius was on his way to San Silvestro. He would go to the Bar Centrale and try to place a call to his grandmother. Could he put through a transatlantic call from San Silvestro? Surely they could get connected to the international exchange. What time was it in Boston? They were several hours behind, but Miffy was an early riser. Then he could put her on the spot re Grandpa and Beatrice Malaspina; he was quite certain that she had a lot to tell him on that subject. And perhaps Olivia would be back at the hotel. It would be a pleasure to talk to her, unencumbered as she was with the knowledge of his affairs that his fellow guests had acquired.

NINE

'Good heavens,' said Marjorie. 'Here's Lucius back already, and with a passenger on the pillion.'

She and George headed for the entrance hall.

'Is it Olivia?' said George.

'No, it's a man.'

'Not the reporter again, what was his name, Slattery?'

'No, and Lucius wouldn't give him a lift to the Villa Dante. This is a tall thin man, with a moustache, a stranger.'

'I heard the Vespa,' called Delia from the top of the staircase. 'Is Lucius back?'

Footsteps on the stone steps, and the two men came in through the front door just as Delia came into the hall.

She stood quite still, an exclamation dying on her lips, staring at Lucius's companion. Then she found her voice.

'What on earth are you doing here?'

'It's Lord Saltford,' Jessica hissed to the others.

Father! Here, at the Villa Dante.

'Delia,' her father said.

Before she could reply, the brisk little figure of Benedetta appeared. She took one look at Saltford, and gave a shriek of joy, followed by a torrent of Italian. Delia could see that

Lucius was as surprised as she was, and he was frowning with the effort of understanding Benedetta's words.

'What's she saying?' Delia demanded. 'Why is she so pleased to see him?' And why did he look so pleased to see Benedetta?

'He's telling her that you're his daughter.'

Another cry of joy from Benedetta, who rushed over to Delia, grasped both her hands in hers and shook them delightedly.

'I simply don't understand,' said Delia.

'I think we can take it that this isn't your father's first visit to the Villa Dante,' said Marjorie. 'Did you say that you never mentioned Beatrice Malaspina to him? Bad move. It seems to me that he may be able to answer most of our questions.'

'Father, what's going on?' said Delia. 'How do you know Benedetta? Have you been here before? Did you know Beatrice Malaspina?'

'Must we stand here in the entrance hall?' he enquired. 'It is a very beautiful room, but perhaps we might go into the drawing room if we are to talk.' He went to Delia's side, and tucked her arm in his. 'I'm happy to see you looking so well,' he said. 'The Villa Dante is a great restorer of health.'

She was touched. 'I do feel better. My cough has gone, and yes, the Villa Dante is a marvellous place.'

'Are Felicity and Theo here?'

'Yes, unfortunately, and so is Richie.'

He frowned, and Delia noticed with a pang of anxiety that there was a tiredness about his eyes.

'That's a pity,' he said.

'And that's an understatement. The drawing room's this way. Oh, you'd know that, since you've been here before.'

'It was nearly thirty years ago. But I don't suppose the house has changed much.'

The angelus was ringing as Lucius opened the door to the drawing room, and stood back to let the others through.

'The bells of San Silvestro,' Lord Saltford said. 'That does take me back.'

'Would you rather we weren't here? Do you want to be alone with your father?' Marjorie said.

'Shall we leave you?' Lucius asked Delia.

'No, of course not,' she said quickly. They would all be keen to hear whatever her father could tell them about Beatrice Malaspina, and she was in no mood to talk to her father about anything else. 'How did you know I was here?' she asked him. 'From Winthrop?'

'Yes. He told me about Beatrice's will, and that you'd come to Italy.'

'This Winthrop appears to be a gabby kind of lawyer,' said Lucius.

Saltford raised an enquiring eyebrow. 'Won't you introduce me, Delia? Jessica, of course, is an old friend. I'm glad to find her here with you.'

Jessica smiled at him, with real affection, Delia noticed. Jessica had always got on well with her father.

'This is Marjorie Swift, also Marjorie Fletcher, the writer. George Helsinger, a scientist from Cambridge. And Lucius Wilde, from America.'

'Lucius Wilde? You must be Lucius J. Wilde's son. And Edgar Wolfson's grandson. Of course. How do you do?' His attention turned to the frieze. 'Oh, is this still here? My word, the line of people is a good deal longer than it was on my last visit.'

'Are you among them?' said Marjorie, with a quick glance at Delia.

Surely he couldn't be there, and she not have recognised him. But he was calling her over. 'Look, Delia, here I am.'

He was, too. Younger, and less severe-looking than she had ever known him. He was wearing a red and blue robe, and holding a bolt of silk in both hands. 'The merchant,' he said with amusement in his voice.

'Who's the woman next to you?' Delia asked. 'The one who looks as though she's pregnant, although maybe it's just the way she's dressed.'

There was a long pause before her father answered. 'That's Miranda Malaspina. Beatrice's daughter.'

George gave a little cry of astonishment. 'It is, it is indeed. Much younger than when I knew her, but now I see the likeness quite clearly.'

'You knew Miranda, of course,' said Saltford. 'You worked with her in America, and you were with her when she died.'

They all stared at him. 'How did you know that, sir?' Lucius asked.

'Beatrice heard from the hospital about your kindness to her daughter; she was most touched by all you did for her. She told me about it, so I'm particularly glad to meet you at last. Poor Miranda. What a terrible thing to happen to her.'

Her father suddenly looked grey and weary. 'Sit down,' said Delia. 'Shall I get you a glass of water?'

'I think,' he said, 'I would prefer a brandy.'

Marjorie was at the decanter before Delia took in what her father had said. 'Brandy? But you never touch alcohol.'

'Not for many years. But here in Italy . . .'

'It's medicinal, in any case,' Jessica said quickly. 'And I'll get a glass of water. I expect the heat's getting to you.'

While Jessica and Marjorie fussed over Saltford, Lucius edged nearer to Delia and George. 'I can understand him knowing my pa – after all, money speaks to money – but what about my grandfather? And if he knows about George and Miranda, he must have been pretty close to Beatrice Malaspina. Ask him, Delia.'

Delia knelt down beside her father. 'Okay,' she said. 'I want the full story. How come you know Beatrice Malaspina?'

'My dear, over a long life I've known a great many people,

although Beatrice was one of the most extraordinary of them.' He looked up at her portrait, and raised his glass of brandy in a toast. 'A unique woman. Now, you tell me about this will of hers, and I'll tell you about Beatrice and Miranda. It's time you learned the truth, in any case.'

Truth? What truth?

'Did Winthrop tell you about the will?' she said. 'When I think how little he said to me, and how gaily he's been passing out information to Theo and you . . .'

Saltford frowned. 'His firm have handled my affairs for many years, but you're quite right, Delia, he's turned out to be rather too – what was the word you used, Wilde?'

'Gabby.'

'Yes, gabby. I think I shall find myself new lawyers.'

'Let me recommend Mr Ferguson, who's handling my divorce,' Jessica said.

'Ah, yes. Your divorce. We must discuss that, my dear, although this isn't the time or the place. Did Winthrop also tell your husband where you were?'

'No, I think Theo did. Or possibly Giles Slattery.'

A look of distaste passed over Saltford's face. 'That man? Has he tracked you down?'

'He's been here, yes. Lucius and Delia managed to get rid of him, but he'll be back.'

'At least he isn't listening at the door at the moment. Tell me why you're here, all of you, and what is in Beatrice's will.'

With help from the others, Delia told him everything. He listened with complete concentration and in silence. When he had all the facts, he pursed his lips and looked up at the starry, vaulted ceiling before he spoke. 'Interesting, and how very like Beatrice. She loved puzzles and intrigue and finding out people's secrets. Never for any ill purpose, you understand, more that she always wanted to have a complete picture of those she cared for.'

'She can't have cared for any of us, sir,' said Lucius. 'She never knew us.'

'No, but all your lives have intersected with hers in some way. And you haven't found the codicil yet? That might explain it all to you without my help, and indeed I don't know the full story, as Delia puts it.'

'Marjorie thinks she knows where the codicil is hidden,' said Jessica. 'I quite forgot, with all the excitement.'

'Out with it, Marjorie,' said Lucius. 'More voices?'

'No, I think Beatrice Malaspina told us, loud and clear, in her notebook.' She laid it on the table. 'I wondered at the time, why those particular incidents, but then we picked up the reference to the tower on the last page and didn't think any more about the rest of it.'

She opened the notebook. 'Delia told us what this is.'

'Wagner,' said Delia. 'Siegfried.'

'Which is part of the Ring cycle.'

'Yes, of course,' said Delia. 'And?'

'The next drawing is a girl sneezing.'

'She had a cold?' said Lucius, looking blank.

'It's the Atishoo that's the clue. Think of the song children sing, Atishoo, atishoo, all fall down.'

'Ring a ring o' roses,' said Delia. 'Okay. What's the next one, a line of verse?'

'By your namesake, and I found the poem in a book of poetry here. The first line goes, "I saw eternity the other night, like a ring of pure and endless light."'

'Twelve days of Christmas, with the five gold rings,' said Lucius. 'And a wedding ring. I'm with you, Marjorie.'

'Tolkien, *Lord of the Rings*,' said Jessica.

'And Saturn, with its famous rings,' said George.

'That's all very well,' Jessica said. 'She wanted you to think ring, but . . .'

'And the ring that's conspicuous in this house is that one on the cardinal's finger,' said Delia, gazing up at the portrait.

'The cardinal's in the frieze, as well,' said Lucius. 'And just look what he's got in his hand, the hand with that poisoner's ring on it.'

'Is he holding a stick of some kind?' said George.

'Look more closely. I think it's a roll of parchment.'

George looked perplexed. 'I do not see . . .'

'Of course,' said Delia. 'Parchment, document, testament. Do you think it's tucked behind the painting of him up there?'

'No,' said Marjorie. 'I think we ought to go and have a look at the case with the ring in it. Was there a ring on a velvet cushion in a glass case when you were last here, Lord Saltford?'

'I remember Beatrice showing me the ring, but she kept it, as far as I know, with her other jewellery in her safe. It's a valuable item, for the worth of the ruby alone, apart from its historical interest.'

'Let's go look,' said Lucius. He went to the door and called out for Benedetta. 'She'll have the key.'

She did, and she handed it over without surprise, but with many nods and smiles.

They gathered round the pillar. 'Almost as if it were an altar,' Delia said to Lucius, who was standing beside her.

'Good thing Theo and Felicity and Richie aren't here,' Jessica said to Marjorie. 'Where do you think they are? They can't know that Delia's father has arrived.'

'Theo and Richie went for a swim, leaving Felicity to keep an eye on you, from what I overheard.'

'So where is she?'

'Snoozing on the terrace under an umbrella. She's not the type to have much sense of duty, and being pregnant makes her very sleepy, I've noticed.'

'Thank God for that. Lucius had better hurry up with that lock, or we'll have them padding in asking questions and making a nuisance of themselves.'

Lucius had finally got the case unlocked. He raised the glass lid and looked at the ring.

'Lift the whole thing out,' said Marjorie. 'The velvet pad and the ring.'

He did so, to reveal a small box with an inlaid top. 'Shall I take it out?'

'Yes,' said Delia, half eager to know what was in it, half not wanting to find the codicil.

'Let's hope it's not another marvel of Renaissance workmanship,' said Marjorie. 'With a spring catch and a poisonous pin to scratch you when you open it.'

'Oh, do be careful,' said Delia.

'Marjorie's being imaginative,' Lucius said, turning his head to smile at her. He took out the box, and carried it over to a marble-topped table which was set between two of the trompe l'oeil doors. Nymphs gazed down at him, and a serving man with splendidly muscled legs gave him a shifty sideways glance.

Inside the box were some papers. 'And what's this?' said Lucius, holding up a piece of stained cloth.

'It's a handkerchief,' said Jessica.

'And those are bloodstains,' said Marjorie.

Delia took the handkerchief from Lucius. 'It has a name tape.' She peered at it. 'Well, what a surprise. Marjorie, this is yours.'

And Marjorie, looking at it, was transported back to London, to a night towards the end of the war, when they were all worked to exhaustion dealing with the terrible destruction wrought by the rocket bombs. A shattered house, a heap of rubble, and weary, red-eyed men concluding that there was no hope of finding anyone else alive. And Marjorie hearing a voice calling out, insisting that there was someone there, digging alongside the men, until the limp, dust-covered, unconscious body of an elderly woman had been lifted out.

'She's still breathing,' said the doctor. 'Hospital, at once.'

He'd looked at Marjorie. 'Although I don't know what you heard, for I can tell you that this woman hasn't been doing any calling for help.'

'Voices in my mind,' said Marjorie now. 'And long before the electric fire in the bath. I'd quite forgotten; there were so many incidents in the war.'

'The woman whose life you saved was Beatrice Malaspina,' Lord Saltford said. 'She found the handkerchief, and later went to great trouble to find out about you.'

'What else is in the box?' said Delia, now longing to find out what linked her to Beatrice Malaspina. Her father? It must be, but why hadn't he been the one named in the will?

'There are two letters,' said Lucius. 'One in an envelope and the other just folded. And there's an official-looking envelope sealed with wax. I think that is the codicil.'

'What are the letters?' said Delia.

He unfolded the one that wasn't in an envelope, and looked at the closely written sheet. 'It begins, "My beloved Beatrice" . . .' He turned the paper over. 'And it's signed "Edgar".'

'Your grandfather.'

'It's a love letter,' he said, his eyes darting down the page.

'Your grandfather, Edgar Wolfson,' Saltford said, 'was the great love of Beatrice's life. She met him when she was already married, and they fell in love. They couldn't marry, of course: Beatrice was a Catholic and so was her husband. So in the end, Edgar went back to America, and in due course met and married your grandmother, Lucius.'

'While he was still in love with Beatrice?' said Lucius. 'My grandmother adored him. How could he do that to her?'

'She wasn't second best, don't think that. Beatrice's love for him wasn't something that would ever fade, but in due course he fell in love with someone else, as she knew he would. She was pleased that he did, and that he found such happiness in his marriage to your grandmother.'

'He told her about Beatrice,' Lucius said. 'I'm sure he did.'

'What about the other letter?' said George.

'That's addressed to you, Delia.'

'To me?' She took it, and stared down at the single word, *Delia*, inscribed in a flowing, characterful script. Then she turned the envelope over, opened it and drew out two sheets of thick cream paper.

The salutation leapt out at her. 'My dearest granddaughter, Delia.'

TEN

Delia walked between the olive trees with her father, more at ease with him here at the Villa Dante than she had been since she was a child.

'I met Miranda Malaspina, your mother, in London, soon after I'd found out that Boswell wasn't my son. Ah, you know about that. From Felicity, I suppose?'

She nodded.

'Fay and I – well, it had always been a difficult marriage, and that discovery wiped out the last vestiges of any real feeling we had for one another.'

'Why didn't you get a divorce? You could have married Miranda.'

'I wanted to, but Miranda didn't. She was a scientist, battling to make a career for herself, which was difficult for any woman in her field, however brilliant, and she knew that if she married at that stage of her career it would make matters even worse. So she decided to have the child, and planned to bring it – you – back to Italy to her mother. That was when I first met Beatrice Malaspina. I came out to the Villa Dante with Miranda. And we discussed it, and I said that I wanted to bring up my child, if Miranda couldn't. In the end, they agreed, although they didn't quite understand how or why my wife would accept the baby as her own.'

'You forced Mother into it?'

'We came to an agreement.'

'That's why she never had the least affection for me!' This revelation gave her the most enormous sense of relief. It explained so much about her childhood. 'Did you keep in touch with Miranda?'

'Yes, and with Beatrice.'

'Did you send her photographs of me?'

'Yes.'

They walked in silence back towards the house. 'We must see what's in the codicil,' said Delia. 'It was kind of the others to wait while I pulled myself together. They must be impatient to open it.'

'I think that whatever are the bequests from Beatrice, she has given all four of you a legacy of inestimable benefit,' said her father. 'I like Lucius Wilde; he's very like his grandfather. He's in love with you, do you know that?'

Delia caught her breath. 'Perhaps,' she said. 'But I'm not falling in love with anyone, thank you. Look what it does for you. Look how dreadful things are for Jessica. Did you know Richie was here? I wish he weren't; it spoils everything. He doesn't belong here.'

'No, he doesn't, but nothing can spoil the Villa Dante. And I think I can come up with a solution to Jessica's difficulties, at least as regards Richie. We'll talk about it later. For now, we're wanted inside.'

To Delia's annoyance, Theo, Felicity and Richie were all with the others in the drawing room. After they had greeted Lord Saltford with varying degrees of surprise, deference and hostility, Delia said to Theo, 'I don't know why you're here. This is a private matter, just between us.'

'Felicity overheard you talking about finding a codicil, and I can see that Lucius is holding what appears to be a legal

417

document. You'd be well advised to have a lawyer present when you open the codicil, if that's what it is. Just in case of any irregularities.'

'There won't be. Beatrice Malaspina was far too canny for that. And there's certainly no need for you to be here, Richie.'

'Oh, if my wife's here, I think I should be, don't you?'

'Never mind them,' said Marjorie. 'Open the envelope, Delia.'

'Why me?'

'You're her closest relation.'

'Relation?' said Felicity. 'What do you mean?'

'Go on,' said Jessica.

'If it's in Italian, I won't understand a word of it.'

It was written in both Italian and English, and was only a few lines long.

Speechless, and with tears pricking at her eyes, Delia read it, and then handed it to Lucius.

'Delia is to have the Villa Dante,' he began. Then he gave a long whistle. 'But I get the land, and Marjorie the tower.'

'Me? The tower?' said Marjorie. 'I don't believe it.'

'And she leaves the books in the tower to George.'

'It's outrageous,' said Theo, who had snatched the document from Lucius. 'It's impossible. Delia, you will have to contest this. You can't own a house but not the land, and how can you have a stranger only yards away in that tower?'

'Marjorie isn't a stranger, and Lucius and I will manage perfectly well about the house and land,' said Delia. 'Please don't try to interfere. The four of us belong here, together, and that's that. George, your room is here for you, always.'

'And the books can stay in the library in the tower, if that's what you want,' said Marjorie at once.

'Thank you, thank you,' said George. 'And I hope I may frequently take advantage of your hospitality. For I plan to study in Rome, and so I shall not be so very far away.'

'Rome?'

'I want to attend the seminary and train for the priesthood.'

'Priesthood?' said Lord Saltford. 'You want to become a clergyman?'

'If they will accept me, I shall join the Society of Jesus.'

'You intend to become a Jesuit?'

'Father, George was raised a Catholic. Let him be.'

Lord Saltford shook his head and sighed. 'What about your work as a scientist?'

George smiled. 'I think I have done enough damage with my scientific work. The Jesuits are a scholarly and a teaching order. I shall teach science.'

'When did you decide this?' Marjorie asked, keenly interested.

The inquisitiveness of the writer, Delia said to herself.

'It has come to me gradually, while I have been at the Villa Dante. I turned my back on religion in my youth, but I now discover that one's religious nature is not so easily quelled. Grateful as I am for the books, this is the real bequest I have received from Beatrice Malaspina: finding my faith once more.'

'Good for you, George,' said Lucius.

Delia and Jessica were sitting outside in thoughtful silence, watching Delia's father walking up and down amid the cypresses, and stopping to admire the fountains.

'Who'd have thought it?' Delia said. 'Father falling in love with Miranda Malaspina like that. Maybe he's not such a dry old stick after all.'

'No, he isn't,' said Jessica, so vehemently that Delia looked at her in surprise. 'I like your father. I like him a lot. He's always been very kind to me, and I don't see him through your distorting glasses. You must have hurt him, over and over, you do realise that?'

'Yes, but he really didn't want me to have my own life, and he still doesn't. Shh, he's coming over.'

Lord Saltford sat down on the marble bench, his hat shielding his eyes from the sun. 'Jessica, my dear,' he said, 'I think we need to have a talk. About Richie, and my wife.'

Delia heard Jessica's sudden intake of breath.

'Richie and Lady Saltford?'

'Yes. I want you to know that I am perfectly aware of the – how shall I put it? – the liaison between my wife and your husband. I understand from Delia that you have no grounds for divorce, because you refuse to name the woman Richie has been unfaithful with.'

'Lord Saltford, I—'

'Let me finish. It is my intention to tell Richie Meldon, who is in my view a thoroughly unpleasant man, and one you should never have married, that you are at liberty to name my wife as co-respondent as far as I am concerned. Should your admirable loyalty to Delia and your kindness to me not permit you to do this, I shall myself institute proceedings for divorce, naming your husband.'

Delia looked from her father to Jessica. She could hardly make sense of what her father had said. 'Do you mean—' She looked at Jessica. 'You were prepared not to name names because it was my mother? For my sake?'

Jessica had gone red. 'For God's sake, Delia, how could I do that to you? Your mother – well, not your mother as we now know, but it doesn't really make any difference. I can't drag your family through the mud. Look how kind you've always been to me, Lord Saltford, and with Felicity married to my brother – no, it's impossible.'

'I don't think any of this need come out,' said Lord Saltford calmly. 'I shall speak to Meldon myself, and I think you'll find he'll go to Brighton and behave, for once in his life, like a gentleman.'

*   *   *

420

Richie had gone, his face sulky and furious. 'Outmanoeuvred, damn him,' said Jessica, who was overflowing with happiness. 'Oh, why can't everything turn out for all of you as well as it has for me?'

'We haven't done too badly,' said Delia. 'I have a new family to find out about, and the Villa Dante. And the others are hardly left empty-handed.'

'But that's things. That's not what matters, not in the end.'

'I think George has found his heart's desire,' said Delia, looking at the end of the table where George, surprisingly, was deep in animated conversation with her father. 'And . . .' She broke off as she heard the unmistakable sound of a taxi.

'Not Richie back!' said Jessica.

Benedetta opened the dining room door and with a beaming smile announced that Signora Hawkins was here. Olivia was on her heels, and there was a scraping of chairs and words of welcome as they arranged a place for her at the table. But before she sat down, to Delia's astonishment, she went over to Lord Saltford and greeted him with a kiss on the cheek. 'Felix, how very good to see you again, and here at the Villa Dante.'

'How do you know my father?' said Delia.

'It's all to do with Beatrice Malaspina,' said Olivia. 'I'm afraid I haven't been entirely honest with you all. You see, I knew Beatrice Malaspina. We met during the war, when she was in England. She supplied a lot of useful information to the department in Intelligence for which I worked. She knew a great deal about the influential advisers around Mussolini, whom she detested, and about Vatican officials, and her insights into their characters and motives was invaluable. We became good friends, and kept up our friendship after the war, when she came back to Italy. And, when she died, she entrusted her memoirs to me.'

'Memoirs?' said Lucius. 'Her life story?'

'Yes. Have you found the codicil? Then many of your questions will have been answered.'

Delia caught sight of Marjorie's face; she was trying to keep her composure, but Delia could see she was fighting a losing battle with disappointment. 'Is that why you came to San Silvestro?' she asked. 'Nothing to do with Marjorie?'

'Oh, no, Marjorie was definitely one of the reasons I came here. I knew she was one of Beatrice's legatees, of course, and why. Beatrice loved your books, Marjorie, and was concerned when you stopped writing. I've always been an admirer of your work, so when Beatrice asked me to help you, I said I would, especially when I found out what had happened to make you stop writing.'

'Okay,' said Lucius. 'So you knew what Beatrice had planned? It wasn't something you found out about when you read the memoirs? Which I reckon we'd all like to read, by the way.'

'Beatrice enlisted my help, and Felix's – Lord Saltford's – as well. I spent a good deal of time gathering information and photos of the four of you.'

'So you were the information expert, were you?' said Lucius. 'Well, I have to hand it to you, you did a pretty good job of it.'

'I always was good at that kind of thing, and my wartime training came in handy. Although Beatrice did much of it herself, let me tell you. She employed private detectives, Pinkerton's in America and a shrewd ex-policeman in London.'

'Why?' said Delia, asking the question they all wanted answered. 'Why go to all that trouble? Why not just write a will, saying I leave you this because of this or that? And why,' she went on, unable to keep the hurt out of her voice, 'didn't she want to see me, when she could have done?'

'That was for my sake,' said Lord Saltford. 'She felt, as a woman of her generation would, that illegitimacy was a stigma, and that it was better for you to believe that the family you grew up in was your actual family. Which was the case: I am your father, and Felicity is your sister, if a half-sister rather than a full sister. And the truth is, she never got on well with Miranda, although she loved and admired her. Miranda was her father's daughter more than Beatrice's. It was from her father that she got her logical mind and dedication to science. As soon as she was old enough, Miranda went to live with her father – by that time, Beatrice and Guido were living apart and rarely saw one another.'

'You mean Beatrice was afraid she wouldn't like me,' Delia said. 'That I might be like Miranda, and she didn't want to rake that up again. I suppose you wouldn't, not when you were that old. Even so . . .'

'Don't blame her, and be happy that she's left you the Villa Dante. It's passed down in her family from mother to daughter for more than two centuries. Now it's grandmother to grand-daughter, but it pleased her that you would inherit it.'

'I'm not sure I understand her,' said Delia. 'I'll read her memoirs, and then I'm going to learn Italian, properly, so that I can talk to people who knew her, here in Italy. Benedetta, for one.'

'You can't possibly live here, Delia,' said Theo. 'There's no point being sentimental about a house you've spent a week or so in. Much better to sell it. And I think the old lady was quite right to keep mum about her daughter and Lord Saltford. That isn't the kind of story you want made public.'

'Shut up, Theo,' said Delia.

'So why the mystery, the tower, the clues?' said Lucius.

'It was her way. I told you she loved puzzles and complex problems. She felt she owed each of you a debt, and went to a lot of effort to find out what had happened to the four of you. When she discovered that each of you was troubled in some way, she laid her plans. What she wanted was for you to put things right for yourselves. Did she succeed?'

'Yes,' said Marjorie, without hesitation. 'I wish she were here. I'd thank her with all my heart.'

'I have already said how much I owe her,' said George.

'I guess she's made me ask myself a few searching questions,' said Lucius. 'And . . .' His eyes strayed to Delia.

'I haven't had time to take it all in,' said Delia. 'I do know that my life will never be the same again.'

Lucius found Delia on the beach, sitting against the rock where he had first seen her, watching the brilliant colours of sunset reflected on a calm sea.

'You look pensive,' he said, dropping down beside her. 'Penny for them, as you English say.'

'I was thinking about Jessica, and Richie, and how pleased I am that she can get her divorce.'

'How has that worked out?'

Delia looked sideways at him, then traced a pattern in the sand with her finger. 'I can trust you, can't I?' she said.

'With your life.'

'Richie was having an affair with my mother. My official mother.'

'With the son of the man who was the father of Boswell?' Lucius stood up, and looked down at Delia. 'Your family are like something out of ancient Greece.'

'I suppose we are. Nothing is what it seemed. But I'm so pleased that I'm not a blood relation of Boswell's. And that Beatrice Malaspina was my grandmother.' She hesitated, then plunged in. 'Does it make it easier for you, about Boswell? That he's not my brother?'

'I'm thankful that the man I killed wasn't your brother, but it doesn't change the fact that I killed a man, who wasn't my enemy, in cold blood. The morality of what I did hasn't changed, and that's something I'm just going to have to live with, I guess. Are you going to go into your father's firm?'

'No. I think that he's finally come to understand that my

424

music isn't just a quirk or a hobby, but an essential part of me. I couldn't sit behind a desk and run the mills, and he agrees that it would probably make me unhappy even to try. So he's promised not to bully me any more, and I don't think we'll hear any more about his leaving everything to charity; he says he'll make other arrangements for the future of the company. And I think I've persuaded him to take Jessica on. She'd be good at it, and she needs a job; she won't take any money from Richie.'

'Good for her.'

'My father went to my flat and collected my post. There's a letter from an impresario who saw me doing impromptu cabaret last Christmas and wants me to audition for a new musical he's putting on.'

'And you're pleased?'

'Nervous, but thrilled.' Delia stood up, brushing the sand off her legs. 'Are you going to marry Elfrida?'

'No.' He laughed. 'With my plans for my future, she wouldn't have me.'

'Plans? Oh, do you mean you're going in for painting? I'm so glad.'

'Yes, I plan on attending art school. In London.'

'London? Why London?' The sea was suddenly loud in her ears. She looked straight at Lucius, then turned away.

Lucius was suddenly serious. 'Delia, I love you. I think I fell in love with you the moment I saw you. I can't live without you.'

'One can, you know. Look at Beatrice Malaspina and your grandfather.'

'Bless the woman, for bringing me here so that I could meet you.'

'Do you think she planned it?' Delia searched Lucius's face, disturbed by what she saw in his eyes. 'Her granddaughter and the grandson of her lover? I'm not sure I like that much manipulation.'

'We could have met anywhere, any time. It turns out our fathers are acquainted, after all. I'm just thankful my trip to Italy happened before I went up the aisle with Elfrida.'

'Well, yes, I grant you that your life will be better without her.'

'But only half a life without you.'

She held out her hand to him. 'Let's not push it. Let's see how it goes.'

'You're full of doubt.'

'Just wary, and I'm still feeling giddy from all the revelations.' She smiled at him. 'Besides, we have to spend time together, like it or not. We've our inheritance to consider.'

She held out her hand and he took it, and turned it over, bending to plant a kiss on her palm. Hand in hand, they turned to look up at the Villa Dante, serene and beautiful in the golden light of an Italian evening.